Little White Lies

Little White Lies

a novel

Ron and Janet Benrey

BROADMAN
&HOLMAN
PUBLISHERS

Nashville, Tennessee

0-8054-2371-0

Published by Broadman & Holman Publishers,
Nashville, Tennessee

Dewey Decimal Classification: 813
Subject Heading: FICTION
Library of Congress Card Catalog Number: 00-060832

Unless otherwise stated all Scripture citation is from the NIV, the
Holy Bible, New International Version, copyright © 1973, 1978, 1984
by International Bible Society. Also used is the King James Version of
the Holy Bible.

Library of Congress Cataloging-in-Publication Data
Benrey, Ron, 1941–
    Little white lies : a novel / Ron and Janet Benrey.
        p.   cm.
    ISBN 0-8054-2371-0 (pb)
    1. Recruiting of employees—Fiction.   2. Businesswomen—
Fiction. I. Benrey, Janet, 1944– II. Title.
    PS3552.E54764 L57 2001
    813'.54—dc21

                                                    00-060832
                                                    CIP

1 2 3 4 5   05 04 03 02 01

IN MEMORIAM

Caroline Osborn
(1906–1976)
Janet's mother

ACKNOWLEDGMENTS

WRITING, IT IS SAID, is a solitary endeavor. We've made it a labor of love. Each of us has helped the other in ways that cannot be measured. This book could not have been finished without the mutual encouragement we gave to one another.

Help came from other sources too. We owe a great debt to our writers' group in Annapolis, who read this manuscript more than once and offered their invaluable suggestions—Ray Flynt, Mary Ellen Hughes, Trish Marshall, Sherriel Mattingly, Marcia Talley, and especially to Carolyn Curtis, who also helped us find the Light that is above all light.

Thanks also to Joyce Hart, our literary agent, for her continued encouragement and support; to Vicki Crumpton, our eagle-eyed editor; and to Dr. Henriette Terwaarbeek, our "Dutch daughter," who freely shared her medical knowledge with us.

Prologue

THEY HAD EATEN TWENTY DOZEN CRAB CAKES for dinner. The 126 enthusiastic partygoers aboard the *Chesapeake Belle* pushed back their
chairs and turned their attention to salesmanship. There were merchants, lawyers, consultants, accountants, and executives from big and
small companies—a true cross section of the business community of
Ryde, Maryland. Most were members of the Ryde Chamber of
Commerce. Many hoped to land new customers and clients while the
big party boat chugged through the calm waters of the Miles River, near
St. Michaels. They greeted their colleagues with eager smiles as they
traveled from table to table, networking with one another and handing
out business cards.

As evening became night, a few hardy souls left the air-conditioned
salon and braved the muggy air on the brightly lit promenade deck. One
of these was a well-dressed woman who stood concealed in the shadows
cast by a tall bin full of life jackets. She watched with intense interest as
Marsha Morgan, the good friend who had helped her achieve so much
success, wobbled unsteadily near the *Chesapeake Belle's* stern railing. If
all went according to plan, Marsha would soon have a dreadful accident.

A few minutes earlier, the watcher had half-steered, half-pushed Marsha up the narrow staircase that led from the main salon and had been very careful not to be seen with Marsha. Her plan was simple. She'd wait until they were alone and then help Marsha over the side.

But they weren't alone. A portly man in a white dinner jacket, one of the *Chesapeake Belle's* musicians, had appeared at the stern to smoke a cigarette, sending the watcher scurrying to her hiding place. He stood a few yards away from Marsha Morgan, occasionally frowning at her.

The watcher felt herself smile. *He has decided that Marsha is drunk. He'll make a splendid witness when the police investigate Marsha's accidental death.*

It had been a spur-of-the-moment decision to give Marsha a drink that contained a shot of vodka. Perhaps Marsha hadn't tasted the diluted spirits in the tall glass, or maybe she decided to tempt the devil. Either way, the alcohol had dulled her caution. Marsha had eagerly knocked back two other drinks after dinner, much stronger cocktails with more than enough vodka to trigger the physical reaction that made Marsha seem drunk. Now Marsha held a fourth and even stronger drink in her hand, which the watcher had given her.

The moon glistened on the Miles River. Here and there on the nearby bank, tiki torches lit backyard barbecues. The watcher could hear faint laughter on the occasional wisps of offshore breeze that reached the *Chesapeake Belle*. *A perfect night for a tragic "act of God,"* she thought.

I only need a few seconds alone with Marsha.

The musician flicked his half-smoked cigarette into the water and pulled open the companionway door. But as he went inside, two other people took his place at the stern railing, a man and a woman. The watcher recognized them immediately: David Friendly, an inquisitive business reporter from Ryde's third-rate hometown newspaper, and Pippa . . . *Something,* Marsha's new business associate.

The watcher sighed deeply. How stupid of Marsha Morgan to take a partner, particularly someone who seemed so competent. Marsha should have known better.

All of this is Marsha's fault.

"Hi, Marsha," David said. When Marsha didn't answer, he added: "Earth calling Marsha Morgan."

There was more chatter and the sound of Marsha's glass crashing against the railing, but the watcher in the shadows hardly noticed. She was focused on getting back to the salon without being seen. Her impromptu scheme to kill Marsha Morgan had gone awry. David Friendly and Pippa *Something* would recognize that Marsha was not well. They would comfort and protect her and certainly not leave her alone at the rail.

Why did they have to arrive now?

The watcher heard Pippa say to David, "You keep Marsha upright, and I'll ask the captain to radio ahead for an ambulance."

She muttered a curse. *Pippa* Something *is a classic do-gooder! You can hear it in her voice. She bubbles over with sympathy and concern and zeal to do the right thing, all of which makes her doubly dangerous as Marsha Morgan's partner.*

And then it happened. Marsha Morgan pulled away from David Friendly, and, to the watcher's astonishment, *folded* herself over the railing. An unexpectedly loud splash followed an instant later, but no shout for help.

"Marsha!" Pippa *Something* screamed.

"Man overboard!" David Friendly yelled. "Turn the boat around!"

"Incredible!" the watcher murmured. "Marsha Morgan fell overboard, and I didn't have to do a thing."

She moved deeper into the shadows. The darkness would help to clear her mind; it would give her a chance to think about loose ends. What else must she do to get completely free of the Morgan Consultancy?

Find the paperwork. Yes! That would be the first chore on the list. Get the wretched paperwork as soon as possible.

A screech of metal caught her ear. She looked up to see David Friendly unhook a bright yellow life ring from its mounting bracket. He flung it into the water behind the *Chesapeake Belle,* then shouted at Pippa *Something,* "Keep your eye on the life preserver! It marks the spot where Marsha fell into the river." Pippa climbed high on the stern rail to obey David Friendly's command.

I wish she would fall in too.

The watcher took a long breath and exhaled slowly as a new thought formed in her mind: *Pippa* Something *is another loose end that must be eliminated.*

She tried to recall Pippa's last name. It was long and unmistakably British, a name that went along with her English accent and her beautiful English complexion.

All in good time, the watcher told herself. *Someone at the table will tell me her name. It will be easy to find her address. But right now you have a more immediate problem. Marsha Morgan is dead, and you have to pretend that you care.*

Chapter One

WHEN THE COPPERS TALK ABOUT MARSHA MORGAN, they start with her death—how she fell off the *Chesapeake Belle* and drowned in the Miles River. But the police can't tell you the whole story. I can. My tale begins five days earlier, with a frenetic telephone call.

It was the last Monday in July. I had begun to peruse *The Baltimore Sun* and drink my second cup of Darjeeling tea when my telephone rang. "Pippa Hunnechurch, here," I said, ready to talk business. On occasion, early morning calls come from eager personnel managers bringing me new assignments.

I heard a deep breath, then a sniff, then a rush of syllables I could scarcely separate.

"We received the most awful news this morning. It's a disaster over here, and we need to talk."

I recognized my caller at once: Connie Hillman, the director of human resources at Simpson Manufacturing Company. I had known her for the past fifteen months as a chipper individual with a buoyant personality. Today her voice reeked of despair.

"Slow down, Connie," I said. "Start at the beginning."

"There is no beginning! This is the *end*. The worst day of my career. The pits. The bottom of the barrel. The . . ."

"I get your point. Something calamitous has happened at Simpson Manufacturing."

Another deep breath. Another sniff. "It's way past calamitous, hon. Our chairman ordered a hiring freeze. Effective today. Throughout the whole company. Starting this morning, I don't have a single job opening to fill."

My hand began to tremble when I guessed what she would say next. I gingerly set my cup atop its saucer.

"You're in the soup too," Connie moaned on. "Forget about any new recruiting assignments. I can't even hire the classy accountant you found for us last week."

"No, I suppose not," I mumbled with Grade-A British reserve, although I wanted to scream: *This can't be happening to me! Not now!* I had spent the better part of a month tracking down the perfect candidate and had earmarked most of my fee, six thousand dollars, to pay down my credit cards and renew my ancient fall wardrobe.

"Did your chairman say how long the hiring freeze might last?" I asked.

"Nine months, minimum. Maybe longer."

Nine months! Intolerable! Simpson Manufacturing generated more than half of my revenues. The company had become my best and most reliable client, the one I could always count on to provide a steady stream of recruiting jobs. Without Simpson paying my monthly bills, I was well and truly done for.

"There must be some way to push my accountant in under the wire," I said, trying to sound less panicky than I felt.

"A prayer might help."

A prayer! I fought to hold my temper. *What kind of an absurd suggestion was that?*

"To be honest, Connie, I had something more practical in mind. Perhaps it might help to send your chairman an E-mail message that explains how much work we did to find this particular accountant. It will be a shame to lose him."

Connie hesitated, then asked: "Don't you believe in God?"

I almost laughed. When Connie grabbed hold of a bone, she didn't let go, but I wasn't in the mood to talk about God, not when I felt scared stiff about my future. I came up with a suitably glib reply.

"Oh, I suppose he is up there somewhere," I said, "but I doubt that he watches over me or cares about my professional problems."

"I believe you're wrong, Pippa. I need God to take an immediate interest in my future. This could be the start of a complete corporate restructuring. If that happens, I'll almost certainly lose my job."

"Good Lord!"

"See! Everyone becomes a believer when the layoffs begin."

"Touché."

We both giggled.

"Well, I'm off to write my own résumé," she said. "It's been swell working with you, Pippa."

My friends call me Pippa because my full name is a right long wheeze: Philippa Elizabeth Katherine Hunnechurch. I am a Brit by birth, a resident of Ryde, Maryland, by choice, thirty-six by the inexorable march of time, and a headhunter by occupation.

Correction! I would be a headhunter until my bank account ran dry. During the past month I had suffered through similar phone calls from three other clients.

"Our markets are terribly weak, Pippa. Lombard Computing won't have any other new assignments for the rest of this year."

"Sorry, Pippa, but Danforth Accounting Services has been forced to downsize its operations."

"Kennally Metals is laying people off, Pippa, not hiring. Senior management has decided to reorganize the company."

The frenzy of corporate cost cutting in my little corner of Maryland threatened to throttle Philippa Hunnechurch & Associates, Executive Recruiters. I had launched myself into business eighteen months earlier with great confidence and enthusiasm, but now I faced the distinct likelihood of not seeing my second anniversary. How could a headhunter survive when her principal customers stopped hiring new people?

I stared at the wall for a while and studied my nineteenth-century print of a whaling ship going to sea. Oh, how I envied the seamen in the picture. A nice steady job for three years with nothing but storms and sea monsters to worry about. How blessed it must be to live one's life without clients.

Ah well, at least Pippa Hunnechurch won't starve, I told myself. *I will become my last candidate. I'll find me a snug, low-stress job that doesn't demand much initiative. I'll collect a regular paycheck, and cleverer people than I will worry about keeping the business solvent.*

All at once the little voice in the back of my brain shouted, *Stop!* My streak of British determination flared like kerosene on a bonfire. I am a Hunnechurch, after all, and a Hunnechurch stands her ground. A Hunnechurch looks the bulldog in the eye without flinching. A Hunnechurch doesn't cower like a trapped rabbit while her livelihood pours down the drain.

Let me explain. When one is raised in Chichester (in the heart of Sussex County in the south of England) by a mother who can trace the family tree back to the very London wigmaker who helped to coif Queen Elizabeth I, one tends to be overstocked with pithy English maxims. At times of stress, they worm their way to the surface.

Maxim or not, I felt my upper lip stiffening nicely. I love my work. Equally as important, I do it well. No way would I let my young recruiting firm go belly up without a fight.

The proper way to launch a new endeavor is to make a list. (Yes. Another piece of practical advice from my mum.) I pulled a notepad from my desk drawer and wrote:

Things to Do at Once to Revive My Sagging Business

1. Don't wait for satisfied clients to call you! *Ask* them for assignments.

2. Find companies that are moving to Maryland. They are growing. They *need* good people.

3. Place calls to every personnel manager within fifty miles of Baltimore.

4. Do more networking.

Right then a notion popped into my head. I rummaged through my "In" basket. *There!* The reminder postcard from the Ryde Chamber of Commerce. The July meeting was scheduled for tonight at Mariners' Hall in downtown Ryde. *Excellent!* A perfect opportunity to collar the local gentry and perhaps uncover a client or two. I amended my list:

5. Begin networking at tonight's chamber of commerce meeting. Take plenty of business cards.

For a moment I was tempted to put down a sixth item: Pray—but my common sense prevailed. God and I had parted company seven years earlier after he demonstrated his complete inability to wisely manage the world we live in. Connie could believe anything she wanted; I felt certain that no one had control of my future except me.

Two weeks later, when I reviewed this curious day for Detective Stephen Reilly of the Ryde Police Department, he responded with petulant skepticism.

"Are you telling me that you went to Mariners' Hall that evening not knowing what would happen?"

"I didn't have the vaguest idea what would happen," I answered calmly. "How could I?"

"Well, one possibility is that you and Marsha Morgan planned your public debut in advance."

"And how could we have done that? I met Marsha Morgan *after* the meeting."

"So you built a relationship with Marsha Morgan . . . became the intended victim of a murderer . . . and almost got yourself killed . . ." he fumbled for the right words, "by accident?"

"Neither by accident, nor on purpose. I am an innocent bystander."

"Why don't I believe you?"

I raised my right hand. "I've told you the whole truth and nothing but the truth, *guv'nor.* I went to the chamber meeting to find a few new clients—not to put myself in the middle of a murderous mess."

```
╔══════════════════════════════════╗
║         Chapter  Two             ║
╚══════════════════════════════════╝
```

I swooped down on Mariners' Hall like a hungry hawk raiding a pigeon loft. There they were: dozens of potential clients shaking hands, patting shoulders, chatting merrily. They were all in a good mood and ripe for networking. And (more's the pity), most of them were total strangers.

Why, I asked myself, *didn't you attend more chamber meetings during the eight months since you joined?*

Because, I answered myself honestly, *you made the duffer's mistake of assuming you had enough clients and didn't need to market your services with vigor.*

I circled the hall slowly, trying to pick out the few executives I had met before or those I had read about in the chamber's monthly newsletter. Several friendly souls looked my way and smiled. I smiled back but kept moving. Now was the time for reconnaissance. I would begin to network at the reception that followed the meeting.

The lights on the big overhead chandelier flashed. I dropped into a chair near the small raised wooden stage as John Tyler, the chamber's president, called the meeting to order. He was in his late forties—gray hair, gray mustache, and gray blazer. His complexion seemed vaguely gray too. The one distinctive touch of color was the solid gold Rolex wristwatch that glittered on his left wrist. Tyler owned a prosperous commercial real estate firm, a family-owned-and-run enterprise of the sort that rarely buys recruiting services.

"Tonight," he began, "I have the pleasure of introducing a good friend. The Reverend Edward Clarke, as many of you know, is pastor of Ryde Fellowship Church, the oldest continuously operating church in Ryde and one of the fastest growing." Tyler smiled at the lanky man in the dark suit standing on the steps that led to the stage. "I say that with great anticipation, Ed, because I sincerely hope that your congregation will outgrow your present sanctuary. Ryde Fellowship sits on a prime chunk of Ryde real estate. I have several clients who would love to build on your site."

Tyler paused to let the audience titter.

"But seriously, folks, Reverend Clarke is here tonight to get us started with an invocation."

Tyler moved aside. Clarke took his place at the podium. I braced myself for one of those lukewarm, one-size-fits-all prayers designed to please everyone (and insult no one), but Reverend Ed surprised me. He clasped the microphone with both hands and said in a velvety voice, "God loves to use businesspeople. Think of what he accomplished with the help of a Judean carpenter, a few fisherman from Galilee, a Palestinian tax agent, a tent maker from Tarsus, a Greek doctor, a dye merchant in Philippi, and the many other businessmen and business-women you'll find in the Holy Scriptures. I am convinced that God wants to use all of you here this evening to advance his kingdom, even if you don't yet have a personal relationship with him. And so, Heavenly Father, I ask in Jesus' name for your blessing on the work of this fine organization and its devoted members."

The woman next to me shouted "Amen" loud enough to make me jump. "He's fabulous, isn't he?" she said as I stared at her in amazement.

"I enjoyed his message. Quite unusual."

"He's *my* pastor," she said proudly. "Have you ever been to Ryde Fellowship? We're a very friendly church with an inspiring new member's program."

Yet another sales pitch for religion. I shook my head and mumbled a little white lie: "Sorry, I am spoken for. Church of England, you know."

Before she could say anything in reply, John Tyler tapped the microphone. "Excellent. Let's begin our program."

The lion's share of the meeting was given over to a long-winded presentation about low-budget TV commercials, the kind that are broadcast in the middle of late-night horror movies. The speakers were two enthusiastic young men in wrinkled suits who ran a small advertising agency in Ryde. They showed us how to create commercials on the cheap and promised us boundless riches if we followed their advice. Not my cup of tea. I gave my attention to the seventeenth- and eighteenth-century portraits that lined the walls of Mariners' Hall—a gallery of austere-looking merchants and seafarers who lived in Ryde back when the town had been one of the most important ports on the Chesapeake Bay.

Ryde was settled in 1654, not long ago compared to Chichester, my English birthplace, but impressive by colonial standards. The founders (a shipload of fisher folk from the south counties of England) sailed up the Chesapeake, turned left into the Magothy River, and fell in love with a charming natural harbor on the river's southern bank. By the time of the American rebellion, most of Ryde's ship traffic had moved to nearby Baltimore, on the Patapsco River. But Ryde's picturesque geography remained intact and became its most valuable asset. Today Ryde has a population of forty thousand, a lovely restored "Old Port" downtown, and a smattering of nonpolluting industrial companies on the outskirts. I, too, fell in love with Ryde the first time I saw it.

The presentation ended. A widespread shuffling of feet signaled that everyone felt ready for the after-meeting reception. John Tyler surprised us by whapping his gavel on the podium.

"Folks, we have one final piece of business to transact before we can adjourn," he said. "Our social chairperson resigned last week. That leaves us in the lurch because our annual conference is only five days away. We need a volunteer to look after the last-minute details. In other words, a pinch hitter who will step up to the plate."

Tyler scanned the Hall hopefully. All around me chamber members shifted in their seats, scrunching down to avoid Tyler's searching stare.

"The social chair is a member of the chamber's board of directors," Tyler went on. "It's an honored position in our community."

Silence.

Tyler cleared his throat. "Come on, people. Where's your public spirit? All the real work for the conference has been done."

More silence.

I was baffled that no one volunteered. Tyler was surely right. This close to the event, all the planning and decision-making would be complete. The chamber's annual conference, a weekend of partying and networking at the Talbot Inn, a posh resort in St. Michaels, on Maryland's Eastern Shore, was the group's yearly summer bash. I hadn't signed up to attend because the benefits (a few seminars and a couple of speeches) didn't seem to balance the cost (more than five hundred dollars).

"I can even offer an incentive to volunteer," Tyler said. "Board members attend the conference for free."

A thought blossomed in my mind. Attending the conference for free would give me lots of opportunity to network with chamber members, especially if I became a board member.

Without thinking any further, I stood up and raised my hand.

"My name is Pippa Hunnechurch, Mr. Tyler. I'll volunteer."

"Wonderful!" Tyler craned his neck to see me better, and his broad smile vanished. "Forgive me, ma'am, but are you a member of the chamber?"

"Card-carrying. Paid in full."

"Strange, I thought I knew all of our members."

"It's my fault that you don't recognize me. This is only the second meeting I have attended."

Tyler frowned. "I try not to look gift horses in the mouth, but social chair is a major post. The incumbent will have other important responsibilities after the conference is over—such as organizing our monthly meetings and arranging our Christmas party."

All at once I understood why no one else had volunteered: being social chair involved considerable contributions of time and effort.

Perhaps I had bitten off more than I wanted to chew? But how could I slink away now that I'd become the center of attention?

"Indeed," I said. "I welcome the challenge."

"Maybe. But are you prepared to do the work? We encourage our less committed members to take on less demanding jobs."

Less committed!

The silly clod had responded to my offer of help with an obvious insult. I stretched to my full five-feet-eight-inches and cranked up my most polished British accent. "It would seem, Mr. Tyler, that no other gift horses have trotted into your corral. Perhaps you should give this one a fair trial *before* you pronounce judgment."

I heard gurgles of nervous laughter around me. Off to my left a woman murmured, "Way to go, Pippa!"

"The fact remains," Tyler said, "that your commitment to the chamber is untested and your abilities are unknown."

"My commitment to the chamber flows from a simple principle. Pippa Hunnechurch always keeps the promises she makes. And, as to my abilities, well, I think they are more than sufficient to execute the responsibilities of your social chair. Shall I explain why?"

Tyler grunted. I took the noise as a yes.

"I am an executive recruiter," I said, speaking more to the room than to Tyler. "Being a recruiter demands acumen, planning skills, a sense of humor, and the ability to get along well with others. One must also be a capable organizer. These are the same attributes a social chair must have. Don't you agree?"

Several people began to clap. Tyler glared at me and gaveled the members quiet. "I accept that you are an able headhunter, *Mizz* Hunnechurch," he said, "and that you are both intelligent and personable. Nonetheless, our annual conference is the single most important event the chamber sponsors. It's much too near the start date to bring a stranger up to speed. We need a more experienced member. We need someone who—"

"Stop talking baloney, John! Pippa Hunnechurch will make a terrific social chair."

The speaker, a woman in a tailored red dress, was tall and shapely with a close-cut hairdo straight out of a designer salon. Everything about her proclaimed elegance—and money to spare. I learned later that she was fifty-one, but at the time, I guessed her age at forty.

"Pippa may be a new member of the chamber," the woman continued, "but she's a well-established recruiter in Ryde. I've heard excellent things about her. She has a wonderful reputation in the consulting community for thoroughness and attention to detail."

I stood there speechless, exhilarated to learn that my little firm had a "wonderful reputation." I started to mumble thank you, but Tyler beat me to it.

"Thanks for your valuable input, Marsha," he said with a plainly audible sigh.

"Input, my foot! I want to make a motion." Marsha's powerful voice reverberated through Mariners' Hall. "Pippa Hunnechurch has volunteered her services. Let's elect her social chair." The woman to my left shouted: "Second!"

Tyler gave up the fight. "OK," he said, evenly. "Marsha Morgan has made a motion that we vote. The motion has been seconded. The question before the membership is this: Shall Pippa Hunnechurch be elected to the position of social chairperson?"

Marsha Morgan.

I gawked at the woman in red. I had heard her name, of course. Every recruiter in Maryland knew about the Morgan Consultancy. Like me, Marsha ran a one-woman headhunting shop in Ryde. Unlike mine, hers had become wildly successful. She specialized in finding top-notch female executives to fill senior management jobs, and she recruited for many of the largest corporations in America. A compliment from Marsha Morgan was high praise indeed. But how had she learned of me? Which of my handful of clients told her that I did good work?

A burst of applause brought me back to the meeting. John Tyler rapped his gavel and said: "Since there are no objections, I declare that *Mizz* Pippa Hunnechurch has been elected the chamber's social chair by acclamation. Our business being completed, the meeting is adjourned."

What do you know? I had become a mover and shaker in the Ryde business community.

Chapter Three

THE CHAMBER MEMBERS TREKKED across the street to the Cinq Ports Restaurant in the Lord Baltimore Inn, with me weaving through the crowd and leaving a trail of business cards. I had taken six steps into the place when a forceful tug on my elbow spun me around.

"Ah, the gutsy *Mizz* Hunnechurch," Marsha Morgan said. She shook my hand with a grip perfected during her many years of dealing with male corporate executives. My fingers tingled as I pulled them away. "Let's find a quiet corner. You and I have lots to talk about."

"Super! I want a chance to thank you properly."

Marsha smiled beatifically at me. "It's the other way around. I need to thank you for taking on a thankless job. I recruited the speakers for our annual conference. I'd hate anything to go wrong with the physical arrangements at the last minute."

We found a tiny two-person table away from the throng and ordered refreshments: a diet Dr Pepper with a twist of lime for Marsha and iced tea with a twist of lemon for me. After we were served, she donned a pair of silver-framed eyeglasses and peered at me for a while.

"So, for whom do you recruit?" she eventually said.

The inevitable question. I had come to the meeting to network—presenting my credentials was part of the game. Still, I found Marsha's thoughtful stare disquieting. A headhunter with her experience would be a tough inquisitor.

"Several local companies," I said. "My biggest client is Simpson Manufacturing. I also consult for Lombard Computing, Danforth Accounting Services, and Kennally Metals." Not a lie. All four were technically still my clients.

Marsha wrinkled her nose. "Not bad, although most of your customers are firing people rather than hiring."

Marsha's simple statement of fact made me blush. "You're right, of course. Business is slow. I need to expand my client base."

"Well, you're off to a good start. Everyone at the meeting tonight knows the name and occupation of our new social chairperson." Marsha grinned at me like the Cheshire cat. "You were smart to volunteer."

"In truth, I made a spur-of-the-moment decision."

"I won't tell if you don't."

We both laughed.

"How old are you?" she asked.

"Thirty-six."

"You look younger. How long have you been a headhunter?"

"Eighteen months."

"No wonder I've never heard of you."

I coughed up a sip of iced tea. *Never heard of me?* "But you gave me a glowing recommendation."

Marsha leaned across the table and patted my arm. "Johnnie Tyler is both irritating and stupid. I said what was necessary to shut him up. It worked."

"Perhaps, but—"

"He's also a world-class male chauvinist, the kind who loves to explain why women can't handle senior positions. I've been told that a staff meeting at his real estate firm looks like vespers at a monastery."

"Perhaps, but—"

"Were any of the nice things I said about you untrue?"

"No. I am thorough, and I do worry about the details."

"There you go!"

"Perhaps, but—"

"No more perhaps or buts. Look old Marsha straight in the eye—tell me what's bothering you."

I nodded. Better to get it all out at once. "To be honest, I am uncomfortable that you invented a reputation for me."

She laughed out loud. "Honey, I didn't invent anything—I merely predicted your future. I know talent when I see it, which is what makes me a great headhunter. You're going to have a fabulous reputation once you get yourself more clients."

"I fervently hope so, but until then, I prefer not to sail under false colors."

"Look. I admit I exaggerated a little, but it's all for a good cause. You deserved a chance to do some marketing among chamber members. I made sure you got it." She poked a finger in my ribs to emphasize the point. "Don't be mad at me."

I smiled at her utter self-assurance. "It is impossible to be mad at you, Marsha."

"You got that right! Now, while we're on the subject of marketing, give me your business card."

I pushed a card across the table.

Marsha fished in her purse and brought out a thick stack of business cards neatly bound with rubber bands. She added my card to the top of the heap.

"Pippa Hunnechurch is now officially in my archives," she said. "Don't be surprised if I call you."

"Please do." I stared at those precious cards covetously. She had to be holding more than two hundred in her hand. All those names. All those addresses. All those telephone numbers. *All those juicy contacts.*

Marsha polished off her Dr Pepper in three large gulps. "Enough gabbing with your elders. Go forth and network. I presume you have a strategy in mind?"

"I suppose so, if you call mingling a strategy."

She grinned at me. "What could be more natural? The new social chair circulating among the members and exchanging business cards. It's a great ploy."

"You make me sound so crafty."

"Honey, there are two kinds of people in this restaurant. Business successes, those who know how to sell themselves, and business failures, those who don't. You have the makings of a success."

"Hear, hear!" I muttered under my breath. Then I downed the rest of my iced tea.

"One thing, though," Marsha said. "Before you paper the room with business cards, make friends with Johnnie Tyler."

"Pardon?"

"At this stage in your career, you don't need the president of the Ryde Chamber of Commerce as an enemy. Buy him a drink, pretend he's charming, and act like you care about real estate. And feel free to blame everything that happened at tonight's meeting on me." She pushed her chair away from the table. "If you ever want my help, holler. I believe that good women should network actively."

Marsha strode off before I could ask what she meant by networking "actively." But she was right. I didn't want Tyler as my enemy. I scanned the Cinq Ports Restaurant. He stood alone in a dark corner, putting away a tall Bloody Mary with determination. A perfect time to make amends.

Tyler squared his shoulders when he saw me approaching.

"Let me buy you a refill," I said quickly.

"Well, well, our new social chair wants to socialize."

"Indeed I do." I waved to the waiter and ordered fresh drinks.

"We seem to have gotten off on the wrong foot," I said to Tyler.

"Not really. Nothing I said was aimed at your person. I just think the chamber needs an experienced social chair."

"I promise to do my best."

He lifted his glass, belched softly, and then said: "And I promise to help you every way I can."

"Many thanks. I am an attentive listener when people offer good advice."

"You want some good advice? I'll give you some. I saw you gabbing with Marsha Morgan. Don't pick up any of her bad habits."

What an odd thing to say, but then I remembered that Marsha had called him irritating and stupid. Maybe he felt the same way about her? "I take it you don't like Marsha."

"On the contrary, she's an awesome-looking babe. I'd love to get her into the sack. Of course, I'd never ask her to do a nickel's worth of business for me."

For a fleeting instant I thought about tossing my untouched glass of iced tea in Tyler's face. But I held my temper and changed the subject. "You said that the social chair has to handle last-minute details for the conference. Does anything need my immediate attention?"

"Yes, as a matter of fact. You have to coordinate the menu for the Friday night dinner cruise."

"We're not dining at the Talbot Inn?"

"Nope. The board planned a special evening for the conferees. We chartered the *Chesapeake Belle*, a party boat based in Baltimore. It's making a special trip across the Chesapeake Bay to pick us up. The first-night get-together will be a dinner cruise on the Miles River."

"What a grand idea."

"Isn't it?" Tyler took a step closer and gave me a cow-eyed look. "Is that an English accent I hear?"

Yikes! The man was becoming amorous.

"Wholly English," I said as he tried to take my hand. I snatched it away.

"You know, you are remarkably pretty," he said. "I'm sure you've heard that before."

"On occasion," I answered truthfully.

I possess your basic British face: long nose, blue eyes that sometimes seem gray, prominent cheekbones, dishwater blonde hair styled in a rather simple, mid-length do. My best feature, and the reason some people say I am pretty, is my English peaches-and-cream complexion. It has stayed with me in America, although, if I spend too much time in the bright Maryland sun, I get homely red spots on my nose.

Tyler made another grab for my hand, but this time he merely tapped my left ring finger. "No wedding ring," he said. "How come a good-looking gal like you isn't married?"

I felt the all-too-familiar tug around my heart, but I wasn't about to show Tyler my grief or tell him my life story. So I merely smiled and offered a who-knows-why shrug.

Tyler tipped forward. Our foreheads almost touched. I leaned backwards and prepared to shove him away if he moved any closer. I balled my right hand into a tight fist.

"We live in a small world," he said. "My newest client is from England. A nice guy with a funny moniker. Derek Wetherspoon."

"Derek Wetherspoon," I echoed. "A fine English name."

"He's from a little burg called Chichester."

Astonished at the mention of my hometown, I relaxed my fist. "I was born in Chichester."

"Didn't I say it's a small world?" Tyler took another sip and belched once again. "You still have family there?"

"My mother and my sister."

"I'll bet that both of them are lovely women, and as pretty as you are."

I forced myself to smile appealingly. "Thank you, kind sir, indeed they are. But you were telling me about Derek Wetherspoon."

"Oh, yeah. Wetherspoon leased the top floor of the Bay View Building. It's gonna be the U.S. headquarters for his company."

"Really? What company is that?"

"Eurokit USA, the American subsidiary of Eurokit Limited."

"When will he move to the Bay View Building?" I asked, trying to sound nonchalant despite my growing excitement.

"Middle of August. It'll take that long to finish all the renovations that Wetherspoon asked for. Until then he and his staff are working out of a temporary facility in Ryde." Tyler put a finger to his lips. "But don't tell anyone. It's still a big secret."

"Oh, mum's the word," I whispered.

I love secrets. But this was more than a mere secret. This was *business intelligence*. Tyler had told me something that no other headhunter in Ryde would know—not even Marsha Morgan. A large company had moved to town. A company that would surely hire more staff. A company that would need the services of an executive recruiter.

"I've never heard of Eurokit Limited," I said.

Tyler leaned toward me and whispered, "It's a very successful company in Europe. A leader in its field. The company builds commercial kitchens for restaurants, hotels, prisons, and company cafeterias. You name it. Wetherspoon seems confident that Eurokit can also do well in the United States."

"No doubt he's right." I picked up my purse.

Tyler frowned. "Are you leaving, Pippa?

I faked a yawn. "To tell the truth, this has been a rather long day." I yawned again for emphasis. "I had better go home. I can hardly keep my eyes open."

It was all rubbish, of course. I felt very much awake, but I had lost interest in doing any more networking that night. The clock on the wall behind the restaurant's bar read six minutes before ten o'clock. I mentally added five hours. It was approaching three o'clock in the morning in England. In a few hours I could ring up my sister Chloe and ask her to send me lots of scrumptious information about Derek Wetherspoon and Eurokit Limited. In a few days, if my newfound luck held, I would have a lucrative new client.

Chapter Four

Wʜᴇɴ I ᴀʀʀɪᴠᴇᴅ ʜᴏᴍᴇ ᴀᴛ 10:38 ᴘ.ᴍ., I felt too excited to sleep, too eager to watch TV, too keyed up to read. I had to do *something* until the sun rose in Chichester. Good cheer took over. I decided to begin my annual production of Hunnechurch's famous Christmas plum puddings. Each year I present a few dozen of them as holiday gifts to my favorite clients and contacts. They taste best when aged several months. I brewed a pot of strong Assam tea and began to organize the ingredients.

Winston, who lives in the kitchen, accepted being awakened with remarkably good grace. He chirped a greeting when he heard me puttering among the pots and pans. I slipped the cover off his cage and let the door down to its horizontal position. "Might as well stretch your wings, laddie. It's going to be a long night." Winston is a parakeet (a *budgie* on the other side of the Atlantic)—a pretty, little bird with light blue feathers and a bright yellow beak. He trotted out of his cage and nuzzled my finger.

Winston perched on my shoulder as I mixed, stirred, sifted, and prepared the bundles for steaming. The clock on the microwave blinked the passing minutes, and in the quiet hours past midnight, my kitchen became quite humid. I opened the window that overlooks my back garden. It was too dark, of course, to see anything through the screen, but I fancied I could smell the tarragon and thyme and the mint in the patch of herbs I had planted behind my little flagstone patio.

Correction! Our flagstone patio in *our* back garden. The Ryde Savings Bank owned 94.6 percent of all that I surveyed.

I live on Magothy Street, not far from Ryde Old Port, in a narrow, two-story row house erected in 1867. Downstairs is my living room, dining room, and kitchen (all tiny). Upstairs are two small bedrooms and a bath. The Ryde Historical Society registry lists the first owner as a Welshman, a rope merchant named Llewellan, whose wife had five kids. Amazing. My friends say my house is barely big enough for me.

Nonetheless, I love "Hunnechurch Manor." I cringed when I applied for a second mortgage to fund Hunnechurch & Associates. Regrettably, I had no other choice. I had put up every dollar (and British pound) I possessed as the down payment on my little house. The equity my home represented was my only ready source of working capital to establish my business. If I failed as a consultant, well, it didn't bear thinking about. I focused on my puddings.

At 3:00 A.M. I foil-wrapped the last of the twelve still-warm puddings lined up on my kitchen table. It was 8:00 A.M. in Chichester. Chloe had slept long enough. She answered her phone on the fifteenth ring.

"Greetings from Maryland," I said cautiously. Chloe and I had shared the same bedroom for twelve years. I had never known her to be a morning person.

"Heavens, Pippa! It must be the middle of the night back in America. Have you gone completely mad?"

"No. I am making Christmas puddings."

"Oh well, then, that explains everything. You've been overwhelmed by brandy fumes."

"In truth, Chloe, I've been waiting patiently to talk to you. Have you ever heard of Eurokit Limited?"

"What a question! Of course I've heard of Eurokit. I will soon be breakfasting amidst one of their deluxe domestic kitchens. The very one you enjoyed on your last visit to Chichester."

"Ah. The white cabinets. The chrome trim. The nifty shelves for pots and pans."

"Precisely. Eurokit makes extraordinary use of space. You should think of putting one in. There's hardly room to swing a cat in your tiny kitchen."

"Definitely something to consider should I ever acquire a cat," I said. "In the meantime, however, I need some information about a chap who works for Eurokit. His name is Derek Wetherspoon. A Chichester laddie who has recently moved to the United States."

"A fellow from Chichester! May one hope that you have found yourself a new gentlemen friend?"

"I'm afraid not, Chloe. My interest in Derek Wetherspoon involves business rather than pleasure. Eurokit plans to open an office in Ryde, and he will be in charge. I want to know where his temporary office is located and anything else that might help me land him as a client. He's bound to hire more people. I want to become his headhunter."

"I do wish you would find a more wholesome label for your peculiar profession, Pippa. 'Headhunter' seems so . . . well, barbaric. It makes me conjure up images of you wearing a flimsy loincloth."

"I would look lovely in a flimsy loincloth."

"No, you would not. You inherited the classic but oversized Hunnechurch bum."

"Rubbish. My bum is adorable. Now, to repeat. The man's name is Derek Wetherspoon. I want all the facts you can gather about him in, shall we say, three hours?"

I heard Chloe sigh. "Heavens, Pippa. I am not a private investigator."

"No. But you are a notorious busybody in Chichester, and your husband is a much-beloved clergyman. The Hunnechurch-Parkers know most of the important people in town, and you can quickly find out about the rest."

"Hmmm. Wetherspoon you say? The name does have a familiar ring. I will make a few inquiries."

"That's my sister Chloe—generous to a fault."

"Don't forget kindhearted."

"Extremely kindhearted," I agreed. "Do you have my fax number on Magothy Street?"

"Indeed, Pippa. Stuart and I both consider it a true curiosity. No other woman we know keeps a fax machine in her bedroom."

"That's because my bedroom is also my home office, as you should remember. My other bedroom is bursting with the several items of Edwardian furniture you shipped me last summer."

"Mum wanted you to have it. She insisted that we send the lot."

"Mum doesn't realize how small a house I live in. You, however, have been here."

"There might come a time, soon one hopes, when you will purchase a larger house and require more furnishings. Then you and your new husband will thank Mum and me for our generosity."

"For the thousandth time, Chloe, the answer is no. I am not anxious to get married again. Neither am I seeing anyone who might want to marry me."

"What can one say after a thoroughly depressing pronouncement like that? Well, I am off to do your bidding. If memory serves, that will make two favors you owe me."

"Your memory is mistaken. Our slate is clean. Remember the large can of maple syrup you needed *instantly* last winter and the three Wonder Bras you wanted by return mail last month?"

"*Hmmm.* You are cursed with the remorseless mind of . . . of a *head-hunter.* One hopes you grow to be more charitable."

"*One* is being presumptuous. I like me exactly the way I am."

Chloe laughed. "I suspect that Mum agrees. She talks about you every day—with great affection."

"How is Mum? Is she in much pain?"

"Of course, though she won't confess it. She soldiers bravely on, arthritis or no." Chloe's voice became serious. "You really should plan another visit to England, soon. I hate to speak in clichés, but Mum is not getting any younger."

"I will, Chloe. I promise." I added in my thoughts, *when Derek Wetherspoon hires me and I have enough extra cash to buy a ticket.*

"*Ta,* Pippa. As always, we'll keep you in our prayers."

"Please do," I said mechanically. Chloe could pray the wallpaper off the walls. I had never found the right way to tell her that her prayers for me hadn't done any good.

━━━━━━

3:28 A.M. I climbed into bed smelling of nutmeg and mace but immensely happy. I dreamed of chrome-trimmed kitchens crammed with executives I had recruited for Derek Wetherspoon. Strange to say, they were all wearing bright white aprons and tall chefs' hats.

Then my fax machine burbled.

7:23 A.M. I leapt out of bed and read the fax as it crawled out of the slot:

> Dear Pippa (it began), Your chap's full name is Derek Geoffrey Wetherspoon III. Age: 47. He used to live not far from us, on St. Paul's Road (marked on the maps as the B-2178 route).
>
> Derek is widely regarded as a marketing genius. He gained his reputation flogging factory machinery, computer parts, and industrial rubber goods for Fieldston-Eberhart, a big manufacturing company in the Midlands. He joined Eurokit Limited three years ago and was soon promoted to executive vice president for international operations, apparently a reward for selling a shipload of kitchens to Saudi Arabia.
>
> By the by, one of the people Stuart queried (a bowler on his cricket team who consults for Eurokit) was aghast that Stuart had heard of Derek's removal to the States. The new U.S. office is supposed to be a *BIG* secret. How on earth did you find out about it? Is one of your clients in the Central Intelligence Agency?
>
> Derek's temporary office is in the Ridley Building, on Gray's Inn Street, Ryde. Stuart's friends describe Derek as follows:
>
> 1. Deucedly smart.
>
> 2. Unreservedly honest.

3. A "workaholic" who puts in twelve-hour days.

4. Prefers to deal with people he knows—can be a tad persnickety about entering new business relationships.

5. Incredibly tightfisted. The man hates to spend Eurokit's money, which is why top management loves him.

Hope this helps. Best of British + Love and Kisses.
Chloe

PS: The man is a bachelor and (so one hears) quite good-looking. You might gain more than a new client if you were to wag your "adorable bum" at him.

PPS: All Souls is "getting wired." Stuart tells me the church will soon have E-mail, which means that I will be able to communicate with you every day. Ha! Ha!

Chapter Five

I WENT TO WAR wearing a navy linen business suit and a pair of matching pumps, a spiffy power ensemble that attracted several approving glances as I hiked through the marble-floored corridors of the Ryde Public Library. A quick visit at the reference desk got me a dozen pages of useful tidbits about Eurokit Limited: financial performance, product lines, key customers, and overall reputation. Everything I read about the firm impressed me. Eurokit was a fast-growing, well-managed, and highly successful company. I craved to make it my client.

My next stop was the editorial office of the *Ryde Reporter*. Our twice-weekly newspaper does an excellent job of following the comings and goings of local businesses, thanks in good measure to the efforts of David Friendly, the *Ryde Reporter*'s business writer. I found him pounding the keys of a video-display terminal.

"Guess who needs a favor?" I said.

David spun around in his swivel chair. "How big a favor?"

"I want to browse through your personal morgue, but I can't tell you what I am looking for or why."

"That's pretty big. It'll cost you a croissant and a double shot of espresso. I'll call the coffee shop. You know where I keep my background files."

David was my age, with a tall, athletic build, curly chestnut-colored hair, and an animated face that one might describe as rugged rather than handsome. We had met a year earlier when he wrote an article about the birth of Hunnechurch & Associates. Our personalities meshed. He soon became my dearest male friend on this side of the pond. I am convinced that our friendship blossomed because there was no chance of us developing a closer relationship. David was a proud papa, irrevocably in love with his wife, a beautiful nurse named Joyce. However, Joyce worked four evenings a week, giving David and me many opportunities to have dinner together.

David was a pack rat. He saved and neatly filed every morsel of information he came across about Ryde businesses and Ryde business people. I found a thin "Eurokit Limited" folder in a file box labeled "Companies Thinking About Moving to Ryde." As I suspected, our mayor had pitched Eurokit management on the joys of relocating to Ryde. David had saved a copy of Eurokit's annual report. Inside, on page twenty-six, was what I came for: a photo of Derek Wetherspoon. Gray at the temples, well-groomed, a ruddy, unmistakably English face. David had clipped a scribbled note, dated the previous December, to the report's cover. It read: Eurokit's management reportedly likes Ryde but won't make a final decision until spring, at the earliest.

He obviously hadn't heard that Eurokit Limited had made a firm decision to establish Eurokit USA in Ryde, Maryland. I ached to tell him, but I couldn't—not yet.

━━━━━━━━━

11:00 A.M. I browsed the lobby directory in the Ridley Building, not expecting to see Eurokit's logo. The company's expansion into the United States was supposed to be a secret, but there should be some sort of entry. I found one: a short list of names topped by "Derek G. Wetherspoon," under the heading "Suite 900."

Suite 900 proved to be the entire ninth floor, a mostly vacant "bullpen" furnished with perhaps a dozen desks scattered about. I could see that Eurokit USA had little more than a skeleton staff. No receptionist said hello as I stepped out of the elevator. Nary an eye looked at me as I strolled around the makeshift office.

I located my quarry sitting at a large desk in the far corner.

"Derek Wetherspoon, I presume?" I said in my most impeccably British accent.

He glanced up at me. "Yes. I am Derek Wetherspoon."

I fought off the urge to bob him a curtsy. Instead, I offered my hand and a warm smile. "My name is Pippa Hunnechurch. I am a fellow expatriate from Chichester."

His bright blue eyes peered at me quizzically. "Do we have an appointment, Mrs. Hunnechurch?"

I sidestepped the question. "It's a pleasure to meet you, sir. Let me be one of the first to welcome Eurokit Limited to Ryde. I'm convinced that your expansion into the Americas will be a rip-roaring success."

"Who *are* you?" His robust voice reverberated in the large, open office. Several heads rose from behind computer monitors to see what the fuss was about. He didn't give me a chance to answer his question. Instead, he asked another one. "How do you know about our . . . our growth initiative?"

For a painful moment, I felt intimidated. I knew his type well: a tough-minded, tight-lipped, *veddy-veddy* proper British gent. I kept smiling and matched him stare for stare.

"I am one of your neighbors in the Ryde business community. Hunnechurch & Associates is an executive recruiting firm. We work hard to keep abreast of new arrivals."

"I see. Well, it was probably inevitable that some fool would spill the beans. No real harm done, I suppose." He paused to look at me over his reading glasses. "You aren't a French industrial spy, are you Mrs. Hunnechurch?"

"It's *Miss* Hunnechurch, but please, call me Pippa. And no, I am not a spy. I am here to introduce my firm."

Without being asked, I sat down in his visitor's chair and placed my business card in front of him. He ignored it.

"Let me guess," he said in a mocking tone. "Your entire purpose for being in business is to make my life easier."

I might have lost my temper, but Chloe's fax had given me the perfect response. "Not at all, Mr. Wetherspoon. My primary goal is to help Eurokit save a packet of money."

His eyebrows rose an inch. "And how do you propose to do that?"

Thank you, Chloe!

"By charging you significantly lower fees than other recruiting firms," I said. "Like you, I am a careful manager who keeps a tight rein on unnecessary costs. I can deliver first-class service at bargain prices."

Wetherspoon picked up my card. I held my breath. Don't say another word, I told myself. He's sniffing the hook. Give him a chance to swallow the bait.

"You interest me, Pippa," he finally said, "but you are three months too late. Eurokit USA has an ongoing relationship with Nailor & McHale."

My stomach did a flip-flop. I knew Nailor & McHale as one of the most respected recruiting firms in the United States. More than a hundred experienced recruiters and dozens of offices around the country. A big organization with an unassailable reputation. Top shelf in every way.

I felt thoroughly foolish. How could I have been so naïve? Wetherspoon might be frugal but probably not the kind of manager to dither around. Of course he would commission a leading firm like Nailor & McHale to staff Eurokit USA.

Ah well, at least you can be a good loser as you leave.

"My earnest congratulations," I said. "You've chosen an admirable firm. I am sure that Nailor & McHale has provided superior service."

"Not completely," he replied.

Another flip-flop.

Wetherspoon began to peer at me intently. I looked away, feeling self-conscious. A framed photograph on the desk caught my eye, a posh racing sailboat with Wetherspoon at the helm. Obviously, the man didn't lack for money. Neither did he mind spending bags of it on himself.

He broke the silence. "That is the *Victoria*. My pride and joy."

"She's lovely."

"Thank you."

We might have been discussing a wife or a daughter.

"Do you race?" I asked.

"Unhappily, I don't have the time to race these days. I won't until Eurokit USA is fully established. But . . . ,"—he pretended to check that none of his staff members were listening—"she's berthed at Ryde Marina, only ten minutes away. I take her for a day sail on the Chesapeake Bay every Friday afternoon, without fail. A small prerogative of rank."

"Hear, hear!"

Wetherspoon gazed at *Victoria's* photo for several seconds more, then turned to me. His wistful grin dissolved.

"What do you know about Eurokit?" he said

"Everything that's available at the Ryde library."

He grunted, an utterance I took to mean, "Satisfactory!"

"Let me add a salient fact to your discoveries," he said. "Eurokit sells kitchens throughout the world, including a few countries that the American government doesn't like."

"You mean, Cuba? Libya? North Korea?"

"All of the above."

"Not surprising, I suppose. After all, Eurokit is a European company."

"True, but the mission of Eurokit USA is to build a major kitchen business in the United States."

I nodded thoughtfully, although I didn't have a glimmer of where Wetherspoon was guiding our conversation.

He went on. "The senior attorney on my staff will be responsible for resolving any problems we may have with U.S. government officials. That's why I am determined to hire a certain kind of chief counsel, someone who has the skills to deal with overzealous bureaucrats, if you take my meaning?"

The penny dropped.

"I take your meaning completely," I said. "You want a lawyer who knows Washington, who has high-level contacts inside the federal government."

"Indeed! A *woman* who can keep us out of trouble."

"A woman?"

"Certainly! Look around." He waved his hand. "There are far too many men on my senior staff. We have to pay *some* heed to America's equal opportunity laws."

"Ah . . . I see."

"I should have thought that recruiting a savvy female attorney is a simple exercise."

"Nothing about recruiting is simple," I said, "but your requirements seem reasonable enough."

Wetherspoon scowled. "Nailor & McHale have made a hash of things. They brought me seven candidates. Not one of them had the kind of credentials we need."

Seven candidates. Poor Nailor & McHale. Derek Wetherspoon had run them ragged. How simply delicious. I felt a smile begin to form.

Wetherspoon tapped the edge of my business card on his thumbnail. "Can you find me the right woman, Pippa?"

I didn't shilly-shally. "Without a doubt."

"How can you be so confident?"

The answer came easily. "Because I know where to look."

"That's what Nailor & McHale said, and a lot of good it did us."

"This is one search where a local firm may be able to do a better job than a national firm. My contacts in the regional business community are exceptional."

He seemed to like my response. "When can you begin?"

"Immediately."

"Excellent. Let's set a date." He opened his appointment book. "Today is Tuesday." He ran his finger down the page. "Shall we say the middle of next week? Wednesday afternoon is good for me. Nailor & McHale have promised to show me another lawyer next Thursday. I want to meet your candidate first." He smiled. "Maybe I'll save the company some money."

"Next Wednesday?" I must have look stunned.

"Is there a problem?"

I recovered quickly. "No problem at all. Next Wednesday afternoon will be fine. You can rely on Hunnechurch & Associates. I'll find the perfect chief counsel for Eurokit USA."

I left Wetherspoon's office in a cheery mood, convinced that I would have no trouble keeping my promise to Wetherspoon. After all, Ryde is barely forty miles from Washington, D.C., and high-powered lawyers lie thick on the ground in our parts. Nailor & McHale might fail, but Hunnechurch & Associates would triumph!

Chapter Six

THIRTEEN PHONE CALLS LATER, I knew why Nailor & McHale hadn't located the chief counsel of Wetherspoon's dreams. Even worse, I began to wonder if I could. We both faced some pretty long odds.

There are thousands of female lawyers working in and around Washington, but Wetherspoon wanted one-in-a-million: an ex-Washington insider with lots of business acumen and a thorough knowledge of international law.

She's out there somewhere, I told myself.

Maybe so, but how are you going to find her? myself answered back. *Perhaps you made too ambitious a promise?*

Headhunting is a great nickname for the work I do. A good head must be stalked with cunning, often by following the trail that its owner left among colleagues and professional associates. The primary tool of the headhunting trade is the telephone. One call leads to another until a suitable candidate is located. Usually the suitable candidate is perfectly happy with the job he or she has, and it's back to the drawing board.

I am often asked why I don't use the Internet. I do use it, whenever I can! My Web site (www.pippahunnechurch.com) occasionally snares great candidates, and if I have the luxury of sufficient time to conduct a cyberspace search, I will post the position on the various employment search engines, then wait for résumés to arrive. Sorry to say, most of my clients are like Derek Wetherspoon, executives in too much of a hurry for me to rely on the Net. Consequently, I am forced to reach for my trusty blower.

That morning my telephone calls turned up nothing but dead ends. Five calls to people in government couldn't steer me toward lawyers with corporate know-how. Furthermore, eight calls to business lawyers didn't lead to any ex-Washington lawyers who were at the right level to be a chief counsel.

Thirteen phone calls, and I was back where I started.

Well, that's not entirely true. I did get the names of two lawyers with the right credentials but the wrong plumbing. I tucked them away in my alternate candidate file. If all else failed, maybe I could convince Wetherspoon to find a different solution for his equal-opportunity problems.

Thirteen phone calls isn't much in the scheme of things, but I had only six business days to find a great candidate, not the usual four or five weeks. I couldn't risk the Internet, and I didn't have time to run an ad in the *Ryde Reporter*, the *Washington Post,* the *Legal Times*, or any other newspapers that lawyers are known to read.

I glanced at my calendar. Six business days—counting the day or two I would need to evaluate her résumé and talk to her references. Philippa Hunnechurch & Associates will not present a candidate who hasn't been fully vetted and appraised.

By noon I felt worried. I sent out for a corned beef sandwich and spent my lunch hour thinking about Washington lawyers. Was there a recruiting approach I had overlooked?

The world headquarters of Philippa Hunnechurch & Associates occupies a two-room office suite on the fifth floor of the Calvert Building, a restored nineteenth-century iron foundry on High Street, in downtown Ryde. The high ceilings and exposed brick walls go beautifully with my antique furnishings. I spend a frightful amount of time in my office, so why not decorate it with furniture I like? An excellent example is the well-padded Victorian sofa in my reception room. I often curl up on it to ponder, frequently while eating lunch.

That lunch hour I seemed to ponder in low gear. There were lots more people I could talk to, but I doubted the calls would do me much good. Most of them were middle managers at local companies. I needed to reach high-level executives at major corporations—the kinds of contacts Marsha Morgan had by the dozens in her thick wad of business cards.

Marsha Morgan.

Marsha is a whiz at recruiting woman executives, which means she has all the right connections. My idea gelled in a flash. What if I joined forces with Marsha Morgan? What if Hunnechurch & Associates became a two-woman firm for the duration of this one search?

I reached for my telephone.

"Marsha, I want to take up your offer of active networking," I said with enthusiasm.

"Well, well, *Mizz* Hunnechurch. That *was* quick! We only met last night."

"True. But this morning I landed an opportunity that I believe will benefit both our firms."

I held my breath, not certain how she would respond.

"Come right over, *darlin'*," she said, in her throaty voice. "It's been ages since I've been hustled by another headhunter."

———————

I breezed into Marsha's office on the heels of her secretary, an eye-catching blonde whom Marsha introduced as Gloria Spitz. She gave me a brisk once-over, apparently decided I passed muster, then disappeared back into the reception room.

Marsha didn't bother to get up. "You look like a woman on a mission," she said.

"I am a woman with egg on my chin, so to speak, because I have bitten off more than I can chew."

"Well, take a seat and spit it out."

I chose the comfy visitor chair near her desk and launched into my spiel. "This morning I accepted a wonderful assignment from an English company entering the American market. The company has chosen Ryde for its new U.S. headquarters."

"A new English company in Ryde? You don't by any chance mean Eurokit Limited?"

I tried not to show my astonishment. "As a matter of fact, it is Eurokit."

"Interesting! I knew they were coming to town, but I heard that Nailor & McHale had Derek *What's-His-Name* all tied up in pretty red ribbons."

"Oh my!" I felt myself gawking at Marsha. "You *are* extraordinary."

"Don't act so astonished. Oscar McHale and I are old friends." She winked at me. "We even share a few trade secrets now and then."

"Well, let me contribute a trade secret that even Oscar doesn't know yet. I met with Wetherspoon this morning. He invited me to find Eurokit USA a chief counsel."

Marsha leaned forward in her chair. "I'm impressed! That's one heck of a catch for a fledgling headhunter like you. But tell me—how did Oscar and company fall off the inside track?"

"They hit a brick wall. Derek gave them an especially difficult assignment. He wants, as he puts it, 'a certain kind of chief counsel,' someone with friends in high places."

"Makes perfect sense to me. A mouthpiece with lots of political clout to shepherd the company through the maze of red tape. In other words, a slick operator."

"Almost. A slick *operatress*."

"Ha! The plot thickens. A woman with clout."

Wetherspoon had given me a two-page job description. I slid it across Marsha's desk. She read it quickly. "Nothing unusual here," she said. "Derek wants a typical big-company, chief-counsel slot, someone to advise the CEO, work with outside law firms, et cetera, et cetera—all standard stuff. Lots of women fill the bill, including a bunch with high-level government experience." A tiny frown creased her brow. "I don't get it. What's your problem? You know where to look for good lady lawyers."

"He wants to meet my first candidate next Wednesday afternoon."

Marsha slapped her desk. "Hoo-ha! Talk about your tight deadlines."

"Hoo-ha, indeed, which is why I need your help."

"Go on," she said.

"I have complete faith that you can find a suitable candidate by the end of this week."

Marsha flashed a sly grin. "What if I told you that I know the perfect candidate? A gal who cut her legal teeth in Washington and is currently head of the international law staff at a major bank in Atlanta."

I clasped my hands as if I were praying. "I'm saved! Tell me her name."

Marsha's grin became a broad smile. "What's in it for me?"

I had expected the question. I thought about my answer on the drive to her office. "Thirty percent of my fee. It's my assignment."

"Fifty percent. It's my candidate."

I hesitated. Fifty percent seemed a lot of brass to pay Marsha, but Marsha held all the cards. The voice in my mind spoke loud and clear. *Accept her offer, Pippa. Half a loaf is better than none. Without Marsha's candidate you will have 100 percent of zero.*

"Agreed," I said. "We split the fee equally."

"Howdy, partner." We shook hands across Marsha's elegant rosewood desk.

She poked at her old-fashioned intercom. "Yo! Gloria! Dive into the candidate files, there's a doll, and get me Linda Preston's paperwork. She is about to become a blue chip."

Five minutes later, we were talking to Linda Preston on Marsha's speakerphone.

"I am sitting in my office with a lovely English lass by the name of Pippa Hunnechurch," Marsha said.

"Hi there, Pippa," Linda said in a soft, melodic drawl. Wetherspoon would probably melt.

"Hello, Linda," I replied.

"Pippa is my brand-new business partner," Marsha said.

I wanted to jump in. "Business partner" struck me as too strong a term to describe our arrangement, but I decided to let it slide. Why risk confusing Linda at this stage? I would explain my relationship later, after we met.

"Let's get right to the point," Marsha continued. "How would you like to be the chief counsel of a brand-new company?"

"I don't know nuthin' about birthin' a new business, Miss Marsha."

"New to the United States, smarty-pants. We're talking about a big, fat, British multinational company that plans to invade our shores."

"Do tell."

"You bet your grits, do tell. This is a once-in-a-lifetime career move. The company is staffing a U.S. headquarters in our little corner of Maryland. The president was very specific about his new chief counsel." Marsha paused for effect, then said: "He wants a woman."

"Hear me roar."

"Who has done time along the Potomac."

"I do declare!"

"Who is a genius when it comes to international commerce."

"C'est moi."

"And by the way is a crackerjack lawyer."

"Guilty as charged!"

"See what I mean, Mrs. Preston? The job is a perfect match for your many skills and charms. What's on your schedule next Wednesday?"

Whoa! We were moving faster than I might have liked. I hadn't even seen Linda's résumé; yet Marsha was already inviting her to come to Ryde for an interview. But what could I say? So I kept silent and let Marsha charge ahead.

Linda came back on the line. "I have two meetings I can postpone with no difficulty."

"Good," Marsha said. "Catch a flight that will put you in Baltimore by mid-morning. Pippa will meet you at the airport and fill you in on the particulars. You'll chat for a while, then she'll take you to meet our client."

"It's a date."

"Fiddle-dee-dee," Marsha said as she broke the connection. "How do you like them apples?"

"I must admit that I am stunned by the pace of what just happened," I said. "But then, she is your candidate."

"*Our* candidate."

"Indeed! Well, I had better read *our* candidate's résumé."

Marsha browsed through the white manila file folder that Gloria had retrieved. She finally glanced up at me and shook her head. "I don't have an up-to-date résumé for Linda, but here is something even more impressive, a profile from her alumnae magazine."

I speed-read the article. Linda had attended Bryn Mawr College and Duke University School of Law. She had been a staff intern at the Department of Commerce, a researcher at a Washington think tank, and a congressional fellow. A few years later she was back at the Department of Commerce as a senior attorney. Then she moved on to the Atlanta Bank of Commerce.

"So what do you think now?" Marsha asked.

"Her background will blow Wetherspoon's socks off, if she knows the right people."

"Her friends couldn't be more right."

"I'll need a fresh résumé that spells everything out."

"You'll have one." Marsha jotted "New Résumé for Pippa" on a memo pad in crisp capital letters.

"Ask her to include a few references."

"Of course. Anything else?"

"Well, we aren't true partners."

Marsha seemed bewildered. "Excuse me?"

"You told Linda we are partners, but we really aren't."

Marsha smiled. "What are we, then?"

"Associates."

"What's the difference?"

I thought about it. "I'm not sure, but 'partner' seems to suggest a more permanent relationship. After all, we are collaborating on only one search."

"Pippa, call me anything you like as long as you call me when its time to divvy up the cash."

I left Marsha's office less than an hour after I had arrived, a fact that Detective Stephen Reilly mentioned more than once during my "official" interview two weeks later.

"Are you telling me that you became associates without a formal contract?" he asked. "In a few minutes? With no lawyers hammering out the details?"

"No lawyers, no documents. We consummated the deal with a simple handshake."

"Just like that? She trusted you, and you trusted her?"

"Of course. Marsha Morgan was a well-respected headhunter with impeccable credentials. Why wouldn't I trust her?"

Reilly grinned at me when he figured out his answer. "Because she offered to trust you—a rookie headhunter *without* impeccable credentials. You should have been a lot more skeptical about her motives."

Unfortunately, the copper was right.

Chapter Seven

IT WAS TRUE. I had trusted Marsha Morgan more than I should have. But at the time everything she said sounded reasonable, and everything she did seemed to move me closer to saving Hunnechurch & Associates from extinction. My apprehension about the future seemed to melt away. I even let myself stop thinking about Eurokit USA. Instead I focused my efforts on the chamber's upcoming annual conference. The next three days were a happy blur of social-chair chores and personal errands.

I visited the *Chesapeake Belle* at its pier in Baltimore and chatted with the chef, a rotund Swiss who insisted in a mélange of English, French, German, Romanche, and hand signals that no "coordination" of his superb menus was ever required.

I drove to the Talbot Inn, in St. Michaels, to inspect the premises. The chamber had booked the entire inn, a gracious, clapboard-sided structure, surrounded by lush lawns and tall oaks, built on a cove adjacent to St. Michaels Harbor. It was exactly the sort of place I would have chosen had I become social chairperson months earlier. I found the events manager, toured the facilities, and pronounced everything ready for the arrival of one hundred and twenty-six chamber of commerce conferees.

The lovely weather on the Eastern Shore amplified my growing optimism. I found a trendy boutique on a side street in St. Michaels and bought a pretty party frock, floral print, slinky long skirt, for our dinner on the water. The price tag gave me pause, but only for a moment. To ease my guilt, I drove back to my office and spent several hours furiously marketing Hunnechurch & Associates. I E-mailed, faxed, and telephoned everyone on my client list, begging and cajoling them to come up with new assignments. Their replies were guardedly optimistic. They *might* need more people soon. Well, *maybe* is better than an out-and-out turndown.

It wasn't until late Friday afternoon, when I returned to St. Michaels for the start of the conference, that I began to feel itchy about Eurokit USA. Marsha Morgan still hadn't given me Linda's revised paperwork, and time was growing short. Derek Wetherspoon wanted to interview Linda Preston in only five days, but I hadn't yet seen her résumé. Nor had I spoken to any of her references. Nor had I prepared a candidate packet for Derek.

Not to worry, I told myself. Monday morning is time enough to sort things out.

———————

The *Chesapeake Belle* towered over the other boats tied up to the Talbot Inn's dock. It was about 150 feet long, painted white, with lots of polished bronze and acres of varnished wooden trim. She struck me as a glorious old tub. The chamber members festooning the top deck seemed happy and relaxed. I made for the gangplank feeling upbeat and confident. Foolish me. Who knew that a three-hour boat ride would nearly capsize my career?

I was halfway along the gangplank when someone sounded an excellent imitation of a bosun's whistle, a strident *tooo-weeee—wooo*. I glanced up. David Friendly stood at the railing saluting me and looking trimly nautical in a blue blazer complete with gold buttons.

"Thar she blows!" he cried. "Avast and amidships! Ahoy the mizzenmast! Spinnaker the scuppers! Which brings me to the end of my seafaring vocabulary."

"Thank goodness."

I hugged David gingerly, dodging the can of ginger ale he held in his hand. "And how be thee?" I asked.

"Annoyed! Weird Lenny had another of his frolicsome brain-storms."

Leonard Smithson, the publisher of the *Ryde Reporter*, is a passionate, serious-minded journalist who teaches on the adjunct faculty of Johns Hopkins University. No one but David calls him "Weird Lenny." They respect each other immensely.

"Believe it or not," he continued, "Weird Lenny has ordered me to write a series of articles about women executives, or the lack thereof, at companies based in Ryde."

"You did that last year."

"And the year before. And the year before that." He took a swig of ginger ale. "If I write one more boring exposé of the fabled 'glass ceiling,' I'll throw up—not to mention what my readers will do."

"One can argue that female executives face many obstacles."

"Well, so do male business reporters. Weird Lenny keeps preventing me from doing what I do best, which is writing about mergers and acquisitions. And financial performance. And shareholder lawsuits." He waved his hand in a dismissive gesture. "You've heard all my complaints before. Let's go see who else has arrived."

We followed the sounds of merrymaking to the main salon. As we walked in, I spotted Marsha holding court in the corner, flanked by four women I didn't know.

"Order me an iced tea," I said to David. "I have a wee errand to perform."

Marsha was engaged in a vigorous conversation about the Ryde economy. I waited off to one side until a lull in the nattering gave me the opportunity to say, "You're looking spiffy this evening, Marsha."

"Why thank you, Dame Hunnechurch. You cleaned up real nice too."

I edged close to her and said softly, "Marsha, we have to talk later. About Linda's paperwork."

"It's a date. I'll save you a seat at our table."

"Save two seats." David had come up behind me. He handed me my iced tea.

Marsha spoke a sham aside to her coterie. "Our favorite business newsmonger will be joining us for dinner. Ladies, mind your tongues."

"Let them flutter without fear," David said. He attempted a gallant bow. "Everything is off-the-record tonight."

"Fair enough." Marsha clinked her glass against David's can.

David tugged my sleeve. We moved toward the center of the salon. "I didn't know that you and Marsha Morgan were an item," he said.

"A minor item. We're collaborating on one search."

"I'm still impressed. We're having dinner with a celebrity."

"Marsha?" I asked.

"Don't be silly! Check out the good-looking redhead standing next to Marsha, the gal with the silver-handled cane and the slight limp. That's Kathleen Isley, deputy secretary for international trade, United States Department of Commerce. She is our keynote speaker tomorrow morning. The lady used to live and work in Ryde."

I had heard of Isley, of course, but I didn't expect a high-ranking government official to have dazzling green eyes and brilliant, brassy red hair. It looked real. Isley had the ruddy complexion of a natural redhead, complete with a few freckles.

"How did Kathleen get her gammy leg?" I asked David.

"I don't know."

"You mean you haven't written a story about her?"

"I tried to, but she politely steered me toward one of her underlings. Perhaps you haven't noticed, but Ryde is hardly a hotbed of foreign trade. Our companies tend to be homebodies."

"Good point," I said, trying to sound less sheepish than I felt. Once again, I couldn't tell my dear friend about Eurokit USA. "I wonder why she agreed to speak to our backwater chamber of commerce?"

David shot me a puzzled look. "You really don't know?"

"I haven't the foggiest."

"Marsha Morgan loves to brag—I can't believe she didn't tell you how she launched Kathleen Isley's career."

"But Kathleen's a civil servant."

"Not originally. About fifteen years ago Marsha talked Militet Corporation into making Kathleen the youngest director of international marketing they ever had."

Militet was a major defense contractor with plants and office buildings scattered throughout the region. Much too big to be my client—yet.

David continued: "Kathleen took off like a skyrocket. She initiated a bunch of deals with Japan, made a bundle of money for Militet, and became known as an expert on Japanese trade. That's why the president drafted her into the Department of Commerce eight years ago. Word is, Kathleen might be our next secretary of commerce." He grabbed my arm. "Did you bring your camera?"

"It's in my room."

"So's mine, which is unforgivable. My editor would kill for a picture of that group. Marsha Morgan and the four superstars she helped launch into orbit."

"Superstars? Then those women aren't chamber members?"

"Nope. They're Marsha's guests. She holds a reunion of her success stories at every annual conference."

"Now I am really discouraged. I don't know any of them."

"Allow me to do the honors." David bent his head close to mine. "The corn-fed gal with the beaky nose and the 'Heidi' braid is Susan McKenzie, Marsha's most recent placement at Militet Corporation. Susan is general manager of the aerospace division. The scuttlebutt says she's on a fast track to become a corporate vice president, and maybe even chairman, some day."

Susan McKenzie had a thin, tanned face and dark eyes. She wore a black linen shift, softened by a triple strand of pearls. David read my mind: "The pearls are real. Two years ago she received a gargantuan performance bonus for cutting the division's head count by 20 percent."

"I cringe at the very thought," I said.

"Trouble is, she cut back too deeply. Militet won a new Air Force communications contract, and the division had to scrounge for engineers to do the work."

"Lay off in haste, repent in leisure."

"There is nothing repentant about Susan. Rumor has it that she spent half her bonus on the necklace."

"A proper Marie Antoinette."

"You got it! Which brings us to the willowy blond in the pale green dress. A vision of delicacy and ethereal charm, but don't be fooled by appearance. Her name is Roxanne Landesberg. She holds an MBA from Harvard Business School. Marsha placed her at Sysex Systems Corporation four years ago as a mere product-line manager. She soon became vice president of business development. I know for a fact that she climbed to her exalted position over the carcasses of four former U.S. Army colonels, all men, of course, who made the mistake of assuming that a former Penn State cheerleader didn't know how to market advanced software to the Defense Department. Her marketing teams nailed five major contracts, close to a half-billion dollars of sales."

"Go Roxanne!"

"She did. She left Sysex last year and opened her own consulting firm: the Landesberg Group."

"A risky undertaking," I said.

"Not the way she did it. She lined up her client list long before she took the plunge. Now she consults for the cream of American industry."

"I wish I could say that."

"Last, but certainly not least, we have the tall drink of water in the pink pants suit. Harriet Beardsley has built one of the country's best-performing mutual fund management groups at Bates-McCann Financial. She is the only BMF portfolio wizard who didn't lose money when the market took a dive two years ago. The others panicked, but Harriet rode it out and made a bundle. She has to be Marsha's richest ex-candidate. Her compensation is astronomical. She owns that massive white mansion on Broad Creek."

"The manor house with all the columns?"

"That's the one!" David tapped his glass against mine. "Notice anything else about the four superstars?"

"They look trim and fit."

"They should. They're all jocks. Susan ran her way through Cornell University's engineering school on a track-and-field scholarship.

Kathleen anchored an Olympic swimming team. Roxanne could be a pro tennis player. And Harriet is a ski fanatic."

I felt the engines grind to life below the decks. We were underway at last. The *Chesapeake Belle* quivered as we moved into the Miles River. David and I went out on deck to watch the blue water take on a pinkish sheen as the sun slipped below the horizon.

━━━━━━━━━━

Dinner was served buffet style. I decided that the social chair was duty-bound to hover near the food until everyone else had been served. When I finally sat down at Marsha's table, she placed a gold-wrapped mint on my plate and said, "Pippa Hunnechurch, you have just set the world record for thoroughness and attention to detail by any board member of this here chamber."

"I don't believe Pippa is a headhunter," Harriet said. "She's much too considerate."

Marsha stuck her tongue out at Harriet.

"Hello, all," I said.

"You sound British," Susan said.

"Born and bred."

"The rhain in Sphain falls mahinly in the puhlain."

"My congratulations. You have the British accent down pat."

"I used to live with a British guy," Susan said.

"Me too," I said. "He was my husband."

Everyone laughed, then went back to eating their dinners. The lull in the table talk gave me my chance to collar Marsha.

"I need Linda Preston's résumé, ASAP, and her references."

"Her résumé's in my office; I typed and proofread it myself. I also added a list of references to my recruiting notes. You'll have everything you need to dazzle *you-know-who*. Pick them up Monday morning. I get in at 7:30."

"Bless you. Now I can relax."

"Hey, no talking about business this weekend," Roxanne said. "Remember *your* rules."

"You are absolutely right," Marsha said with a smile. "I humbly apologize for myself and my industrious new partner."

Someone coughed. Harriet dropped her fork on her plate. "Since when do you have a *partner?*" she asked Marsha.

"Since Pippa asked for my help," Marsha replied.

I jumped in. "Perhaps partner is too strong a word."

"I'll bite," Roxanne said. "What kind of relationship do you have with Marsha?"

"We're strategic teammates," I said.

"I'll go along with that!" Marsha said. "I like 'strategic teammate' a whole bunch better than 'associate.'"

"It's a cute phrase," Kathleen said, "but what does it mean?"

"It means they're collaborating on a search," David said, then turned to me. "Did I get that right?"

"Indeed you did."

"What kind of search?" Susan asked.

"I prefer not to reveal that." I answered.

"Why not?" Roxanne said.

"Whoa! Time out!" Marsha said. She made the "T" hand gesture that referees make at American football games. "We're back to talking business."

"Not at all, Marsha," Kathleen said. "We're trying to understand your alliance with Pippa Hunnechurch."

"It's a simple story," Marsha said, her voice almost icy. "Pippa needed my help. And you know me—I enjoy helping women advance their careers."

David weighed in. "I like it, Marsha! It's a great story—with lots of interesting angles. Two professional women working together. Old pro helps newcomer. Women mentoring women in the Ryde business community. I think I'll write it."

"Good!" Marsha said, her smile returning. "I'd love a little limelight. We recruiters spend our careers working behind the scenes."

I networked for a while after dinner, but my heart wasn't in it. After all, I had a grand, new, corporate client—why try to hustle a local accounting firm or a small software company? David and I went for a walk on the near-deserted promenade deck to enjoy the breeze that blew off the river. We watched the *Chesapeake Belle* turn around in the Miles River and point its bow toward St. Michaels, and we listened to the pleasant jumble of sounds on the air: the gentle thump of the party boat's big diesel engines; a snippet of dance music; and, a car horn somewhere on the nearby shore. We soon began to chat about Marsha's four superstars.

"My congratulations, Pippa," David said. "You seem to have been accepted by Ryde's high-flying overachievers."

"They did seem a little intense, didn't they?"

"*Intense?*" David laughed. "I worried they were about to self-destruct, although I also think that particular quartet could do wonders for Hunnechurch & Associates."

"I suppose so. I guess you need a big ego and a powerful drive to get to the top. People in high places are not known for their gentility."

"Yeah, well, life's too short. I leave the joys of dealing with big egos to you and Marsha."

"Speak of the devil . . ."

Marsha Morgan stood at the stern rail, a blank expression on her face.

"Hi, Marsha," David said.

No answer.

"Earth calling Marsha Morgan," David said.

Again, no answer.

We moved closer.

Marsha's temples glistened with beads of sweat. She seemed to be having trouble focusing her eyes and coordinating her fingers. She dropped her purse and used both hands to grip the tall glass she held. She drank; a dollop ran down her chin. She took another gulp.

"All gone," Marsha said softly. "No more *drinkies*."

David touched Marsha's cheek, then her forehead.

"Does she have a fever?" I asked.

"No. She feels clammy. Maybe she's drunk?"

"She doesn't look drunk. Besides, I've never seen Marsha drink anything stronger than diet Dr Pepper."

I tried to sniff Marsha's drink, but the wedge of lime riding on the rim overpowered any other smells the glass might have held.

"OK," David said. "Maybe she's seasick?"

"Being seasick doesn't make you inert. She's acting like a zombie." I had a thought. "Is she wearing a medical warning bracelet?"

"No bracelet, no locket. Check her purse."

I picked up Marsha's purse, a small black-beaded clutch. "Nothing in here but her keys, her driver's license, and a couple of twenty-dollar bills."

Marsha pulled away from David. "Ooooh. Look at the moon," she said. She tried to point at the reflection of the full moon on the calm black water. Her glass struck the mahogany rail and dropped glittering shards at our feet.

"We have to do something," David said. "She's definitely getting shakier."

"We'll be in St. Michaels in a few minutes. You keep Marsha upright. I'll ask the captain to radio ahead for an ambulance."

What happened next took only an instant.

"I want to touch the pretty moon," Marsha said.

Before David could catch her, Marsha lurched to the railing, pulled herself up, and tumbled over the edge.

"Marsha!" I screamed.

"Man overboard!" David shouted. "Turn the boat around!"

David grabbed a yellow life ring and threw it into the ebony water. "Keep your eye on the life preserver! It marks the spot where Marsha fell into the river."

I stood on a fitting at the base of the stern rail and leaned over as far as I could.

"It's too dark. I can't see a thing."

The boat began to turn. Other people rushed on deck. Someone shouted, "There's her head!"

Crew members shone spotlights on the river. Two at first, then a third, and a fourth. The bright disks of light danced over the still and silent water, but all they illuminated was a crab pot float and what looked like a white plastic coffee cup.

For nearly forty minutes, the *Chesapeake Belle* moved in ever-widening circles as more than a hundred pairs of eyes searched the Miles River. We were joined by two police boats and five crabbers from St. Michaels, but no one saw anything.

At ten o'clock, the *Chesapeake Belle* turned for home—without Marsha Morgan aboard.

Chapter Eight

As it happened, David and I were the only Chamber conferees who saw Marsha fall off the *Chesapeake Belle*. We sat in the captain's cabin and told our story to a pair of corporals from the Maryland Department of Natural Resources Police who clucked their tongues, made sympathetic noises, and offered several clichéd comments about the perils of drinking while boating.

"Marsha wasn't drunk," I said.

"Lots of people who don't look drunk die in alcohol-related accidents," the tall corporal said.

"She wasn't drunk," I repeated.

"We have a witness who says she was," the short corporal said. He glanced at his notebook. "One of the ship's musicians. But it will be the medical examiner's call."

"Right," Tall said. "They will perform an autopsy when the body is recovered."

I nodded. So did David. Neither of us expected Marsha to be plucked from the water alive, but now we were prattling with the police about cutting her up. In less than an hour, we had gone from partygoers, to witnesses, to gossips. The metamorphosis made me queasy.

"Excuse me," I said. "Where can I throw up?"

It was half past eleven when David and I returned to the Talbot Inn. The screened-in back porch was crowded with people watching a flotilla of small boats move back and forth in the distance. The police had enlisted the help of the U.S. Coast Guard and the St. Michaels Fire Department to search for Marsha.

"I'll stay out here for a while," I said. "Maybe something will happen."

"I doubt they'll find her body tonight, but who knows? I'll join you later, after I call Weird Lenny and tell him what happened. Marsha's death is news."

I felt myself shudder. "I keep remembering what she said a few hours ago. 'I'd love a little limelight.'"

"Now she's going to get some—with a vengeance. Can't you see the headlines tomorrow morning? 'The Party's Over for Vacationing Headhunter Lost in the Miles River.'"

"No one, not even a journalist, can have so little taste."

"Wanna bet?" David abruptly became a working reporter: "Who is the keeper of Marsha's biographical information? I need enough to put together a brief obituary."

Good Lord! His simple request made me realize how little I knew about Marsha Morgan.

"I haven't a clue where to send you," I said. "We never discussed her personal life. I don't even know if she's married."

David gave me a good-bye hug, then marched inside the Talbot Inn. I found a vacant dark corner on the porch and sat alone, staring at the black water, and thinking about the fragility of humankind, the uncertainty of our futures, and the absurd whimsicality of bizarre accidents that, without warning, claim the lives of people you rely on.

Inevitably, I began to imagine a quiet two-lane road in the south of England. I could see the buds of early spring on the trees and here and there birds perched on branches. Then I saw the elderly pensioner driving west into the evening sun, squinting at the yellow glare, not realizing he had steered his old Austin Mini across the centerline. And finally, the shower of glass and metal bits as the Mini plowed head-on into our new Ford sedan.

Enough! It happened seven years ago.

"What difference does seven years make?" I muttered to myself. "You'll never forget that terrible day."

I had been sitting in the back seat, which is why I came away from the crash with only a few cuts and a broken ankle. The two people in the front seat weren't as lucky: my husband, Simon, and my daughter, Margaret (whom everyone, of course, called Peggy). Peggy was three when she died. And Simon, how old would he be now if he had lived? Thirty-eight? Or was it thirty nine? Sometimes I have trouble remembering his face but not Peggy's. I glimpse an echo of her features every time I look into a mirror. No, I'll never forget that awful day.

"How are you feeling, Pippa?"

I glanced up at Susan McKenzie. I didn't want to explain the tears in my eyes, so I said, "I suppose I'm grieving. Odd, I miss Marsha, though we only just met."

"We saw you sitting all alone, and well, maybe that's not such a great idea right now. Come join us." She pointed across the porch. Marsha's superstars were gathered at a round wicker table. They waved in unison when I looked their way.

Why not join them?

"I'll bet that Pippa wants a pint of strong ale," Harriet Beardsley said.

"Nope," Susan said. Pippa looks like she could use a double Scotch."

"They don't serve booze out here," Roxanne said, "but a nip of my bourbon will do the same job." She held up a palm-sized pewter flask.

"I'm not much of a drinker."

"As my mother used to say," Harriet said, "even teetotalers will knock a few back for medicinal purposes."

The other three watched in silence while Roxanne poured two fingers of bourbon into a plastic tumbler.

"Why am I being plied with liquor?" I asked.

"The jig is up," Kathleen Isley said. "We had better tell Pippa the truth." Then she turned to me. "We have an ulterior motive for disturbing you. We think you are the right person to call Gloria Spitz."

"Oh my! I forgot about Marsha's secretary."

"We don't want her to hear about Marsha on the late-night news."

"I agree, but why elect me for the job?"

"First, because you were Marsha's business partner. Second, because you were there when it happened."

"Ah."

"We think you should call Missy too."

The name meant nothing to me. "Who is Missy?"

"Marsha's sister," Susan said. "We think she is the next of kin."

"Marsha never told me she had a sister."

"In that case, you take Gloria, and I'll do Missy," Kathleen said. "I wonder if the front desk has an Atlanta phone directory?"

I nodded mechanically, and then the word "Atlanta" hit home. Linda Preston lived in Atlanta. Her résumé, typed and proofread, was waiting for me in Marsha's office along with a trove of other information I needed.

I could ask Gloria to find it for me, but was it still mine to take?

"Is there a lawyer at the table?" I asked.

"Me," Harriet said.

"Gloria may ask me about her job. Should she show up for work on Monday morning? Should she do anything special," here I spoke with care, "about the papers and things in Marsha's office?"

"Good point. Well, I would certainly advise Gloria to start looking for a new position. In the interim, she should secure the office, lock up every drawer and file, and sit tight. I assume that Missy will be Marsha's executor and dispose of her property, including all of the chattels related to her recruiting practice."

Rats! Ask a lawyer a silly question and you get an ironclad answer. The papers I needed were trapped in a limbo of legal mumbo jumbo.

I took a swallow from my cup, forgetting it contained straight bourbon. The burn in my throat made me gasp. I began to cough.

"My goodness, you really aren't much of a drinker," Harriet said as she pounded my back with her bony fist. "Here, have a cup of water."

I sat quietly, sipping my water and thinking about my options.

I could try to locate Linda Preston at her home on Saturday or Sunday, but I didn't have her phone number, and it was possible that there might be several women named Linda Preston in the Atlanta phone book. Furthermore, what if mine lived outside the city or had an unlisted telephone number?

My other option was to wait until Monday morning and call Linda at her bank. That would get me her résumé by return fax, but not the other useful recruiting materials Marsha had prepared, most important of all, her notes and comments.

The notion of the résumé being "Marsha's property" struck me as beside the point. All I needed was a copy of Linda's file, not the file itself.

I realized I had a third option.

What if I went to Marsha's office tonight?

What if I used Marsha's copying machine to make a copy of Linda's paperwork?

After all, I had the means of getting into Marsha's office. Her keys were inside her little purse, which was crammed deep inside my own handbag. (I meant to turn the purse over to the police, but I had forgotten.) If I left right away, I could be back at the Talbot Inn by 2:00 A.M., a reasonable hour, with no one the wiser.

"Look, this is going to sound silly," I said, "but after I call Gloria, I'm off for a drive to clear my head."

"Not silly at all," Roxanne said. "Do you want any company?"

"Thanks, but no. I have some serious thinking to do."

"About your *partnership* with Marsha?"

"Exactly."

"It's a pretty night. Go topless," Kathleen said.

"Pardon?"

"You arrived yesterday in a little red convertible," Kathleen said. "So I thought . . ."

"Ah. Yes, my trusty Mazda Miata roadster. You know—I will put the top down."

"You own a Miata?" Roxanne said with genuine pleasure in her voice. "I haven't ridden in a two-seater sports car since my college days."

"Then tomorrow you shall take her for a spin. She's a charming machine. Great fun to drive."

"And also a hazard to life and limb," Susan said grimly. "There are too many monster pickup trucks and sport utility vehicles on the road for anyone to put her faith in a tiny convertible. These days you need a hefty vehicle with energy-absorbing crumple zones, and big side-impact door beams, and . . ."

Harriet interrupted, "Don't mind Susan. She's a nerd engineer to the core. Naturally, she drives a big, green Volvo station wagon . . ."

"Of course I do," Susan interrupted in return. "I'm not ready to donate my organs yet."

I pushed back from the table, anxious to escape any more discussion about car crashes. "I promise I will drive defensively. In the meantime, should David Friendly come looking for me, tell him where I went."

<hr>

I called Gloria as I drove west on Route 50-301, using the palm-sized personal phone I keep in the Miata's glove box.

"It's Pippa Hunnechurch. I'm afraid I have some rather terrible news . . ."

When I finished my story, Gloria reacted with a soft, "Poor Marsha. God rest her soul. Let's pray for her."

"What?"

"Pray. You know, talk to God. We can do it together."

Maybe it was the shock catching up with me, or maybe I was just tired. Either way, I lost my temper. "By all means let's talk to God. Let's find out what he had in mind when he let Marsha fall off the *Chesapeake Belle*."

"Oh, Pippa, you can't feel that way about God."

"Spare me the theology lecture, Gloria. I am in no mood to shoot the breeze about religion right now. Besides, there's something important I have to tell you." I related Harriet's advice about securing Marsha's office on Monday morning. The long silence that followed made me wonder if we were still connected.

Gloria eventually said, amidst several sniffles. "I don't believe it! I *won't* accept that you care more about Marsha's office than her soul."

"Neither am I in a mood to be snapped at," I said. "I thought you might find the information useful. It seems I was wrong."

I rang off. Ahead were the lights at the western end of the Chesapeake Bay Bridge. I put Gloria Spitz out of my mind.

━━━━━━

Marsha's office was in the uptown end of Ryde High Street, about a mile north of mine, in a five-story, red-brick edifice that had started life as an eighteenth-century leather warehouse. A decade ago a local developer had transformed the old pile into a trendy office block. It seemed an exotic structure by day but forbidding by night. I made a U-turn and parked across the street.

High Street was deserted and dark. There weren't any restaurants in this part of Ryde, and no stores remained open past six-thirty. The sound of my shoes hitting the pavement bounced off the building's brick exterior and made a lonely, clip-clopping echo. I felt in jeopardy—a woman alone on a lonely street. I jogged toward the converted warehouse, my senses alert.

Don't get mugged. Don't get your photo printed alongside Marsha Morgan in tomorrow's Ryde Reporter.

Curiously, the thought of David Friendly forced to write two obituaries struck me as funny. Most of my fear drained away. I used the largest key on Marsha's key chain to unlock the tall glass front door.

A single fixture illuminated the lobby, providing barely enough light to read a hand-lettered sign on the information desk: "The security guard is making his rounds. If you want to sign in after-hours, please press the call button."

Ouch! I hadn't expected security guards or sign-in books. I didn't want to explain my presence, not when I was about to bend the estate laws of Maryland.

I heard the hum of machinery. An elevator in motion. The numbers above the door flashed 6, 5, 4 . . .

I scampered to the stairway and tiptoed up three flights of stairs to Marsha's office.

Detective Stephen Reilly would later say: "First, you didn't identify yourself to the security guard. Second, you didn't sign in. Third, you pranced around like a cat burglar. You *must* have known that your actions that night came perilously close to breaking and entering."

"I saw no need to check with the guard," I mumbled. "I visited the building merely to copy a few pieces of paper." My claim sounded feeble, even to me.

I used a middle-sized key to unlock the outer door to Marsha's suite. It was dark in the reception room; only a slight glow from the hallway made its way through the door's frosted-glass panel. Silly me, I hadn't thought to bring the powerful flashlight I keep in my glove box. No matter. I remembered that Gloria's desk sat against an interior wall. I inched my way along the carpet until my knee hit something large and wooden. I groped for the desk lamp and yanked the chain. The sixty-watt bulb was more decorative than practical. It cast scarcely enough light to search the file cabinets, but more than enough to signal anyone in the hallway that I had entered the office.

I had to find Linda's paperwork before the security guard stumbled across me. He might be in the lobby right now. If he decided to patrol the fourth floor, how long would it take him to get here?

I gave myself sixty seconds, but I took only eight.

The middle drawer of the file cabinet closest to Gloria's desk was labeled *"Na to Pr."* Its lock succumbed to a smallish key. There! A white manila folder tagged "Preston, Linda." Inside was the alumni magazine article I had read at Marsha's desk, plus one item she hadn't shown me: a five-year-old letter of reference signed by someone named James Huston. But I found no résumé. No notes. No list of current references.

Blast!

Think, Pippa! If you were Marsha, where would you put Linda Preston's résumé?

In my desk drawer, of course. With my other current files.

I doused Gloria's desk lamp. The dark felt wonderful. I unlocked Marsha's blessedly lightproof door, made my way into her office, and poked all the switches. It didn't matter if someone in a passing car saw a light on in a business office.

Marsha's office smelled of lemony furniture polish. There were deep vacuum tracks across the dark blue carpet, her wastebasket had a fresh plastic liner, and the books on her shelves had been straightened. All of it the work of a professional cleaning service, the kind I couldn't afford. I felt a twinge of envy. Some people have all the luck. . . .

Snap out of it, Hunnechurch! The woman is dead.

I laughed at my misplaced greed and got to work.

Marsha's big desk had drawers on both sides of the foot well, but only the bottom drawer on the left seemed tall enough to hold file folders. The smallest key on her chain did the trick. I pulled the drawer open. Its contents glowed back at me like a patch of periwinkles—a brilliant, electric blue.

I had found a stash of brand new file folders, all of them bright blue. I riffled through the tabs with my index finger. Five were neatly labeled in Marsha's precise handwriting: "Beardsley, Harriet." "Isley, Kathleen." "McKenzie, Susan." "Landesberg, Roxanne." "Preston, Linda."

Bingo!

Linda's folder contained everything I needed: her résumé, a typed list of references, and several sheets from a yellow legal pad that were covered with Marsha's precisely printed recruiting notes. Then I remembered Marsha's words to Gloria. "Linda Preston is about to become a blue chip."

Blue chip people deserve bright blue folders. It made perfect sense.

I took the opportunity to lean back in Marsha's chair and savor the moment. Ryde's leading headhunter had thought enough of Linda Preston to place her among the superstars. How wonderful to know that I would soon present Derek Witherspoon with a candidate who was the peer of Kathleen Isley.

The more I thought, the more curious I became. *What does it take to be a superstar? What is special about, say, Kathleen Isley?* I opened her folder, expecting to see a current résumé. Instead, I found several pages of notes in Marsha's now-familiar handwriting. The last page, headed "Linda Preston Reference," seemed to summarize Linda's working relationship with Kathleen Isley at the Department of Commerce.

Stop dawdling, Pippa! You don't have time to read interview notes, or whatever they are.

Where does Marsha keep her copying machine?

I remembered. Behind Gloria's desk.

I gathered up Linda's paperwork and turned out the lights in Marsha's office. I fumbled in the dark reception room for several moments before I located the machine's power switch. The innards whined and complained as the copier warmed up, which is why I nearly didn't hear the elevator arrive at the fourth floor.

The security guard!

The copy machine fell mercifully silent as heavy footsteps approached the outer door, then receded. I stood still as death, my hand over my mouth.

I moved to the outer door and listened. Nothing. I counted to one hundred. Still nothing. I opened the door an inch and peeked out. Empty.

The copy machine was new and fast. Even so, I winced at every wheeze and squeak as it reproduced the contents of the two "Linda Preston" folders I had retrieved, one white, one bright blue. I replaced both in their respective file drawers and locked the respective locks, enjoying a surge of exhilaration about my skulduggery skills.

I walked through the office twice, double-checking that I left everything as I had found it. Then I locked both doors and tiptoed down the stairs to the lobby.

A mere fifty feet stood between the street and me. Fifty blooming feet. I began to jog. But halfway across the lobby, the men's room door opened. A burly bloke in a tight uniform peered out at me.

Perhaps I could pull the wool over.

"Good night," I said, still jogging. "See you on Monday morning."

I reached the sidewalk before the security guard could realize that he had never seen me before. I don't know if he tried to confront me. I ran like the dickens for my Miata, feeling the same kind of remorse that I felt thirty years ago when I nicked a Jaffa orange from my mother's favorite greengrocer.

We Hunnechurches are not natural-born criminals.

Chapter Nine

I SKULKED INTO THE TALBOT INN through the side door at 2:00 A.M., hoping I wouldn't meet any members (or guests) of the Ryde Chamber of Commerce. I felt knackered to the soles of my feet, eager to slip between the sheets and bury my head in my pillow and anxious to put an end to this horrid day.

"Pippa! Where on earth have you been?"

David Friendly bounded out of the bar. Roxanne Landesberg, glass in hand, was a step behind him.

"Motoring through the countryside," I said.

"So everyone told me. But it makes no sense—not for three hours."

David knows me too well to fall for a little white lie. I changed the subject. "Any news about Marsha?"

He shook his head. "They'll resume the search tomorrow."

Roxanne raised her glass. "Come have a drink with us."

"The company is tempting, but I am exceedingly tired. Perhaps tomorrow night."

Roxanne frowned. "Party Pooper Pippa." She swung open the door to the bar and tugged David back inside. Raucous laughter spilled into

the lobby, the sounds of people having fun. Life goes on, and so would
the chamber's annual conference, despite Marsha's death. The thought
depressed me as I trudged up the stairs to my room.

When Peggy and Simon were killed, the people around me ex-
ploded with sympathy and thoughtfulness. They cooked my meals, ran
my errands, wrapped me in the kindness I needed to get through those
terrible days of grief. But the crowd in the bar required no sympathy.
Less than four hours later, they had all but forgotten this evening's
tragedy.

Don't be so sanctimonious, Hunnechurch. You're one of them.

Once again my conscience was dead right. My recent agenda did
not include grieving for Marsha Morgan. I had put the problems of
Hunnechurch & Associates first. How odd that I hadn't considered
rescheduling Linda's interview? In truth, the notion hadn't entered my
head. Thoughts about saving my business had filled every available
nook and cranny.

"Not your finest hour, Pippa," I murmured as I climbed into bed.

I was bone tired and should have drifted off in seconds, but con-
templating my flaws keeps me awake better than caffeine. So why not
do a spot of work? I sat up in bed, spread my loot across the surface,
and began to read.

Linda's beautifully formatted résumé echoed all that the alumni
magazine article had reported, and added a critical new fact. During her
tenure at the Department of Commerce, Linda had worked hand in
glove with Kathleen Isley for close to a year on a program to improve
trade relations with the former Soviet republics.

My first thought was, *Wow!* Linda has the deputy secretary for international trade as a friend in high places. What more could
Wetherspoon want from his chief counsel?

On second thought: *Wait a minute!* Kathleen heard Marsha and me
talking about Linda Preston. Why hadn't she reacted? Why hadn't she
mentioned that she knew Linda?

On third thought: Kathleen didn't get the chance to react. The table
had begun a weird four-sided discussion about the Morgan-
Hunnechurch "partnership."

The memory set me snuffling. It began to sink in that our association—call it what you will—had ended. I would never see Marsha Morgan again.

═══════

The weekend went off more or less as planned. John Tyler asked for a moment of silence for Marsha before Katherine Isley's keynote address, and several other presenters offered kind remembrances. The pall I felt on Friday night seemed to decrease with each hour the conference progressed. I found myself enjoying the working sessions and the social gatherings.

On Sunday afternoon after the final session, the inn's front-desk manager waylaid me as I returned to my room. "We understand that you are Miss Morgan's business partner," he said with more than a touch of fawning. "Someone has to pack her suitcase, then bring it to her family. We were wondering . . ."

What could I say? I agreed to take on the burden of Marsha's belongings but then discovered that Marsha's suitcase was an enormous, leather-trimmed "check-through" that would never squeeze into my Miata's miniature trunk. It was even too big to sit next to me in the passenger seat. I tried to enlist the help of her four superstars, but they spewed out excuses like water from a fire hydrant.

Kathleen Isley: "I would, Pippa, but I have to race back to Washington."

Susan McKenzie: "Sorry, Pippa. I brought two other people, and there's not an inch of space left in the Volvo."

Roxanne Landesberg: "Oooh, I'm hopeless doing that kind of thing. I don't tolerate death well, if you know what I mean."

Harriet Beardsley: "*Mea culpa*, Pippa. I suggested that the man at the front desk talk to you. Your relationship with Marsha was much deeper than mine."

And so, I loaded Marsha's clobber into her oversize valise and strapped the thing on the Miata's trunk lid with the bungee cords I keep aboard for carrying extra-large items.

Winston chirped when he heard me step on a creaky floorboard. "Mummy's home," I called out, "and mighty glad to be here."

I heaved Marsha's suitcase into the hallway and gave it a robust kick. It toppled onto its side and slid to a stop next to the walnut buffet table that holds my mail. Good! It could stay there forever for all I cared. I had other things to worry about.

I made myself a pot of tea and began to prepare the "candidate package" I would give to Derek Wetherspoon before Linda arrived for her interview.

The excellent notes I had found in Marsha's office were dotted with occasional asides to me. For example:

- FYI: Linda is forty-one years old. Remind Wetherspoon that forty-or-so is a perfect age for a new chief counsel. But be discreet! We don't discriminate on the basis of age in this country. *Ha! Ha!*

- NOTE: Linda provided five references in Washington and Atlanta. (They adore her dearly. Of course they would, or she wouldn't list them as references!) I told all five to expect calls from you, since I know you'll want to hear the gushing praise for yourself.

- IMPORTANT: Kathleen Isley is *not* among Linda's references because the honorable deputy secretary for international trade seldom returns phone calls from mere headhunters. Nonetheless, she loves and respects our gal.

Linda's reference list included home phone numbers. Perhaps one or two would be home on Sunday afternoon. The first name on the list was Emily Baxter, a recently retired senior attorney at the Department of Commerce.

"Good afternoon." Her voice sounded soft and melodious.

"Pippa Hunnechurch, here." I introduced myself and offered a quick apology for disturbing her Sunday. "Would you have some time to chat about Linda Preston?"

"My pleasure. She's a wonderful attorney . . ."

We spoke for more than a half hour about Linda's assignments and triumphs at the Department of Commerce. I merrily scribbled Emily's kudos: "hard worker; totally reliable; a genius at doing international deals; a quick learner; really knows her stuff; not afraid to stand her ground."

I thanked Emily and tried the second person on the list. No luck.

Linda's third reference, Daniella Holms, a partner at an Atlanta law firm that worked closely with Linda's bank, answered on the second ring.

"*Ah* am expecting a summons from *mah* husband," she explained in a thick Georgian accent, "to join him for dinner. So let's cut to the chase. Linda Preston is a superb lawyer and an exceptionally *nahce* lady. She will make an imposing chief counsel. Any questions?"

I had a few about Linda's experience in shepherding overseas transactions.

"Linda has initiated any number of foreign deals for companies in Atlanta," Holms said. "We have worked together on several. She has always shown a high degree of professionalism."

I thanked her, hung up, and looked at the clock. It was 6:50. Too late to make more calls. I heated a frozen Cornish pastry in the microwave and finished organizing the bits and pieces of Linda's dossier. I went to bed that night in a happy mood, altogether pleased with myself.

Chapter Ten

I AWOKE TO A DELIGHTFUL MONDAY MORNING IN RYDE. I was refreshed, energetic, and confident that Derek Wetherspoon would be unreservedly impressed by Linda Preston's credentials. Then I remembered that Linda Preston didn't know that Marsha fell off the *Chesapeake Belle*. I had meant to telephone her on Sunday afternoon but plumb forgot.

Correction! In truth, I didn't want to make the call. What if Linda balked at being my candidate? What if she refused to come to Ryde for her interview?

I stared at the telephone as I ate breakfast and ran alternative phrases through my mind. Should I announce, Marsha is dead? Or was it kinder to say, Marsha has disappeared?

Don't be daft, Pippa! There's only one way to do this.

Linda's résumé provided her unlisted telephone numbers at home and at work. A woman in her position wouldn't keep bankers' hours. I dialed her private number at the bank and held my breath.

"Good morning. This is Linda Preston."

"Hello, Linda. It's Pippa Hunnechurch."

"Oh, Pippa, isn't it awful about Marsha."

I nearly swooned with relief. "You've heard!"

"Missy Morgan told me on Saturday morning."

I felt bewildered for a moment, but then I recalled my conversation with the four superstars. "Of course, Missy is Marsha's sister. You both live in Atlanta."

"We've been good friends for years and years. In fact, she is the kind soul who sent my résumé to Marsha for her consideration."

"How interesting." My mind raced to invent more small talk, but I needn't have bothered.

"We really should talk about my interview on Wednesday," Linda said. "I intended to call you this morning. You beat me to it. But then, a great headhunter thinks of everything."

I sopped up the compliment. "Indeed. I want you to have full confidence in me."

"Oh, I do. Marsha told me to put *mahself* completely in your hands."

"Wonderful!" I said, savoring every syllable. "Have you made flight reservations?"

"Delta Airlines. Nonstop from Atlanta. Arriving at 10:10 A.M."

"Excellent. I'll meet you at the gate."

Much relieved, I lingered in my bath and dawdled over another cup of tea. Why rush? Three more reference checks, and Linda's candidate package would be complete. I enjoyed the dusty sunbeams in my little parlor and resolved to become as effective a recruiter as Marsha Morgan thought I could be.

I had begun to rinse the breakfast dishes when my telephone rang.

"Pippa, it's Gloria. I need you at Marsha's office."

The mix of anger and distress I heard made me stiffen. "What happened?"

"Something awful."

"But what?"

"I can't describe the problem on the telephone, Pippa. You have to see it for yourself."

I hesitated. I didn't want to return to that particular office building so soon after my visit on Friday night. What if the burly security guard also worked Monday mornings?

Gloria broke the silence. "Pippa, I need you over here, *now.*"

Her tone had become unyielding. But who could blame Gloria for being upset? Her boss drowned, her job gone, her morning filled with some sort of unexpected crisis.

"Chin up, Gloria. I'll be there by ten."

"My chin is all the way up, Pippa. In fact, I'm so mad I could . . ."

———————

I found Gloria at her desk in the reception area, head resting on her arms. She looked up at me with weepy eyes that had sent thin dribbles of diluted mascara down cheeks made puffy by crying. Even so, those slate blue eyes were full of fire.

"There, there," I said in as motherly a tone as I could muster. "Let it all out. Marsha was a wonderful woman. We are all going to miss her."

"I'm not crying because Marsha is dead. Well, I guess I am, but that's not the only reason this morning. Have you seen our front door?"

I had breezed through it when I came in. I turned and looked again. This time I saw jimmy marks on the jamb and slivers of splintered wood on the carpet.

"Some jerk pried the lock open," Gloria said, "then he forced the door to Marsha's office. That's where the real damage is."

Marsha's door stood ajar. I peeked cautiously. The office beyond looked like Christmas in the Scottish Highlands. A snowfall of paper confetti covered the desktop, the credenza, the chair seats, and every flat surface I could see. Hundreds of white file folders, all empty, lay higgledy-piggledy on the floor, concealing the dark blue carpet. Two men, both wearing latex gloves, toiled among the paper drifts. One spooned debris into a small plastic bag. The other held a peculiar flashlight that cast an eccentric blue light. I remembered seeing the same gadget in a recent TV show about police procedure. The bloke was scanning for fingerprints.

I recognize plain-clothes coppers when I see them. I leapt back from the door.

"Someone used the paper shredder in Marsha's office to chop up our files," Gloria said. "*All* of them." She cocked her head toward the bank of file cabinets near her desk. The bottom drawers protruded half open and empty. "I'm furious about what happened, but I don't know who to yell at."

"Your file drawers were locked . . ." I started to say. "I mean—I'm sure you keep your file cabinets secured."

"Marsha and I had a deal. The last one to leave the office locks the file drawers. She kept her key with her, but I buried mine in the paper clip dish where it wasn't hard to find." Gloria honked into a tissue. "The cabinets are full of old résumés and interview notes. I never imagined they deserved much protection."

An excellent point. Why would someone destroy Marsha's candidate files?

"Perhaps a burglar did the damage?" I mused out loud. "To cover his tracks."

"Maybe. But nothing valuable seems to be missing." She opened her desk's pencil drawer. "See! All our petty cash is still here, more than four hundred dollars, and our company credit cards too. The police don't think we had a burglar."

I'd almost forgotten the two men in the other room. "Ah, yes, the police."

Gloria tossed her tissue into a wastebasket and reached for a new one. "What should *we* do next?"

"*We*? As in you in me?"

"Well, I could use a friend, and you were Marsha's business partner."

"So people keep insisting." I knew that arguing the point would get me nowhere. I had a simple choice to make: abandon Gloria or help her sort things out. I took a deep breath and said: "OK. First things first. *We* will arrange to have the jumble cleaned up."

"Good idea, Miss Hunnechurch," said a male voice, "but not while Miss Morgan's office is a designated crime scene."

I spun around. The copper I'd seen holding the plastic bag stepped out of Marsha's office. He was about my age, tall, with light-brown hair, a longish nose, and piercing brown eyes that made me feel blame-worthy enough to do a scarper. He knew my name. Did he also know about my after-hours visit the other evening?

I thrust my hand forward and in my best British accent said, "You have the advantage on me, sir."

He tapped the ID card hanging around his neck on a blue lanyard. "Detective Stephen Reilly. Ryde Police Department. I know your name because Gloria Spitz told me she called you."

We shook hands. He was smiling; I was anxious and trying my best not to look guilty.

"Gloria also told me that you have a business relationship with the Morgan Consultancy," he said. "I understand you joined forces with Miss Morgan shortly before her—*ah*—disappearance on Friday night."

"I suppose that's a fair description of our dealings. I met Marsha last Monday. We agreed to team on one recruiting assignment."

"She tell you about her enemies?"

"I didn't know she had any."

"She had at least one." Reilly grasped my arm near the elbow and guided me into Marsha's office. "I've been a detective in Ryde for a dozen years, but this kind of vandalism is a first for me. Do you have any ideas about who did it, or why?"

"No. Neither." I couldn't help staring at the snow-white paper fragments. Something about the clutter struck me as wrong.

"A penny for your thoughts," Reilly said brightly.

"What?"

"You look pensive."

"I was wondering—when did it happen?"

"Early this morning. The building is wide open during daylight hours. The night guard went off duty at 6:00 A.M. Gloria arrived at nine o'clock. That leaves a window of three hours."

How long would it take to shred so much paper? At least an hour with Marsha's shredder going full tilt, which eliminated the possibility of Gloria's doing it in a fit of mania. She called me at 9:30 and the coppers before that.

Then I figured out what was wrong. *It's all white.*

The bright blue folders I had seen on Friday night would be as conspicuous as ink stains on a satin sheet. *Where were they?*

I knew the only possible answer. Reilly's "vandal" had taken Marsha's blue-chip folders, the five labeled: Beardsley, Harriet; Isley,

Kathleen; McKenzie, Susan; Landesberg, Roxanne; and Preston, Linda.

I felt a chill and a glimmer of an explanation. Shredding the other files in Marsha's suite made sure that no one, maybe not even Gloria, would realize that the five "private" folders had been snatched from Marsha's desk drawer.

No one, that is, but me.

Five blue folders. One for each current and future superstar.

But why would anyone go to so much trouble to steal old recruiting materials? It made no sense, not for a handful of handwritten interview notes.

I should have told Reilly, but I couldn't, that is, not without admitting what I had done on Friday night.

"I can't think of a reason for anyone to be so destructive," I said. "It certainly is bizarre."

"Uh-huh. And a remarkable coincidence too. Sixty hours after a prominent woman is lost in an extraordinary accident, her office gets trashed."

I shrugged.

"We usually let a beat cop respond to a vandalism call, but I decided to investigate this one myself."

I nodded.

"Where were you at 7:00 A.M. this morning?"

"*Me?*"

His voice hardened. "I don't believe in remarkable coincidences."

"Why would I want to mangle Marsha's files?"

"My questions come first. Where were you at seven o'clock?"

"At home. In my bathtub, if you must know."

"Alone?"

"I beg your pardon?"

"I take that as a *yes*. Gloria says that Marsha Morgan didn't give you a key to this suite. Why not?"

"I didn't need a key. I have my own office."

"Do you own a crowbar?"

"Why would I own a crowbar?" I thought for a moment, and in the silence that filled the room, I imagined Reilly and his men invading

Hunnechurch Manor looking for evidence that I was the culprit. "Well, perhaps I do. I inherited an old box of tools with the storage shed in my garden."

"We'll need a set of your fingerprints. Drop by Ryde Police Headquarters at your convenience, but no later than tomorrow morning."

"Why do you want my prints?"

"You've been here before. I expect to find your fingerprints all over the place."

How true! I had probably touched everything in the suite on Friday night—from files to cabinets to the copying machine.

"Oh, I guarantee that you will find my prints here and there," I said.

"Now, let me answer your question." Reilly switched to a credible English accent: "Why would Pippa Hunnechurch want to mangle Marsha Morgan's files?"

"Why indeed?"

"I can think of an excellent reason. Now that Morgan is presumed dead, destroying her files destroys the Morgan Consultancy forever. You will have one less business competitor to worry about in Ryde, Maryland." Reilly smiled at me in triumph, pleased as punch with his inane theory.

"Ridiculous!" I shot back. "Marsha's success depended on her skills and her contacts, not the paperwork in her files. Moreover, I would love to have every résumé that Marsha had collected. It would be insanity for a headhunter to destroy them."

"OK. Here's another possibility. Marsha Morgan killed herself on Friday night. You did her a favor and obliterated the embarrassing facts that drove her to suicide."

My head began to spin. "You *can't* be serious. I saw Marsha fall off the *Chesapeake Belle*. She didn't kill herself."

Policemen don't have to fight fair. Reilly chose to ignore my sound argument. "Thank you, Miss Hunnechurch," he said. "No more questions, for now. Have a good day."

Have a good day!

I barely held my temper and returned to the reception room, just as Kathleen Isley limped into the suite. She peered at Gloria, then me.

"Excellent!" she said in a tone hard enough to scratch glass. "Both birds with one stone. I want my property back. My résumé and the other biographical materials that Marsha kept in her files. I assume that one of you will know where I can find them."

Gloria stiffened. Her head came up, and her cheeks filled with color. I could picture her brain assembling the perfect insult to hurl at Kathleen, something like, *you pompous arrogant twit.* The woman definitely deserved a dressing down.

Nonetheless, I jumped in front of Gloria's desk. No way could I let her pick a fight with the former supervisor (and mentor) of Linda Preston. I needed Kathleen's cooperation in the days ahead. Derek Wetherspoon might want to chat with her about Linda, and I had a question I wanted to ask about Linda's role when she, too, worked at Commerce.

"Good morning, Kathleen," I said. "I am sorry to report that there has been a problem with Marsha's files."

"What kind of problem?"

I didn't get the chance to answer. Kathleen's arrival had piqued Reilly's interest. He stood solidly in the doorway to Marsha's office and said, "Who are you?"

Kathleen threw back her head and became Her Royal Highness, the princess of Greenbacks. "My name is Kathleen Isley. I am the deputy secretary for international trade, United States Department of Commerce. Does that satisfy your curiosity?"

"Oh." Reilly seemed to lose several pounds of pressure. He made dainty but ineffectual gestures toward his badge. I seized the opportunity.

"I am going to take Gloria downstairs for a nice cup of tea, *Detective Reilly,*" I said. "You don't need us to explain what happened here this morning."

Kathleen swung her silver-headed cane like Charlie Chaplin. "You're a policeman? *What* happened here this morning?"

I pushed Gloria into the hall and pulled the glass-paneled door shut behind me, purposely distancing us from Isley and Reilly.

If two people ever deserved one another . . .

Chapter Eleven

A COUPLE OF TOURISTS DISCOVERED MARSHA'S BODY as they strolled along the St. Michaels waterfront munching their lunch. I learned the details later on Monday afternoon.

I had returned to my office to finish my telephone interviews of Linda Preston's other references: an import-export banker in New York City, a lawyer at the Department of Commerce in Washington, D.C., and a retired diplomat who now lived in Maine. To a woman, they praised Linda's brilliance, her legal judgment, and her management skills. I added their compliments to Linda's candidate package and finished by penning a brief note to Derek Wetherspoon, which read, "Here is some background information about Linda Preston, the candidate I will present to you on Wednesday. I believe she will make an ideal chief counsel for Eurokit USA."

I heard a knock on my outer door. I ran to open it, expecting to find the messenger I had called to deliver the candidate package to Wetherspoon. Instead, there stood John Tyler, grim faced and red eyed.

He lurched into my office and put his hands on my shoulders. "It's over," he said, his nose inches from mine. "The police recovered

Marsha's body on the shore of the Miles River, near the Chesapeake Bay Maritime Museum." I took his hands, lowered them to his side, and gently pushed him out of my personal space.

"Sit down. I'll make us a pot of tea."

While I fiddled with the kettle, John related a horrific tale of Marsha's clothing caught on a piling and generation of gas inside her body cavities and facial damage done by crabs. Tyler spoke with a grim intensity that made me queasy, but I heard pain behind every word. Perhaps he cared for Marsha more than he had let on? He surprised me by ending with, "Now we can get started."

"Started on what?"

"The chamber must devise an appropriate memorial to Marsha. I realized immediately that you and I are the logical people to take charge of the project."

Blimey! Another responsibility to worry about.

We drank our tea and discussed a few possibilities Tyler had in mind: a bronze bust in the chamber's office; a commemorative lecture series; a flower garden somewhere in Ryde.

"Those are ideas off the top of my head. I know you will come up with equally good suggestions as we work together on the memorial." He reached out and took my hand.

I yanked my hand free and told him a little white lie. "Indeed we will work together, but not today. I have a pressing business engagement."

Tyler grunted. He stood up to leave but hesitated. "One last thing. The comments I made in the Cinq Ports Restaurant the other night about never doing a nickel's worth of business with Marsha—I spoke out of turn, and I regret it. Please forget what I said. The woman had her faults, and she may have occasionally shaved the truth a tad, but *de mortuis nil nisi bonum.*"

One of Chloe's favorite Latin phrases, which means *of the dead say nothing but good.*

I should've asked Tyler to explain what he meant about Marsha "shaving the truth a tad," but my chief concern was getting him out of my office.

"I know nothing bad about Marsha Morgan." I said. "She was an exceptional woman."

He beamed at me as he stepped into the dim hallway. "And so are you, Pippa."

Oh my. I had a gentleman admirer I didn't want.

━━━━━━━

Toward the end of the day, I visited the *Ryde Reporter* and found David reading an advance copy of the issue that would be distributed on Tuesday morning. Marsha's face filled three columns on the front page. Thanks to David's efforts, the headline was respectful and subdued: "Miles River Accident Claims Local Business Leader."

"I've heard about Marsha's body," I said. "John Tyler did the honors."

"And I know that you toured Marsha's tattered office." He gave me a sly glance. "A little birdie told me."

"Ah. You spoke to Detective Reilly."

"Stephen and I go way back—to my junior reporter days, when I occasionally got assigned the police beat. He's still one of my best sources."

"My mum likes to say that gossip and rumor breed well in cramped places. Ryde is a small town at heart, and you deal in tittle-tattle."

David grinned at me. "Reilly is a terrific cop. He's a virtuoso at solving tough cases and cracking hardened suspects."

"Very amusing."

"Don't get snotty. I'm your number-one character witness. He called this morning and asked if I knew you. He wondered if you were capable of an act of senseless destruction. I told him you were polite to a fault and would never create chaos, unless you had time to sweep up afterwards."

"Ha ha."

David opened his advance copy to an inside page that featured a large photograph of the shredded debris. He read the caption aloud. "In a possibly unrelated incident, Miss Morgan's office was vandalized on Monday morning. Detective Stephen Reilly stated that 'we have no evidence to support an inference that the damage done to Miss Morgan's library of files is related to her apparent accident.'"

Oh no!

The thought hadn't occurred to me. Could the destruction of Marsha's files be connected somehow to her death? Reilly had said that he didn't believe in remarkable coincidences, but I had ignored the full implications of his words.

David shook his head. "Reilly's my friend, but have you ever heard such a blatant bunch of weasel words?"

"You don't believe him?" I asked, cautiously.

"Oh, I believe that he doesn't have any evidence," he said, "but Reilly knows that someone worked hard to destroy Marsha Morgan's records after she fell off the *Chesapeake Belle*. He also knows there has to be a good reason for that."

I understood part of the "good reason." The villain shredded Marsha's files to conceal the theft of a handful of blue file folders. One for each of the superstars. But for what purpose? Why go to so much trouble to abscond with old résumés and recruiting notes?

I was tempted to share my thoughts with David, but then I would have to confess my late-night visit to Marsha's office. Instead, I changed the subject. "I need another favor."

David cocked his thumb toward the corridor. "My file cabinets are thataway."

"I doubt that mere clippings will suffice this time. How would one make inquiries about a person who worked with Kathleen Isley six years ago?"

He eyed me with interest. "Why would Pippa Hunnechurch need to know something like that?"

I saw no reason not to tell him.

"You may recall that Marsha and I discussed a candidate on Friday evening at dinner."

"I remember. A woman named Linda Preston. The fruit of your per-haps—partnership. I wrote her name down for future reference."

Oh, did you? I made a mental note. Be careful what you say in front of reporters—even if they are good friends.

"Yes, well, Linda worked awhile for Kathleen Isley. I want a clear picture of her responsibilities at the Department of Commerce."

"Why not ask Isley yourself?"

"It seems that Kathleen tends to ignore questions from mere recruiters."

David guffawed. "I'll bet she does."

"I don't know where else to look."

"I do. A famed personage like Kathleen Isley attracts a big spotlight, which often illuminates the people around her. I'll see what I can find."

"Bless you."

David reached for a pad and pencil. "Where does the lady live?"

I hesitated.

"Come on, Pippa," David said. "Linda Preston is a common name. I need *some* distinguishing information."

"She lives in Atlanta. Her specialty is international commerce."

"When is Linda coming to town?"

"Wednesday."

"*This* Wednesday?"

"You sound surprised."

"I am surprised. I expected you to postpone your recruiting effort a week or so because of what happened to your partner."

I didn't want to take this particular guilt trip again. "Headhunting is like the theatre," I said with conviction. "The show must go on. After all, my client has an important post to fill."

"What company is she visiting?" David asked. He slipped the question in so skillfully, I almost told him about Eurokit.

I wagged a finger at his nose. "Nice try, but I can't reveal my client's identity yet."

"In that case, you can buy me dinner tonight at The Crab Palace. I have an irresistible yen for crab cakes."

"Crab cakes? You know as well as I that the price of Maryland crab has gone through the roof this month."

"My services cost. Pay me with useful information or fancy food. Your choice."

"I have often heard it said there are no reporters in heaven. Now I know why."

Chapter Twelve

I HUGGED DAVID GOOD-BYE around seven o'clock—both of us feeling well-fed, me feeling uneasy about spending seventy dollars of my scarce working capital on a dinner. Two weeks earlier I wouldn't have cared, but that morning I had received the final payment on the last invoice I had sent to a client. My accounts receivable had sunk to zero, but my creditors kept sending bills: American Express, Visa, the Ryde Savings Bank, the telephone company—on and on they went, an endless queue of open hands, each one a depressing reminder of my financial peril.

Like it or not, the future of Hunnechurch & Associates depended on Linda Preston, a woman I'd never spoken with face-to-face. Unless she generated new revenues for me, I'd soon be living on my savings. And when they were gone?

"When worry comes to call," my mum likes to say, "keep your mind distracted by doing something useful." That night I had a perfect busy-work chore to perform. I set out to deliver Marsha's suitcase, purse, and key ring to her home.

The address on Marsha's driver's license turned out to be a posh three-story townhouse on an exquisite cul-de-sac off High Street, not

far from Mariners' Hall. I unlocked the front door a few moments before an oak-cased grandfather clock in the hall began to chime eight
o'clock. In between the loud bongs, I heard a thump upstairs that
made the hairs on the back of my neck jump to attention. I wasn't
alone in the house.

"Hello?" I called out. "Who's there?"

When no one answered, I climbed to the second floor to investigate. I found a hallway with three closed doors. The noise had seemed
to come from the top of the staircase. I chose the door nearest to me
and pressed my ear against the cool varnished wood. *Nothing.* I turned
the knob and gently pressed.

An orange fur ball streaked past the ajar door and bumped to a stop
against my leg. Crickey! Marsha owned a cat. I hoisted it by the scruff.
Small. Cuddly. Female. I read the metal tag on her collar: *My Name Is
Ginger.*

Ginger started mewing, a hungry meow that brought out the British
pet lover in me. "Okay, pussums, I'll find your *din-dins* after we check
for other felines."

I pushed the door all the way open and stepped into Marsha's
bedroom.

It was a lovely, large, airy room, full of expensive Colonial-style
furniture, the sort of bed chamber one sees in a restored eighteenth-
century mansion. Elegant wallpaper, elaborate draperies, and a huge
four-poster bed with a white chenille spread. A small indentation near
the center of the bed marked the spot where Ginger had spent the
weekend alone.

I pirouetted slowly, taking in the accessories that Marsha had placed
throughout the room: a friendly ceramic dog, a bouquet of silk flowers,
an antique cast-iron boot puller.

Then I saw the huge photograph of Marsha hanging in a corner, except the Marsha in the picture was not the Marsha I had known. I
moved closer for a better look.

The photo was a festival of pink. Marsha reclined sexily on a pink
chaise lounge in front of a pink backdrop, dressed in a scanty pink neg-
ligee that would be right at home at a bordello. It took me a moment to

realize that Marsha had posed for one of those "glamour shots" beloved by teenage girls. The lighting was as soft as butter—no wrinkles or age spots here. She might have been thirty years old when the photo was taken. Wrong! The date on the bottom edge proved that it had been taken several months earlier.

Marsha, this is a side of you I never suspected.

I wondered why Marsha, so attractive in her own right, would want to look like someone else.

Ginger mewed in my arms. "Sorry pussums, I forgot about you. Let's find your food bowl."

I guessed that Marsha had left Ginger a weekend supply of food in the bathroom that adjoined the bedroom. Behind the open door I found Ginger's litter box, plus a stainless steel gizmo that held food and water bowls. Both had been licked empty.

I carried the lot downstairs to the kitchen where I found an assortment of canned cat food in the pantry.

"Poor Ginger," I said as I filled her bowls. "We didn't know about you."

I plucked the odd strands of cat hair from my black linen blazer while Ginger chomped on Liver Paté Treat. Each bite seemed to restore a portion of her feline haughtiness. When she finished eating, she moved to a cool spot near an air-conditioning vent and licked her paws, without so much as a thank-you glance at me.

"Ungrateful rotter. Give me a loyal budgie any day."

Perhaps Ginger understood me. In any event she lifted her tail high above her head and padded out of the kitchen with great dignity. I followed her to the den where she leapt from footstool to wing chair to the top of an elegant ladies' writing desk.

"Oh, no you don't, cat. I doubt that your mum let you roost on the antiques."

But Ginger curled up in one corner—serene as a ceramic statuette and smug in her mastery of her little world.

"My apologies, m'lady. Marsha clearly enjoyed your company when she worked."

The cat replied with a disdainful flick of her white-tipped tail. It brushed against a stack of business cards, the very same stack Marsha had flashed when we first met.

I undid the rubber bands, fanned the cards open, and perused the pantheon of chairmen, presidents, vice presidents, chief financial officers, lawyers, marketing directors, and consultants. Marsha had jotted comments next to many of the names. The scribbles on my own card said: "ambitious, hardy, straitlaced."

Straight-laced? Never! Well, maybe just a little, I allowed to myself.

Most of the executives hailed from Maryland, Virginia, and the District of Columbia, but several lived in Georgia. One well-worn card caught my eye: James L. Huston, Managing Director, Peachtree Consulting Group, Atlanta. It took a spot of thinking to remember where I had seen the name before. Then it came to me. James Huston had provided a reference for Linda Preston five years ago. I had found his letter in the white "Preston, Linda" file and had made a copy of it. Marsha had written on the bottom of Huston's card: "Knows everyone, a hunk, straight-laced."

Well, well, Marsha thought we had something in common: straight-lacedness.

On a whim, I sat down at Marsha's desk, picked up her telephone, and dialed Huston's home number.

A silky voice, deep and resonant, answered: "Huston."

"My name is Pippa Hunnechurch. I was an associate of Marsha Morgan."

"Is that so? And how is Marsha?"

Huston doesn't know.

Get a grip, Pippa. Why should he know? Most of Marsha's professional contacts in other parts of the country probably haven't heard about her death.

I focused my eyes on a spot on the wall. "I'm sorry to be the one to tell you, Mr. Huston, but Marsha Morgan is dead." I explained what had happened. When I finished, Huston said, "Thank you for phoning. I presume that you will inform her many business acquaintances in Atlanta."

His question startled me. Why would a headhunter based in Ryde, Maryland, have "many business acquaintances" in Atlanta?

"That's an excellent idea," I said noncommittally. "In fact, I called you to talk about Linda Preston. You may recall that you provided a reference for her five years ago."

Huston was silent for several seconds, then said, "Yes, I did provide a reference for Linda Preston when she left the federal government and joined the Atlanta Bank of Commerce."

"Did you also work for the Department of Commerce at the time?"

"In a way. I led several studies for Commerce under contract as an outside consultant."

"How interesting. Well, Marsha and I teamed on a recruiting assignment before her death. We identified Linda Preston as a leading candidate for a senior position at a large company based in Ryde, Maryland. She has exceptionally impressive credentials."

Huston *hmmmed* for a while. "Believe me, I understand why you think so."

"That's an odd way of agreeing with me."

"I misspoke, Miss Hunnechurch." His voice had become stiff and distant. "I have nothing to say to you about Linda Preston. I make it a point not to gossip about former colleagues with total strangers."

His abrupt change in tone bewildered me.

"I don't expect you to betray any confidences, Mr. Huston. I'm just asking you to review a few publicly verifiable facts. Linda worked closely with Kathleen Isley at Commerce. What were her roles and responsibilities?"

"Ask Linda. Ask Secretary Isley. Don't ask me."

The anger in his voice increased with each word. I worried that he might hang up, so I tried a different approach.

"Indeed I will ask them, Mr. Huston, but you offer a unique perspective. Your letter of recommendation helped put Linda Preston in her present position. I thought you might have—well, a special knowledge of Linda's strengths and credentials."

"Her strengths, perhaps. Her credentials, no."

"I don't grasp the distinction. May I ask? . . ."

"No you may not ask. I refuse to engage in scandalmongering with faraway headhunters."

"How can I resolve your concerns about me?"

"I might feel more comfortable if we spoke in person."

"Regrettably, I have no plans to travel to Atlanta."

"Call me again if your plans change. Good evening, Miss Hunnechurch."

Click.

I put the phone down feeling angry and on edge. Men like Huston talk freely to me about their coworkers every day of the week. It's no big deal.

Unless one has something unpleasant to relate.

I caught the cat blinking at me. "What do you think, Ginger?"

She yawned at me from her corner of the desktop.

"I agree. Forget James Huston! Perhaps he had an affair with Linda that turned sour? Or maybe he's jealous of her success? In any event, who cares? The man is yesterday's news. Linda's current references are spectacular."

Ginger began to purr.

I reassembled the stack of business cards and snapped the rubber bands in place.

"One more question, Ginger. Do you think anyone will mind if I nick Marsha's treasure trove of contacts?"

A genuine dilemma. One part of me urged, *Take them! Marsha's collection of business cards has no monetary value and is destined for the trash bin.* But another voice insisted, *Don't! Hunnechurches are brought up to believe that character is what you do when no one is watching.*

Ginger yawned again.

"Excellent advice, mate. The only person who might want these cards is me." I dropped the stack into my purse. "By way of thanks, I'll serve you another can of cat food."

I had begun to putter around the kitchen when I heard a car door slam. A few moments later the front door opened. I stepped into the hallway.

"Oh!" said the woman I had startled.

"I'm Pippa Hunnechurch," I said quickly. "You must be Missy Morgan."

Missy resembled Marsha. An inch or two shorter, a year or two older, perhaps a few pounds heavier, but the same youthful features and the same alert eyes. Only hers looked tired and full of pain. I felt a pang of sympathy.

"Miss Hunnechurch. Of course! Marsha told me about you." She spotted the opened can of cat food in my hand. "Good. You fed Ginger. Thank you."

She took a step forward and nearly fell over Marsha's suitcase.

"That's Marsha's, isn't it?" she said.

"Yes. She had it with her at the hotel. The manager asked me to take charge of it. I also have her purse and her keys."

"Her keys! That's how you got in. Now it all makes sense. Forgive me, I know I sound disconnected. But Marsha's death, the flight, too little sleep . . ."

She looked wobbly enough to keel over where she stood.

I offered to do what any well-brought up Brit would do in similar circumstances. "Let me make you a cup of tea," I said.

Her face lit up. "I'd kill for a cup of tea."

I led her into the kitchen and sat her down at the dinette table. I found tea bags in a cabinet above the stove and filled the kettle.

"It's pleasant here in Maryland," she said, "although the summers can be hotter than Atlanta, which is much farther south. You must miss England."

"Er . . . sometimes." I said, not sure of which bit of small talk I had replied to.

"Ginger is a pretty cat."

"Indeed. Intelligent too."

Missy made a *psss-psss-psss* sound, and Ginger jumped into her lap.

The kettle boiled. I brewed our tea strong—two bags in each mug. We sipped in silence.

"I often forget that tea is so soothing," she finally said. "I mostly drink coffee in Atlanta."

"How long have you lived there?"

"About twenty years. Marsha and I grew up in Florida and began our businesses there. She moved to Maryland; I moved to Georgia."

"What made you choose different parts of the country?"

Missy set her mug down hard. The sharp noise made me jump. "Let's not prattle about geography," she said. "Gloria faxed the newspaper story to my office. I know you saw Marsha fall off the boat. That's what I want to talk about."

I nodded. "It happened in an instant. She simply, well, slid over the rail."

"Why?"

"I don't know. She looked quite ill before she fell."

"Ill? In what way?"

"Distant. Ashen. Unresponsive. Almost in a trance."

Missy's face seemed to melt into a flood of tears. "Stupid! Stupid! Stupid!" she shouted, and then she began to sob. I felt inches away from crying myself. I looked around for a box of tissues but settled for a stack of paper napkins.

"Sorry," she said as she blew her nose. "Did Gloria tell you? She has arranged to have Marsha cremated in Ryde."

I shook my head. "She didn't tell me."

"We can't do it before Saturday. We have to wait until the medical examiner finishes—you know."

I knew. The autopsy.

Missy continued: "I plan to take her ashes back to Georgia with me."

"Ah."

"I thought it might be appropriate for her closest friends to get together before Saturday in her home."

"A less formal good-bye . . ."

"Exactly! Thursday at noon seems a good time. Will you come?"

"Certainly, I'll come. I'll also make phone calls, arrange for food, help in any way I can."

Missy brightened a little. "Gloria is doing all that. She's a wonderful secretary. Marsha planned to find her a management job some day."

The grandfather clock began to chime nine o'clock, inviting me to remember what a long day I had had.

"It's late," I said. "We both need a good night's sleep."

Missy guided Ginger gently to the floor. "Thanks for shepherding Marsha's belongings."

"Her purse is in the den. Her keys are inside."

Missy started to stand, but I waved her down. "Finish your tea. I'll see myself out."

I turned to leave, but she gripped my hand and squeezed tight. "Before you go, I have a question about the vandalism to Marsha's office. Gloria told me you saw it."

"Indeed I did. A policeman named Reilly took me for a tour of the ruins. A horrible sight. A sea of shredded paper and file folders."

Her eyes fastened on me. "Were all of Marsha's files destroyed?"

I found the question curious, yet startlingly to the point. I didn't want to lie to Missy. I fished for an ambiguous answer.

"It looked that way to me," I said.

Her relief was palpable. "I'm so pleased!"

She released my hand and said, "All gone!" over and over again as I stood speechless with surprise. Why would a pile of confetti make Missy so happy?

Chapter Thirteen

I ARRIVED AT MY OFFICE in the Calvert building at the crack of dawn on Tuesday morning, reeling from a sleepless night filled with unhappy dreams about what would happen to Hunnechurch & Associates if Derek Wetherspoon didn't fall into instant love with Linda Preston. With no other assignments on the horizon, all my eggs lay in one southern basket—a state of affairs that kept me uneasy. At the same time I felt great confidence in Linda Preston. She had ideal credentials for the Eurokit job. The candidate package I had sent Derek was one of the strongest I'd ever put together. Why worry about a sure thing?

I stepped into my reception room, and there at my feet was a thin manila envelope that someone pushed underneath my front door. The logo on the envelope read: *Calvert Management Company.* A letter from my landlord. Now what? I settled behind my desk and tore open the flap.

Dear Miss Hunnechurch. The lease on your office will expire in 30 days. If you wish to renew your lease, please sign the enclosed copy of this letter and return it to Calvert Management Company no later than seven (7) days from the above date. Please note that because of the rising costs in maintenance, insurance, and utilities, we are forced to raise your rent by 8 percent.

Wonderful! On top of everything, I had a week to decide about my office. I stared at my calendar, wishing it were a crystal ball, when a small voice inside my head coaxed me into remaining calm. "Don't panic!" it said clear as day. "This will all work out. Make yourself a cup of tea."

"An excellent idea," I said out loud as I reached for my electric kettle.

I am convinced (as is my mum) that a watched pot will never boil. While I waited out of eyeshot of the kettle, I switched on my computer and read my E-mail. Much to my amazement, the first message was from Chloe.

From: Chloe_and_Stuart
Subject: We Have Joined the Information Age!
Dear Pippa—

Guess what? Our humble shire church now has a computer network, which gives me access to E-mail, so I won't have to trouble your boudoir fax machine whenever I want to contact you quickly.

Stuart assures me that the computer I am using right now to send this message is completely *au courant*. "Sophisticated enough to be simple to operate" was the phrase he used. I believe him, although I wish I had your insightful mind regarding computers. You understand the beastly things while I am a total idiot when it comes to anything with a keyboard. All thumbs.

If you actually receive this message, please be kind enough to reply by return E-mail (Is that the correct terminology?) so that I will know I've done everything right. (I certainly hope I have because I look forward to chatting with you endlessly over the Internet.)

Blessings,
Chloe

PS: I have discovered today that British Airways is having a super sale. I can actually afford to visit you in Ryde if I buy my tickets before the end of next week. Let me know if you're up to having me.
PPS: Stuart sends his love.
PPPS: ISN'T THIS FUN!!!

Chloe's E-mail cheered me enormously. A visit from my sister might prove the perfect medicine for what ailed me. She was a good listener, someone I could tell my troubles to with the hope of receiving reasonably sensible advice. She would even understand my reluctance to share my financial woes via the telephone. We Hunnechurches don't like to worry each other when we're thousands of miles apart.

Her visit would cost me almost nothing. She would kip in my overflowing second bedroom, and we would take inexpensive day trips to sights in Maryland, Virginia, and Washington, D.C. When I had to work, Chloe would happily shop 'til she dropped.

I moved my mouse and touched the *new message* button.

From: PippaHunnechurch
Subject: This and That
    Congrats on getting E-mail. It is a wondrous invention and will help you do an even better job of keeping tabs on Stuart's parishioners.
    About your visit . . . DO, DO, COME TO MARYLAND!
    I am in the midst of a recruiting assignment, but I should be out from under the heaviest work in a week or so. You choose the date (I will be incredibly flexible).

Love,
Pippa

I was still musing about Chloe's visit when my telephone rang. I snatched up the receiver. Perhaps a new client wanted to give me an assignment? Hardly an outrageous wish.

"Pippa Hunnechurch," I said, trying to sound both perky and prosperous.

"Stephen Reilly. Ryde Police Department. I am sitting here in my office wondering why we haven't yet had the pleasure of your company."

I stared at the mouthpiece. "I beg your pardon."

"We asked you to come in and be fingerprinted. Remember?"

Oh dear. I had forgotten my date with the coppers.

I backpedaled furiously. "You said no later than this morning."

"Which means that you are late," Reilly snapped. "I suggest you leave now."

My good mood evaporated like the steam that had begun to pour from my teakettle.

"I'm on my way," I said sullenly.

I added silently, *Without a hot cuppa to keep me going.*

━━━━━━━━━━

It was my first visit to The Department of Police, Ryde, Maryland (to quote the sign over the front door), but regrettably, not my last. The department's headquarters is a modern glass-and-steel annex tucked discretely out of sight behind the redbrick Ryde Town Hall, which was built in 1809. I parked the Miata in the visitor's lot and told myself I was being foolish to feel as nervous as I did.

An aging desk copper peered at me through a hole in the glass information window and asked, "How can I help you?"

"I am Pippa Hunnechurch," I announced boldly, "here to have my fingerprints taken, per Detective Reilly's instructions."

Had I said it right? Did one have her fingerprints "taken," as with a photograph?

The desk copper told me to wait on the bench in the corridor. I sat down meekly and tried to ignore the corkboard full of *Wanted* posters on the opposite wall. Two of the criminals were women. I wondered if either had entered a locked office building late at night.

A stocky female police officer arrived and said, "Pippa Hunnechurch?"

She seemed comfortable with my unusual name. Had I become a talked-about person at police headquarters?

I stood up. She ushered me along the corridor and into a tiny, windowless room where the only piece of furniture was a tall metal table. I recognized the equipment necessary for capturing my fingerprints. I held out my left hand.

"You've been fingerprinted before?"

I nodded. "When I emigrated to the United States."

"Then you know it doesn't hurt a bit."

Having one's fingertips rolled first on an inkpad and then against a piece of cardboard is painless, but the process made me feel every inch a criminal. At least the job was being done in private, with no onlookers to add to my discomfort.

I had relaxed too soon.

Reilly swooped through the door, followed by a big man I had never seen before.

"Ah, Miss Hunnechurch," Reilly said. "Just the woman we want to see."

"I wish you would stop using the royal 'we,'" I said to Reilly. "You are not the queen of England. 'We' sounds rather bigheaded."

Reilly worked his lips into a tight smile. "'We' is wholly accurate. Meet Corporal Ken Miller, a Maryland State Police detective working out of Easton."

I gave Miller my warmest smile.

"*We* want to talk to you about Marsha Morgan," Reilly said.

"You do? But I don't know anything about Marsha—well, nothing important."

Miller took over. "We are intrigued, Miss Hunnechurch, by how quickly you ended up in the middle of things. You met Miss Morgan a few days before her death. Yet you were one of only two people who saw her fall off the *Chesapeake Belle,* and you were the business partner her secretary Gloria called when her office was ransacked."

"I never was her business partner."

"Really? Several women at your table during dinner that evening heard Marsha Morgan describe you as her new partner."

I started to explain, but Reilly interrupted. "Let's move this discussion to our interrogation room. We'll be more comfortable there."

Interrogation room! Yikes!

"I'm finished," the policewoman said as she released her iron grip on the pinkie finger of my right hand. She gave me a solvent-dampened towel to remove the ink that coated my fingertips. I started wiping.

Reilly and Miller led me back though the corridor to a simply furnished office with a large mirror set into a short wall. They sat down on one side of a gray steel table; I sat down on the other side. Exactly like on TV.

"Want some coffee?" Reilly asked. He pointed to a coffeemaker on a shelf in the corner. "There are fresh donuts in the waxed paper bag."

I shook my head. I couldn't stop thinking about the expanse of one-way glass. Was anyone behind the mirror watching us?

"You seem nervous, Miss Hunnechurch," Miller said.

"Yes . . . well . . . all of this police-precinct ambience is strange to me."

"Then let's get you back to civilization as quickly as possible. Tell us what you saw and did on Friday night. Start at the beginning. Why were you aboard the *Chesapeake Belle?*"

I told Miller about the Ryde Chamber of Commerce's annual conference and our dinner cruise. I explained how David Friendly and I went topside for a stroll and found Marsha behaving oddly.

"You tried to speak to her?" Miller asked.

"We tried, but she was too befuddled to answer."

"Although *not* too befuddled to jump off the boat?"

"Marsha didn't jump. She murmured something about touching the reflection of the moon in the water and tried to lean over the stern railing. She lost her balance and fell into the river."

"You didn't attempt to grab her—pull her back to safety?"

"David did. But he was too late."

"Where were you when she fell overboard?"

"Going for help. I thought she needed a doctor."

"It's nice to run into a helpful person. We don't meet many of them in our line of work."

Reilly chimed in: "We certainly don't. But if Miss Hunnechurch wants to be helpful, I wonder why she never mentioned to me that she was an eyewitness to Marsha Morgan's death. We had such a friendly conversation in Miss Morgan's vandalized office on Monday morning."

His "aside" to Miller caught me off guard. I said something silly. "You never asked me about Marsha's disappearance."

"She's right!" Reilly said to Miller, in a voice that oozed sarcasm. "I didn't ask her."

"Oooh!" Miller replied. "I bet you also forgot to ask her about taking charge of Miss Morgan's possessions. Her suitcase, her . . ."

"Her purse." I finished his sentence. "I was talked into that particular chore. I took them to Marsha's house on Monday afternoon. Missy Morgan has the lot."

"There's no end to her helpfulness," Miller said to Reilly. "I have no more questions for her. Do you?"

"A small one." Reilly turned to me: "Now that we have your fingerprints for comparison purposes, I need to know how frequently you visited Miss Morgan's office."

My mouth went dry as talcum powder as I told the little white lie. "I went to Marsha's office only once—the day after I met her."

Reilly looked at me but said nothing. I use the same technique when I interview candidates. Silence often encourages people to babble things they didn't plan to say, but not someone who knows how to play the game. I gritted my teeth and stared him down.

"Have a good day, Miss Hunnechurch," Reilly said at last.

I felt like a convict freed after a twenty-year sentence when I emerged into the sunlight. I had become the first Hunnechurch to be interrogated by the police, a distinction I decided not to share with Chloe and Mum.

The flight from Atlanta arrived on time—another good omen. The first passenger ambled out of the jetway, a man, middle-aged and portly. Then, another man, young and athletic, wearing blue jeans—and an elderly woman, tugging a carry-aboard suitcase on wheels—and a woman, dressed for business, but too young to be Linda—and two kids, a boy and a girl, followed by their frazzled mother.

The trickle of arriving passengers became a flood. But where was Linda Preston? My personal goosey gremlin whispered in my ear, *Maybe she missed the flight?*

Ridiculous! Linda is a no-nonsense professional.

Can you be sure about that? Remember your peculiar exchange with James Huston? He refused to talk about Linda. So you never verified the one credential that Derek values the most—Linda's clout at the Department of Commerce.

True. But Marsha Morgan did, and Marsha knew her stuff.

But Marsha didn't know everything. What if Derek Wetherspoon and Linda Preston discover that they hate each other?

What, indeed! Personal chemistry between candidate and client is the major factor no headhunter can control. On occasion, recruiting can be as chancy as arranging a blind date, but not this time. Linda Preston didn't climb to her present high-ranking post at a major bank by being difficult to like, and Derek Wetherspoon seemed less vexatious than many other chief executive officers.

Get thee behind me, gremlin!

Then a stunning woman stepped into the arrival area. She carried a folded garment bag in one hand, a narrow tooled-leather briefcase in the other.

Please. Let this be Linda. P-l-e-a-s-e.

She wore a trim designer suit, tailored in crisp beige linen. Her brunette hair was short and curly, and her makeup flawless. She moved with poise and assurance—the very model of a modern legal officer.

I raised my arm. Our eyes locked.

"Linda?"

"Pippa?"

I pushed through the throng of arrivers and greeters.

"I am so very pleased to meet you at last," Linda said in her ambrosial drawl. "It is positively disquieting to surrender your career to a voice on the telephone."

I took her garment bag. "I know a perfect place for a *tete-a-tete* before your interview."

"Lead the way, Pippa. Marsha told me to put myself whole hog in your capable hands. Here I am."

As we walked through the busy concourse, I heard the garment bag clink.

"A little gift for you," Linda said, "wrapped in my Sunday-go-to-church clothing."

"Pardon?"

"I worried that a proper British gentleman like Mr. Wetherspoon might find my favorite suit too *chichi*. So I brought an alternative getup—just in case. A little navy number. Cautious and quiet."

"Fear not. Derek is not stodgy, nor, I suspect, all that proper. He will," I searched for the perfect word, "*appreciate* your outfit."

"I am genuinely relieved to hear that. The photo in Eurokit's annual report makes the man look like he swallowed a riding crop."

I couldn't help laughing out loud. If Derek Wetherspoon didn't immediately fall in love with Linda, well, he'd be a hopeless fool.

We settled at the end of a row of plastic chairs in the back of a deserted departure lounge. Linda unzipped the garment bag and presented me with a white gift box tied with a red satin ribbon.

"Iced tea glasses and spoons," she said. "The kind my mother uses, and she is an expert on iced tea. Marsha told me you like the stuff."

"Indeed I do!"

"A small token of gratitude that you chose me as a candidate. Marsha also told me how important this search is to you."

"She did?"

"She explained that many of your smaller accounts have dried up and that you are relying on Eurokit. I appreciate your faith in my abilities."

I kept smiling and tried not to show my amazement that Marsha had me all figured out. I hadn't fooled her, not for a millisecond.

"Yes, well, the focus today is on you, not me. Let's talk about Eurokit Limited."

"By all means. What do you want to know?"

Her self-confidence struck me as refreshing rather than arrogant. "You have done some homework, I presume?"

"More than mere homework. I have performed a full day of legal research."

Linda opened her briefcase and turned down her accent. "I identified several precedents and agency rulings that may impact Eurokit, and to be blunt, I can see a couple of areas where Mr. Wetherspoon might have severe regulatory problems if he isn't careful. For example, there's the case of *Porter v. Quantum Importing.* . . ."

I listened as Linda elucidated the various minefields Eurokit USA had to tramp through once it began its expansion into the U.S. market. Most of what she said went careening over my head. When she paused for breath, I responded, "I can see why Derek wants an attorney who knows people in high places at the Department of Commerce."

"Which brings us to Kathleen Isley," she said.

"Derek is bound to ask about your relationship."

"I know the deputy secretary, and she knows me. In fact, we spoke last week about old times at Commerce."

"How long did you work with Kathleen?"

"Eleven months." She snapped the locks on her briefcase shut with two loud clicks. "Eleven months that seemed like eleven years. There were ten of us on the team. Six negotiators, three lawyers, and Kathleen—the slave driver. I've never worked harder in all my life, but I also learned a lot."

"Most impressive."

"Ah, but will I impress Mr. Wetherspoon?"

"Without question! Derek understands that few female attorneys have the unusual combination of skills and experience that Eurokit needs. You fit the bill perfectly."

Linda beamed at me for a while and then said: "What else should I know about my new boss?"

I summarized what I had learned about Derek, then added: "He will be an interesting man to work for, but not always an easy one. British-born executives tend to be a tad behind the times when dealing with women."

"No problem! My boss at the bank is a classic good ole boy who wishes his momma had named him Bubba. I whupped him into shape in a few weeks."

We both laughed.

"You say that Mr. Wetherspoon works hard; I'll bet he also plays hard," she said.

"Indeed! He relaxes by racing sailboats."

"I declare! So do I. Two-person catamarans. On Lake Lanier, in Georgia. My daughter serves as my crew."

What daughter? "I didn't know you had a child. Or that you were married."

"I divorced a decade ago. My daughter's name is Franny. She's seventeen years old."

My gremlin returned. *Something else you didn't know about Linda, Pippa. Something important. Remember those three past recruiting assignments that came to screeching ends when your recruits decided not to move their teenagers to a new city.*

"Have you spoken to Franny about the move to Ryde?" I asked cautiously.

"She adores the idea. We'll be able to do lots more racing on the Chesapeake Bay."

I could sense Linda's enthusiasm. Her voice bubbled, her eyes gleamed, and her hands fidgeted. I can always tell when a candidate is anxious to land a new job. Linda showed all the symptoms.

"Now, Pippa, I want your honest advice," she said, her drawl back at full power. "Do you suppose it will be OK if an occasional 'y'awl' slips out? Or should I restrain my southern accent?"

"You may *y'awl'* to your heart's content. I am confident that Derek will find your accent charming."

A cleaning crew invaded our lounge with a loud vacuum cleaner. Linda rose to her feet and adjusted her skirt.

"Tallyho!" she said. "I do believe it's time to make the English gentleman's acquaintance."

Poor Derek. He didn't stand a chance.

━━━━━━

He stood when we approached his desk. His eyes left me the instant he caught sight of Linda. I watched his experienced eye take in the swell of Linda's figure beneath her jacket, the curve of her hip beneath her skirt, the line of her leg where it reached her ankle. His face began to glow.

I said, "Derek Wetherspoon, allow me to introduce Linda Preston."

"A long-awaited pleasure, Miss Preston." His voice oozed elegance and breeding as he took her outstretched hand. For a moment I thought he might kiss her fingertips.

"Why, thank you, kind sir," she said with a smile that lit up the ninth floor.

"I'll be back for Linda at three," I said.

"Quite right," he said without looking at me.

Three cheers for the power of personal chemistry! I spun on my heels and made for the elevator.

My calendar was open for the rest of the day—no appointments, no interviews, no urgent phone calls. I exercised my privilege as a successful self-employed consultant to play hooky. I telephoned my answering machine and revised the message:

"Hi. You have reached the offices of Pippa Hunnechurch, who is busy tending to a satisfied client. I plan to call in for my messages, so please leave yours."

What can I say? I felt happy.

I spent an hour browsing the shops in the High Street, cataloging the goodies I would buy when the fresh infusion of Eurokit money recharged my bank account. I made a mental list: an autumn frock, a more modern printer for my computer, a bread-making machine.

Late morning turned warm, but not oppressive. I walked to Ryde Old Port and meandered past the sailing yachts moored in the marinas. They rocked in their slips as small powerboats, moving back and forth through the harbor, made waves in the Magothy River. Maybe someday I would own a modest sailboat—say a thirty-footer? Big enough to sail the Chesapeake, small enough to single-hand.

Behind me a deep-toned horn tooted. A crowd of tourists hurried aboard the *Pride of Ryde,* our local excursion boat. I looked at my watch. It was eleven-thirty. I could have lunch on the water. What a grand idea!

I was the last passenger up the gangplank before we cast off. I bought a chicken-salad sandwich and a cup of tea in the snack bar, then found an empty deck chair under an awning near the starboard rail. Several tourists peered at me as they strolled past, doubtless wondering why their shipmate had come aboard in an elegant silk business suit. I answered every quizzical stare with a contented grin.

The navigable section of the Magothy River is about eight miles long—from its wide mouth on the Chesapeake Bay to a low bridge upstream that carries Maryland Route 648 across the narrowing river. The *Pride of Ryde* cruised a big loop: first a brief jaunt out into the Bay, then an unhurried motor close by the Magothy's north shore, then the journey back to Old Port, along the southern shore. We traveled perhaps twenty miles in three hours, moving along at seven knots, the perfect speed to create a scrumptious breeze.

Could life get any better than this? Indeed it could.

━━━━━━━

The *Pride of Ryde* docked at two-thirty. I swung the Miata's top down and drove to the Ridley Building. Derek and Linda stood waiting for me out front, licking ice cream cones, looking thick as thieves. I knew at once that her interview had been a smashing success.

Derek bade Linda farewell and helped her into the passenger seat. She chattered all the way to the airport. On and on she went about Eurokit's business strategy, Derek's vision for the future, and the essential role that the new chief counsel would play. I finally interrupted. "Did you talk about money?"

"We had a lovely conversation! Derek asked me if I would consider twenty-five percent more than I earn now. Plus a hefty bonus."

Huzzah! Hunnechurch & Associates would soon be flush for months!

I dropped Linda at the terminal and then called Derek on my cell phone.

"We need look no further," he said. "Linda is perfect. I want her back for a second interview to meet more of my staff, and I can't make a formal offer until my managing director in England gives the nod, but those things are mere formalities."

"I'm so glad." And not only for Linda. I'd soon be back on my financial feet, able to pay my bills.

"Your performance has been exemplary," he said grandly. "I am more than pleased. You have done precisely what you promised to do. I look forward to offering you many more assignments, Pippa. Soon."

Ta da! Hunnechurch & Associates was back in business.

Chapter Fifteen

I KEEP MY TELEPHONE ANSWERING MACHINE at home in my hallway, atop a glass-front curio cabinet. I felt a surge of excitement as I unlocked my front door and saw the red light blinking. Perhaps Wetherspoon had left a message announcing that he had spoken to his boss in England and cleared the way to hire Linda.

Get a life, Hunnechurch! Afternoon in Ryde is late night in Great Britain. Eurokit's execs went home hours ago. Besides, the mills of big companies grind slowly. Nothing's going to happen for a few days.

I punched the playback button. Gloria Spitz said, "Hi Pippa! I hate to bother you at home, but I need to see you—tonight if possible. Missy Morgan is saying extraordinary things, and I want your advice. Please call me so we can arrange to meet."

So much for a quiet evening at home.

Winston began to chirp. An insistent squawk that meant, in budgie-speak, "Why haven't you unlocked my cage yet?"

"Forgive me, matey. It has been awhile since you stretched your wings."

I undid the latch. Winston flew to the rim of my sink and gazed at me with beady black eyes for a few moments. He took off again, whizzed twice around my head, and then soared down to a neat landing on the floor. He explored the kitchen on foot, his claws skittering on the polished oak while I drank a mug of tea. The cheerful cuppa added to the warmth I still felt from Derek Wetherspoon's amiable parting words.

I lifted Winston back to his cage. "I'll be back, laddie—after I find out why Gloria's knickers are in a twist."

—————

I arranged to meet Gloria for supper at The Remorseless Gourmet, a stylish bistro not far from my house that served sinfully fattening food. Neither of us could resist the special of the evening, seven-cheese lasagna.

"OK," I said, "tell me about Missy's extraordinary statements."

"I will—after I apologize."

"Apologize? For what?"

"The way I behaved on Friday night when you phoned me."

"Ah. The night Marsha died."

You called me out of kindness, and I made the mistake of judging you. I'm sorry for what I said. I was out of line, and I should have told you so when you came to Marsha's office on Monday morning. Please forgive me."

"Put it out of your mind. We were both upset on Friday night." I sprinkled a few bits of red pepper atop my lasagna. "Missy is upset too. Does that explain the odd things she said?"

Gloria hoisted a chunk of hot lasagna on her fork and blew gently to cool it. "I don't think so. It started this afternoon at the townhouse. I went over to help Missy sort through Marsha's clothing closet. We began to chat—to pass the time while we worked. In truth, she did all of the talking, mostly about the silly things that the Morgan sisters did when they were kids in Florida. She admitted that both the Morgan girls are sentimental about the past and like to keep souvenirs. That's when I jumped into the conversation. I told Missy that nothing of sentimental value was destroyed in Marsha's office. I know that for a fact because I helped Marsha put everything away after our last redecoration."

Gloria sighed. I kept silent.

"Well . . ." Gloria continued. "Missy got very quiet—as if she was thinking. Then she went all goofy on me. She offered to find me a new job in Atlanta."

"Missy wants you to move?"

"She *insists* that I move."

"She must have told you why."

"Sure. She put her arm around my shoulder and said, 'You have to leave Ryde because too many people here know that you worked for Marsha.'"

I mulled over Missy's behavior while I chewed my lasagna. Grief is a strange emotion. One never knows how a person will react when a sibling dies. Still, I agreed with the label that Gloria had come up with—*goofy*.

Gloria went on: "I couldn't think of anything clever to say, so I told her the truth, that I plan to ask you to find a job for me in Ryde."

"I'll be delighted to help." I added silently, *assuming, of course, I'm still in the recruiting business.*

"Thanks, but mentioning you was a big mistake. Missy went ballistic. She shouted, 'Stay away from Pippa Hunnechurch. She's one of *them*. You can't trust anyone but me.'"

"Blimey! Did she explain what she meant by that remark?"

"Nope. We spent the next hour in the den writing my résumé on Marsha's computer." Gloria handed me a white manila folder. "More goofiness."

The "Résumé of Gloria Ellen Spitz" filled two handsomely formatted pages. I read them carefully. Few of my candidates did a better job of organizing their skills and experience, or describing their talents and education.

"I'm dazzled."

"Don't be. The first page is chock-full of make-believe. For starters, I've been Marsha's secretary for four years, but Missy put down five years, so I don't need to reveal that I got fired by Kendall Tax Preparers."

"I see."

"No, you don't see! Kendall claimed I was insubordinate. In fact, they gave me my traveling papers because I chose to attend a two-week drill during tax season. I'm a tech sergeant in the Maryland National Guard."

"Gloria Spitz is a *weekend warrior?*"

"*Ten-hut!*"

"You handle guns? And things that go boom?"

"My specialty is maintaining antitank missiles, but I hold a marksman rating with an M-16."

"That is *fascinating*."

"I think so too, but Missy wouldn't let me put the National Guard on my résumé. She said, 'Atlanta-based companies prefer ladylike women.' Too bad! I don't even know what 'ladylike' means. I've always liked to roll around in the mud with the boys."

Never judge a book by its cover. An ancient proverb they teach kids in kindergarten. Sensible advice for every headhunter. But there I sat, staring at buxom, beautiful Gloria Spitz, trying to reconcile my memory of the teary-eyed secretary in Marsha's office with my new image of Gloria wearing a helmet and aiming an assault rifle.

"You have worked in recruiting long enough to know that many job hunters do what Missy suggested," I said. "They omit career details that are embarrassing or troublesome to explain."

"Sure, but she also invented lots of stuff about my job with Marsha."

The first page of Gloria's résumé included a succinct account of her accomplishments at the Morgan Consultancy. I hadn't seen anything outrageous or unbelievable, so I read the paragraphs again—this time more carefully. They described Gloria as Marsha's executive assistant, with broad responsibilities for evaluating candidate backgrounds: performing reference checks, developing candidate packages, and coordinating candidate interviews. The activities all seemed credible to me. If I had an executive assistant, she would do all of these things.

"Everything sounds true," I said.

"I don't care how my résumé *sounds*. It's all a bunch of hokum." Gloria rapped the table with a knuckle to emphasize each of her points.

"First, Marsha never gave me the title of executive assistant.

"Second, I never evaluated anyone's background. Marsha always did that, although she sometimes asked my opinion about a candidate's résumé.

"Third, I never developed candidate packages, unless you consider the task of assembling the paperwork in a file folder as 'development.'

"Fourth, Marsha even took over that for her blue-chip candidates. I could keep going, but why bother? Even a little white lie upsets our God of Truth."

The phrase "blue-chip candidate" caught my ear. I hadn't thought of asking Gloria about the five blue file folders that had been taken from Marsha's desk, but now I had the perfect opportunity.

"I presume that a 'blue-chip candidate' is a highly skilled person destined for a first-rank company?"

"Beats me." Gloria stirred sugar into the cup of cappuccino she had ordered instead of dessert. "With some candidates, Marsha would do everything herself: check references; arrange for interviews; even type their résumés. She called them her 'blue chips' but never gave me a reason why."

"I suppose that Linda Preston became Marsha's most recent blue chip?" I said.

"I think so. Marsha did all of the follow-up work for Linda herself."

"And Kathleen Isley, a while ago?"

"Uh-huh. Marsha often talked to Mrs. Isley. I got the idea that she wanted Marsha to find her a fat job when she left the Department of Commerce. Anyway, they spoke last week. I arranged a conference call between Marsha in Ryde, Kathleen Isley in Washington, and Linda Preston in Atlanta—all three talking on the same line."

"So that's how they did it."

"Did what?"

"Linda mentioned that she spoke with Kathleen Isley, but she didn't tell me where or when."

"'When' was right after you left the office."

That made sense to me. I had asked Marsha to fill in the missing bits of Linda's file. She decided to do it quickly.

Gloria tapped the manila folder with her cappuccino spoon to recapture my attention. Each tap left a small spot of brownish froth on the smooth white surface.

"Do you know what really frosts me about the résumé that Missy invented?"

"Enlighten me."

"It doesn't say that I did a sensational job as Marsha's secretary—her good right arm during the past four years. It makes me sound more like a management consultant than an administrative assistant."

"Perhaps that was Missy's goal? She told me that Marsha thought you had the capability to fill a managerial post some day."

Gloria scrunched up her face. "I don't want to be a manager at some big company. I don't crave the hassle or the stress or the empty striving for advancement. I don't envy the candidates I've met while working for Marsha." She looked straight into my eyes and said, "I have seen all the works that are done under the sun, and behold all is vanity and vexation of spirit."

"Pardon?"

"Ecclesiastes. First chapter. Verse 14."

It was then that I noticed the two tiny fish symbols she wore in her earlobes. All at once I understood her mention of our "God of Truth," and her unexpected apology an hour earlier. Gloria took her Christianity seriously. I found myself hoping she wasn't one of those religious kooks who came knocking on my door offering quick and easy salvation. I also wondered if Gloria's in-your-face religiosity might be distorting her view of Missy's behavior. Perhaps Gloria, not Missy, was the goofy one?

"Yes, well, perhaps Missy described you somewhat enthusiastically on paper," I said, "but we both know that modest exaggeration is taken for granted in the world of résumés. I will admit, though, that this seems a more skillful piece of work than most. I wonder where Missy Morgan learned the art of résumé writing?"

Gloria gaped at me as if I had gone bonkers.

"No one told you?" she half-shouted.

"What should I have been told?"

"Missy is a headhunter too. The Morgan Consultancy has—*had*—two offices: one in Ryde and one in Atlanta."

I managed to nod and say, "Now I understand." But of course, I didn't. Not much of what I heard that evening made sense to me at the time.

Mercifully, Gloria moved to another topic. "Hey, before I forget to ask you—you are going to come tomorrow, right? To Marsha's wake?"

"Marsha's what?"

"Missy calls it a memorial get-together for Marsha's friends. But, well, the truth is she organized an old-fashioned Irish wake, complete with great food. I bought a ton of elegant hors d'oeuvres at the French Chef. The only difference from a traditional wake is that Marsha won't be in her casket, propped up in the corner of the living room. Too bad—I think she would have enjoyed the experience."

I couldn't help but smile. No doubt about it—Marsha would relish being the guest of honor at a wake. But what about me? Did I actually want to attend? Perchance the time had come to untangle myself from Marsha, Missy, and Gloria—the whole goofy lot of them.

"I had planned to come," I said, "but now I'm not sure. Perhaps Missy would prefer I didn't come. After all, *I'm one of them*."

"*Please*, Pippa, don't let the weird stuff that Missy said stop you from coming. Marsha would want you at the get-together."

She looked so crestfallen that I took her hand. "You're right, Gloria. The gathering is about Marsha, not Missy. I'll be there."

But as I spoke, I began to wonder, *What does Missy mean that I am "one of them"? One of whom?*

Chapter Sixteen

SOMEONE HAD TACKED A HAND-LETTERED SIGN on the crab apple tree in front of the townhouse, which read, "Welcome Friends of Marsha Morgan." Gloria yanked the front door open before I had a chance to ring the bell.

"Missy doesn't know that we met last night," she whispered. "She's acting less goofy today. No more nonsense about me moving to Atlanta."

"Where is she?"

"In the living room, puttering around. I'll be in the kitchen. Holler if you need me."

Three people I didn't know, two women and a man, stood chatting in the hallway. One of the women held Ginger in her arms like a baby. I smiled, nodded, then walked past them quickly. Unlike the cat, I didn't feel in a mood to make new friends.

I found Missy alone in the living room, near the fireplace, fiddling with a large silver frame that held a recent photograph of Marsha. She draped a black ribbon diagonally across the left corner, centered the frame on the mantelpiece, and then stood back to examine her work.

"Perfect," I said.

"Pippa! Thank you for coming." Her voice sounded more ragged then when we last met, and the lines around her eyes had become darker and deeper—as if she hadn't slept since arriving in Ryde. Still she seemed pleased to see me.

"Gloria told me about her plans," she said. "I hope you'll help her find a new job?"

I had expected the question. Nonetheless, I felt awkward when the moment came. Gloria seemed both competent and scrupulously honest (an admirable aspect of her Christian faith), but I had no personal knowledge of her secretarial skills or capabilities. My safest course was a vague reply. "I'll schedule a thorough interview with Gloria after things get back to normal."

"Do it quickly. Gloria is a gem; someone will snap her up when you aren't looking. I'd hate to see you lose a recruiting fee because you waited too long."

"Speaking of recruiting, I didn't learn until yesterday that the Morgan Consultancy had a branch office in Atlanta."

She smiled. "I understand that you had worked with Marsha for only a few days and that you know very little about the Morgan sisters."

"Alas, that's true. Marsha never told me she had a sister, or that you are a recruiter."

"I've been in the game for twenty years."

"Then you should have these." I dug Marsha's stash of business cards out of my purse and pressed it into Missy's palm. "I found them—lying about."

She gave the stack back to me. "You keep them, Pippa. In fact, take anything else you find useful." Her face went grim. "All I ask in return is that you watch out for Gloria."

"Gloria has a good head on her shoulders. I'm sure she will land another job in no time at all."

"That's not what I mean." Missy pulled me into the corner. "You saw what happened to Marsha's office. The files, Pippa. Someone destroyed the files. You must protect Gloria."

Missy's intensity startled me. I pried her fingers from my wrist and tried to move away. She cast her arms around my shoulders.

"No! We have to talk about Gloria." Missy spoke loud enough to attract the attention of the woman who held Ginger. She poked her head around the archway and stared inquisitively at our clinch.

"OK, Missy," I said. "Let's talk about Gloria. In private."

I broke loose from Missy's bear hug and led her through the hallway, past the trio of chatterers, into Marsha's den.

"Why do you think Gloria needs protection?" I asked as I shut the door.

"Because the only reason to shred a headhunter's files is to eliminate the information they contain."

"You are speaking in riddles."

"No, I'm not. Someone *obliterated* Marsha's files. Think about the implications for Gloria."

I thought about it.

"Ah," I said, "the villain may assume that the information still survives in Gloria's head."

"It's a scary possibility." Her eyes darted about the room, landing on everything but me.

"Tell me, Missy," I said, "about *whom* are we talking? Do you know who wrecked Marsha's office?"

"I can't tell you."

"You mean—you won't tell me."

"No. I *can't* tell you." She laughed at me. A coarse, ugly laugh that made me take a step backwards. "That's my problem. I don't know who did it. There are several likely suspects. I can't begin to guess which one is responsible."

"Why would 'several' people have reasons to destroy Marsha's files?"

"My goodness, Pippa! What a foolish question for another headhunter to ask. Your office must be full of information that some candidates might consider embarrassing. Imagine how they would feel if you died without warning."

I took a moment to imagine my unexpected demise. "I see your point. Marsha's accident made her confidential records . . ."

"Unconfidential!"

Missy was right. An unexpected death changed the rules. Who knew what fate would befall her files. Her heirs might store them in cardboard boxes, send them to a paper recycler, even give them to another headhunter. Me, perhaps, along with her cache of business cards.

Who says my files contain embarrassing information?

"Whoa, Missy!" I shouted. "My cabinets hold heaps of résumés and interview notes. Nary a secret or scandal anywhere. What else did Marsha squirrel away?"

I became annoyed when she didn't answer my question. I spoke the first thought that came into my head. "Did Marsha collect nasty tittle-tattle about her candidates?"

Missy gasped. "How can you say something so hurtful? Especially today? Marsha loved all her candidates. She helped her women get outstanding jobs. You know that."

"Yes, I know that," I said, feeling painfully contrite. "I apologize for my foolish remark."

Missy became calm. "And I apologize for overreacting. It's no wonder you think I am foolish—all this weeping and gnashing of teeth."

"I don't think you are foolish."

"Well, I am. I was wrong to involve you in a situation that only I can fix."

"Missy, what is going on?"

"Nothing much, really. A few loose ends I have to clean up. That's all."

"What about Gloria?"

"Oh, she'll be fine. I will make certain of that. Now, I must see to my other guests."

Missy strutted away with a raised chin that declared her fervent annoyance with Pippa Hunnechurch.

Blast you, Miss Morgan!

I stood there awhile, feeling an unpleasant mixture of bewilderment and disquietude. Perhaps Missy had deduced the correct answer? Perhaps a former candidate had panicked when Marsha died without warning, then broke into her office and chopped up every file in sight?

"There are several likely suspects," Missy had said.

Why not *hundreds?* There must have been hundreds of file folders strewn across Marsha's office.

The answer came to me, complete with a memory of the five electric blue folders I had seen in Marsha's desk drawer. Missy believed that one of Marsha's "blue-chip" female candidates did the deed. One of *several* special women who received special attention at the Morgan Consultancy: Harriet Beardsley, Kathleen Isley, Susan McKenzie, Roxanne Landesberg, and Linda Preston.

Why hadn't I thought of it myself? After all, I had guessed that the vandalism was designed to cover up the theft of the blue folders. I suppose I had assumed that Detective Reilly's "perpetrator" must be a man, though I don't know why. One doesn't need brute strength to use a prybar on a door or work a paper shredder.

But one does need a reason. What lurked inside those bright blue folders that no one else should see?

Harriet Beardsley. Kathleen Isley. Susan McKenzie. Roxanne Landesberg. Linda Preston.

No! Not Linda Preston. I had spoken to her on Monday morning at her home in Atlanta, seven hundred miles away from Marsha's office. Besides, I had copied the contents of Linda's blue folder. One typed résumé and a few pages of handwritten notes—nothing that anyone could construe as embarrassing.

Harriet Beardsley. Kathleen Isley. Susan McKenzie. Roxanne Landesberg.

The more I thought about it, the less likely it all seemed. I couldn't picture any of them breaking and entering Marsha's office—not to recover a few pages of old interview notes prepared by Marsha Morgan.

And as for Gloria being in danger, well, could any of those rather prissy females pose much of a threat to a robust tech sergeant in the Maryland National Guard?

Gloria interrupted my musings.

"Missy has gathered everyone in the living room," she said, "so that we can all make speeches about Marsha."

"How does she seem?"

"In complete control. She's meeting and greeting the mourners like a pro."

"That's a relief."

With luck, no one else would see Missy's goofy side.

═══════════

The living room was awash with people—perhaps thirty in all—most of them strangers to me. I searched for a familiar face and found five: John Tyler, sober and grim visaged, conversing with Marsha's four superstars. The women wore fetching black outfits that made the quartet resemble a coven of high-fashion witches.

Which one of you wrecked Marsha's office?

Forget it, Pippa. It's not your problem. It's not even much of a crime. An episode of minor vandalism that everyone will soon forget, including the coppers.

Kathleen Isley's face lit up when she saw me elbowing my way toward her.

"I hear that Linda Preston will soon be Eurokit USA's new chief counsel," she said.

"I take it that you spoke to Linda."

"Last night. My congratulations to both of you."

I glanced at her biceps. Did she pump iron? Was she brawny enough to pry open a front door?

"Thank you, Kathleen," I said. "I'm quite optimistic that Linda will be offered the post."

"*Optimistic?* You sound like an overripe bureaucrat. Linda is a shoo-in. She told me so herself."

Oh, oh! It's not that I am superstitious, but I worry when a candidate is overconfident. The deal isn't done until the ink dries on the employment contract.

"By the way," Kathleen went on. "I meant to call you about Linda and add my unofficial recommendation. But, well, Marsha's death intervened."

"Indeed. Now that you mention it, I am surprised that Linda didn't name you as a formal reference."

"I did volunteer. After all, Linda reported to me for almost a year. She's an excellent attorney and a dependable employee. However, Linda declined. She said she didn't want to come across as a name-dropper."

I wondered when all this had been decided and whether Marsha had offered her advice and why Marsha had written a completely different explanation in the notes I found in Linda's folder. Before I could ask Kathleen any questions, Gloria maneuvered past us with a tray of hors d'oeuvres.

"The smart money is on the miniature crab cakes," she said. "Grab a couple before they are gone."

I harpooned two crab cakes—each the size of a quarter—with a plastic toothpick. Kathleen made a grimace and said, "Why would Missy serve canapés that are dripping with gobs of grease? Genuine fat pills!"

"So that's why they are so yummy. I'll have another." I skewered a third crab cake. When I looked up, Kathleen had moved away.

"Well, excuse me for trying," Gloria murmured. Then she said, "That woman is proving exceedingly difficult to love."

"Don't take it to heart. Photogenic females lead lives of fat-free desperation."

I stood on tiptoes and looked around the room. "Have you seen Missy?" I asked Gloria. "I can't spot her in the crowd."

"She's probably in the kitchen. I'll go check."

I wasn't alone for long. Harriet Beardsley sidled up to me as she nibbled a square of melba toast that held a big dollop of pink goo.

"Have you tasted the shrimp paté?" she said. "It's fabulous."

"Not yet."

"You must." She brought her mouth close to my ear. "Call me if you have any questions about your partnership with Marsha. I've had lots of experience with tricky financial issues. You know—profit sharing when a partner dies in the middle of a major piece of business."

Harriet's ill-mannered shift from shrimp paté to the private details of my business caught me unawares.

"I beg your pardon?"

"I take for granted that you arranged to split your fee with Marsha, but she died before the main transaction, namely, the hiring of your joint candidate, took place. There may be valid ways to rescind your agreement and save yourself some money."

I ached to scream, *Who asked for your silly advice? Mind your own business!* Instead, I said, "I intend to fulfill the bargain I made with Marsha. Her estate will receive the agreed-upon share of any fees I earn."

Harriet looked at me with amazement—the way she might gaze at a slow-to-learn child who repeatedly touched a hot stove—then rejoined her peers.

Silly twit! Take your codswallop with you.

I gave my full attention to my crab cakes. I had downed two when Gloria—this time without a tray—reappeared and said, "Pippa, Missy is in the den with a policeman."

She didn't speak all that loudly, but silence spread through the room like wildfire on a California hillside. Everyone turned to stare at Gloria, none with more curiosity than the four superstars. Kathleen Isley made the mistake of asking Gloria the obvious question, "A policeman? Is he an invited guest?" she asked.

"Not unless you invited him, Madam Deputy Secretary," Gloria answered sweetly.

"Me?"

"He's your favorite detective, Stephen Reilly, the cop who was in Marsha's office when you came to get your stuff back. You reduced him to quivering jelly. I'm sure he remembers you."

Kathleen reddened, Gloria snickered, and the other folks murmured. Most of them knew that Kathleen would soon regain her composure and try to fillet Gloria.

However, Kathleen never got the chance because Missy stormed into the room—her back stiff, her mouth a thin, tight line. Gloria and I looked at each other. Had the goofiness come back? What would we do if Missy let loose?

The crowd parted like the Red Sea before Moses. Missy marched to the mantelpiece, took down Marsha's photograph, and—in the manner of Hamlet speaking to Yorik's skull—spoke to the smiling image:

"You know, Sis, you often used to talk about your life in Ryde and about the many wonderful friends you made. That's why I thought it would be nice to have this final get-together. I figured that the people you helped to find great careers would want the chance to say good-bye in a more pleasant setting than a funeral parlor. Makes sense, doesn't it?"

Missy rocked the silver frame to "nod" Marsha's face.

"Yeah. I knew you would agree 'cause the simple fact is that lots of people in this room owe their careers to the Morgan Consultancy, especially the four women who were with you that night on the *Chesapeake Belle*."

Missy made a sweeping gesture with Marsha's photo that took in the four superstars.

"Four very famous ladies with impressive titles and loads of money and lots of responsibility and great futures, which sounds funny when I say it, because you, dear sister, don't have a future."

Missy looked at me, then back at the photo. "Oh, and we mustn't forget a not-so-famous lady who wanted to follow in your footsteps, a fellow headhunter who couldn't find the perfect candidate until you generously gave her a helping hand. She was also aboard the *Chesapeake Belle*."

With care she replaced Marsha's photo atop the mantelpiece, then looked at us one by one. "The five of you came here today prepared to make pretty speeches about Marsha. Well, you are not going to say a word. Do you want to know why? It's because of what a nice detective from the Ryde Police Department just told me. He shared the autopsy results with me. They prove it was *your* fault that Marsha fell off the boat."

I'm sure I went ashen faced. I heard a sibilant gasp—I think from Roxanne Landesberg—and a moan from Kathleen. Missy seemed to be enjoying our reactions. I moved forward, hoping to do something to calm her, but Susan McKenzie stopped me. "No. Let Missy have her say."

"I agree," Missy said. "Let me have my say. The subject on the table is friendship—or the lack thereof. The five of you claim to be Marsha's friends, but when it counted, you didn't look out for her. You let a diabetic drink lots of alcohol. Worse, a diabetic who is also a recovering alcoholic. Then you let Marsha wander around the open deck of that blasted boat—when she probably was heading for a diabetic coma."

A diabetic?

Now I understood what had happened aboard the *Chesapeake Belle*—Marsha's vacant expression, her zombie-like behavior, the way she tumbled over the railing. It all made sense. I glanced around. The superstars seemed as surprised as me by Missy's revelation.

"I'm so sorry, Missy," I said. "Marsha never talked to me about her illness . . ."

"I don't believe you!" she bellowed. "Marsha told *everyone* that she had diabetes. She wanted people to know because she often had problems regulating her blood-sugar level. She knew that she was in constant danger of losing control, just as she did on the *Chesapeake Belle*."

Missy had begun to cry. She wiped her tears away with her sleeve. "I don't want any of you to come to Marsha's funeral. You are all uninvited. The police may call it an accident, but it was your callousness that let it happen. Well, I can be callous too. Remember ladies, I knew you when you weren't so high and mighty. I won't forget what you did to Marsha. I can get even, and I will."

She dropped to the floor and began to sob.

Chapter Seventeen

To MY AMAZEMENT, Missy Morgan's outburst left me feeling calm rather than distressed. Her illogical rage seemed to sever once and for all my alliance with the Morgan sisters. Hunnechurch & Associates was a one-woman firm again, thank you very much.

I decided to call it a day. The last I saw of Missy, she had surrendered herself to the care of the superstars. Susan McKenzie half-dragged, half-carried Missy to the sofa. Kathleen Isley and Harriet Beardsley hovered nearby, making sympathetic sounds and worried grimaces. Roxanne Landesberg went off in search of a cup of hot cocoa. Good riddance to the lot of them. With a bit of luck, our paths might never cross again.

Gloria waylaid me on the threshold before I could slam the door on the madness I had witnessed. "Don't run off," she said.

"I've had all I can stand of Missy Morgan," I said loudly. "I don't like being yelled at publicly—or threatened. I hope I never see Missy again."

She grasped my forearm so tightly her fingernails nearly pierced my skin. "Aren't you going to attend Marsha's funeral?"

I pried her fingers open and freed my arm. "Missy doesn't want me there. It's her call."

"No! Both of us should be there on Saturday. For Marsha."

I took a deep breath and struggled to let go of my anger. It wasn't Marsha's fault that Missy had a screw loose. "OK . . . OK. I'll be there."

━━━━━━━━

I hadn't eaten much that afternoon, only the three miniature crab cakes, so I stopped at a no-name drive-through, bought a deluxe double cheeseburger, and dined alfresco in a tourist overlook that offered a grand view of Ryde Harbor. My little car's top was down, the afternoon sun felt warm and comforting, and I had no reason to hurry back to my office.

As I munched, I realized that Kathleen Isley had silenced the last little niggle of concern I felt about Linda Preston by confirming their friendship. Now I could, with confidence, stamp Linda *approved* to join the leaders of Eurokit.

Perhaps I sent a telepathic signal to Atlanta because my personal telephone rang a few moments later.

"Hi, Pippa, it's me," Linda drawled. "I tried to call your office, and then I remembered you have a cell phone in your car. Frankly, I'm dyin' of curiosity. Has Derek said anything to you yet?"

"No. But then, it's less than twenty-four hours since your interview."

"True, but I want this job so bad I'm close to peeing in my pants."

I laughed out loud.

"What's so funny?" she asked.

"You. Your enthusiasm. Your vocabulary. Everything about you is charming."

"From your mouth to Wetherspoon's ear."

"I had the impression that you thought you were a shoo-in to get the job," I said, paraphrasing Kathleen's words.

"That was yesterday. Today I am awash in trepidations. What if the man had second thoughts? What if he wants someone less expensive?"

"Relax. The hiring process takes time. You have been through a recruitment before."

"Oh yes, but not with an inscrutable Englishman on the other end. I wonder if Derek is still shopping around?"

"I doubt it. He seems hopelessly smitten with you."

"Oh, how I hope so."

"Tell you what, let's get you something else to think about while you wait. I'll ask a local realtor to send you a relocation package that describes the joys of Ryde, Maryland."

"Are you joshing me? I called two realtors yesterday. They overnighted a ton of pretty brochures about homes and schools and sailboat marinas. I've been pouring over the stuff for hours. Why do you think I have the vapors?"

"Hang in there, Linda. All will be over before you know it."

"Amen. Amen. And amen."

═══════

When I returned to my office, I found a fax waiting for me:

> *Pippa: Word of Eurokit's arrival in Ryde has leaked far and wide. An infernal reporter called to ask questions. Methinks the time has come to hire an experienced public relations person. I presume you can complete the task quickly? Call at your convenience.*
>
> > *Derek*
>
> *PS. I have just discovered that my boss went to France on some sort of "retreat" with a major customer. The HQ approvals I need before I can make Linda an official offer will grind slowly through the mills of Eurokit. Don't allow our catch to wriggle off the hook. Linda is definitely the one I want. You have my permission to tell her so.*

I recall a fleeting period of pure bliss as I crooned over and over again, "I have a new assignment," and "Linda is definitely the one." I didn't even notice David Friendly come through my front door until he said rather gruffly, "Stop grinning like a booby. We have to talk."

"How can I stop grinning? I have two reasons to be overflowing with happiness. First, I am about to call a frantic candidate and give her some wonderful news about a fabulous job. Second, I have received a new search assignment, which means I no longer look forward to a winter of economic discontent."

"How peachy!" The flinty edge to his voice grew even sharper.

"Very peachy, in fact. And there's even a tidbit of joy for you. My newest client wants a senior *flack*. Do you know any talented business journalists who want to enter the exceptionally high-paid world of corporate communications?"

"Gee. I'll bet your newest client is Eurokit USA."

I stopped grinning.

"Oh! You've heard about Eurokit USA?" I said, trying not to sound as guilty as I had begun to feel.

"Yeah, but not from you."

"Is that why you seem so annoyed?"

"Congratulations, you figured me out. Of course I'm annoyed. You uncovered a juicy discovery and didn't share it with me, which I think is pretty rotten because we're supposed to be good friends."

He had a point. "I wanted to tell you about Eurokit; I really did. But I couldn't, not without breaking a confidence."

"Pippa, you have a bad case of selective morality. You think nothing of asking me to dig up information that other people consider confidential."

"Touché."

"I prefer *gotcha*. But let's not quibble. I'm not finished pulling your chain. You haven't asked me how I learned about your relationship with Eurokit USA."

"I assumed you used your reportorial wiles."

"Nope. Your assignment to recruit a female chief counsel was a topic of lively conversation at Marsha Morgan's memorial get-together, along with 'I wonder why Missy wigged out,' and 'Isn't it strange the way Pippa Hunnechurch disappeared without saying good-bye?'" David shot me a wry smile. "I arrived at Marsha's townhouse a few minutes after you bailed out."

"How is Missy?"

"Eerily calm. She walked around the room, personally apologizing to everyone—even me. Then she *re*invited the crowd to Marsha's funeral."

"Well, I apologize to you also. I won't hold out on you again." I added a silent, "unless utterly necessary."

"Good, because I have an interview with Derek Wetherspoon in twenty minutes. Describe him in fifteen words or less."

I swallowed a snigger. David Friendly must be the "infernal reporter" Derek had complained about.

"Derek is your typical upper-class British gent," I said. "Self-confident. Traditional. A tad pompous. A bit of a *toff*."

"A *toff*? Is that like a buffoon?"

"Not at all. A toff is a chap who likes to exaggerate his Britishness. Derek is quite charming—in a *toffy* sort of a way."

"What does he think of the news media?"

"He sees all reporters as creatures of the netherworld, allied with the devil."

"Hmmm. A better opinion than most."

"Stare him down if he growls at you. His bark is worse than his bite."

"A good choice of words. I brought a small bone to toss your way."

"In addition to the bone you came to pick?"

"Ha. Ha." He reached into his jacket pocket and brought out three photocopied pages. "You asked me about Kathleen Isley's subordinates, specifically, the bureaucrats who worked for her six years ago."

"Indeed I did."

"Well, you goofed. Big time. I dug through an old reel of microfilm and found a relevant article in a gossip sheet for nerds called *Electronics Industry Insider*. Six years ago Isley was up to her hips in secret negotiations about Japanese microchips. It was a solo gig; she didn't have any subordinates."

David glanced at his watch. "Fee fie foe fum, it's time to visit the Englishman. Cheerio, old chum. Pip pip, tallyho, and all that rot."

I didn't offer a suitable reply or see David out. I was too busy reading the article he had unearthed. Its title was "Kathleen Isley: America's Unsung Chip Warrior." The writer described Kathleen's Ph.D. in economics and the nine separate trips she had taken to Japan to meet with bureaucrats in the Ministry of Trade and Industry. Not a word about

Linda Preston or any efforts to increase commerce with the former Soviet republics. One enlightening tidbit: Kathleen had been injured in an automobile accident on a rainy night in Tokyo. Her leg had been broken in several places and healed two inches short. Hence her limp.

My niggle of concern began to ring as loud as my alarm clock. Linda had been quite specific about her responsibilities at the Department of Commerce. "There were ten of us on the team," she had told me. "Six negotiators, three lawyers, and Kathleen—the slave driver." And what had Kathleen Isley said a few hours earlier? "Linda reported to me for almost a year."

The article can't be right.

I found the writer's name beneath the title: Sophia Cooper, Associate Editor. I called the Ryde Public Library and told the reference librarian what I knew. She quickly informed me that *Electronics Industry Insider* was published every other week by Industrial Newsletter Corporation, in Towson, Maryland, the distributor of a dozen different specialty newsletters. Sometime during the past six years, Sophia Cooper had been promoted to editor-in-chief.

I took a shot and called the editorial offices.

━━━━━━━

"Of course I remember that piece," Cooper said. "It was my first story about the U.S. socking it to Japan. The secretary of Commerce received most of the credit, even though Kathleen Isley hit the home run. She persuaded the Japanese government to open their market to more U.S.-made circuit chips. *Electronics Industry Insider* was one of the few publications to give Isley the recognition she deserved. I got the story right. The lady took a significant career risk—stuck her neck out repeatedly. Hardly anyone else in Commerce thought her mission would succeed."

"You wrote that she worked alone."

"She did work alone, for more than a year. On paper, she managed a small group of lawyers and economists who focused on Russian trade, but the project was a cover. The Department of Commerce kept her Japan assignment a secret."

I hung up feeling confused.

Linda had said, "There were ten of us on the team—including Kathleen."

Kathleen had affirmed. "Linda reported to me for almost a year."

Cooper claimed: "We got the story right. . . . Kathleen worked alone."

I made myself a cup of tea and tried to make sense of the three statements. Maybe I could reinterpret them—put a different spin on their meaning? But no matter how I looked at the facts before me, I kept reaching the same inescapable conclusion: Cooper had made a mistake six years ago. *Or . . .* Kathleen had lied to Cooper. *Or . . .* Linda and Kathleen had lied to me. *No!* The third possibility made no sense at all.

I picked up my phone and pressed the redial button.

"Good afternoon, Sophia Cooper speaking."

"It's me again, Pippa Hunnechurch."

"Did you forget to ask me something?"

"I need to talk to you face-to-face. It's important."

"About Kathleen Isley?" I heard the excitement build in her voice. I could imagine her thinking, *Perhaps this woman has the makings of another "right" story about the deputy secretary of Commerce?*

"Yes. About Kathleen. And about your article."

"Can you be here by 4:30?"

My clock read a quarter to four. I had just enough time to drive from Ryde to Towson if I ignored the speed limit on the Baltimore Beltway.

"I'm on my way."

Chapter Eighteen

THE TRIP TO TOWSON took me forty-two minutes. I drove aggressively, my foot on the accelerator, my hand on the horn, and my mind on what I was going to say to Sophia Cooper. I gave up trying to invent a clever reason for my visit. The truth would have to do. She would undoubtedly be disappointed when she heard my explanation. There's nothing newsworthy about a headhunter checking a credential on a résumé.

Industrial Newsletter Corporation had its own six-story glass and aluminum building in a square-block style that was popular thirty years ago, but which now looked dated. The *Visitor* slots in the parking lot were full. I eventually found a spot in the main lot next to a restored Triumph TR6, a vintage British sports car that was built in the early 1960s. The TR-6 was Simon's favorite car. He wanted to buy one in disreputable condition and rebuild it himself. The sight of the friendly green roadster buoyed my spirits. I felt certain that Cooper would sweep away my confusion about the working relationship of Linda Preston and Kathleen Isley.

Cooper was thirtyish, tall, and businesslike—with clear blue interviewer eyes, the sort that can read your mind. She ushered me into a comfortably furnished office, past easy-maintenance plants and a colorful assortment of Chesapeake Bay prints.

"You came a long way at high speed to talk about Kathleen Isley," she said. "So talk."

I had brought the slender attaché case I own but seldom carry. Inside was my complete "Preston, Linda" file. I propped the attaché case on my knees and dug out my copy of her *Electronics Industry Insider* article. I placed it on her desk.

"What you wrote about Kathleen six years ago has me concerned."

"Concerned? About a short piece in an obscure newsletter that had fewer than one thousand subscribers at the time?" She sat back in her swivel chair. "Give me a break! Hardly anyone read *Electronics Industry Insider* back then. I can't even guess how you managed to get a copy?"

"A friend of mine is a business reporter. He found it on microfilm."

"Very enterprising. But why bother?"

"I am an executive recruiter. One of my clients is interested in a candidate who worked with Kathleen Isley at Commerce six years ago. The candidate made various statements on her résumé. I felt a need to verify them because that's what recruiters do."

She chewed on my explanation for moment. "I get it! My article disagrees with your candidate's résumé."

"Yes. Unfortunately."

"And now you want to know who's telling the truth."

"That is my problem, in a nutshell."

Cooper smiled. "Six years ago I was a kid fresh out of journalism school. With loads of ambition, but lower than average grades, I couldn't get a job with a high prestige publishing company. *Time, Newsweek, Business Week* didn't want me. Then along came an opening on *Electronics Industry Insider.* I jumped at it and made myself a promise. No shortcuts. No mistakes. No half-baked writing. Every article done with total integrity. When you called, I told you the Isley piece was my first story about the U.S. socking it to Japan. Well, it was also the first full-length article I ever wrote. I ran my butt off to do a good job. I had to beat the bushes inside and outside Commerce to dig out the details because Kathleen Isley refused to be interviewed. I remember the work I did like it was yesterday."

"I see." She hadn't left much room for discussion.

"And yet . . ." Cooper picked up the copy of her article and looked at it thoughtfully. "Who's to say that a minor error didn't creep in? I was a green kid back then. If you really have doubts about what happened six years ago, why not go directly to the horse's mouth? Talk to Kathleen."

"Perhaps I should."

"You sound hesitant."

"Kathleen isn't my candidate. One of her former subordinates is."

"I don't think so," she said in a sing-songy voice. "Kathleen had no subordinates six years ago. That fact I'm absolutely sure of. You know what I think?"

"No, I don't," I said, although I had begun to guess.

She grinned at me. "I think that Kathleen Isley is your client. I think she is leaving Commerce for a bigger and better job in industry, and I think you are trying to decide what to put on her résumé. Should it be her triumph in Japan? Or her make-believe project in Russia?"

I gawked at her. How had an intelligent woman come to such a ridiculous conclusion?

"Not so . . . not at all," I stammered. "I have nothing whatsoever to do with Kathleen Isley."

Her grin widened. "Thanks for the tip. Maybe I can turn it into a story."

The look of delight in Cooper's eyes made it clear that nothing I could say would change her mind. I stood, retrieved my copy of her article, and said, "I won't take any more of your time. Thank you for seeing me."

She was grinning like a loon when I left her office.

=========

In an odd way, my trip to Towson had been a success. I came away certain that Linda Preston and Kathleen Isley had misrepresented their past working relationship, but my questions about Linda's résumé had been replaced by bewilderment. Why would two successful women lie about something so trivial? Derek Wetherspoon didn't care if Linda had reported to Kathleen six years ago. All that mattered was that Linda could make the occasional phone call to Kathleen to help Eurokit USA.

Forget it, Pippa! It's probably a typing mistake, a careless slip of the fingers. Don't worry about a minor discrepancy that's ancient history. Go home and make a cup of tea.

Perhaps I was being silly. Linda was a superbly qualified lawyer with sterling credentials and impeccable references—an ideal candidate for the chief counsel post at Eurokit USA. What could I accomplish by continuing to gnaw at this inconsequential bone?

Except, I couldn't let go. Sophia Cooper had talked of striving for "total integrity" in her writing. "No shortcuts. No mistakes. No half-baked writing." I understood what she meant. A headhunter must accept the ultimate responsibility of making certain that nothing but the truth is presented to her client. Linda and Kathleen had told the little white lie, but my name was on the candidate package delivered to Derek Wetherspoon.

I knew what I had to do next.

———

"Go directly to the horse's mouth," Sophia Cooper had suggested. Easier said than done. I doubted that this particular horse would let me visit her office or even answer my telephone calls. That left one option: drive to her house and simply knock on the front door. Linda's paperwork gave me Kathleen's home address in the Georgetown district of Washington, D.C.—more than seventy miles from Towson, Maryland. I glanced at my watch. Nearly six o'clock. *Blimey!* I would be driving through the stop-and-go traffic of the last half of rush hour—not much fun in a low-slung sports car equipped with a stick shift.

Wait 'til tomorrow, Pippa. What's your rush?

I didn't have the answer, except that *something* urged me to make the trip immediately.

I crawled along the Baltimore-Washington Parkway and shuffled through downtown Washington. I finally inched into Georgetown, regretting that I had not left my Miata at a suburban metro station and finished my journey by train. I managed to find a tight parking spot three blocks from Kathleen's house. It was ten past eight when I tapped the S-shaped brass knocker that hung on her bright red front door.

"Hunnechurch!" she exclaimed ungraciously. The look of bother on her face made me feel like a door-to-door magazine salesman. "What do you want?"

"Merely a quick word about Linda Preston. May I come in?"

"No you may not come in! I'm shocked to find you parked on my pavement at this hour. You have imposed on our acquaintance."

"I apologize for the late hour," I said sweetly, trying to pretend that I had *not* noticed her use of the word "acquaintance" rather than friendship. "But I do need a moment of your time to ask a question about Linda."

Kathleen kept a firm grip on her front door. "No questions! No quick words! I told you all that I intend to say about Linda Preston this afternoon. I have no interest in your firm or in any of your activities. I have nothing further to communicate to you on any topic, and I expect not to see you again. If you persist, I will turn the matter over to the Federal Bureau of Investigation. It is against the law to harass a high government official."

She slammed the door shut. The brass knocker bounced twice, making a pair of gentle clicks. An instant later, the lights on either side of the door blinked off, leaving me in the dark—both physically and emotionally.

What have I done to trigger Kathleen's overreaction?

I trudged back to my car in a daze. My traditional English upbringing stressed the importance of good manners. One simply didn't slam a door in the face of a recent dinner companion. Even allowing that redheads lose their tempers easily, Kathleen Isley's spiteful behavior seemed extraordinary. Perhaps she had a rotten day? Or had I caught her at a bad moment?

Or maybe she simply dislikes Pippa Hunnechurch?

I sang along with a CD of vintage Broadway showstoppers on the drive home to Ryde. Ethel Merman, Carole Channing, and Mary Martin quickly restored my good spirits, but I still had the problem of resolving the petty misstatement on Linda Preston's résumé.

Who else might know what really happened at Commerce six years ago?

The answer popped into my head: James Huston, the consultant who once provided a reference for Linda Preston and the man who refused to do any "scandal-mongering with far-away headhunters." I steered the Miata to the shoulder of the Baltimore-Washington Parkway, flipped open my cell phone, and dialed his number in Atlanta.

"Good evening. This is James Huston."

"Hello, Mr. Huston. This is Pippa Hunnechurch."

"Ah, yes, the recruiter with the charming English accent."

"You offered to chat with me about Linda Preston if I came to Atlanta."

"That's not quite the way I remember leaving things, Miss Hunnechurch, but I am agreeable to a brief meeting."

I gritted my teeth and charged ahead. "As it happens, I can arrange to be in Atlanta tomorrow."

"My schedule is chock-full tomorrow. I am conducting an all-day seminar at Georgia State University."

"You must take breaks during the day?"

The line went quiet. I wondered if he had rung off. "Mr. Huston?"

"Why are my observations so important to you?"

"Because you strike me as someone who tells the truth."

He chuckled. "We take our mid-morning break at ten-thirty. I'll set aside fifteen minutes to meet with you—mostly out of curiosity. I want to see how you cope with the truth."

I booked a 6:00 A.M. flight to Atlanta. The cost of the ticket consumed nearly half of my dwindling supply of working capital.

The truth may be precious, but why does it have to be so expensive?

Chapter Nineteen

I GAZED OUT THE WINDOW as the plane took off to the east and made a sweeping turn to the south that gave me a perfect view of the Chesapeake Bay.

There were a few sailboats catching the early on-shore breezes and a big, green container ship plodding toward Baltimore. I could pick out Poplar Island, lying north of the Choptank River, and the drawbridge across Knapps Narrows on the Eastern shore.

The scenery might have held my interest if I'd been able to forget about catching Linda Preston and Kathleen Isley in a little white lie about their long-ago relationship at the Department of Commerce.

Little white lies don't count, Chloe had instructed me when we were children. "It is frightfully impolite to tell the truth all the time. I would be a mean sister if I told you that your nose was put on your face funny, and I would be a nasty daughter if I told Mum that her shepherds' pie is too runny."

Perhaps only an overzealous headhunter concerns herself with a meaningless discrepancy on a résumé. I tallied the arguments I had made the day before:

First—Linda's past working relationship with Kathleen has nothing to do with her competence or her qualifications to be Eurokit USA's chief counsel.

Second—Derek Wetherspoon wouldn't care that Linda didn't report to Kathleen six years ago.

Third—The whole thing is probably a harmless typographical error made by Marsha Morgan when she retyped Linda's résumé.

Unfortunately, my exercise in logic didn't drive away my niggles. I continued to feel vague worries that I couldn't quite put into words. Not woman's intuition exactly, but a deep concern that something serious was amiss.

I hoped that James Huston would have a sensible explanation.

The cabin attendant came by with coffee. I asked for hot tea and earned a sour glance. "It will take some time, Ma'am. I have to go back to the galley to prepare tea."

"I'll be patient," I said impatiently. My last-minute ticket had cost more than nine-hundred dollars I couldn't afford. I certainly deserved a cuppa to help soothe the pain.

"Do you know Atlanta?" the cab driver asked me as we exchanged smiles in the rearview mirror. She was a plump black woman who spoke with a lilting accent I couldn't place.

"This is my first trip," I said, "although I saw *Gone with the Wind* five times."

She chortled merrily. "Atlanta has changed substantially since General Sherman burned the place flat in 1864. Did you know that Atlanta is the only major American city ever completely destroyed by war?"

"You say that with excitement."

"Oh, all metropolises are exciting to me. I'm working toward a Ph.D. in urban planning at Emory University."

"Where are you from?"

"Ethiopia. And you, of course, are a Brit."

"Of course."

"From the South of England, probably the County of Sussex."

"How did you guess?"

"I never guess. I have an ear for accents. My nickname at Emory is Henrietta Higgins. Accents are kind of a hobby with me, especially British accents and southern drawls."

"An odd combination."

"Not at all. I firmly believe the theory that the American southern accent has its roots somewhere in England. It makes perfect sense—the Brits settled the South."

"I'm afraid that my accent is fading. A few more years in America, and I'll probably sound like a *New Yorka*."

"Nonsense!" she said with a beautiful Oxfordian lilt. "You are a splendid purveyor of the Queen's English."

"Indubitably!"

We left Interstate 85 and drove into downtown Atlanta. On our right we passed an enormous building sheathed with bronze-colored glass. A big bronze sign proclaimed, The Atlanta Bank of Commerce. At this hour of the morning, Linda Preston would be at her desk, probably reading the *Wall Street Journal*, although today she might be composing her resignation letter. *After many happy years at ABC, I have been offered a wonderful opportunity in Ryde, Maryland.* I wondered if her boss would make a counteroffer that Linda couldn't refuse, then quickly squashed the thought. Why worry about something else I can't control?

"Georgia State University is that tall cluster of buildings up ahead," the cab driver said.

I looked at my watch: nine-thirty.

"I'm early for my meeting," I said. "Tell me a pleasant way to spend an hour in this part of town."

"Underground Atlanta is worth a look."

"Underground . . . *what?*"

"Underground Atlanta is an area of old buildings that were literally buried back in the 1920s, when the city built concrete viaducts that elevated the streets around them. The original storefronts have been transformed into boutiques and eateries."

"I'm game."

I emerged from the air-conditioned taxi into humidity that felt like it could wilt rock, then descended an escalator into Underground Atlanta—a cool, dark thoroughfare with brightly lit shops designed to attract the millions of tourists and conventioneers that pass through Atlanta each year.

I consumed fifteen minutes of my hour waiting in a queue to purchase and arrange to have shipped to Chloe a nightshirt custom-embroidered with "Frankly Stuart, I don't give a damn!" I spent another quarter hour in a gourmet coffee shop that roasted and ground its own coffee beans. The luscious smells had drawn me like a magnet. It is a common misconception that Brits don't drink coffee. We do. The problem is, most of us don't brew it very well.

I allowed a full twenty minutes to amble, on the shady side of the street, the four blocks to Georgia State. I arrived reasonably dry and un-rumpled and followed Huston's directions to a basement lecture hall. As he had promised, I found a large cardboard sign on an easel next to the door, "The Secrets of Selling Overseas. A Short Course for Entrepreneurs by James Huston, International Marketing Consultant." Huston's photograph filled the bottom half. I had expected an academic drudge, but he looked decidedly dishy. Early forties, craggy features, dark, wavy hair swept off his forehead, blue mischievous eyes, a wonderful smile. . . .

Yikes! You've been smitten by a photograph.

I had to laugh at myself. It had been a long time since Pippa Hunnechurch had reacted like a starstruck teenager. Yet, how could I be surprised that those stunning blue eyes captured my attention. . . .

Get a grip girl! You've come to interrogate the lad, not moon over him.

I brushed my amorous thoughts aside and pulled open the door. A few dozen casually dressed people chatted in small groups. Break time. I spotted Huston at the refreshment table at the side of the hall, filling a coffee mug. Happily, he was alone.

"Good morning, Mr. Huston. I am Pippa Hunnechurch." I laid my accent on thicker than usual. The cab driver had seemed impressed. Maybe Huston would be too.

Huston turned. "Ah, the Englishwoman who traveled nine hundred miles to speak to a truthful man," he said with a smile warm enough to set a woman's knees knocking. His photo didn't do him justice.

"The very same," I said, doing my best not to blush. I scolded myself for acting like a schoolgirl, merely because James Huston was more than a bit of all right.

Well, what did I expect? I was out of practice dealing with good-looking men. I'd met Simon when I was twenty-one. A year later I became Pippa Hunnechurch-Scott. When Simon and Peggy were killed, I decided to move to the United States. Over the Atlantic I stopped thinking of myself as a widow. I took off my wedding ring and switched my last name back to Hunnechurch. For the first few years I had no interest in dating. I threw myself into the work of making a living. More recently, the struggle to get my business off the ground kept me too busy to contemplate a serious relationship—at least that was what I kept telling myself.

"May I pour you a cup of coffee?" he asked.

Huston's courtly manner encouraged the rusty emotions his photograph had aroused. My eyes automatically flicked to his left hand. *No wedding band.*

"Thanks, but no," I said. "I just had a cup."

"Then let's find ourselves a quiet spot."

I followed him to a wooden bench in a rear corner.

"What can I tell you about Linda Preston?" he began rhetorically. "Well, the Linda I knew at the Department of Commerce was intelligent, well-educated, meticulous, dedicated, amiable, creative, quick-witted, always prepared, generous, thrifty, and kind to animals." He paused to catch his breath. "I liked Linda. She was an excellent attorney and a superb manager."

"But you refused to provide a formal reference for her."

"I still do. I'll deny everything good I said about her."

"But that's unfair. Your attitude suggests that Linda is less than qualified."

"I don't suggest anything about Linda, except that she is a skilled lawyer. I fully expect her abilities to take her to the top of the legal profession. Is that what you came to Atlanta to hear?"

"In part. I also want to resolve a minor question relating to Linda's professional credentials."

Huston peered into his coffee cup awhile and then took a healthy swallow. When he finally spoke, his voice seemed laden with mockery. "A minor question of professional credentials," he said with a shake of his head. "Why am I not surprised?"

"Excuse me?"

"Miss Hunnechurch, are you in cahoots with the Morgan sisters?"

I bounded midway to my feet. "I'm not *in cahoots* with anyone," I said loudly enough to turn a few heads, but my gush of self-righteousness dissolved as quickly as it arose. I sat down and lowered the volume. "The late Marsha Morgan helped me identify an exceptional candidate."

"I'll bet she did," he said, adding a little chuckle. "How did you and Marsha get together?"

"It's fairly common for headhunters to collaborate on a search. I needed assistance, and I asked Marsha Morgan."

"And Bob's your uncle—as you English say—she came up with a world-class attorney. Perfect in every way."

"Yes."

Huston shot me another smile, this one dripping with acid. "I'll bet that she forgot to mention that Missy Morgan had found Linda her job at the Atlanta Bank of Commerce."

All at once I understood the source of his displeasure.

"You think that the Morgan sisters *churned* Linda," I said.

"Yup. Missy Morgan giveth Linda to the bank. Marsha Morgan taketh her away, with your help, that is."

My mind reeled as I considered the implications. Churning is one of the most unethical things a headhunter can do. One doesn't accept a fee for finding a top-notch employee, then recycle the candidate after the dust has settled. The unwritten rule is quite clear. Don't "steal" an employee you have recently placed.

"You look perplexed," Huston said. He patted my hand. I pulled it away.

"I *am* perplexed," I said. "How can you possibly know all this?"

"Four years ago the board of directors of MidSouth Manufacturing hired me to serve on a selection committee to choose its new vice president of international marketing. Three headhunting firms, including a one-woman shop in Atlanta, presented candidates. Her candidate turned out to be an old friend of mine, a woman I had worked with at the Department of Commerce. We were close friends at the time, if you get my drift—*exceptionally* close friends. We were an item even after she went to work for Gateway Aerospace in Virginia."

"And so you knew the details of her life."

"Everything about her, starting with her shoe size. That's why I spotted the flaws in her résumé. The descriptions of her professional accomplishments overstated what she actually had done. I'd be hard pressed to call it lying. Her résumé simply overstated a few small details. For example, it said that she participated in a major trade mission to Asia. Not so! She prepared some position papers for the team but didn't make the trip. Further down the page it declared that she framed a series of new regulations designed to simplify the export of high-tech manufactured products. Sorry! All she did was to help edit the final words."

"Quite distressing, but not unusual. I meet many candidates who overstate their skills and achievement."

"That's not what happened. When I confronted the headhunter, she admitted that she was working with the Morgan Consultancy and that Missy Morgan had personally prepared the résumé. That's when I remembered that Marsha Morgan had placed my friend at Gateway Aerospace."

"Did you also confront the Morgan sisters?"

"Sure. They told me they were proud of their 'system,' as they called it. They insisted that their primary goal was to get highly qualified women the great jobs they deserve. They said it was terribly unfortunate that I was too straight-laced and conventional to applaud their success in placing promising women in top posts." Huston's voice became harsh. "Basically, they told me to get lost."

"They openly confessed to falsifying professional credentials?"

He thought a moment. "Not falsify, exactly. Missy didn't invent a phony college degree or concoct a fictitious job on my friend's résumé.

The Morgan Consultancy specialized in exaggeration for a good cause. Marsha and Missy would stretch the truth a little to get the candidate hired—some fine-tuning here and there and a touch of embellishment to attract more interest." He stared at me thoughtfully. "Professional credentials are whimsical things. They can be enhanced with a tweak of a pen to fit the job at hand. I think you'll find that the Morgan sisters owned a great many pens."

I felt my mouth go dry. Everything I knew about Linda Preston had been provided to me by Marsha Morgan. She had prepared everything in that folder I had so sneakily copied that night in her office, even the "fresh copy" of Linda's résumé, which, thanks to me, now sat in Derek Wetherspoon's office.

"Now you look green." Huston took my hand. This time I didn't pull back. "I didn't mean to upset you."

I shook my head and tried to smile. I knew it wasn't a convincing smile. "It's nothing, really."

Huston drew closer. "Let me make it up to you. I'll buy you dinner."

"Many thanks, but I am winging back to Baltimore on the 3:30 flight."

"How about a delayed rain check?"

"Again, thank you, but I doubt I'll have business in Atlanta any time soon."

"Maybe not, but I will soon have business in your neck of the woods. I learned this morning that I have to spend two days in Washington, D.C., with a firm that's organizing a seminar for me in the District. May I call you when I'm up north?"

"Please do." I slid a business card from my wallet and placed it in his hand.

"Perhaps I'll see you in Ryde."

"Perhaps you will," I said, almost indifferently. It is hard to be polite when the center of one's universe has come crashing down.

```
┌─────────────────────────────────────┐
│        Chapter  Twenty              │
└─────────────────────────────────────┘
```

I TRAMPED THE STEAMY STREETS around Georgia State University—Decatur, Washington, Piedmont—hoping that the heat bouncing off the pavement would thaw the lump of ice that James Huston dropped in the pit of my stomach.

I had wanted a sensible explanation of what seemed like a little white lie. Well, he certainly provided one. I now knew with painful clarity that Marsha Morgan had chosen me to help her churn Linda Preston and that the heart of Marsha's scheme was a jiggery-poked set of professional credentials adapted to fit Eurokit's requirements. I had taken the bait like a bluefish chomping a minnow and hurried to convey Marsha's fabrications to Derek Wetherspoon.

Clearly, I had been played for a fool, and it was my own fault. I should have seen it coming. Three people don't coordinate a cock-and-bull story without a purpose. How had Huston put it? The Morgan sisters specialized in "exaggeration for a good cause. A little fine-tuning here and there and a touch of embellishment to attract more interest." It was a perfect description of how Marsha Morgan "sold" me to the members of the Ryde Chamber of Commerce and the way Missy Morgan slanted the facts in Gloria's résumé.

Even John Tyler's "chauvinistic" comment about never doing a nickel's worth of business with Marsha had been a warning. "The woman had her faults; she may have occasionally shaved the truth a tad." Tyler tried to tell me how she operated, but I had paid no attention.

Now I felt guilty and abused. Above all, I felt torn by a dilemma. What should I do about Linda Preston?

On the one hand I wanted to "give her the push," as we Brits say. Linda had lied to her headhunter—the one truly unforgivable offense a candidate can commit.

On the other hand I still believed that the "unembellished" Linda Preston would make a super chief counsel for Eurokit. Who would be hurt if I forgot Linda's sin? Who would benefit if I raised a great ruckus?

My haphazard walk brought me back to the entrance of Underground Atlanta at ten minutes before noon, feeling sticky, gloomy, and hungry. I made for an ersatz English pub I'd seen earlier. I forced myself to endure the mock-Elizabethan decor and the waitresses dressed in Moll Flanders costumes and ordered a "plowman's lunch," an assortment of cheeses, a hunk of paté, and a small loaf of bread.

A bite of Double Gloucester cheese helped one more piece of the puzzle fall into place. I had wondered why Kathleen Isley, a high-ranking government official, would embroider a former associate's background. Now it seemed obvious. Kathleen was repaying previous services rendered. No doubt Marsha and Missy had amplified Kathleen's résumé years ago to ease her way into Militet Corporation and start her career.

I felt disgust at the Morgans for what they had done, but I found myself admiring the elegance of their "system." We help you to succeed today; you help a younger candidate tomorrow.

Which brings you back to Linda Preston. You have to make a decision— now!

Both of my alternatives seemed lousy. I couldn't ignore Linda's lies, but giving her the push would put me out of business.

There has to be a better option. . . .

The answer leapt into my mind. Why not reverse the lie? Why not *undo* the damage by sending Derek a memo that corrects the embellished facts in Linda's candidate package?

Why not, indeed! It would be easy to set the record straight. A handful of well-chosen sentences should do the trick. To wit, a brief explanation that although Linda technically reported to Kathleen Isley, they worked on separate projects.

I had a further thought. I could counterbalance the bit of "bad news" with a barrage of "good news," a few pages of additional information about Linda's current experience at the Atlanta Bank of Commerce.

A fabulous idea, Pippa. Linda's office is only a few blocks away.

I dug my cell phone out of my attaché case and dialed her work number. Her voice mail announced, "I am sorry to miss your call, but I'm not at my desk right now. Please leave a message or press 0 to talk to a live person."

I looked at my watch: 12:32. Linda was probably at lunch.

I pressed 0.

"Mrs. Preston's office," said a youngish female voice.

"This is Pippa Hunnechurch. When do you expect Mrs. Preston to return?"

"Not before 2:30, at the earliest."

Rats! My return flight to Baltimore left at 3:30. Well, I'd have to take a later plane home.

"Please tell her that I'm in Atlanta. Ask her to call my cell phone." I gave the number and repeated my name.

Had I put my cell phone in my pocket or my purse, the lives of several women might be different today, but I chose instead to return the phone to my attaché case. When I lifted the lid, I saw the folder of Linda Preston's paperwork I had brought with me, and I remembered that the lawyer who had spoken so highly of Linda also worked in Atlanta.

I found her name—Daniella Holms, a partner in a large law firm with a Peachtree Road address, probably a short taxicab ride from Underground Atlanta. I checked my interview notes—*Said she worked with Linda on several foreign deals.*

I had ample time for a short visit before Linda called me. With luck I'd collect even more good news for her rejuvenated candidate package.

━━━━━━━

Daniella Holms greeted me with a firm handshake, a synthetic smile, and a curiosity-filled gaze from her pretty brown eyes. She was in her early forties, my height, with the rangy build of a successful athlete.

"My, my, *Mizz* Hunnechurch," she said as I followed her into an office three times as big as mine. "This is a pleasant surprise. *Ah* never expected to meet a Yankee headhunter in the flesh."

I settled into a cushy leather-upholstered sofa. Daniella, her arms crossed, leaned half-standing, half-sitting against the edge of her desk. It was the pose of a woman who liked to dominate her territory.

"Thank you for seeing me without an appointment," I said.

"My pleasure. We tend to be less formal down here. And I must admit that I am dyin' to know what brought you to my doorstep. But where are my manners? You look thoroughly parched. May I have my secretary get you something to drink? Iced tea, perhaps?"

"I would love some iced tea."

She picked up her phone, mumbled a few words, then flashed another pretend smile. "Now then, how can I help you?"

"I came to Atlanta to meet with a gentleman who provided a professional reference for Linda Preston, and, well, I couldn't resist the opportunity to speak to you in person. You were on your way to an engagement when I called you last Sunday. We couldn't do more than scratch the surface of Linda's capabilities. Besides, telephone interviews are so limiting, so impersonal. Don't you agree?"

She cut through my small talk like a laser. "Whom did you visit today?"

"I prefer not to be specific, but I will say my meeting took place at Georgia State University."

She arched her eyebrows. "Georgia State. Imagine that. I didn't think any of Linda's former colleagues taught there." Her soft drawl had disappeared, leaving a hard-as-nails edge to her voice.

Down to business. I opened a small notebook and perched it on my knee. "How would you rate Linda's experience with overseas transactions?"

"Extensive. That's the best word to describe it. Linda has oodles of years at the Department of Commerce."

"Doing deals with the Russian republics?"

She nodded. "Scores of little countries whose names end in *stan*."

I let her lecture me awhile about the huge potential market in Asia and the Far East for U.S. companies and the legal intricacies of doing business in newly emerged nations. Nothing lubricates an interviewee more than talking about oneself.

The door opened. A young man in a sleek charcoal-gray suit sidled into the room clutching a rattan tray that held two crystal tumblers full of cold tea decorated with sprigs of mint. The ice cubes clinked as he set the tray down on a side table next to my chair. I took one glass, he carried the other to Daniella, then shut the door behind him.

"Moving beyond the Department of Commerce . . ." I said. "Tell me about Linda's more recent experience. When we last spoke, you mentioned that you worked together on several foreign deals here in Atlanta."

She frowned. "You must have me confused with one of Linda's other references."

"I don't think so." I took a long, slow sip of tea. Cold. Dark. Strong. Much sweeter than I like it.

"I *know* so," she said. "I would never make such a statement. Linda and I have not worked together on any legal transactions."

I coughed as the tea went down the wrong way.

"Is something wrong with your tea?" she asked.

"No. It's fine, thank you," I answered, fighting to disguise my confusion. Could I have made a mistake? Definitely not—my interview notes proved the point. I pressed on.

"I believe you told me that Linda Preston managed many foreign transactions for large companies in Atlanta." I looked Daniella square in the eyes and added, "Do you still agree with that statement?"

"Well, it certainly makes sense to me," she said. She seemed to be evaluating each syllable before she uttered it. "After all, the Atlanta Bank of Commerce serves many local corporations."

"Can you tell me about specific transactions?"

She said nothing for several seconds, then, "No. Not *specific* trans-actions. Not chapter and verse. All I can report with certainty is that I presume that Linda Preston, in her role as director of international law, has initiated several major deals for bank customers situated in and around Atlanta."

Weasel words—every last one of them.

I stared at Daniella while she stared at the crystal tumbler in her hand.

She's in it with the Morgan sisters. She lied about Linda Preston.

I stood up. "Tell me, Daniella, did Missy Morgan help you land this posh job?"

Her eyes flared. "My professional life is none of your business, *Mizz* Hunnechurch."

"Your answer tells me she did."

"Get out of my office."

"How many lies have you been forced to tell for the Morgan sisters?"

Daniella hurled her glass at the wall behind me. I jumped sideways as cold tea and lead-crystal shards rained down on the sofa.

"Don't you dare to confront me," she bellowed. "You are nothing but an employment agent with delusions of grandeur. Well, let me tell you how *my* world works. If you make any public attempt to cast aspersions on me—if you defame me in any way—I will haul your sorry carcass into court and make you wish you had stayed in England."

Her violence and venom amazed me. Daniella was more upset than she had any right to be. Why launch such a vicious attack?

The cornered look on her face answered my question.

She's terrified of what I might do.

"Calm down, Daniella," I said. "We have to talk about our mutual problem."

"I'll call the police if you don't leave."

Blimey! The very same threat that Kathleen Isley had made to me, and doubtless for the very same reason. Kathleen was also frightened.

"No. I don't think you will call the police." I pulled two visitors' chairs away from the bits of broken glass that glittered on the rug near the sofa. I sat on one. "You have a tiger by the tail, and we both know it. You fibbed on your résumé, and you provided misleading references for other women."

She stood motionless, silent.

Something clicked. "I've been a complete duffer," I said, "but now I understand. Lying to a headhunter isn't a criminal offense, but it could be more than enough to wreck a promising legal career. Your law firm won't take kindly to a scandal that makes your untruthfulness public."

My words scored a direct hit. Daniella seemed to shrink in stature as I watched. Her shoulders fell; her chin drooped. For a moment I thought she might faint. Instead she sank into the empty chair. She folded her hands in her lap and waited for me to speak, but I was busy thinking about the neatly printed names on the tabs of four blue folders: Beardsley, Harriet; Isley, Kathleen; McKenzie, Susan; Landesberg, Roxanne. Four senior executives who had climbed to the tops of their organizations. Four unimpeachable references, whom Marsha Morgan called upon to exaggerate the capabilities of her lesser candidates.

The several pages of notes I had seen in Kathleen's blue folder must have been a log of the various references she had provided. Marsha would need to maintain precise records, if only to keep track of the different little white lies she asked Kathleen to tell.

Marsha planned to add Linda Preston to her collection of "blue chip" executives. Five blue folders chock-full of deception, locked away in her desk, where Gloria Spitz couldn't see them.

Potent stuff. "Embarrassing information," to use Missy Morgan's words. No wonder someone decided to shred the lot.

"What are you going to do about me?" Daniella asked, her eyes wide, her voice soft.

"About you? Nothing."

"You aren't going to—tell the world that I . . ."

". . . that you puffed your credentials to land this job? No, I'm not going to tell anyone."

Her southern charm resurfaced. "Why, thank you, Pippa," she said.

"Don't thank me, Daniella. You aren't my candidate, but more to the point, I prefer to build careers, not destroy them."

She smiled at me. This time it seemed genuine. "I thought you would say something like that. I even think you mean it, which really takes the cake."

"Pardon?"

"So few people I meet are serious about the scruples they profess."

"I'll take that as a compliment."

Daniella sighed. "What's going to happen to Linda Preston?"

"I haven't decided yet."

Daniella worked hard to stifle a grin. "Who's fibbing now? You plan to fire the lady. I can see it in your face."

There wasn't much point in arguing. I had hoped to salvage Linda's candidacy, but now I knew that Daniella had also added fluff to her credentials. No way in good conscience could I continue to represent Linda Preston.

"Correct, Daniella," I said. "Linda Preston is history."

"But don't you see? To get rid of her, you may have to let the whole ball of yarn unravel. Think about it."

I thought about it.

Oh my! She was right.

How would I convince Linda to withdraw? My sole weapon was to threaten her with the truth, but the truth was a gun aimed at *everyone* who participated in Marsha Morgan's "system." If I pulled the trigger, David Friendly would get wind of the story, and that didn't bear thinking about. David was an even better reporter than Sophia Cooper, and look how she had pounced on my mention of Kathleen Isley. David would prod and poke and dig, and in the end he would create Ryde's scandal of the century. The four superstars, four successful women who had done me no harm, might fall like dominos, beginning with Kathleen Isley. Then the taint would spread to the people they helped, and, in time, down to Georgia. And yes, also to Pippa Hunnechurch.

By no means did I want to travel down that road.

"I was wrong," I said. "You don't have a tiger by the tail—it's a full-grown Tyrannosaurus Rex."

"You know, you can always forget that Linda lied."

I shot Daniella a sour look.

"Or," she went on, "you might make Linda's departure her own idea."

"I'd rather wring her silly neck in public, but I take your point. I will tread lightly, maneuver deviously, and encourage Linda to withdraw on her own." I added, "Assuming I can figure out a way to do it."

Daniella slumped in her chair. "I have every confidence you will, *Mizz* Hunnechurch. You are intelligent and wise and have the makings of a fine lawyer."

I remember thinking. *There's an idea. When Derek Wetherspoon fires me, I'll be free to find a new occupation.*

Chapter Twenty-one

I HEARD MY CELL PHONE RINGING in my attaché case during the cab ride to the airport, but I wasn't ready to speak to Linda Preston, not yet, not until I figured out the best way to give her a firm heave-ho. My detour to Daniella Holmes had ended all thoughts of visiting Linda at her office. I wanted to fly back to Ryde on the first plane leaving Atlanta.

I felt remarkably tranquil on the flight home. And why not? All the stressful uncertainty had left my life. Hunnechurch & Associates could not possibly survive the loss of Eurokit USA as a client. I believed with conviction that my last acts as an independent headhunter would be to:

1. Deal with Linda Preston.

2. Pay my rent and phone bill while I still had some money in the bank.

3. Find myself a safe, humdrum job, with health insurance, two weeks paid holiday each year, and a nice pension.

There's nothing wrong with working for someone else. Most Americans do it every day.

Nothing at all, except a lifetime of knowing that my own stupidity caused my little consultancy to fail.

I emigrated to America a year after the accident that killed Simon and Peggy. My plan (Chloe's plan, really) was to stay for no more than two years—an extended change of scenery designed to help me recover from the loss of the two people I loved most in the world. I would live cheaply, move from city to city, and change jobs when the mood encouraged me. In short, I set out for a "spate of wandering on a foreign strand," to use Sir Walter Scott's words.

"Living cheaply" was essential. Simon had recently begun a promising career as a chartered accountant, what Americans call a CPA. We spent his earnings freely and put little into our savings or his life insurance. Thus, I came to the United States with more optimism than money.

Who knew that Ryde, Maryland, would catch my fancy, or that my brief sojourn in the United States would become permanent? I certainly didn't when I answered the advertisement for a "junior in-house personnel recruiter" at CentreBank in Baltimore. The human resources manager I chatted with didn't seem concerned that I had not attended a four-year college in England. "Formal training is not as important as the right temperament and attitude," he had said. "I think you might have a knack for recruiting employees."

He was right.

I found more than a hundred top-notch employees during my five-and-a-half years at CentreBank. I often worked with outside recruiting firms, and inevitably perhaps, I began to think, *Hey! I can do what they do. I can run my own consultancy.*

Perhaps I was wrong.

Ah well, with no alternatives left, why bother moping? As Scarlett O'Hara put it after her own misadventures in Georgia, "Tomorrow is another day."

The closer we got to Baltimore, the more my outlook seemed to improve. The plane made a smooth landing on time; the shuttle bus to the parking lot stood waiting for me at the terminal door; the traffic moved freely on Maryland Route 2; and, my house seemed to glow in the late afternoon sunlight. With my mind idling, I didn't even notice the police cruiser lurking across the street.

I had scarcely greeted Winston when my phone rang.

"Good afternoon," I said. At the time, I really meant it.

"Hunnechurch!" Detective Stephen Reilly barked back. "Don't you check your answering machine? I've been trying to reach you all day."

"About what?"

"I'll explain when I see you. My office. Ten minutes."

"You want me there? At the police station?"

"Didn't I just say that? Look outside your front window. You'll see one of my men sitting in a black-and-white. He notified me when you got home. He'll follow you downtown."

"Can't this wait until tomorrow? I've had a trying afternoon."

"Me too!" The line went dead with a loud clack as Reilly hung up on me.

My bad mood surged back.

━━━━━━━━━━

The copper from the cruiser, a hefty chap in a rumpled uniform, escorted me into the Ryde Police Headquarters.

"Do you know what this is about?" I asked as we clomped down the asphalt-tiled corridor.

"Sure, but you'll enjoy it more hearing the details from Reilly. I've never seen him so bent out of shape." He gave me a gentle shove into Reilly's office. "Have fun."

The room was as large as my office, but it held about a ton more paper, which was stuffed in cardboard boxes, piled on the window sills, and balanced on one of his two visitor's chairs. The only uncluttered surface in view was Reilly's desk. He sat behind it, reading an official-looking document. *Oh, oh!* Even upside-down, I could make out my name typed near the top.

"Hello," I said.

"Sit down." He didn't even look at me.

I perched on the edge of the clean chair. "I regret that you had difficulty finding me today, Detective Reilly, but I took a business trip to

Atlanta today and didn't think to call my answering machine." I added, "Your harsh behavior strikes me as excessively theatrical."

Reilly seemed annoyed by my criticism. His eyes moved from the paper to my face and glared at me for several seconds.

"You don't like my theatrics, huh? Well, I don't like a material witness who withholds important information and repeatedly lies to the police."

Yikes! I had been found out. I felt my cheeks begin to burn.

"By the way, 'material witness' is my idea. Corporal Miller considers you a suspect. You illegally entered Marsha Morgan's office on Friday night. On the following Monday morning we found it trashed."

I half expected Reilly to whip out his handcuffs and read me my rights.

"No sir! Not at all!" I said forcefully. "You have no reason to accuse me of . . ."

Face it, luv. You've been caught with your fingers in the jam pot. No point telling another whopper.

I took a breath and began again. "Marsha's office was intact when I relocked the front door on Friday night. That's the unblemished truth."

Reilly grunted. He pulled open a desk drawer and brought out a yellow pad. He selected a pencil from one of several standing in a coffee mug. "Tell me everything you did on Friday night—from the beginning."

"'Everything' begins with a personnel file in Marsha's desk drawer. We were working together on a search assignment. The file contained our candidate's résumé. Marsha intended to give it to me on Monday morning, but then she fell off the *Chesapeake Belle*."

"Which you somehow took as an invitation to evade the security guard, enter the building surreptitiously, and break into Morgan's office?"

"Yes, yes, and no. I didn't break into Marsha's office. I used a key to unlock the front door."

"Which you pilfered from her purse. Technically, that counts as a break-in."

"Under normal circumstances, of course, I would never have borrowed her keys or entered her office, but the future of my firm was at stake. I desperately needed to find the paperwork, and—"

Reilly interrupted. "Do I look like I care about your business?"

"Sorry. Well, I retrieved the file from the bottom drawer of Marsha's desk. Then I copied the contents, replaced the file, exited the building, and—"

"Don't forget your brief encounter with the security guard, who got very annoyed when you ran past him."

Reilly turned over the document he had been reading when I walked in. My photograph grinned at me. A clipping from the *Ryde Reporter.* The lead illustration from an article that David Friendly had written a year earlier. "The guard remembered seeing your picture in the local paper."

"Ah, so that's how you found me out . . ."

Reilly leaned back in his chair. "OK, you visited Morgan's office to get a file from her desk. Tell me why we lifted your fingerprints from more than thirty locations, including most of the drawer handles in the suite?"

"I had to browse for the paperwork I wanted. I began with the file cabinets, then moved to Marsha's desk."

"While you were browsing far and wide, did you come across Kathleen Isley's name?"

"Kathleen Isley?" I did my best to look befuddled.

"Kathleen Isley," he continued. "deputy secretary for international trade. You had dinner with her a few hours before you broke into Morgan's office?"

"Oh, Kathleen."

"You are a lousy liar, Miss Hunnechurch."

I beamed at him. "How kind of you to say so. I really do prefer to tell the truth."

"Now's your chance."

"I did find a file folder labeled 'Kathleen Isley' in the bottom drawer of Marsha's desk."

"Did you happen to see what was inside?"

"Three or four sheets of lined yellow paper, from a pad like yours. Covered with Marsha's handwriting. I remember thinking they were interview notes."

"Nothing else?"

"No."

"Are you sure? Isley claims that Morgan had her résumé on file, plus some confidential biographical materials."

"Those items were not in the folder I found."

Reilly popped forward in his chair. "Let me ask you an unrelated question. You're a headhunter, so you might know the answer. Why would Isley make such a fuss about an old résumé? You saw her chew my tail this past Monday morning."

I nodded. "She did seem rather upset."

"The Honorable Madam Deputy Secretary called the chief, visited the mayor, and threatened to have the FBI search through the debris. There must be a reason why."

I knew the reason why. Kathleen feared that her catalog of "exaggerations" would be exposed, but explaining things might encourage Reilly to conduct a deeper investigation and trigger the very scandal that Daniella Holms and I wanted to avoid. My best course, I decided, was to pretend that he had asked a rhetorical question. I gave an agreeable shrug and said nothing.

"I take your silence to mean, 'I don't know,'" he said.

"How can I comment on Kathleen Isley's motivations? I met the woman a week ago. We exchanged a bit of small talk at dinner. That's all."

Reilly drummed a rhythmic tattoo on his pad with his pencil. "No more lies? No more evasions?"

"Certainly not!"

"Good. A nice unambiguous statement. It had better be true."

A uniformed officer appeared in the doorway. "We have an incident."

"Stay put," Reilly said, "and resist the urge to explore the private paperwork on my desk." He shut the door behind him, leaving me rankled by his impertinence. My truly rotten day had been crowned by a shabby jeer from a copper.

Not quite! Your day isn't over.

I remembered Linda Preston.

I had planned to call her when I arrived at Hunnechurch Manor, but Reilly's "invitation" had driven the thought from my mind. Now it was past seven o'clock. Linda was probably at home riffling through Maryland brochures and communing with her daughter.

Too bad, Linda. You put me in this pickle.

My cell phone was still in my attaché case, sitting in my front hall. I dragged Reilly's telephone to my side of his desk and charged the long-distance call to my credit card.

"Pippa! I tried to reach you this afternoon. I hear you're in Atlanta."

"Actually, I'm back in Ryde."

"You sound funny. Is something wrong?"

"I'm afraid that we face a serious predicament. One of your sham references overplayed her hand."

A pause, then, "You weren't supposed to know that my credentials were *Morgandized*. I guess Missy told you."

I coughed to hide my gulp of astonishment. The Morgan sisters had even coined a cute moniker for their "system." Talk about gall!

"Your *Morgandizing* has sprung a leak," I said.

"Who was it?" she asked.

"Kathleen Isley."

She cursed, then said, "I warned Marsha not to overstate our relationship on my résumé."

"Yes, well she did exactly that, and therein lies the nub of the matter." I launched into the medium-sized white lie I'd invented during the plane ride. "A local business reporter approached me last night, all agog. He wants to do a feature article about Eurokit's arrival in Ryde and their new chief counsel who is an old friend of Kathleen Isley."

"Oh boy! Who told the reporter about me?"

"Someone at Eurokit, I presume. In any case he has seen a copy of your résumé, and he is asking awkward questions."

"Such as?"

"Such as, when did Linda Preston and Kathleen Isley work together on the Russian republics?"

Silence.

I continued. "He seems to know a lot about Kathleen's activities at the Department of Commerce."

"That poses a problem. Kathleen and I didn't actually work together at Commerce."

No kidding! "How easy will that be for him to find out?"

"Easier than I can risk. This thing could blow up in my face."

Talk about understatement!

"Aren't you being melodramatic?" I said, almost enjoying myself.

"Not at all, Pippa. I'm a lawyer. I have my license to worry about. I can't risk getting disbarred."

Another silence. Then she said: "We may have to cut our losses."

I wanted to shout, *Hurrah*. Instead I said, "It has to be your decision, Linda. The last thing I want to create is a brouhaha that could harm your career. You have too much at stake and a daughter to think about."

"Let's say I decide to pull the plug . . ."

There you go. "Well, I suppose you could offer a reasonable excuse to Wetherspoon."

"For example?"

"Invoke your daughter's happiness. Tell him that Franny refuses to leave her friends in Atlanta and move to Ryde. Wetherspoon will understand that adolescent children can force a change in one's plans."

"I'll consider your suggestion," she said.

"Do."

"And Pippa, thanks for being so understanding."

I bit my tongue so I wouldn't scream with joy.

I was cradling the receiver when Reilly returned. I thought he might yell at me for using his telephone, but he sat down without saying a word. His face looked pale and pensive. He finally spoke to me:

"Go home. The interview is over."

"I'm free to go?"

"Yeah. I have more important work to do."

"What has happened?"

He stared at me for a while before he decided to answer. "Someone shot Missy Morgan. She's dead."

Chapter Twenty-two

I DOUBLE-PARKED MY RED SPORTS CAR, with the engine running, a half block from the police headquarters' "official vehicle" lot. I didn't know what kind of car Reilly would be driving, but I had a good view of the exit through the Miata's squat windshield. A few minutes later an unmarked blue sedan nosed into the street. The sky was still light enough for me to spot Reilly at the wheel. I shifted into gear and slipped into the flow of traffic behind him. With luck he wouldn't recognize me, though I didn't much care if he did.

The arrogant clod!

I had crumpled into a near faint when Reilly told me about Missy. He leapt around his desk, pushed me back in my chair, and offered to call the public health nurse.

"No need," I managed to croak. "I'm feeling better."

"You look awful."

I *felt* awful. A few days earlier I had proclaimed, "I hope I never see Missy again." Well, my wish had been granted. I took several deep breaths and said, "I've never before known a murder victim. Where did it happen?"

Had Reilly given me a grain of encouragement, I might have told him everything I knew about the Morgans. Instead, he spun away from me and said, "Beat it, Hunnechurch! Tune-in the TV news like everyone else."

I bolted from the room, royally mad at Ryde's finest.

━━━━━━

Downtown was crowded with carloads of singles going to Friday evening "happy hour" at the saloons along Ryde High Street. Music and laughter wafted on summer breezes, along with the smell of locally brewed beer. I followed Reilly as he skirted double-parked cars and outflanked jaywalkers. The address numbers on High Street climbed, and the traffic decreased. *I know where he's going—the old leather warehouse.*

Four police cruisers, their red and blue lights blinking, and a boxy ambulance, with its tiara of strobe lamps flashing, were in front of the restored brick building that contained Marsha Morgan's office suite. Reilly pulled up next to the ambulance. I parked the Miata around the corner and made my way back to the small crowd that had gathered to watch. Most of the crowd looked like business people from nearby offices who must have been working late on Friday night and had seen the fuss outside.

The sidewalk in front of the warehouse was cordoned off with yellow plastic tape strung between parking meters. I remembered the fear I had felt walking that same patch of pavement in the dark. Someone had erected a tentlike enclosure made of green canvas. Missy must be behind it. Had she recognized her killer? Had she smiled at a familiar face, one of Marsha's beloved blue-chip women, then been amazed when bullets tore through her body?

Stop speculating! You don't know anything for certain.

Sound advice. I had made more than my share of guesses during the past week.

Without reading their contents, I had surmised that the blue file folders recorded the lies that the superstars told. I had supposed that one of the bunch rifled Marsha's office, but where was my evidence?

Now I fancied that the same superstar shot Missy Morgan in cold blood on Ryde High Street—merely to protect her career.

Perhaps you are too willing to believe the worst about people?

The crowd around me murmured as two paramedics pushed a covered gurney into the ambulance. Missy in a body bag. No guessing. No surmises. A horrible fact.

I thought about the frenzied panic in Daniella Holms' eyes as she threw her iced tea at me. Fear can be a potent motive for murder. Where might I be now if she had been holding a gun rather than a tall glass?

The superstars would be equally concerned about their futures, and Missy had made an extravagant threat at the memorial get-together when she said, "I won't forget what you did to Marsha. I can get even, and I will." I hadn't understood Missy's meaning that afternoon, but the four superstars surely did.

"In revenge and in love, woman is more barbarous than man." That was the one fragment of Friedrich Nietzsche's writing I still remembered from *Introduction to Modern Philosophy,* an evening course I took at Anne Arundel Community College.

Missy had threatened revenge, but she had also feared revenge for Gloria Spitz. What had Missy said? "You must protect Gloria."

The memory came as a jolt. I looked around and spotted a pay phone booth at a gas station a half block away where two TV news vans were setting up their antennas. I jogged toward it, fumbling in my purse for quarters as I ran.

Directory assistance found Gloria's telephone number on the first try.

"I can't believe it!" she said. "We were just talking about you."

"*We?* Who's there with you?"

"A friend of yours. David Friendly." Her voice became somber. "Pippa, something awful happened."

"I know. Missy is dead."

"Isn't it terribl—"

I cut her off. "Yes, it's terrible. I'm coming to see you. Give me directions and tell David to stay put."

"You sound worried about me."

"I am."

"Well, this is going to sound funny, but we're terribly worried about *you*."

━━━━━━━━

Gloria lived in a gracious gingerbread Victorian on a tree-lined street of immense older houses that had been chopped into affordable flats for the twenty-something set. The scent of mowed lawns sweetened the air.

I climbed to the second floor. Gloria opened the door the instant I rang the bell. We simultaneously asked one another, "Are you OK?"

She answered first. "Of course I'm OK. It's headhunters who are dropping like flies this month, not secretaries."

"Where's David?"

"In my kitchen, getting something for you."

David called out, "*Mizz* Spitz doesn't have any iced tea, or anything tealike, for that matter, but she does own a world-class collection of weird coffees. How does hazelnut-amaretto-cherry-cappuccino sound?"

"Impossibly flavorful," I replied.

Gloria's living room smelled of vanilla—courtesy of a scented candle that burned brightly on a glass-topped coffee table. Four over-stuffed armchairs circled the flame like Conestoga wagons around a campfire. I sank into the fattest chair and curled up, my feet tucked out of sight. The comfy embrace of the upholstery reminded me that I had rolled out of bed at 5:00 A.M. I began to feel tired.

"What kind of music do you like?" Gloria asked.

"Anything but heavy metal."

"I was thinking more of some gentle classical music."

Gloria went off to fiddle with her stereo. I took the opportunity to check out her living room. I had expected to see a multitude of Christian paraphernalia, but the only spiritual objects in view were a rather large Bible on the bookshelf near my chair and a framed photo of Gloria teaching what looked like a Sunday school class of a dozen five- and six-year-old kids.

David arrived with a giant ceramic mug. "You look awful," he said.

"So everyone insists."

He cocked his head. "I know that tune, but I forget the name."

"*Music for the Royal Fireworks,* by Handel."

"Just the thing to soothe an agitated Englishwoman," Gloria said.

Gloria and David made parental smiles as I sipped my coffee. The "weird" brew tasted delicious. I'd been thirstier than I realized.

"Why are you worried about me?" I asked David.

"Let me think . . ." he said as he struck a sarcastic pose that included staring at his fingernails. "Could it be that I don't want to write any more obituaries for executive recruiters?"

"Very droll."

"No. Very scary. Someone has declared open season on headhunters."

"It might be an appalling coincidence, you know—a freak accident followed by a random mugging on a dark street corner."

"Both deaths happening within a few days of each other? With a wrecked office in between? No way they're not related!"

"Well," I said without thinking, "Stephen Reilly is on the job. Beneath his unpleasant exterior, he seems to be a competent copper."

David lurched to attention. "Who told you that Reilly caught the case?"

Oops! One must speak carefully around an ex-police reporter.

"The call came in when I was at the police station," I said, hoping that part of the truth would cover my blunder.

"With Reilly?"

"Yes."

"He invited you to the Ryde Police Headquarters for an interview?"

"Sort of."

"Why?"

"He wanted to tie up a few loose ends."

"Like what?"

I took another sip of coffee while I thought up a logical reply. Telling David that I'd been called on the carpet for an impromptu visit to Marsha's office would bring a torrent of other questions I didn't want to answer. I settled for another fragment of truth.

"It seems that Marsha had Kathleen Isley's résumé in her office," I said, "plus some other biographical information. Kathleen considers her paperwork confidential. She made a bit of a fuss the other day."

"A bit of a fuss?" Gloria said with a snort. "She sliced and diced Reilly like cold cuts for a picnic. He didn't know what hit him."

"Indeed!" I said, eager to move the conversation away from me. "Reilly asked me if I knew why she reacted so strongly?"

"Do you?" David said.

"I'll tell you what I told Reilly. 'How can I comment on Kathleen Isley's motivations? I met the woman a week ago. We exchanged nothing but small talk.'"

Once again I had deceived my loyal chum, not with a bold-faced lie, but with a neatly done piece of equivocation that had the desired effect—David lost interest in interrogating me.

"It's Reilly's problem, not mine," he said with a shake of his head. "But none of what's happened makes much sense. One drowning. One shooting. A trashed office. An irate civil servant. And last but not least, a British headhunter who helps the police clean up loose ends but won't tell her friends how or why."

Gloria broke the awkward silence that followed. "I've been thinking about Missy," she said. "I wonder if I was the last person to see her alive?"

"Not unless you shot her," I said.

"The last person *before* the shooter." Gloria stuck her tongue out at me. "I spent the day with Missy, helping her inventory the furniture and equipment for shipment to Georgia. I left at five o'clock. I didn't think Missy would last much longer. We were both dead on our feet." She looked horrified when she realized what she had said. "Darn!" she murmured. "I didn't mean it like that."

"Be glad you left when you did," David said.

"Maybe she would still be alive if I had hung around?"

"Or maybe you would also be dead," he said.

"I don't think so." Gloria patted her waist. "I've been carrying this ever since the office was trashed, in case the perpetrator came back."

"*Carrying?*" David said. "As in a *gun?*"

"You guys aren't observant." Gloria lifted the bottom of her sweater, revealing a compact holster clipped to her belt. She tugged a small pistol from its sheath and displayed it in her open palm.

"A Walther PPK automatic," she said. "Seven 380 Auto cartridges. More than enough stopping power to get a bad guy's attention."

She drew back the slide. The pistol made a *snick-snack* sound that sent the hairs on my neck standing. David sucked in a mouthful of air.

"Do you have a permit for that shooting iron?" he asked.

"Of course I do," she answered. "I sometimes moonlight as a bodyguard."

Gloria removed the Walther's magazine and worked the slide again to unload the cartridge she had chambered. "This little fella will be my constant companion until further notice."

"Unbelievable," David murmured.

Gloria pulled the trigger. The empty pistol made an ominous click. "I qualified as an expert pistol shot in the National Guard, something else Missy didn't want to put in my résumé."

"Onward Christian soldier!" I said.

Gloria peered at me for several seconds, then said. "I've been called a Christian soldier many times before, both by fans and critics."

I raised my mug in a toast. "Consider me an affectionate fan."

"In that case, let me ask you a sociable question. How are *you* fixed for self-defense?"

"I am snug and secure in Hunnechurch Manor. An Englishman's home is his castle."

"Yeah, but a castle is only as strong as its armory," Gloria said. "I stow a twelve-gauge shotgun in my bedroom. How about you?"

"I suppose I could cosh an assailant with the heavy-duty British umbrella I keep in the hallway. And of course, there's Winston, my watchbird. Get him mad, and you are in for a nasty nip."

Neither Gloria nor David smiled.

"The perpetrator probably still has the gun he used to shoot Missy," Gloria said. "You can't stop bullets with clever banter."

"I agree with little Miss Annie Oakley," David said. "You are frighteningly defenseless."

"Bunk here for a while," Gloria said. "It'll be a hoot. We'll send out for pizza, stay up late, tell corny jokes, like a mini-vacation."

"I appreciate your concern," I said, "but there is simply no need—"

"What are you doing?" David interrupted with an intensity that made me blink. "What kind of game are you playing?"

"Game? I hardly think—"

"Precisely! You're hardly thinking. In fact, you talk like your brain stopped working. Either you've become a fool, or you're putting on an act for our benefit." David stared at me. He began to drum his fingers on the arm of his chair. "Let's review the bidding. You rush over here concerned about Gloria, but you pooh-pooh our concerns about you."

"True, but—"

"Shut up! I'm on a roll." His voice had the punch of a whip. "You spend some quality time with Ryde's leading detective, no doubt at his invitation, and you give us a nonsense explanation. Loose ends, baloney! You know more than you are telling us. That I can accept. Maybe you have a good reason for not sharing your information with me. We'll sort that out later—if you stay alive. But don't pretend you aren't involved in what's happened, and don't say you aren't in danger. We both know that two women have been murdered since last Friday night."

"Two?"

"Are we sure that Marsha's death was an accident? I doubt it's all that difficult to send a diabetic into a coma."

"We saw her fall off the boat. It was an accident."

"The murderer got lucky. I'll bet the plan was to wait until Marsha was alone on deck, then give her a well-timed shove over the rail."

"More guesses," I said, although I knew that David was right. I could feel it in my bones. Worse, I even knew the motive: *me*. The talk of my "partnership" with Marsha during dinner on the *Chesapeake Belle* had frightened one of the superstars. Bringing an outsider into the scheme increased the risk of exposure. So the killer had acted swiftly to terminate my relationship with Marsha Morgan.

"Stop arguing with us," David said. "Spend a few days with Gloria. You can take care of each other while Reilly chases the bad guy."

"Well, if you put it that way . . ."

"Good deal!" Gloria said.

"I'll call the pizzeria," David chimed in.

"I will need fresh clothing," I said.

"We'll stop by your house tomorrow afternoon." Gloria studied me keenly. "The business suit you have on will do for tomorrow morning."

"The morning? I don't understand."

Gloria scowled at me. "Don't tell me that you forgot about Marsha's funeral."

Chapter Twenty-three

I KIPPED IN GLORIA'S GUESTROOM on an old brass bed next to a wall full of military memorabilia: certificates attesting to her prowess in rocketry, ordinance assembly, and hand-to-hand combat; surprisingly handsome illustrations of antitank missiles; a framed collection of colorful patches from her uniforms; and in the center, a large photograph of Gloria decked out in battle dress and face camouflage.

"Didn't I tell you you're in good hands?" she had said when she made sure I was tucked in.

"I am in awe. Truly."

"Tomorrow after the funeral, we'll lay in a supply of food, video-tapes, magazines, and anything else we need for a siege."

"I vote for a teapot and a packet of Darjeeling tea."

"Fine with me. I'll get some more ammo."

"And when we fetch fresh clothing from my house, I need to make sure that my parakeet has enough seed and water for a few days."

"Affirmative. We'll infiltrate your residence after we shop."

"What happens on Monday when I have to go to my office?"

"I'll tag along as your point man."

"Is that like a bodyguard?"

"Sort of."

My own bodyguard! Whatever would Chloe think?

"I appreciate all you are doing, Gloria," I said.

"Then how come you sound so uptight?"

"Well, the police may take their time. I can't live here forever."

"Why not? It beats dying somewhere else."

Indeed it did.

"Now get some sleep," she said. "Defensive logistics can be tough work."

I threw her a half-baked salute. "Yes, ma'am."

She paused at the door. "And you might consider putting yourself in God's care."

"I put my faith in you."

She gave me a wry smile. "I'll pray for Pippa Hunnechurch even if you won't."

Sleep remained elusive that night. I tossed and turned into the wee hours and thought about the tough question David had asked. *What was my game?*

Why was I so reluctant to reveal the Morgan sisters' scheme to Detective Reilly? Was it moral (never mind legal) to hold one's tongue when a policeman might benefit from a quick whisper in his ear? More to the point, why stay silent when I might be the shooter's next target? One didn't need much genius to realize that the killer might consider Marsha Morgan's "partner" as great a threat as her sister.

I understood my obligations, and I appreciated the risk. Nonetheless, I seemed ready to tell little white lies by the dozens to keep the Morgans' scheme a secret.

One reason, I had to confess, was the annoyance I felt. Reilly had treated me shabbily. Why should I offer him any help? He could bloody well solve these crimes all by himself.

Another consideration was that I wanted to avoid embarrassment. I hoped that my career as a headhunter would end on a high note, not with the public revelation that I'd been bamboozled and played for the fool.

Most important of all, I had made a covenant with Daniella Holms when I told her, "I'm not going to tell anyone. I prefer to create careers, not destroy them."

The more I thought about my promise, the more I realized that it had meaning far beyond the borders of Georgia. A scandal here in Maryland would destroy the three superstars who had not committed murder and might taint the careers of women I hadn't yet met. Legend says that we Brits have a strong sense of fair play. No matter what happened, I decided that night that I would never ruin the lives of the women caught up in the Morgan sisters' scheme.

I fell asleep thinking, *Pippa Hunnechurch always keeps the promises she makes.*

I awoke the following morning feeling forlorn. The thought of going to a funeral weighed heavy on my heart. I kept recalling Simon and Peggy's interment. The memory of their caskets sitting side by side at the cemetery brought tears to my eyes. I blinked them back and crawled out of bed, wondering how I would get through the day.

I found a pink terry bathrobe on a hook behind the bedroom door. I slipped it around my shoulders and padded into the kitchen where Gloria stood at the counter attacking a fresh loaf of bread with a long knife. She looked up. "Good morning! Did you sleep well?"

I shrugged. "Pretty well. I had a lot on my mind last night."

"Me too. I kept thinking about Marsha and about today."

"I trust you know where the funeral will be. Missy never told me the arrangements she made."

Gloria popped two slices of bread into her toaster. "I took care of the arrangements."

"I will say again what I said last night. I am in awe." I really was. How many secretaries or assistants would take over such an unpleasant chore?

For a moment she seemed bewildered by my praise. Then she rolled her eyes. "I keep forgetting that you don't have a church. One phone call to my pastor, and I had all the help I needed."

"Did Marsha belong to your church?"

"No, but what difference does that make?"

"None, really." I added, "Your church seems a lot like a family."

Gloria lobbed a chunk of crust at me. "Wow! Why didn't I think of that? You headhunters are sharp!"

"Spare me the sassy banter until after I've had my first cup of tea."

"Tea? In my house?"

"*Please* tell me you are joking."

"I'm kidding. Look to your left."

I did—and spotted a chubby teapot wrapped in a thick dishtowel, its spout steaming merrily.

"I zipped out while you were asleep for some Darjeeling," she said.

"Bless you!" I lunged for an empty mug.

I had eaten two pieces of toast and drunk my second mug of tea when Gloria said, "We do have a decision to make this morning. *We*, as in you and I."

"About?"

"Marsha's body will be cremated, which is apparently a Morgan tradition. One of us has to take responsibility for her ashes."

"Oh dear."

"Well, now that Missy is gone, it's up to you and me."

"I thought that ashes were . . . scattered."

"Lots of people keep them in their homes, in urns."

"No thank you. I barely knew Marsha Morgan. I don't want her remains sitting on a shelf in my bookcase."

"Of course, but now we also have to worry about Missy. She'll probably be cremated too. You can have two matching urns on your shelf."

We both shouted, "Bookends!" at the same instant and started giggling. Our giggles grew into chortles, and our chortles became belly laughs. We laughed for only a minute, but it seemed like an hour.

"Oh my!" I said as I caught my breath. "That was amazing."

"Now I know what they mean by a good laugh. I feel better."

"Me too, although I hope that Marsha doesn't mind us hooting on the morning of her funeral."

"No way! She had a wonderful sense of humor."

I pushed aside my breakfast and gave Gloria a big hug.

———

We drove to the Nyquist Funeral Chapel and Crematorium in Gloria's Dodge pickup truck, a full-size, four-wheel-drive model equipped with heavy-duty suspension and off-road tires. I felt a mile high in the white behemoth, and oddly in danger, as we barreled past the expensive homes on Founders Lane. I heard Gloria snicker as I tugged my seat belt extra tight.

I hung on tight as she made a quick left turn on Waterman's Way and an even faster right into a winding driveway fringed with large oaks. A moment later we were parked in front of the chapel, a white clapboard building that might have been a New England meetinghouse.

Several of Marsha's neighbors (whom I recognized from the ill-fated memorial get-together) were waiting near the front door. They followed Gloria and me into the sanctuary. We took seats up front. Marsha's simple casket lay on a rolling table a few feet away, adorned by a large wreath of white roses. The polished wood gleamed in the beam from an overhead spotlight.

"The wreath is exquisite," I said.

"Marsha loved white roses."

When I saw a tear course down Gloria's cheek, I also began to cry. Gloria, seemingly prepared for every eventuality, reached into her purse and brought out a fresh handkerchief for each of us.

I heard chairs scrape at the back of the sanctuary. Marsha's four superstars—Harriet Beardsley, Susan McKenzie, Roxanne Landesberg, and Kathleen Isley—entered as a group. They wore nearly identical black dresses. I acknowledged their presence with a nod, but only Harriet bothered to nod back at me.

Gloria whispered in my ear, "They look like a quartet of nuns."

"Shhh! You'll start me laughing again."

More people arrived, and an organ began to play. The music was somber, mournful, beautiful. Gloria patted my hand. "Here we go."

But my mind was on the blue-chip superstars. I couldn't help murmuring, "One of that lot shot Missy last night."

"What did you say?" Gloria asked.

"I'm merely mumbling to myself," I answered quickly.

A tall, slender man wearing a purple pulpit robe took his place at the podium behind Marsha's coffin. "Good morning," he said. "Let us begin with a few minutes of silent prayer and reflection."

I was about to bow my head when David Friendly slid into the seat next to me. "Why do reporters always arrive at the last minute?" I whispered.

"Beats me," he whispered back. "Now I'll ask you a dumb question. Why are the superstars so closedmouthed? None of them are willing to say anything quotable about the Morgan sisters."

"You spoke to the superstars?"

"You bet! Weird Lenny wants an in-depth article about Marsha and Missy in the next issue. I called a dozen people this morning. Everyone cooperated, except the fabulous four."

Of course they stonewalled David! I could imagine their fear when he called to ask about their relationship with the Morgan sisters and their relief when they realized he knew nothing about Morgandized résumés. One of the four must have been especially relieved.

"Gosh," I whispered, not being able to think of anything else to say.

"Like I said, it was a dumb question. I know the answer. The superstars think they are too important to respond to a humble reporter from the *Ryde Reporter.*" David's expression abruptly switched from annoyed to amused. "Hey, I see a cop I know in the back of the sanctuary."

"What cop?" I said louder than I meant to.

"Shhh!" Gloria poked my ribs with her elbow. I turned my head.

"David says there's a copper in the sanctuary."

"He's right. The guy in the dark blue suit sitting in the last pew. We can talk about him later. You're supposed to be reflecting."

In truth, I didn't want to be reflective that morning. I feared the consequences. If I wondered about death, a flood of memories of Simon and Peggy might overwhelm me. If I thought about life, well, that would trigger a new round of worrying about the killer and whether I had put myself at risk.

The pastor began the service, and I gradually realized that he looked familiar. Where had I seen him before? Of course! At Mariners' Hall at the Ryde Chamber of Commerce meeting. The minister with the velvet voice who gave the unusual invocation. I fished for his name and remembered, Reverend Ed Clarke.

The penny dropped. Gloria must be a member of Ryde Fellowship Church.

Clarke spoke words of Scripture that I recognized as part of a psalm. "God is our refuge and strength, an ever-present help in trouble. Therefore we will not fear, though the earth give way and the mountains fall into the heart of the sea."

Did anybody here today really believe that? I certainly didn't. If anyone felt out on a limb all by herself, it was me. I feared the inevitable loss of my consulting firm; I feared for my safety, I even feared another summons from Detective Reilly. A few pie-in-the-sky religious platitudes couldn't eliminate my problems.

The service moved forward. We sat, we stood, we sang, and we read responsively. Toward the end Reverend Clarke asked if anyone wanted to speak. John Tyler leapt to his feet. He strode to the podium and lauded his longtime friendship with Marsha, her role in the Ryde business community, and the many hours of volunteer work she had done for the chamber of commerce. Tyler talked eloquently. Clearly he had taken *de mortuis nil nisi bonum* to heart.

Roxanne Landesberg spoke next. She eulogized Marsha's determination to help women succeed in business. Her praise sounded distant and impersonal, the kind of tepid tribute delivered out of a sense of obligation. I decided that Roxanne must be representing the superstars. They probably drew straws to choose a speaker, and she lost.

To my astonishment Gloria stood up and gave the best speech of all. In a loud clear voice, she talked about Marsha's funny superstition of wearing "her lucky brand of pantyhose" when candidates went for first interviews, her charming habit of not wearing her wristwatch during interviews so that she never seemed to rush a candidate, and of the many young women she placed for free to kick start their careers. There was nothing sentimental in Gloria's words, but I'm sure that everyone in the chapel realized that Gloria loved Marsha and loved working at the Morgan Consultancy. That job was gone, and I had offered to find Gloria a new one. I would have to do something about that soon.

The service nearly over, I congratulated myself for making it through. Then the organ struck the opening chords for the final hymn. We rose to our feet.

> There is a blessed home,
> Beyond this land of woe.
> Where trials never come
> Nor tears of sorrow flow.

The words were at once familiar, haunting, and painful. They carried me across three thousand miles of ocean to a little churchyard near Chichester where I had stood staring at two holes in the ground while a cold, hard rain drummed on the umbrella someone held above my head as we sang the same hymn.

No!

I pushed past David, bolted up the aisle, and ran from the building. I plunged into the shade of a friendly looking oak tree and began to sob. When my tears stopped, I began to feel foolish. I was in no mood to be seen by the mourners leaving the chapel. I stayed behind my tree and listened to engines starting and cars moving along the driveway. At last the car noises ended, and a velvety voice called, "Are you there, Pippa?"

I walked around my tree. The Reverend Ed Clarke grinned at me. Gloria and David hovered a few feet behind him.

"I'm here," I said, mustering a cheerful smile.

"Funerals can be tricky."

"Yes, well, the truth is, that last hymn set off some unpleasant memories."

"Perhaps you'd like to chat about them?"

"Thank you, but no. It's all rather silly—something that happened long, long ago."

"You know best."

I nodded.

He took my hand. "If you change your mind, call me." He laid his business card on my palm and closed my fingers around it.

"Let's go to my place for lunch," David said when Reverend Clarke had returned to the chapel.

"Count me in," Gloria said.

"What about the remains?"

"You don't take the ashes with you, Pippa. They deliver them the next day."

"Oh, in that case, let's get away from this place as fast as your pickup truck will move."

We followed David's car over hill and vale until, past the few remaining farms in Ryde, we arrived at a quiet residential area that locals call the Dells. David's house, a trim Cape Cod, sat beside a small creek, screened from Forest Road by a dense patch of scrub oak and pine trees.

"I'll walk the perimeter before you get out of the truck," Gloria said.

"Pardon?"

"I see lots of places for a shooter to hide."

I gaped at her. "You can't be serious. It's the middle of the day."

"Yep, it is, and I am your point man. So stay put."

Gloria hopped out of the Dodge and trotted off to peruse the boundaries of David's yard.

He came over and tapped my window. "Is she doing what I think she's doing?"

"Behold! My bodyguard in action."

Gloria trotted back. "I didn't expect to find anything. The shooter has no way of linking you to David."

"Quite right!" I lied earnestly. Unfortunately, the superstars knew that David and I were friends. He sat next to me during dinner aboard the *Chesapeake Belle*. His secluded house would make a fine spot for an ambush, but I couldn't tell any of this to Gloria, not without breaking my promise to keep Marsha's scheme a secret.

"Let's see what Joyce has cooked up for us," David said. He led us to the brick-paved patio behind his house. "We thought you'd like to eat back here. There's a nice breeze off the creek today."

"A grand idea," I said as Joyce stepped out of the back door looking svelte as a brunette cover girl, bearing a tray laden with bottles, pitchers, and glasses.

David took the tray. Joyce and I exchanged pecks on the cheek.

"Iced tea or lemonade?" she asked me.

"Make it lemonade," David said before I could answer. "Pippa needs something stronger than iced tea. She had a rough morning, full of bad memories."

Joyce filled a tall glass full of lemonade. "Just what the nurse ordered."

I dropped into a wicker rocking chair and promptly changed the topic of conversation.

"It's too quiet around here," I said. "Where is little Peter?"

"With his grandparents," Joyce said, "for the whole blessed weekend."

David ducked through the back door and brought out another tray—this one piled high with cold fried chicken, potato salad, and cold green-bean casserole.

"Yum! My favorite." Gloria reached for a chicken leg and then surprised everyone by giving it to me. "Don't even think of picking at your food. You ate toast for breakfast. You had better put something substantial under that lemonade."

"Yes, mummy."

In fact, after Joyce said grace, I ate like a hog. And, I must admit, I began to feel less gloomy. I even remembered the casual promise that Gloria had made in the sanctuary.

"*Mizz* Spitz," I said, "you still owe me an explanation about the copper in the back pew."

Gloria sighed theatrically. "Am I to understand, *Mizz* Hunnechurch, that you don't know why the police often attend the funerals of people who die suspicious deaths?"

"You're right. I don't know why."

"To mingle with potential suspects."

"At a funeral?"

David took over. "Funerals are great places to spot murderers because most murder victims are killed by people they know."

"Ah ha!" I said. "The very people who are likely to attend the victims' funerals."

"Right! So the cops look for bizarre behavior."

Gloria added, "like someone racing out of the sanctuary."

"Oh dear."

"I'm joking."

"Perhaps, but my hasty exit must have surprised you."

Gloria grinned sheepishly. "Yeah, until David told me about England."

I had no reason to start crying, but I couldn't stop my tears.

"I'm being silly again," I said. "Forgive me."

Joyce crouched next to my chair and took my hands. "It's not silly to cry when you hurt, Pippa. I can only imagine what it must be like to lose a child and a husband at the same time. But try to remember that God cares deeply about you, and—"

I pulled my hands free. "No. I don't believe that. A caring God would not allow stupid accidents to happen. Either he doesn't care—or else he doesn't have the power to stop them."

"God doesn't cause pain, Pippa," Gloria said. "And he doesn't always prevent it, but—"

I didn't let her finish. "What a perfect excuse! Oops—sorry! Not my fault."

"*But,* as I started to say, God can always help you cope with the pain that comes your way."

"Then why didn't I feel that help seven years ago? There were days I felt I couldn't go on. The pain seemed endless."

Gloria smiled at me. "You have free will, Pippa. You chose to distance yourself from God. Perhaps it's time to come home?"

I shook my head and tried to invent a witty reply, but Gloria's gentle words kept getting in the way. *You have free will, Pippa.* I found myself wondering, had I given God a chance to comfort me seven years earlier?

Probably not.

"Are you OK, Pippa?" David asked. "You look . . . *strange.*"

"I am perfectly OK," I said, "and thoroughly tired of talking about me."

"Great! Let's play badminton."

Chapter Tewnty-four

ON MONDAY MORNING we drove to my office in the Calvert Building in Gloria's Dodge pickup truck.

"Your little red Miata is much too recognizable," Gloria had said as we ate breakfast, "and too easy to force off the road. We'll stash it behind my house and use my big four-by-four instead. From now on we pay for valet parking. No more walking through lonely garages. And we'll arrive at your building at nine o'clock. We want plenty of people near us in the lobby and the elevator."

"All of these precautions seem rather involved. I may not be anyone's target."

"That's the thing about security; most of it is a waste of time. The problem is, we don't know which parts to eliminate, so we have to do everything right."

"I see your point," I said, and stopped arguing.

I unlocked the outer door to my office at five minutes past nine. Gloria lunged past me into the reception room, holding her pistol in a two-handed grip.

"Clear!" she called.

"Good heavens! What are you, a one-woman SWAT team?"

"Don't dawdle in the hallway!"

"Aye, aye sir!"

"Secure the door behind you!"

I did as instructed, then filled the kettle for my morning cuppa and turned on my computer. I gave the kettle the privacy it needed to boil quickly by reading my E-mail. Perhaps lightning had struck in the form of a new assignment. No joy. Three of my four messages were advertisements; the fourth was a message from Chloe:

> From: Chloe_and_Stuart
> Subject: I Am Coming to Maryland!
> Dear Pippa—
>
> Roll out the red carpets . . . polish the fine silver . . . de-louse your budgie . . . put in a fresh supply of those delightful Maryland crab cakes. I will arrive on Friday, a mere five days hence, via British Airways, at 2:46 P.M., ready and eager to do battle with the shopping malls of greater Ryde.
>
> Love and blessings,
> Chloe.

Blast! I had forgotten about Chloe's visit.

"Did you say 'blast'?" Gloria asked.

"No. I *shouted* it. My sister Chloe is coming to Ryde on Friday. On top of everything else, you and I will have to deal with a family visit."

Gloria surprised me by saying, "Don't sweat it. I like to see you surrounded by people."

"Chloe isn't *people*. She can be stubborn . . . stiff-necked . . . argumentative. . . ."

"A typical Hunnechurch, huh?"

I laughed out loud and then sent Chloe an I-can't-wait-to-see-you E-mail.

The morning passed without further incident. Gloria read the first half of a Christian novel she explained was about spiritual warfare. I paid a few bills, downed a pot of tea, made several futile marketing calls, and wondered when the axe would fall on Hunnechurch & Associates.

The executioner arrived promptly at 11:30.

We heard an impatient pounding on the outer door. Gloria opened it, her hand in easy reach of her holster. Derek Wetherspoon saw me and said, "Hunnechurch, I have come to wring your miserable neck."

"Good morning, Derek. Let me introduce my new assistant, Gloria Spitz."

Derek grunted at Gloria, then glared at me. "I suppose you know what has happened?"

"Oh, yes. Linda Preston doesn't want to move to Ryde."

"Correct. She offered an inane tale of a daughter who loves Atlanta. Poppycock! I'll wager that she used Eurokit to lever herself a higher salary at her bank."

"I doubt that's the case. You shouldn't blame Linda."

"I don't blame Linda. I blame you. In full. You sold me damaged goods. A competent headhunter would discern that Linda never intended to make a move. You don't seem to know the fundamental aspects of identifying a proper candidate."

"There are other lawyers out there," I countered feebly.

"So Nailor & McHale assures me. I have invited them to try again." Wetherspoon snorted. "They are a *real* recruiting firm—not a recycled secretary with delusions of grandeur. Oh, yes, this time I took the trouble to make inquiries about your background. I only wish I had known about your humble beginnings before I made the mistake of trusting you."

Give the rotter his due, he knew how to wound.

"Do you know what you remind me of, Pippa?"

"What do I remind you of, Derek?"

"A trifle. A huge, sticky English trifle. Sponge cake, custard, whipped cream, almonds, sherry. I'm sure you enjoyed many, back in Chichester."

I nodded and stared at the vein that throbbed in his temple.

"Do you want to know why you remind me of an English trifle?"

"Not especially."

"You remind me of a trifle because you are good-looking, enticing, even pleasingly sweet at first, but ultimately you turn out to be an insubstantial confection—all sugar and froth."

With that he stalked out of my office, leaving me feeling humiliated. I sagged into a chair.

"I'm proud of you," Gloria said. "I half expected you to kick that jerk where it hurts the most, or ask me to shoot him. Instead you demonstrated the Christian virtue of forgiveness."

"The man deserves to be upset. I let him down."

Gloria patted my shoulder. "This is where I brew more tea. I'm beginning to understand what makes Brits tick."

She refilled the teakettle; I thought about my future.

What happens now?

A good question, that! I tried to dredge up an answer, but my mind was numb. I gazed out the window at Ryde High Street until the cheerful teakettle whistle drove my gloom away.

"Feeling better?" Gloria asked hopefully.

"Much, and also a bit hungry."

"I figured you might be, so I called the delicatessen across the street."

We sat at the antique card table in the reception room and devoured corned beef sandwiches, cherry cheesecake, and mugs of strong tea. The telephone rang at about one o'clock.

Gloria answered. "Good afternoon, this is Hunnechurch & Associates. How may I help you."

Her eyes went wide. She put her hand over the mouthpiece and said, "It's a man with a gorgeous Southern accent. Says his name is James Huston. Are you in?"

I had forgotten that James intended to call but not how dishy he was. I scooted into my office and picked up the phone on my desk.

"Hello, James. How are you?"

"Happy. I'm in Washington today, as promised, and free to take you to dinner tonight."

"Tonight? Dinner? I don't think so."

"Really? Why on earth not? I hope you aren't mad at me."

Gloria appeared in the doorway, still holding the receiver, her hand covering the mouthpiece. "Don't say no," she stage-whispered. "You can use a night out."

"Go away!" I stage-whispered back. Gloria made a funny face at me.

"I'm afraid I would be rather poor company, James," I said. "A wealth of unpleasant news is weighing me down."

"Do you mean Missy Morgan? I read about her this morning. Terrible."

"There's Missy—there's Marsha—there's the irate client who gave Hunnechurch & Associates the old heave-ho this morning because Linda Preston won't be his next chief counsel."

"Linda turned down the job?"

"Yes. For personal reasons."

"My, my—it's no wonder you sound dispirited."

"Indeed. I'm sure you will understand why dinner is out of the question."

"To the contrary, Miss Hunnechurch. I understand that a pleasant dinner with a friend can be an excellent way to cope with a passel of bad news. My mission this evening will be to cheer you up."

"Thank you, James, but—"

"I won't take no for an answer, Pippa. The truth is, I already made a reservation. A place called Stanley's. In Ryde. Do you know it?"

"Stanley's? No."

"My friends in Washington tell me it's worth a trip, but if you have another suggestion . . ."

Gloria reappeared in the doorway holding a yellow pad upon which she'd scribbled: "STANLEY'S = GREAT!" "Go!" she mouthed.

Oh, why not!

"You win, James," I said, willing myself not to laugh out loud at Gloria who had begun to celebrate. "Stanley's it is."

"Can you meet me there at seven o'clock?"

"Let me check."

I shielded the receiver with my hand and said to Gloria, "Two demands. One, I don't want you hovering over me at dinner. Two, I don't want James to take me back to your house after dinner."

"No problem. I'll drop you off at Stanley's, then take up position outside—with maybe an occasional sortie inside. I'll see you; you won't see me. Mr. Huston can drive you to Hunnechurch Manor after dinner. I'll zip ahead and be waiting inside. We'll go back to my place after your date."

"It's not a date," I insisted.

"Whatever," Gloria said as she ducked back into my reception room.

I sat back in my chair and wondered how I should spend the nearly six hours before I met James Huston. I had no recruiting work to do, and I knew that trying any more last-gasp marketing would merely annoy the people I telephoned. I certainly didn't feel like playing hooky or cruising the Magothy River. In the end I checked my handwritten *Things to Do* list and found two obligations to fulfill.

Tackle the unpleasant chore first.

I'm sure that I sighed ten or twelve times as I drafted a two-sentence letter to Calvert Management Company:

> Gentlemen. Because of change in the direction of my recruiting business, I do not plan to renew the lease for my office suite. Many thanks for the fine service your organization has provided Hunnechurch & Associates.

I decided to fax my letter to Calvert Management. It would save the price of a stamp and also consume another sixty seconds of my increasingly interminable afternoon.

"I would have done that for you," Gloria said when she saw me at the fax machine in the reception room.

"Indeed, but I have another chore for you to perform. Knock out a one-page résumé that summarizes your inimitable capabilities."

"My résumé? Now?"

"As quickly as you can. We'll need it when we visit Bill Hastings."

I had often worked with the William Hastings Administrative Skills Agency during my human resources days at CentreBank. Bill was a headhunter of sorts. He had built a successful consulting business after retiring from the U.S. Navy by specializing in one narrow area. Bill recruited first-rate administrative staffers. His two most popular job categories were executive secretaries and office managers. We liked (and more importantly) trusted each other. I figured that Bill owed me a favor or two from the old days. What better way to balance the books than by asking him to find a permanent job for Gloria?

The opulence of Bill's digs surprises most visitors. His corner suite on the top floor of Ryde's tallest building has a fabulous view of Ryde Old Port and the river beyond.

Gloria said, "Wow!" as Bill welcomed us into his office.

"Well now," he said, "this is a treat. How long has it been, Pippa, since you were my client? At least a year."

"Nearly two. I left CentreBank twenty months ago."

"To start your own business. So, how's business?"

"Exciting." I might soon become one of Bill's administrative candidates, but he didn't need to know that yet.

Bill shed the well-tailored sports jacket that made him look taller and less round than he really was and settled behind his impressive desk.

"Well now," he said again as he scanned Gloria's résumé. "As I understand it, Miss Spitz, you presently work for Pippa."

"Yes."

I felt a need to amplify Gloria's answer. "Gloria is temporarily in my employ, Bill. She is my point person on a rather complex issue that emerged from a current search."

He smiled at me. "I heard that you partnered with Marsha Morgan. You're beginning to talk like her."

"Marsha and I were not partners; we were associates." I suddenly realized how silly my denials sounded. I took a breath. "The point is, Gloria is available to consider a more permanent opportunity."

Gloria added, "If I can find one with the same challenges that

Hunnechurch & Associates offers me. I enjoy working on the front line, so to speak."

"Sounds reasonable to me," Bill said in a tone that told me he didn't think it reasonable at all. "Although your résumé suggests that you might benefit from a few more years in rear-guard positions to build your skills and experience."

Oh dear! What had Gloria put, or not put, in her résumé? I had intended to read the document before we left my office, but my haste to leave got in the way.

"I'm surprised to hear you say that, Bill," I said. "Gloria has oodles of experience, most recently five years as Marsha's assistant where she evaluated candidate backgrounds and performed reference checks. She also helped Marsha develop candidate packages and performed a myriad of other recruiting activities. Gloria is a natural for a senior administrative post in a human resources department."

Bill had returned his attention to the résumé, so he didn't see the bewildered look on Gloria's face. I discreetly held my finger up to my lips.

"Hmmm." he said. "Yes. I see. Or rather, I don't see." He glanced at Gloria. "All of your credentials should be highlighted in your résumé. As St. Paul so eloquently instructed, don't hide your light under a bushel."

"I think you'll find it was Jesus who said that no man—"

I jumped in again. "The truth, Bill, is that I would hire Gloria myself if I could afford her."

"I take it that you will provide a reference for her."

"A glowing reference!" I meant every word. Although I had known Gloria only a few days, I respected her intelligence, her wit, and her spirit. I would miss her as a colleague, but I was resolved to keep her as a friend.

"Excellent. I have a few questions for Gloria," Bill said, a clear signal for me wait outside. I stood, winked at Gloria, and retired to his marble-tiled reception room.

Less than a minute later, Gloria marched out of the office, her head high.

"My goodness! That was a short interview."

She glowered at me. "It was long enough to straighten out the lies you told."

"Not quite lies," I said feebly.

"Lies! A bunch of hooey from the résumé that Missy prepared. I'm ashamed of you."

"I wanted to help you to find a good job, one that uses your talents and experience."

"I won't lie to get ahead. I thought you knew that."

"Why make such a fuss about a little white lie? Your résumé doesn't show how good you are. I simply exaggerated a bit, for a good cause. . . ." The words froze in my mouth. *Blimey!* I could almost hear the Morgan sisters give the same explanation for their little white lies.

"Oh my. What have I done?"

"I'd say you put your foot in your mouth—up to your ankle."

"Forgive me, Gloria."

"Of course!"

As we hugged, I thought, *How easy it is to start down the twisty road of deceit.* I wondered why I had not learned that simple lesson many years before.

Chapter Twenty-five

"A̲H̲ ᴀᴍ ꜱᴏ ɢʟᴀᴅ ᴛᴏ ꜱᴇᴇ ʏᴏᴜ ᴀɢᴀɪɴ, Pippa," James said with a charming drawl that caused two women in a nearby booth to turn their heads. "Moreover, it seems that I will be spending a good deal of time in Hunnechurch territory."

"Your seminar, I presume."

"My seminars," he said with an emphasis on the final s. "A series of them in Washington, Baltimore, and also this fair metropolis."

"Here? You're going to lecture in Ryde?"

"Yes, ma'am. I signed the contract this afternoon." He leaned across the table and put his hand atop mine. "You will attend, of course. As my honored guest."

I nodded, hoping that my foolish grin didn't reveal that his touch was sending sparks into the small of my back.

Snap out of it, Pippa. You are acting like a schoolgirl again.

The specialty at Stanley's was, no surprise, Maryland Crab Norfolk, a luscious creation of lump crabmeat in an impossibly rich butter and wine sauce. James felt it the duty of all first-time visitors to try it. Naturally I agreed.

The waiter arrived with our dinners. As we ate, James told me all about his consulting business and his favorite techniques for educating American business people about overseas markets. I tried to listen attentively, but my mind wandered. For the first time that day, I began to think about the superstar who shot Missy Morgan and (probably) murdered Marsha.

Here I sat in a public restaurant, an easy target, if she was so inclined, and I had made James Huston a target too. I wished that Gloria were sitting in the next booth. I wished that I had never heard of the Morgan Consultancy.

Oh, Pippa, you are in a fine mess.

James tapped my hand.

"A penny for your thoughts," he said. "I presume they don't include any of my Secrets of Selling Overseas."

"Oh, dear. I apologize for drifting, James, but I did warn you about the shaky state of my psyche."

"Yes, you did, and I apologize for boring you with a lot of talk about me. My goal, of course, was to keep your mind away from headhunting tonight, but will you indulge me a brief detour into the subject?"

"Carry on," I said.

"I know Linda Preston too well to believe that she would turn down a chief counsel job with a major corporation for—how did you put it— 'personal reasons.'"

"Oh."

"*Ergo,* you fired her and not long after we chatted in Atlanta."

"Well . . ."

"*Ergo,* I cost you an assignment. The least I can do is to provide a replacement." James took a business card from his breast pocket. "Here. This lady is an even better qualified international lawyer than Linda Preston. I jumped the gun a tad and told her to call your office."

I read the lines of small type in the glow from the candle on our table: Angela Jennings, Attorney at Law. A sole practitioner based in Washington, D.C.

"Her pals call her Angie. You can count me among her enthusiastic references." James spoke with the kind of warmth that made it clear he really thought highly of Miss Jennings.

I tucked the card in my purse. When I looked up, James smiled at me.

"I don't know about you," he said, "but I'm in the mood for one of those high-falutin desserts I see on the cart across the room."

We ordered French pastries and a pot of strong Assam tea.

"How are you feeling?" James asked as I devoured the last few crumbs on my plate.

"Much better, thank you. It's impossible to be glum after so much comfort food."

"Good. Then let me ask you a pair of questions I've been bursting with all evening. They are about the very pretty blonde woman who brought you to the restaurant in that impressive pickup truck. First, do you know she is carrying a gun? Second, why is she watching over you like a guardian angel?"

I told James enough of the truth to satisfy his curiosity yet not send him rushing from the restaurant: that the violent deaths of the Morgan sisters had made Gloria Spitz and David Friendly concerned about my safety. That Gloria had volunteered to be my bodyguard. That beneath her knockout looks lurked the gallant heart and combat skills of a female Rambo.

"She's good, and that's a fact," he said with a laugh. "The way she scanned the parking lot while you climbed out of the truck was impressive. My cousin works for the U.S. Secret Service—his eyes are always moving back and forth like Gloria's. 'Course I spotted her gun right away. It's impossible to hide a weapon on hips like hers."

"I hadn't realized that Southern gentlemen were so observant," I said with a touch more sarcasm in my voice than I had intended.

"Ha!" James slapped the table with his palm. "*Ah* am properly chastised, ma'am. Shall I correct the error of my ways by saying even nicer things about your hips?"

"Don't you dare."

Neither of us spoke much during the ride home in James' rented Ford sedan, but we both nattered like sappy teenagers when I unlocked my front door.

"Welcome to Hunnechurch Manor, kind sir." I punctuated my frivolous greeting with a delicate curtsey.

"An honor, ma'am," he drawled and bowed from the waist. "*Ah* presume that your protector is in residence."

"Upstairs—*I hope.*"

"In which case I shall be on my best behavior, a perfect gentlemen." He spoke louder. "Gloria can uncock her six-shooter."

Gloria's voice drifted down from the second floor. "It's a *seven-shooter.*"

We laughed, and then I said to James, "Make yourself comfy in the living room. I'll make us a pot of tea."

I bumped into Gloria in the hallway.

"James Huston is one stupendous guy," she whispered. "I'm jealous."

"And jealous you shall remain!" I whispered back. "He came all the way from Atlanta to visit me."

"Hey! I know that a young woman like me can't hope to compete with a mature, thoroughly grown-up female like yourself."

"Very funny."

"Anyway, can I trust you two alone for ten minutes? My truck is running on fumes. We'll never make it back to my place unless I gas up."

"See ya around!"

"I know you're happy to get rid of me. However, let's not forget the person who's bumping off headhunters. Magothy Street looks clear, but lock the door behind me and stay away from windows while I'm gone."

"Anything you say."

I dutifully turned the dead bolt behind Gloria, then went exploring in my kitchen for the pair of Wedgwood tea cups and saucers my mum had sent two Christmases ago. I found them roosting in the uppermost cabinet above my refrigerator. I had scarcely finished folding up my stepladder when James came up behind me and yanked me into the hallway.

"There's a prowler outside," he said. "Behind your house. Listen!"

I listened.

I heard soft scratching. It was an insistent, purposeful sound that seemed to come from the far end of my hallway.

"Maybe it's an animal," I said.

"That's metal against wood. Someone is trying to pry open your back door."

Someone with a gun.

She's come for me. Missy's killer has come for me.

"Where's your personal protector?" he said.

"At a gas station."

"Then I had better take a look."

I tried to stop him by grabbing his middle. "Don't go! Stay here. We'll call the police."

"Good idea! You call the police. I'll take a look."

"I won't let you go outside. What if the intruder has a gun?"

James wriggled free. "Not in this part of town. It's probably some local kid. Do you have anything I can use as a weapon?"

"No."

"Sure you do. All single women own *something* deadly."

I remembered. "There's a Louisville Slugger in my coat closet."

"A baseball bat. Perfect."

"Not against bullets."

James tiptoed to the closet and began to rummage. I crept to the hallway telephone extension and dialed 911. The dispatcher answered on the first ring.

"This is Pippa Hunnechurch, 735 Magothy Street. There's a prowler outside trying to get in my house."

A brief delay, then, "OK, Pippa. A car will be there in two minutes. Stay on the line please."

"Abso-bloody-lutely!"

She has a gun. She will use it.

Across the hallway, James whispered, "I found your bat." He smacked it against his palm, and I recalled the happy noises at a block-party softball game two summers ago. My neighbors cheered when I won the drawing and took home the game bat.

"Don't go," I begged. "The police are coming. They want us to stay on the line."

But James moved toward my back door.

"If you are going, so am I."

My legs felt like stone. I couldn't take another step down the hall-way. I could hear the dispatcher calling over the telephone: "Pippa, are you still there? Pippa, is everything all right?"

The scratching at the door seemed louder now.

James flung open the back door. New sounds floated on the air: James shouting; Winston screeching; a car stopping out front; a loud bang; the crash of broken crockery on a shelf above my head; me screaming; a rush of footsteps; a furious pounding on my front door; then James, blessedly alive, growling, "Unbelievable! A woman wearing a ski mask took a shot at me before she vaulted your fence."

━━━━━━━━

The bullet had whizzed past James' head, through the open door, down the hallway, and into my knickknack shelf—demolishing two Toby Jugs (William Shakespeare and Falstaff) and lodging in the wall. The two po-liceman who responded to my 911 call *tsk-tsked* at the damage, made sure my garden was shooter-free, and told us that detectives would come calling in the morning.

We had decided to spend the night at Hunnechurch Manor on the theory that my house was safer than driving around Ryde—me in my bedroom, Gloria on the nineteenth-century chaise lounge in my furniture-filled guest room, and James on an overstuffed sofa in the living room. James fell asleep almost immediately; I heard gentle snoring wafting up the stairs. I labored past 2:00 A.M., trying to con-vince Gloria that she shouldn't stay up all night on "guard duty." She refused to listen. Gloria finally sacked out when I awoke at 7:30 A.M. The coppers arrived an hour later.

"I can tell you right now," Detective Stephen Reilly said to James, "the lab won't be able to match this slug to a specific pistol."

He held up a plastic bag that held a misshapen blob of lead and copper. A perky young woman from the Maryland Crime Laboratory had recovered the spent projectile from my woodwork.

"Even so," James replied, "they should be able to estimate the caliber."

"True. It's a small bullet. My guess is that it weighs less than a hun-dred grains."

We were in my kitchen, gathered at my dinette table, me sipping tea, the boys talking guns over mugs of black coffee and slices of a frozen coffee cake I had found deep in my freezer.

"A small bullet," James said, "definitely not from a magnum cartridge. I heard the distinctive *pop* of a conventional round fired by a short-barreled revolver. If I had to guess, I'd say a snub-nose thirty-two."

Reilly nodded. "You're a man who knows his ballistics. A thirty-two is consistent with the bullet's shallow penetration into the wall. The round doesn't have much punch."

"It also makes sense. A thirty-two is a good belly gun for a burglar—compact, reliable, easy to carry."

"And, luckily for you, hard to aim with accuracy, except at close range."

James chuckled, but Reilly turned to me stone-faced, "As it happens, Missy Morgan was shot at a range of three or four feet. The medical examiner recovered three thirty-two caliber slugs from her body."

I asked the obvious question, "From a similar gun?"

"Oh, I'd say from the very same gun, Miss Hunnechurch. In fact, it's beginning to look like an unknown person has decided to rid Ryde of its pesky headhunters." He held up his hand. "Scratch that! Thanks to Mr. Huston, we know that the shooter is a woman. It's incredibly helpful to have a reliable eyewitness."

"Unfortunately, *ah* am not much of an eyewitness," James said. "I only caught a brief glimpse of her when she turned to shoot at me. She was wearing a black jumpsuit, with a ski mask covering her face. I didn't try to memorize her features. When I saw her taking aim, I ducked for cover."

I hadn't even done that much. I froze in the hallway at the first hint of danger. How had Mrs. Hunnechurch's daughter become such a coward? Why hadn't I rushed forward and tried to identify the shooter?

Reilly turned back to me, "Have any ideas about who that woman might be?"

"No." My answer came at once, almost instinctively. A direct attack on me didn't change the fundamental moral arithmetic. Dozens of relatively innocent women outweighed one horrendously guilty psychopath.

"No." Reilly seemed to roll the word around on his tongue. "Another nice unambiguous statement, the kind I like to hear. Trouble is, I think you are holding out on me."

I said nothing. Neither did James, bless his heart, although the urge to shout at me was written all over his face. *I agree with Reilly. You look like you are keeping secrets from the police.*

Reilly peered at me. I watched the sunlight spilling through the window and listened to traffic moving along Magothy Street.

"I can't make you stop being stupid," he said, "so I'll give you some advice. Vary your routine and keep out of sight until we catch the shooter, which may not happen until you start cooperating."

James walked Reilly to the door.

I smiled at James when he came back, but he didn't smile at me. In fact, he looked decidedly grim.

Brace yourself, luv. He's mad at you.

"What happens next?" he asked.

"I'll take Reilly's advice and lie low for a while."

"You'll be safer away from Ryde. Come to Atlanta. You can stay with my sister."

His offer caught me off guard. James wasn't angry after all. He wanted to rescue me.

"Thanks, but no. I refuse to drag you, or your family, any further into this morass," I said. "You might have been killed last night."

"We'll be safe in Atlanta. The shooter won't know where you've gone."

"Perhaps, but that would be running away. I was a coward last night. I don't like the feeling."

"Pippa, I won't ask what Reilly meant about your not cooperating, but I'm going to be mighty unhappy if you wind up dead."

I jumped out of my chair and hugged him. "That's the nicest thing a man has said to me in years."

"Well, if you won't come to Atlanta, I had better stay here."

"Oh, but you must return to Atlanta."

"Pippa—"

"James, don't fuss and don't argue. I'll be fine—with a little help from you."

"My help? You just told me to go back to Atlanta."

"Indeed! But lend me your rental car and a credit card. That's all the help I need."

His mouth opened in surprise.

"I have decided to lie low, keep out of sight, and wait for Reilly to catch the shooter."

"With my car and credit card?"

"I have been thinking about the challenge of keeping out of sight. It is widely known in Ryde that I own a red Mazda Miata. I won't drive it until the crisis is over, and I won't be able to use my own credit cards either—it has become so effortless to check databases and locate people."

"I see," he said slowly as the gears in his head meshed and turned. "My rental car and credit card will help you stay invisible."

"Precisely!"

"While you demonstrate your courage by not running too far away from Ryde."

"True, but I don't intend to do anything foolish. I will take all necessary precautions to ensure my safety. I won't even use my faithful old cell phone because it is easy to eavesdrop on the kind I own."

James stared into my eyes. "I hope you're telling me the truth."

"The absolute truth, *luv!*"

"In that case . . ." He reached into his pocket. "One set of car keys, one Visa card, and this."

"This" was a small gold cross he took from a hideaway in his wallet.

"It originally belonged to my grandmother," he said softly. "She gave it to my grandfather who carried it in Korea. My dad carried it in Vietnam, and I carried it in the Persian Gulf. We all came home." He smiled. "*Ah* am mighty glad I had it with me last night."

"I won't take your favorite good-luck charm," I said, without thinking.

James looked at me quizzically. "I know that some people put a cross into the same category as a rabbit's foot, but I'm kinda surprised that you are one of them."

"I'm sorry, James. . . ."

"No. I apologize. When I saw the fish symbol on the back of Gloria's truck, I guess I jumped to the wrong conclusions." He pressed the cross into my hand. "But I still want you to have this. If you seek what's behind the symbol, you'll find the substance that miracles are made of."

"I could certainly use a miracle."

"You saw one last night in your backyard. That woman was a few yards away when she shot at me. I'm sure she can't understand how, or why, she missed."

"But Reilly said—"

"That I was lucky, that belly guns are hard to aim. *Baloney!* I can hit a tin can at twenty yards with my snub-nose thirty-two. *Anyone* can hit a man at closer range. Something made the shooter point high. You may think it's luck, but I call it the hand of God."

I studied the little cross. About an inch-and-a-half high. Worn smooth with age. Surprisingly heavy in my palm. And remarkably reassuring.

"I'll keep it in my purse."

"Good. I feel better knowing it's with you."

A car pulled up outside. James stretched to get a glimpse of Magothy Street.

"More police officers?" I asked.

"I don't think so. A tall man with curly hair and a really nasty scowl on his face."

"Oh dear! David Friendly."

"Who is he?"

"A good friend, a nosy reporter, and a self-appointed big brother— all at the same time."

"Hmmm. He looks *determined.*"

"Incredibly so! Nothing stops David Friendly when he wants to give me a lecture."

I moved to my sink and filled the kettle with water. Doubtless I would need a fresh pot of tea to see me through the morning.

Chapter Twenty-six

JAMES BORROWED HIS CAR KEYS BACK and departed for Ryde Police Headquarters to provide a formal statement, giving David an unfettered opportunity to climb atop his soapbox. He ushered me into my living room, demanded that I sit down, and held forth:

"My friends in the police department told me what happened last night," he said. "The other night I thought you were in trouble. Now I know for sure that Pippa Hunnechurch is in deep doo-doo. If you hadn't invited that sharp-eared Southerner into your home—"

"His name is James Huston," I offered.

"Well, if James Huston hadn't been in your living room, you would be dead, and I would be digging around for your biographical trivia because I'd have another obituary to write for the *Ryde Reporter.*"

"I appreciate your concern."

"*Appreciate* this! Stephen Reilly announced to the world that the police are hunting for an armed female prowler who may also be responsible for the murder of Missy Morgan. I asked myself, *What's the link between Pippa Hunnechurch and the Morgan sisters?* The answer is simple. The shooter is a woman connected to your partnership with

Marsha Morgan. The name Linda Preston springs to mind. Am I right? Is she involved?"

"I don't have an answer."

"Yeah? Well, maybe Reilly will agree with me. I'm going to tell him what little I know, and everything I've guessed, *before* you get shot."

David hadn't connected Missy's death to Marsha's superstars, but his notions came ominously close to the truth. Alas, he even remembered Linda Preston's name. She was the loose thread on a knitted sweater. One tug and everything comes unraveled. All I could do was bluff.

"If you go to Reilly," I said, "he'll ask for the shooter's motive. What will you say? How will you fit the facts into a coherent story that makes sense? All you have to offer is the name of a woman who lives seven hundred miles away. Linda didn't shoot Missy Morgan."

"So what? Incomplete reporting is better than none. Maybe Reilly can fill in the missing pieces. My alternative is to do nothing, which would be totally irresponsible. I won't stand around and wait for you to get killed."

"Me neither. I'm going underground, per Detective Reilly's suggestion."

The kettle began to whistle. David followed me into the kitchen.

"Ah, then you're leaving Ryde."

"Within the hour. For points unknown to anyone but me. I won't even tell Gloria where I am going."

David settled in the dinette chair that Reilly had recently vacated. "My, my, a sensible decision," he said. "What brought that on?"

"I don't like my friends being shot at."

"That's certainly a noble sentiment. But I'd be even happier if you announced that you had begun to look after your own safety."

"I plan to take appropriate precautions—"

"That's not what I mean, Pippa. You are enmeshed in this—this—*whatever* it is, but you seem to be doing nothing to get yourself disentangled. You aren't cooperating with Reilly, and I don't understand why."

At that moment I was far from certain myself.

I fussed with my teapot and wished that David were a dentist or a florist or a computer programmer—*anything* but a devoted journalist. I craved to share my secret with my best friend, but the moment he understood the "why" of my actions, he would feel duty bound to tell the world about the Morgan sisters' scheme.

Someday I would explain everything to David, that is, if our friendship survived that long.

———————

A book I leave sitting on my coffee table, *The Visitors' Guide to Maryland Bed and Breakfasts*, pointed me to a perfect bolt hole, a small bed-and-breakfast in Ellicott City, a historic mill town on the Patapsco River, about thirty-five miles west of Ryde. The advert for the Flour Mill Inn invited guests to bring their pets. I booked a room for Winston and myself, preregistering as "Mrs. James Huston" of Atlanta, Georgia.

I trotted upstairs, found my large canvas tote bag in my bedroom closet, and packed a week's worth of business and casual clothing. I made a nest amidst my clothes for the fitted leather toiletry case that Chloe had given me two Christmases earlier, and then I remembered, *Chloe is coming to Ryde.*

Today was Tuesday. She would arrive on Friday.

Blimey! My head spun at the thought of coping with Chloe amidst the growing chaos of this impossible summer. Even worse, my sister would be in danger, along with me. Why, oh why, did I let Gloria talk me into the visit? More to the point, how could I get Chloe to revise her plans?

For one giddy moment I considered telling her the truth, but honesty would bring Chloe to Ryde on the next available flight from England. Her streak of British fortitude is even stronger than mine.

Like it or not, I needed to craft another little white lie, and that posed a tricky challenge. Although Chloe doesn't mind telling an occasional fib, she prides herself on being a living lie detector. One must invent a good tale, indeed, to put the wool over Chloe Hunnechurch-Parker.

I perched on the edge of my still unmade bed and pondered a few possibilities.

A feigned illness? *No.* Chloe lives to tend the bedridden.

An unexpected business trip? *Hardly.* She would spot the untruth instantly.

A plumbing catastrophe at Hunnechurch Manner? *Don't be silly.*

I was about to heave a colossal sigh when Gloria staggered into the bedroom.

"Why are you up?" I asked.

"I just remembered something. . . ." She rubbed her eyes. "Your sister is coming to the United States. We need to stop her before she becomes another target for the shooter."

"Great minds think alike."

"Huh?"

"Never mind."

Gloria yawned. "I need coffee."

We trooped downstairs to my kitchen.

"Forgive me," Gloria said as she sipped. "I underestimated the shooter's ruthlessness. She's willing to kill innocent bystanders."

"You are forgiven. However, I can't simply call Chloe and say *stay home!* I must invent a reason for her to change her mind."

"In other words, tell Chloe a 'little white lie.'"

"Yes. Do you have another suggestion?"

Gloria shook her head sadly. "No—although you know how I feel about falsehood."

"I'm beginning to feel the same way. But this particular falsehood will help keep her safe." I hesitated a moment, then added, "Take your coffee and scram. If I must tell a humongous half-truth to my sister, at least let me do it in private."

I telephoned Chloe, hoping that she wasn't at home. No such luck.

"Pippa! Stuart and I were talking about you this morning. He wishes he could visit too, but he can't get away from the church this week."

"Yes, well, that is why I am calling. This is quite embarrassing, Chloe, but would it be possible for you to postpone your trip for a few weeks?" I cringed and delivered the only falsehood that Chloe would believe. "You see . . . I . . . uh . . . have met someone."

"A chap! You have a new man in your life?"

"Indeed."

"Derek Wetherspoon by any chance?"

"No, not Derek. His name is James. He hails from Atlanta, Georgia."

"Oh happy days!" she squealed. "Pippa has her own Rhett Butler! I can't wait to meet him."

"And so you shall." Then I came to the heart of the lie. "The problem is, James will be in Maryland this weekend. He has asked me to—how shall I put it?"

"Go off with him to some idyllic spot."

"Precisely."

"Heavens! This has happened so quickly. I am—"

"Flabbergasted?"

"Certainly that, but also thrilled for you—and thankful that my prayers have been answered. Seven years is a long to time to be on one's own." She added, "I fully understand why you want me to delay my visit."

"Thank you, Chloe."

"Of course, I shall have to invent an appropriate excuse for Stuart. I can hardly tell him that my sister has planned a naughty weekend with a new gentleman."

Yikes! My little white lie would soon lead to another. As Walter Scott wrote, "Oh, what a tangled web we weave, when first we practice to deceive."

We chitchatted a while before I rang off. I was feeling guiltier with every word.

Gloria returned to the kitchen. "Did it work?"

"Yes! My tall tale worked magnificently."

"Don't rub it in." She refilled her mug with hot coffee. "I hate to hear anyone telling lies, but I can't bodyguard both of you."

"Ah. I'm glad you brought that up. I have decided to leave Ryde for a few days."

"How few days?"

"Until Reilly catches the shooter."

Gloria frowned. "Alone?"

"It seems the sensible thing to do."

I expected an argument from Gloria, but a wry smile broke across her face. "Sure! Why not give it a try? See if you can survive on your own. The worst that can happen is that you will wind up dead."

━━━━━━━━━━

The Flour Mill Inn was a nineteenth-century gingerbread house, three stories tall, on a quiet cul-de-sac off Frederick Street in old Ellicott City. We made a funny sight traipsing up the broad staircase: the innkeeper (a charming biddy in a denim skirt), me (with Winston's cage), Winston (chirping to beat the band), and James (carrying my large canvas tote).

My room was decorated with calico-print wallpaper and furnished with maple furniture that looked to be as venerable as the house. It faced south, giving me a partial view of Frederick Street and Ellicott City's many summer tourists.

"Hiding out will be jolly in such pleasant digs," I said to James after the innkeeper left us alone.

His sour glance signaled that I had said the wrong thing.

I corrected myself. "That was a poor choice of words. I meant tolerable, not jolly."

He grabbed my arm. "Promise me you that you will be prudent."

"As prudent as a zebra at a lion's watering hole."

"And that you will keep the cross in your purse."

"Without fail."

"Call me every day—no, twice a day."

"Ditto."

"And if you change your mind about coming to Atlanta—"

"I know, I know. Use the credit card to buy an airplane ticket."

A horn beeped in the street outside.

"My taxi to the airport has arrived," James said. "Enjoy the Ford."

I felt a pang of impending loneliness. "I'll miss you." I gave him a peck on his cheek.

He gave me a more substantial kiss on my lips. I put my arms around him and kissed him back.

I hadn't been a participant in such a sincere kiss for seven years. Happily, one does not forget how to join in.

"*Ah* didn't plan for that to happen," James drawled, a boyish grin on his face.

"Me neither."

"But, *ah* am awfully glad that it did."

"Me too."

The horn beeped again.

"I have to go," he said.

"But you will be back soon."

"Count on it."

"Indeed I shall."

As I watched his taxi drive away, I found myself musing, *A naughty weekend with that particular gentleman might be an excellent idea.*

━━━━━━━

I decided not to unpack my canvas tote bag on the theory that I hadn't really run away from Hunnechurch Manor. Ellicott City was a strategic retreat, a temporary retirement from the field of battle. I put Winston's cage on a chest of drawers that had its own mirror. "There, laddie, a familiar face to keep you company. I'm off to reconnoiter and communicate, as Gloria might say."

I found a pay phone hanging on the wall in a bookstore two blocks from the inn. I dialed my office, prepared to punch in the code that makes my answering machine regurgitate its stored messages. Imagine my surprise when a human voice answered my call.

"Hunnechurch & Associates," Gloria said brightly. "How may I help you?"

"Gloria? What are you doing in my office?"

"With you gallivanting all around Maryland, I don't have anywhere else to be, so I decided to play your secretary again. Where are you?"

"Nice try, Miss Spitz. I'm lying low somewhere southwest of Baltimore where no one will find me."

"I certainly hope so. You're my only living reference. I need you alive to help me find another job."

"Any telephone calls I should know about?"

"Detective Reilly is looking for you. He called about twenty minutes ago. He sounded more than a little annoyed."

"Being annoyed seems to be a permanent condition with Reilly. Pay it no mind."

"He said he wants to know where you are."

"Let him look for me. He is the one who suggested that I keep out of sight."

"You also had calls from a couple of reporters. One from the *Baltimore Sun,* another from a TV station."

"I would sooner sit down amidst a pack of ravenous lions."

"And a woman named Angela Jennings wants to talk to you. Her message reads, 'Please tell Pippa Hunnechurch that I want to be Eurokit's next chief counsel.'"

"Oh dear! I forgot all about Angela. She is a friend of James Huston. He gave me her card last night. If I recall, he spoke to her yesterday."

"Apparently, he told her that you were the most honest, most easy to work with headhunter he's ever known."

"Goodness!"

"Of course, that was *before* someone took a shot at him from your backyard."

I laughed loud enough to draw a cold glance from the sales clerk in the bookstore, an austere woman with long, stringy hair and thick-framed eyeglasses.

"Tell you what," I said. "Call Angela Jennings and ask her to fax us a current résumé."

"She did that on her own. I'm looking at it. The lady has terrific credentials. Now all we need is a client who wants a top-notch chief counsel."

"*Hmmm.* Now that I think about it, Derek Wetherspoon didn't actually order me *not* to find him another candidate."

"No. He was too mad at you to think coherently."

"Ha. Ha."

"What's the next step?"

"I want you to bring me Angela's résumé. We need a convenient location to meet later this afternoon. Someplace safe, say about twenty miles north of Ryde."

"I know the perfect spot."

━━━━━━

Gloria chose the Anne Arundel County Law Library inside the courthouse, a facility equipped with metal detectors on the front door. "No guns inside," she explained. "Guaranteed!"

We met in the lobby at three o'clock and found a battered table and a couple of metal chairs in the stacks, far away from the attorneys and paralegals doing research. We could talk without disturbing anyone.

Gloria dropped a manila envelope on the table. "Angela's résumé."

I reached for it, but she stopped my hand with hers.

"Not yet," she said. "First, we talk about what's going on. You can mislead the police, you can mislead David Friendly, but you *never, ever* mislead your point man." Gloria spoke without her usual bravado. In its place was a quiet determination that riveted my attention. "We know for sure that you're a target. Well, if you are in harm's way, then so am I. That's why I need to know everything you know, starting with, Why did Marsha and Missy Morgan die?"

She was right, of course. I had an obligation to tell her the truth. I inched my chair closer to the table.

"Once upon a time," I said, "a headhunter whose business was in serious trouble accidentally discovered that two headhunters had invented a surefire scheme for placing good women in great jobs. . . ."

I told Gloria about Hunnechurch & Associates' sagging client list and plummeting bank account, about my first meeting with Marsha Morgan, about the blue folders I had seen in Marsha's office, and about the facts I had learned from Sophia Cooper, James Huston, and Daniella Holms. I reviewed my strange meetings with Missy Morgan and my futile visit to Kathleen Isley. I explained the conclusions I had reached and my reasons for playing the dunce with Reilly. "My guess," I said finally, "is that one of the superstars has decided to close the books on the Morgan Consultancy—for keeps."

"By eliminating you and possibly me?"

"Precisely."

"But you don't know which superstar?"

"It could be any of the four. Like my mum often says, 'You pays your money and takes your choice.' Full stop. End of story."

Gloria smiled a gritty smile without humor. "No wonder we call Satan the *deceiver*."

"Pardon?"

"He tempted the superstars to tell *harmless lies*—the kind that are supposed to do no damage. I can imagine his arguments. *Why worry about a few little fibs? Everyone puts some modest exaggeration in their résumés. Besides, who will ever find out once you have the job?*" She sighed. "But there are no 'harmless lies.' The four of them are trapped like bugs on flypaper. Living in fear. Terrified that their modest exaggerations will destroy their careers."

"But only one superstar killed Missy."

Gloria nodded. "Which you have taken as a valid reason *not* to help Reilly load his howitzer."

"His *what?*"

"Ever hear of a friendly fire accident? That's when an artillery shell falls short and blows up the good guys instead of the bad guys. You're worried that Reilly will destroy three reasonably innocent women with friendly fire."

"Indeed! I refuse to be a part of it. I'll keep my head down until Reilly catches the killer—on his own."

"But what if Reilly can't nab the shooter without some help from you?"

"Aye, there's the rub. It's hard to know if I've made the right decision."

"Have you checked to see what the Bible says?"

"I don't own a Bible."

I watched an eyebrow arch. "No Bible? I'll buy you one today."

"You don't have to buy me a Bible."

"Oh, yes I do! I'm one of those stubborn people who believe that the Bible is life's instruction manual, and you know what people say: 'When all else fails, read the directions.'"

Chapter Twenty-seven

I HAD SHIFTED THE FORD to reverse to back out of my parking space in the courthouse garage when I saw the flash of headlights in my rearview mirror and recognized Gloria's pickup truck. She pulled into the vacant slot next to mine. I killed the engine and unlocked the doors.

Now what?

Gloria slid into the passenger seat, pushing a gym bag ahead of her. "I just remembered the extra gear I stow in my truck," she said. "I thought it might be good stuff to have with you when you're lying low."

I unzipped the bag. The first item I found was a personal phone.

"It's digital," Gloria explained, "impossible to eavesdrop on unless you have the capabilities of the National Security Agency."

"I'll borrow it with pleasure," I said. "I left my portable phone locked inside my Miata."

The next item was a small plastic pouch shaped like a miniature leg of lamb. It felt surprisingly heavy in my hand, and ominous, even hidden behind supple plastic.

"Is this what I think it is?" I asked.

"My backup Walther PPK automatic pistol. Loaded and ready to shoot."

"I have never held a gun, much less shot one."

"No big deal. I can teach you everything you need to know for short-range personal defense in thirty seconds. Load. Cock. Point in the general direction. Squeeze the trigger."

"And hope I don't shoot myself in the foot. I think not. Besides, I don't have a license to carry a gun." I eagerly returned the pouch to Gloria.

"OK, but you can't object to carrying a canister of pepper spray." Gloria delved into her gym bag and emerged with a palm-sized aerosol can. "This baby looks like a can of hair spray, but it's loaded with *cap-saicin*—pure essence of red pepper."

"Red pepper? As in the spice I sprinkle on pizza?"

"Yeah, but a thousand times stronger. One squirt will immobilize an assailant for several minutes. Capsaicin is most effective when sprayed on the face, but it feels like liquid fire wherever it hits."

I switched on the Ford's dome light and examined the little canister. It fit my hand perfectly and had an ingenious plastic doohickey on top to guide my thumb over the push-button nozzle.

"This contraption won't actually kill anyone, right?" I asked.

"No, but the person you squirt will wish she was dead for a good half hour."

"I like it. Pippa packs a potent punch of pepper power. *Perfecto!*"

"Check out what's in the bottom of the gym bag."

I reached inside and lifted out a heavy garment—a lumpy cardigan sweater that seemed to be made of gray nylon.

"My spare bulletproof vest," Gloria said. "A professional model—the kind cops wear. It weighs only three pounds, but the Kevlar reinforced armor plates will stop any slug up to a 357 Magnum."

"Reilly says the shooter has a thirty-two."

"A popgun. You'll be perfectly safe inside this vest. Try it on."

I was wearing a skirt and a summer blazer; I took off my jacket.

"And your blouse," Gloria said. "The vest goes over your bra and under everything else."

I surveyed the garage. No one around. I unbuttoned my blouse.

The fabric shell felt coarse and unyielding against my skin. As

Gloria helped me adjust the Velcro straps, I asked her what well-endowed female police officers did with their bosoms.

"I'll show you," she said and yanked the straps tight.

"Ouch!"

"What did you expect? Built-in cups?"

"No. I suppose a man invented the silly thing."

I tried to imagine what I looked like with a woman's head atop a bulky male-shaped torso. Chloe would wet her knickers laughing if she saw me.

"Your shirt and jacket may feel tight," Gloria said as I did up the last of my buttons.

"Indeed they do. This vest is also remarkably warm."

"Get used to it, Pippa. You may need to wear body armor for a long time."

I fought an ethical skirmish with myself on the drive back to the Flour Mill Inn. On the one hand I noted that Angela Jennings was waiting for my call, that she had an extraordinary résumé, and that (most significant) she wanted the Eurokit job. For all these reasons I should contact her at once.

On the other hand I remembered Gloria's sage remark, "Now all we need is a client." My snappy comeback had been bluster and blowing. Derek Wetherspoon might not have said the specific words, "Don't find me another lawyer," but he clearly meant to give me the boot. It would be unethical and unfair to string Angela along if I didn't have an official recruiting assignment.

What to do?

The big Ford sedan was blissfully snug, with a quiet engine, comfy seats, and a powerful stereo. I tuned in a classical music station and leaned my head against the headrest. The Brahms violin concerto swept over me like a soothing wind. The miles ticked off, and I wrestled with my conscience until a new argument popped into my mind—James Huston expects you to follow through with Angela. He's bound to be upset if you don't.

Game, set, and match.

I pulled into a restaurant parking lot and reached for the personal phone Gloria had lent me.

"Miss Jennings," I said. "This is Pippa Hunnechurch."

"Ah. Jimmy's favorite headhunter."

Jimmy? I needed a moment to connect "Jimmy" with James Huston. He didn't seem like a "Jimmy" to me.

"Indeed! I was most impressed by your résumé. We need to meet."

"Pick the *when* and *where*," she said with enthusiasm. "I can clear my calendar for the rest of the afternoon."

I felt an unpleasant twinge of guilt. I had come to the boundary between truth and misrepresentation. Angela didn't know that Wetherspoon had all but fired me. I realized that she was eager to be recruited and would go the extra mile—if I let her. "Please don't alter your schedule on my account. Perhaps we can meet somewhere after hours?"

"Sure. At my health club—if you don't mind driving to Chevy Chase, Maryland. I work out every day."

She gave me directions.

"I'll be there by six," I said. "How will I find you?"

"You'll see several unbelievably gorgeous women stretching their abs. I'll be the average-looking gal with envy on her face."

I wheeled the big Ford out of the parking lot and headed south.

━━━━━━━━━━

Many people sweated that afternoon at the Suburban Gym and Athletic Club, but none more than me. I had decided to follow Gloria's advice and keep wearing my bulletproof vest. It seemed like a reasonable idea while I was sitting in the Ford, with its powerful air conditioner blowing a tempest of cold air at me.

I made good time on the Washington Beltway and arrived at the club—a big, square cement building near Connecticut Avenue—at 5:20. A cheerful exercise coach with big muscles checked his clipboard and told me Angela Jennings would be in the swimming pool. Another coach, standing next to the pool, suggested that I try the women's locker room.

The locker room was as humid as a swamp. A fast-turning ceiling fan swooshed the damp air in all directions but did nothing to raise my comfort level. Beads of sweat soon formed on my upper lip, and my hair fell limp on my neck.

I heard water running in one of the shower stalls. "Angela," I called.

A soapy head poked past the plastic shower curtain. "Pippa?"

"It's me. I'm afraid I arrived a bit early."

"Wonderful! Give me a minute to rinse off." She disappeared back under the shower.

I sat on a cement bench near a wall of metal lockers, aware of a trickle of sweat moving down my ribs under my bulletproof vest. I wondered if anything in the vest was prone to rusting.

Angela made her entrance wrapped in a white towel. "It's an honor to meet you," she said. We shook hands. She had a no-nonsense grip and an intelligent face. She was tall, blonde, and thin, and radiated the glow of frequent exercise. The quick calculations I had made with the dates on her résumé suggested that she was in her early forties, but, dripping wet, she looked considerably younger.

"So," she said, "tell me about the job. Jimmy didn't know any of the specifics."

Jimmy again. Said with a definite nuance of familiarity that I found discomfiting. Were they personal friends as well as business acquaintances? Might they have an even closer relationship? *Think about James later. You are conducting an interview.*

There was no point in beating about the bush. I decided to "sell" Angela with even more zeal than Marsha Morgan had employed on Linda Preston. I didn't bother to talk about a vague opportunity at an unnamed "international conglomerate." Instead, I gave her a detailed spiel about the joys of Eurokit while she toweled off. I described Derek's vision of the role of chief counsel as she wiggled into her underwear (her abs looked fine to me). I reviewed Eurokit's excellent compensation package and fringe benefits as she gathered her hair in a ponytail.

"My kind of job," she said when I stopped talking. By now she had put on a silk frock. Angela's look would definitely appeal to Derek's sensibilities. I wondered if "Jimmy" felt the same way.

We moved to the cooler surroundings of the club's snack bar and ordered glasses of iced tea. Sitting in a low, soft chair encouraged my bulletproof vest to hike up and bulge through my blazer. Angela gave my
shoulders the occasional odd glance but said nothing. Neither did I. How
does one explain body armor while trying to make a good impression?

"You seem to have a successful solo law practice," I asked. "Why are
you eager to switch to a large organization?"

"I see my practice as a transition from government work. A temporary solution. I prefer to be part of a large enterprise where I can practice law without worrying about the messy details of keeping a business
afloat—if you know what I mean?"

Indeed I did.

"I take it you worked with Kathleen Isley at Commerce?" I said.

"Kathleen the Solo Samurai, we called her. Forever off on some one-
woman crusade to Japan and points East. Sure I know Kathleen, and
her boss. Why do you ask?"

"Derek Wetherspoon wants a counsel with clout."

Angela gawked at me. "Surely he doesn't think that Kathleen Isley
can do him any favors?"

"Well, she is deputy secretary for international trade."

"Right, which means her focus is *policy*. She thinks deep thoughts
about treaties and country-to-country trade deals. She goes to economic conferences and has dinner with foreign trade ministers who
wear funny hats. Eurokit needs friends among the people who make
the day-to-day decisions at Commerce."

"I take it you know such people?"

Angela nodded. "More importantly, they know me."

She gave me a list of references, starting with James Huston. I
would call the others eventually—if I could get Derek to consider
Angela's candidacy.

We shook hands and parted, me feeling like a working headhunter
once again. I enjoyed the sensation of being at the top of my form—
without doubt the result of my kissing an attractive man and arranging
a promising interview on the same day.

A combination that rare makes one ignore a gunshot or two.

Chapter Twenty-eight

DEREK WETHERSPOON TOOK PRIDE in working long hours, so I used Gloria's digital phone to ring his office as I drove north in the slow lane on Maryland Route 29. The clock on the dash read 7:19 P.M.

"What do you want, Hunnechurch?" he said, adopting his stuffy, *veddy-veddy* British tone of voice.

"An hour of your time," I replied. "At your convenience, of course."

"Why? Do you want to compare our combat experiences? I'm really not surprised that someone took a shot at you. You must have droves of irate ex-clients."

So the rotter had heard about the incident at my house. I didn't expect sympathy, but what would it have taken to say, "Sorry to hear about your unhappy evening, Hunnechurch," rather than deliver a jolt of sarcasm? I suppressed my fierce desire to call him an insufferable clod.

"Actually," I said, "I have identified an exceptional candidate for the chief counsel slot—"

"Pull the other leg, Hunnechurch."

"She is a woman with far better credentials at Commerce than Linda Preston."

"Not interested! Not in the least."

"She lives near Washington D.C. You won't have to deal with relocation."

"Nailor & McHale are on the case."

"She is eager to pursue the opportunity with your company."

"I told you, Miss Hunnechurch, I'm not interested. Don't call me again."

Then he hung up.

Blast!

I felt more concern for Angela Jennings than myself. She must be excited this evening, pleased as punch that "Jimmy" Huston had taken an interest in her career, delighted that a headhunter had driven forty-odd miles for an interview, and intrigued by the thought of working at Eurokit USA. In a day or two I'd have to call her and explain that Derek was not interested in her candidacy—

Nonsense! Angela deserves better than a pliable wimp willing to take no for an answer. I jammed the little telephone into my purse, punched the gas pedal, and swore to myself that Wetherspoon would read Angela's résumé, even if it meant visiting his office and personally nailing it to his door. My British determination was fully as strong as his.

Alas, I lost my concentration for a moment and swerved the Ford in the fast lane—almost side-swiping a Mercedes-Benz roadster that had crept into my blind spot. The blameless driver honked his horn, applied his brakes, and fell far behind the obviously loony woman who didn't know how to use her side-view mirror.

Double alas, a Maryland state trooper witnessed my incautious maneuver.

The pull over, document check, and subsequent lecture about the hazards of aggressive driving (happily in lieu of a ticket) consumed more than twenty minutes. I noted from the bulges on her shirt that the trooper, a woman of my age and size, was also wearing a bulletproof vest. I scrunched my shoulders when she asked for my driver's license, hoping she wouldn't notice that we wore similar undergarments.

Finishing my journey to Ellicott City at the pace of a parson, I pulled into the parking lot next to the Flour Mill Inn as the streetlights were blinking on. More out of force of habit than anything else, I used Gloria's phone to call the answering machine in the hall at Hunnechurch Manor. The perky artificial female voice said that five messages arrived during the day, the first a bit before noon. I pushed the buttons to start message replay. The five messages were all alike— two seconds of silence followed by an ominous click.

Yikes! The superstar with the gun was trying to find me, and she didn't care if I knew.

I stepped out of the Ford feeling vulnerable. The parking lot seemed enormous in the late-evening darkness, and dangerous too, with dozens of unlit crannies where a woman with a gun could lurk. I clutched my can of pepper spray and half-ran, half-skipped to the side entrance. No sooner had I grasped the polished brass doorknob, than a disembodied voice said, "You'll have to do better than that, Pippa."

I spun around and aimed the canister at the gloom. "Who's there?"

Gloria stepped out from behind the inn's utility van and grinned at me.

"Congratulations," I said. "You scared me half to death."

"I certainly hope so. I was tempted to say *boo!*"

"You would be a lot less smug right now if I had doused you with elixir of pain."

"Not a chance. The nozzle is pointed at your face. We need to re-view your operational procedures."

It was then I remembered that I hadn't told Gloria I was hiding in Ellicott City.

"How did you find me?"

"With my trusty telephone. It took me two hours to track you down. I started calling hotels, inns, and bed-and-breakfasts within fifty miles to the west of Ryde and told the desk clerks a sad story. 'Excuse me, sir, but I own a guesthouse in Ryde. I'm trying to locate a British tourist who checked out this morning—a pretty lady named Hunnechurch who left her medication in her room. We think she is still in the region.' Everybody was real cooperative and accommodating. The lady at the Flour Mill Inn was a peach. 'Oh, isn't that amazing. We have a British lady who checked in today, but her name is Huston, not Hunnechurch.' We had a good laugh over the coincidence."

"I'm overwhelmed by your skill."

"Don't be. Your security stinks. You also committed the potentially fatal blunder of being outside at night. *Bang!*" Gloria shot her finger at me and then blew away the imaginary puff of smoke. "This shooter operates in long shadows. She ambushed Missy on a dark, lonely street. She tried to bust into your house late at night. She may have poisoned Marsha during dinner."

"I take your point. But—"

"But?"

"You have a distinct advantage over the shooter. I gave you a head start when I told you I was staying southwest of Baltimore. For all she knows, I could be hiding out in downtown Kuala Lumpur, Malaysia."

"Not likely. If I were the shooter, I'd make three key assumptions about your location.

"First, the police will want you close at hand, so they'll stash you someplace nearby.

"Second, you have no idea what's going on. You probably didn't connect last night's fuss in your backyard to Missy's death, so why go far away? After all, the shooter doesn't know you broke into Marsha's office and saw the blue file folders."

I raised my hand. "I didn't break in. I had Marsha's key."

"Shut up and let me finish. The third assumption is that you have a successful business to run and can't be too far from Ryde."

"My business is on the rocks," I said with a sigh.

"I didn't know that until you told me this afternoon. I thought you had lots of clients, not just Derek Wetherspoon. Now I understand why you tried to fob me off on Bill Hastings."

"Oh dear. Did it really seem like I was fobbing you off?"

"Yes, but I forgive you. Let's talk about your strategy to stay alive." Gloria launched into an abysmal imitation of a Cockney accent, "I'll keep my head down until Reilly catches the killer."

"It's a perfectly sensible plan of action."

"For me, maybe. With you doing the hiding, it simply won't work. You'll be dead before the end of the week."

"Why are you trying to put the wind up me? I'm frightened enough on my own."

"Face it, Pippa. The time has come to stop fooling around." She linked her arm in mine. "Are you hungry?"

"Surprisingly, I feel ravenous."

"Let's find a pizza joint," Gloria said. "We'll have dinner, and I'll explain how we're going to keep you alive."

═══════════

We chose the Pizza Palazzo, a small restaurant on Frederick Street, two blocks from the Flour Mill Inn. There weren't many diners in the restaurant that night. Nevertheless, Gloria asked for an out-of-the-way booth in the back, where, as she explained to me, she could keep an eye on the comings and goings of the other patrons. We ordered a large pepperoni pizza, two Caesar salads, and a pitcher of iced tea. Our food and drink arrived quickly.

"I think you're safe tonight," Gloria said, "but it's only a matter of time before the shooter gets lucky and finds you."

"Not if I keep moving."

"That's one of your four alternatives." Gloria lifted a slice of pizza and chewed at the edges. I slipped an especially runny slice onto my plate and cut it into several pieces.

"I have alternatives?"

"The way I see it, you have four choices. One—you go into hiding big-time. That means changing your name, finding a new career, maybe returning to England. If you're lucky, the shooter will figure you've gone for good and forget about killing you. Of course, I may still be in her crosshairs, but I know I can take care of myself.

"Two—you fess up to Reilly and put all of the superstars on the spot. Now Reilly may not believe you. After all, he knows you lied to him before. But assuming he does believe you, he *may* be able to identify the shooter by checking alibis and doing other cop stuff. Your problem is that the shooter is a smart cookie. Who's to say that Reilly will find any real evidence against her? If he doesn't, well, Pippa is back on death row.

"Three—you can hang around Ryde and wait to get killed, which won't take long the way you operate. Somebody as good as me could find you in a morning, starting from scratch. But let's be optimistic about the shooter's skills. She'll need three or four days."

My pizza began to taste like ashes. I washed it down with a gulp of tea and waited for Gloria to continue. When she didn't, I said, "That's only three choices. What's the fourth?"

Gloria leaned back in her chair and stared straight at me. "You eliminate the problem, with my help."

I needed a moment to understand what Gloria had said.

"You don't mean—*kill the shooter?*"

"No. What we need to do is to nab the lady in the act." Gloria pulled at a long string of mozzarella cheese. "Our objective is to wrap her up tight and deliver her to Reilly—complete with the gun she used to kill Missy. But we have to be prepared to defend ourselves."

I felt the blood drain from my face. "I don't fancy myself an executioner."

"Do you fancy yourself a murder victim?"

"Of course not!"

"You will be if you keep your head in the sand and pretend all is right with the world."

"Once again, let me say, I am in awe. Your analysis is . . . *comprehensive.* But I'm also surprised that you didn't mention the Christian virtue of forgiveness? The one commandment I still remember from Sunday school is 'turn the other cheek.'"

"I encourage you to forgive the shooter—*after* we turn her over to the authorities for the trial and punishment she deserves. 'Turn the other cheek' doesn't mean you don't defend yourself when she tries to shoot you."

I sat up straight. "Please explain, '*when she tries to shoot you.*'"

"I should have said '*if* she tries to shoot you.' Look, what we have to do is simple. We know that she wants to kill you, so we create a trap she can't resist. We'll arrange an ambush, using you as bait. I want to catch her without any violence, but we have to be prepared to defend ourselves."

Gloria finished her slice of pizza while I (too agitated to eat) searched for the logical flaw in her arguments. There had to be a better and safer solution. One does not volunteer to become "bait" for a murderer by a simple process of elimination.

"So what do you think?" she said.

"That you have gone bonkers. I *must* have other choices."

She shrugged. "Maybe you do, but I can't come up with any."

"OK, here's one. I act as a lure, as you suggest, but we dangle me at a distance. Once we know who the killer is, we can tell Reilly."

"It won't work." She shook her head slowly, like a teacher trying to convince a dull student that the earth is round. "Say you manage to identify the shooter before she kills you—how will you get Reilly to pay attention? What are you going to say? Excuse me Detective, but a well-respected business executive killed Missy Morgan, took a shot at the gentlemen caller in my hallway, and wants to shoot me."

"Something like that."

"Where's your evidence, *Mizz* Hunnechurch?"

"Well . . ."

"What's this lady's motive?"

"I . . ."

"Surely you must know *why* someone wants to kill you."

"Not really . . ."

"See! Reilly will start asking all sorts of questions you can't or won't answer, and . . ."

"And the whole story will come out."

Gloria nodded, then hefted another slice of pizza. "There may be no way to stop that from happening, Pippa. What you want to achieve may be impossible—the shooter in prison and a happy ending for the innocent superstars."

I stared at my nearly uneaten slice of pizza for a while, once more pondering the moral arithmetic of my predicament. Were the lives and careers of three liars worth more to society than capturing a murderer?

"Notice I said 'may be impossible.'" Gloria beamed at me over her fresh slice. "It *could* happen your way if the superstars are as smart as you say they are."

"How could it happen my way?" I spoke louder than I meant to. Gloria smiled at my reaction.

"I thought that would get your attention," she said.

"Indeed it did. Now, please explain."

"I've been thinking about things from the shooter's perspective. If she's caught in the act, it doesn't make any sense for her to explain why she tried to kill you. In fact, she's better off keeping silent about everything, including her sleazy deals with the Morgan sisters."

The penny dropped.

"You're right! She'll never talk about her blue folder, or about the lies on her résumé. She'll hire a clever lawyer who'll argue that she was criminally insane when she killed Missy and shot at me, but her defense falls to pieces if the full story of her premeditation comes out." I leaned back in my chair and began to applaud. "Gloria, you are a genius!"

"One tries," Gloria said in a mock English accent.

"It's inescapable! If the shooter keeps her mouth shut, there's no way for Reilly to learn the details of the Morgan sisters' scheme."

"Unless you tell him the whole story."

My merriment froze in its tracks. "Yikes! I forgot about me."

"Indeed!" she said, again with a sham English accent.

"Am I obligated to tell Reilly everything I know—everything I've guessed?"

"That's a question only you can answer, Pippa. With God's help, of course, which reminds me . . ."

She put a manila envelope on the table.

"More self-defense weaponry?" I said.

"The best there is."

I looked inside and found two more envelopes, one small, one big. I tore open the small envelope and turned it upside down. A tape cassette spilled into my hand.

"What's on it?" I asked.

"A familiar old hymn. Play the cassette the next time you feel stressed. You'll recognize the tune immediately, but listen closely to the words. They could have been written just for you."

I pulled open the flap on the large envelope. In it was a pocket-sized Bible, leather-bound, with my name embossed in gold letters on the front cover. I riffled through the pages and watched the names of some of the books whiz by: Genesis; Leviticus; 1 and 2 Kings; Job; Psalms; Isaiah; Daniel; Matthew; Luke; Romans; Galatians; Revelation. All of them were vaguely familiar, yet surprisingly alien. I had studied the Bible as a girl in England, but hardly any of it had stuck with me.

"Enjoy it," Gloria said.

"Thank you." I smiled, genuinely touched by the gift. "Perhaps I will browse through the Bible again."

"I even know when!" she said brightly. "A chunk of bait has lots of spare time on its hands, not to mention a headhunter in hiding."

"Ah. You want me to decide."

"Yep. Which alternative shall it be?"

"Let's get one thing straight," I said. "This particular chunk of bait is not prepared to prowl the streets of Ryde like a tethered goat until the killer decides to shoot me like a fish in a barrel." With that absurdly mixed metaphor, Pippa Hunnechurch announced her decision.

You're in for it now, luv.

Gloria reached across the table and patted my hand. "Definitely no prowling the streets, but you will stop hiding. We want the shooter to attack you inside your house at night."

"We do?"

"Absolutely. Setting the trap on your turf will give us the best chance to capture her alive."

"What if she decides not to come after me?"

"We'll make sure that's not a problem." Gloria's eyes gleamed with the strategies percolating in her mind. "The first thing we do tomorrow is to make you an irresistible target. It's kinda like putting a slice of especially smelly cheese in a mousetrap."

"And how do you propose to turn me into Gorgonzola?"

"You're the headhunter, you tell me. How can we jump-start the four superstars? The idea is to get their attention—to really startle them."

The answer came to me in a flash. "I know the perfect enticement. Fake blue file folders."

Gloria raised her glass of iced tea. "To fake blue file folders," she said.

I clinked my glass against hers.

Chapter Twenty-nine

A CHILL COURSED UP MY SPINE when I woke up on Wednesday morning at seven-thirty. Today would bring me into direct contact with a murderer. My mission was to yank the lion's tail—to all but invite the shooter to launch a fresh attack on me.

"The good news is that we make the rules," Gloria had said the night before as we strolled the streets of Ellicott City licking ice cream cones. "And we choose the battlefield."

Gloria's plan was simple.

On Wednesday afternoon I invite the superstars to my office and put on a bit of a show, designed to rouse their interest. Then I quickly disappear back to the Flour Mill Inn.

On Thursday morning I relocate to Hunnechurch Manor. I spend the day out and about in Ryde, involved in highly visible pursuits calculated to pique the shooter's interest.

On Thursday night we spring the trap in my living room.

I couldn't bear to think about Friday morning. True, if all went well, I'd be out of danger, but I would still be an executive recruiter without any clients or any assignments—unless I could somehow change Derek Wetherspoon's firmly made-up mind.

Equally distressing, Gloria announced that she intended to "invest" most of my few remaining dollars on "combat intelligence," as she called it.

"We need to know as much as we can about the superstars," she said.

"OK, let's browse the files at the *Ryde Reporter.*"

"Don't waste your time. I'm talking about private stuff that never gets into print. We need their secrets—the nitty-gritty details that reveal their personalities."

"How does one acquire such knowledge?"

"I moonlight as a bodyguard, remember? The private detective agency I work for can fill our order in a few hours."

━━━━━━━

I donned a peculiar outfit that Wednesday morning—dressy black slacks (appropriate for the gathering we intended) and a loose silk blouse (ideal for camouflaging my body armor). The bulletproof vest seemed lighter today. Strapping it on made me feel intrepid, if not invincible.

I checked my watch. Twelve minutes past eight.

"Careful timing is critical," Gloria had said. "It's a tool that we'll use to keep you safe. You'll be on your own in public places because we can't let the shooter know we're working together, but I'll try to watch your back whenever I can."

I entered the Calvert Building at 9:15 on the dot, strolled nonchalantly into the lobby, and climbed the fire stairs to the fifth floor ("Don't ride any elevator without me," Gloria had instructed). I found her waiting in the shadows outside my office.

"Your suite is clear," she said, "but this building scares me. It has too many entrances to watch and too many convenient locations for an ambush." She glowered at the skimpy light fixtures that did a poor job of illuminating the hallway. "I want you out of here as quickly as possible after your shindig is over."

My shindig would be a proper late afternoon tea, the sort my mum and her cronies still enjoyed every afternoon in Chichester.

I called the Remorseless Gourmet and arranged a catered menu: estate-grown Darjeeling tea, cucumber sandwiches, scones (with thick Devonshire cream and black cherry preserves), sugar cookies, a selection of fruit tarts, and chocolate-dipped strawberries.

"Amazing!" Gloria said. "I've been to kids' birthday parties that laid out fewer sweets."

"Spoken like the crass colonial you are. I will take charge of British traditions; you focus on the mundane details that must be seen to."

"All done. I ordered a dozen pink tea roses from the florist across the street and a box of blue file folders from Denby Office Supply. Both will be delivered before noon."

"Good. We are ready to whack the beehive."

Marsha Morgan's stash of business cards, now stowed under lock and key in my desk drawer, provided private fax numbers for the four superstars. I sent them the following invitation:

> TO: *Harriet Beardsley*
>   *Kathleen Isley*
>   *Roxanne Landesberg*
>   *Susan McKenzie*

> *Good morning, ladies!*
>
> *I have scheduled an open house at my offices at 5:00 P.M. this afternoon for Marsha Morgan's distinguished friends, that is, her circle of blue-chip executives.*
>
> *It is my intention that Hunnechurch & Associates will raise the fallen banner and carry on Marsha's fine work, with no change in procedure.*
>
> *I am sure I can rely on you, as Marsha did, to enthusiastically support worthy candidates.*
>
> *I look forward to your continued participation and also to your attendance this afternoon. It is essential that we get better acquainted if we are to work together successfully in the future.*

I apologize for the abysmally short notice. Missy Morgan's death and the recent excitement at my home prompted me to accelerate my implementation schedule.

Tea and light refreshments will be served.

Come as you are. No need to RSVP.

Pippa Hunnechurch

"I'm impressed!" Gloria said. "You have a talent for hiding nasty threats in polite words."

"Thank you—I think."

"Your invitation will get their attention. They'll come to tea because they can't afford not to. I wish I could watch their faces when you explain what the note means."

"So do I. The thought of your leaving me alone this afternoon gives me humongous butterflies."

"There's no place for me to hide in this office."

"Or any place for me to duck for cover."

"She's not going to shoot you in front of other people."

"A comforting thought. I hope you are right."

"I'll be in the corridor, near your front door. It'll be easy to hear what's going on through the glass panel."

"You have scads of ammunition, I trust."

"Two magazines of custom-made, high-power hollow-points."

"I've been thinking. What if the shooter also has body armor?"

"No sweat. If she tries to shoot you, I'll aim for her head."

═══════════

Imagine a gaggle of unusually haughty geese pecking at scones and chocolate-dipped strawberries. The superstars gathered in my reception room radiated conceit and self-confidence. Any concerns they felt were concealed behind their smug smiles. I flitted among my guests, offering plates of goodies, and wondering which of them shot Missy and craved to shoot me.

"Won't you try a cucumber sandwich?" I said to Kathleen.

"No thank you, Pippa," she said as she sat (rather heavily) on my Victorian sofa. "I have a dinner engagement this evening in less than an hour. Can we begin our—agenda?"

"I second that," Susan said as she brushed cookie crumbs off her pastel blue power suit.

"In that case," I said, "I shall pour the tea."

"None for me," Roxanne said.

"Of course you will have tea," I said. "Everyone drinks tea at a tea party. Besides, how can I read your tea leaves if I don't give you a cup of tea first?"

Four pairs of eyes looked at me as if I had gone daft.

I filled and passed four cups in turn. As I filled mine, I said, "Our good friend Marsha Morgan had an uncanny ability to place unique women in unique posts. Her untimely death has left a void in the Ryde recruiting community. I propose to carry on her valuable works. Naturally, I will need your continued cooperation—your willingness to provide special recommendations when circumstances require."

I paused, but no one challenged me. No one shouted, What in the name of heaven are you talking about, Pippa?

I had figured the scheme right.

Harriet spoke first. "Frankly, Pippa, I'm surprised by the *suddenness* of your decision. You might have said something last week."

Translation: Why didn't you let on earlier that you knew about Marsha Morgan's "system"?

"Indeed I might have spoken sooner. My only excuse is that I felt discombobulated by Marsha's accident. We were quite close, you know."

"No! We didn't know," Susan said. "I thought you met Marsha a couple of weeks ago."

"True, but the calendar is such a misleading measure of intimacy," I said. "Marsha and I were kindred spirits, birds of a feather. Our friendship jelled in an instant."

Another interval of silence, then Kathleen said, "This continued cooperation you ask for, what level of effort do you have in mind? Marsha appreciated that we are busy women. She asked for our help infrequently."

Translation: How often are you going to stick it to us?

"I plan to operate in much the same way. Special assignments don't come along every day. I should anticipate needing your individual assistance, shall we say, no more than once every two years."

My answer seemed to satisfy the geese. Kathleen grunted. Roxanne nodded. Harriet offered a thin smile. Susan looked at me thoughtfully. "Our cooperation every two years would be a reasonable expectation if you were a close friend," she said, "but, let's be honest Pippa, we hardly know you, and you hardly know us. Don't you think it's presumptuous to assume that you can pick up where Marsha left off?"

Translation: What makes you believe you can threaten us?

"If I seem presumptuous, I apologize. I keep forgetting that we met less than two weeks ago. You see, I consider the four of you as members of my recruiting team because Marsha told me everything about your careers when we established our partnership."

"Partnership!" Roxanne sputtered. "On the *Chesapeake Belle* you insisted that you had no partnership with Marsha Morgan."

"Certainly! We were talking in loud voices at a dinner attended by many of Ryde's leading executives, including several clients of the Morgan Consultancy. Picture their reactions on learning that Marsha and I were partners. We would be accused of churning each other's candidates. I didn't want that to happen."

Once again no one argued with me. These were smart women who understood the full extent of what the Morgans had been doing and their roles in the scheme.

Harriet picked up Susan's earlier thread and gave it a lawyerly twist. "I accept that Marsha told you many things about us, but spoken words are so unreliable."

Translation: Do you have any real proof?

"I agree. Spoken words are subject to dispute, but Marsha also gave me copies of her notes that detail the many ways you helped the Morgan Consultancy place highly qualified candidates."

It was the cue I'd been waiting for.

I reached under my chair for my attaché case. Then I undid the locks, lifted the lid, and tilted the case forward so that everyone could see the four blue file folders that Gloria had labeled to resemble those I had found in Marsha's office. After everyone saw them, I closed the lid and snapped the locks shut.

My "hard evidence" of their deeds transfigured the atmosphere. Gone was any pretense of goodwill. The superstars wore expressions that ranged from hatred to fury. At that moment they all wanted me dead, and one in particular knew that I understood everything.

There's no turning back now.

"Have you finished your cups of tea?" I asked. "If you recall, I promised to read your tea leaves."

"Enough nonsense," Kathleen said.

"This is getting too weird for me," Roxanne added.

Susan stood up to leave, but Harriet realized I had something else to say. "Where are you going with this?" she asked.

"The times we live in are so unpredictable," I said. "Minor indiscretions get blown into major scandals. One must have a means of looking ahead. My older sister taught me to interpret tea leaves when I was a child."

I lifted my cup, swirled the leaves clockwise in the dregs, then spilled the excess liquid into my saucer.

"Consider my tea leaves," I said. "A most interesting pattern. I see a woman"—I smiled at them—"me, no doubt, surrounded by flowers, circles, and horseshoes, all symbols of good luck. My future looks bright. I think I would see much the same sights in your cups. A clear sign that our futures are entwined. Don't you agree?"

No one stayed long enough to answer my question.

Chapter Thirty

THE FOUR SUPERSTARS DIDN'T WAIT to be ushered out of my office. They rose in unison and marched into the hallway, leaving my front door open behind them. I heard their heels click on the floor tiles with the precision of a tap-dance quartet, then disappear into the elevator.

In my haste to congratulate myself for throwing a triumphant tea party, I didn't consider the obvious. The women were able to walk directly into the elevator because someone else had ridden to the fifth floor.

I glanced up, and there was John Tyler standing in my doorway. He peered at the plates of food on most of the flat surfaces in the reception room and then smiled.

"I get it!" he said. "You and those four gals had a wedding shower. I hope you're not the one getting hitched."

I swallowed my urge to throw the teapot at the chauvinist lunkhead. "Good afternoon, John. What brings you to Hunnechurch & Associates?"

"Our project, of course."

"Pardon?"

"The chamber of commerce's memorial for Marsha Morgan. It's important that we do it right."

He swung the door shut. I could see Gloria's faint shadow on the glass panel. She had returned to her listening post. I wondered why she didn't simply come in. Then I realized that she thought John Tyler was a client and was leaving us alone to talk business.

"You mentioned a few ideas the other day," I said. "A bronze bust, if I recall, and a lecture series."

"Clichés. Both of them. I know we can do better if we work together as a team. I think that women can be just as creative as men. Don't you?"

Tyler took my silence as a signal to continue. "You have exquisite taste. I can tell by your furnishings and your clothing." He reached out and touched my lapel. I pushed myself out of my chair and moved away from him. Tyler followed me and put his arm around my waist.

"You smell nice today, Pippa," he said.

"Unhand me, John."

"Your mouth says no, but your eyes say yes." He pulled me toward him, lips puckered.

"All of me says no!" I shouted and spun out of his grasp.

The door flew open and in roared Gloria. She grabbed Tyler's hand and levered him away from me. A moment later he lay face down on my carpet, his arm held securely in an impressive lock.

"Are you OK, Pippa?" she asked.

"Splendid!"

"Let go of me!" Tyler squeaked.

Gloria hoisted him to his feet but continued to hold his arm firmly.

"Not until Pippa tells me to let you go," she said.

I moved close to Tyler's grimaced face. "John, I will be happy to work with you on a suitable memorial for Marsha Morgan, but our relationship stops there. Understood?"

"Let go of me!"

Gloria must have tightened her grip because Tyler suddenly shouted, "OK! OK! I understand."

"Let him go." I said.

"My pleasure," Gloria said.

Tyler took a giant step sideways and began rubbing his arm. He looked at me, then at Gloria, then back at me. "I didn't realize you were *that kind* of woman."

I was still laughing when Tyler slammed my front door behind him.

I gave Gloria a hug. "Thank you for rescuing me from an evil suitor. I was about to wallop his face, which would have left a mark."

"Mark or no mark, I think you just lost a friend."

"I dearly hope so. I want John Tyler as a business colleague, nothing more."

"Hey, I see you have lots of food left."

"A mountain of scones and tarts and cookies."

"Let's get out of here and eat them. We'll have a junk food supper."

Gloria whizzed about my office like a bumblebee with its tail on fire, shoveling the leftover goodies into a paper shopping bag, pouring a half pot of still-hot tea into a thermos, and tidying up my reception room, while I did little more than watch. Her frenzied way of working struck me as odd, and then I saw the tears in her eyes.

"Why are you crying?" I asked.

She tried to smile. "Don't mind me. I cry a lot."

"So I have noticed, but only when you have a good reason to be upset. Tell me what's bothering you."

She punctuated a sigh with a resigned shrug. "OK," she said, "I am upset, but you won't understand if I tell you why, so let's forget the whole thing."

I wish I could report that I reacted calmly. Regrettably, "you won't understand" and "forget the whole thing" made my hackles rise. I tossed a crumpled napkin at Gloria and said, "Suit yourself! Where shall we go to eat?"

"Somewhere beautiful."

"Beautiful is easy in Maryland. Follow me."

I had parked the rented Ford alongside the cashier's kiosk in a pricey ground-level parking lot a few steps from the Calvert Building and paid the baffled Sikh exchange student inside the kiosk twenty dollars to watch over it like a mamma hen, which eased my somewhat

outlandish fears that the shooter might try to wire a bomb to its igni-
tion switch.

The Ford didn't explode when I turned the key. I nosed into the
rush hour traffic on High Street, and looked around for Gloria's Dodge
truck. I spotted her waiting for me in a No Parking zone next to a fire
hydrant.

"You want beautiful," I muttered to myself, "you'll get beautiful."

I drove to my favorite tourist overlook on a bluff above the Magothy
River, laid claim to its one picnic table, and began to unpack the shopping bag. A few moments later Gloria trudged up the short hill from the
parking area.

"Good choice." She sat down opposite me and smiled. "The view is
wonderful."

"Ah! The old Gloria is back. Now, tell me why you were upset."

"I meant what I said earlier. You won't understand."

This time I kept my cool. "Try me."

I listened to the afternoon breeze rustle the leaves in the big chest-
nut tree that shaded our picnic table while Gloria considered my request. At last she held up a manila envelope. "Here's the report I ordered
about the superstars. I read it while you were pouring tea. See how it
makes you feel."

I opened the envelope and found two closely typed sheets of paper.
"The four subjects you asked us to investigate (the report began) have
colorful private lives:"

Harriet Beardsley

Marital Status: Currently divorced. (Her two failed marriages were
to successful men who were away from home much of the time.)

Children: None.

Hobbies: The subject is an enthusiastic gourmet. A recent graduate
of Ryde Culinary Institute's amateur chef training program, she is co-
author of the cookbook, *Eastern Shore Dishes Your Mother Might Have
Made.* The kitchen in her new house is larger than the living room.

Financial status: Wealthy. Owns property in Florida and the
American Virgin Islands estimated to be worth in excess of $15 million.

Other: The subject's former secretary reports that Ms. Beardsley has a well-deserved reputation for "bed hopping." A former "significant other" we interviewed claims that the subject "switches men at the start of each season like clockwork."

Susan McKenzie

Marital Status: Currently divorced (one previous marriage).

Children: None.

Hobbies: The subject spends much of her spare time restoring 78-rpm phonograph records (primarily historic jazz recordings made during the 1920s and 1930s) in the elaborate sound studio she built in her basement. She owns a celebrated collection of rare jazz record albums and has written several magazine articles on record collecting.

Financial status: Perilous!

Other: The subject attempts to lead a wealthy lifestyle and frequently overspends her only source of income, her monthly paycheck. A former personal trainer (currently suing her for unpaid fees) reports that the subject "throws money around lavishly" and is in debt "up to her ears."

Kathleen Isley

Marital Status: Currently divorced (two previous marriages).

Children: None.

Hobbies: The subject is reputed to read three novels a week (a habit picked up during her years of globe-trotting). She is a self-professed "connoisseur" of sixteenth- and seventeenth-century English poetry. Her personal library is said to include more than fifty rare volumes of poems by English poets, including John Donne, Ben Johnson, and John Milton.

Financial status: Comfortable.

Other: A former housekeeper reports that the subject "takes great pride in living on the edge" and "often engages in risky behavior." The subject's driver's license was recently reinstated after a six-month suspension for multiple speeding and reckless driving convictions. Subject was arrested twice for shoplifting in Washington, D.C. during the past thirty-six months (charges were dropped, reportedly because of her influence).

Roxanne Landesberg

Marital Status: Currently divorced (one previous marriage).

Children: None.

Hobbies: The subject is known throughout Maryland as an expert gardener. She maintains her own greenhouse, an acre of esoteric ornamentals, and a pond stocked with Japanese carp (the kind with long, flowing fins).

Financial status: Wealthy.

Other: The subject has two convictions in Maryland for driving while intoxicated (most recent was last October when the subject's driver's license was revoked). A former employee claims that two years ago subject spent several weeks in a mental health facility specializing in addictive behavior, "then jumped back off the wagon."

I looked up into Gloria's curiosity-filled face.

"So, what do you think?" she asked.

I didn't know what to think. The descriptions of the superstars' hobbies seemed wholesome enough. Nothing to bring tears to anyone's eyes. And as for the "other" details, well, my first reaction was discomfort. Perhaps we had pried more deeply into the superstars' lives than was fair? What right did we have to ferret out their shabby little secrets?

"You have me at a loss," I said. "I can't imagine that any of this would make you cry."

She considered my answer for a while, then said, "Those pages tell a story of four unhappy women. Don't you feel sorry for them?"

Without knowing why, I felt an immediate need to challenge Gloria's opinion, to defend the superstars.

"Aren't you overreacting?" I said. "We all have a skeleton or two in the closet, and why would I feel sorry for them? They seemed utterly content when I ate dinner with them aboard the *Chesapeake Belle*. I'll probably be content, too, when I reach the pinnacle of my career."

"Success in worldly affairs is not the same thing as contentment."

"Perhaps not, but it can be a great start."

"Don't their lifestyles tell you anything? One superstar's an alcoholic. Another's promiscuous. A third is addicted to expensive toys. The fourth has to take crazy risks to feel she's alive. All of them have been divorced at least once; none of them have families. . . ."

"Whoa! Not every woman needs kids—or a husband—to make her content."

"Perhaps not, but it can be a great start," she said in an eerily faithful imitation of my accent.

Gloria's impersonation kicked my anger into high gear.

"I know where this is going. I feel a sermon coming on. The gospel according to Saint Gloria. A Bible-thumping attack on successful women who lead unconventional lives. Well, I say, judge not, that ye be not judged. Isn't that the Christian precept you ignored when I called you on the night that Marsha died?"

"Very good, Pippa! But no, I haven't judged the superstars. I feel pity for the lot, including the murderer."

Oops! In my exuberance I'd forgotten that one of the four had shot Missy Morgan in cold blood. Gloria noted my momentary confusion and launched her offensive. She moved to my side of the picnic table and poked my bulletproof vest.

"You don't get it! You *really* don't get it. It's not their lifestyles that are tragic or their sins. Those four women have turned away from the things that are important in life. They have no family, no fellowship, no love, *no God*." Gloria grabbed my shoulders. "Like you!"

"Like me?"

"Yeah, just like you." She sat down heavily next to me. Our bench shuddered. "It won't be long before you are a lonely superstar, and the thought made me weep."

"You cried about me?"

"See! I said you wouldn't understand."

I turned toward the Magothy River in time to watch the *Pride of Ryde* bump to a halt against its pier at the end of its late afternoon cruise. Most of the tourists on the upper deck wore similar red T-shirts, probably an organization on an outing.

Was Gloria right? Had I too become a loner?

It was easy to understand why she thought so. I'd moved away from my family and friends in England, opened a one-woman firm, bought a one-person house, kept myself too busy to date, and (something that Gloria knew well) declared myself independent of God.

"I've never considered myself *solitary*," I said.

"We're all born solitary, Pippa. The question is whether we stay that way. Each of us has the choice. We can remain the biggest thing in our own lives, like the superstars, or become part of something much bigger."

Without meaning to, I murmured, "A communion of fellowship in the presence of a loving God."

"I like it!" Gloria whacked my bulletproof vest again. "That's a neat description of Christianity. I suspect you didn't come up with it yourself."

"Hardly. My sister sent me a sampler embroidered with those words."

She picked up an apricot tart and took a big bite. "I'd love to see Chloe's sampler."

"Sure. Look in my bedroom closet. Top shelf, in the back, under a stack of old sweaters."

Gloria let out a fine "Ha! I knew it! You're punishing God."

"Don't be silly."

"I once punished God too. When I was eight years old, I wrote, 'God stinks,' two hundred times on a sheet of composition paper. I was furious. He let my sick turtle die even though I prayed for its recovery."

"I am not mad at God."

"Why not?" She polished off the tart. "It would have been no trick at all for God to warn Simon or to delay your trip a few seconds that day."

My first thought was: *No trick at all. Not for a God that cared.* But then I recalled Gloria's words to me several days earlier. "God doesn't cause pain. That's why he doesn't prevent it."

"Please believe me. . . ." I fought to keep my voice from cracking. "I am not mad at God."

"Oh, I believe you. You're far too refined to stay angry with anyone for seven years. Instead you punished God by chasing him out of your life. You put him away on your highest shelf, under a stack of old sweaters."

I shrugged. "Perhaps I did. I felt that God wasn't paying attention to me."

"Not true, Pippa. God pays attention to everyone." Gloria reached for a cherry tart. "Look, you can't blame God because an old man lost control of his car. God never promised that tragedies wouldn't happen, but he did promise to help you get through the pain. It was foolish of you not to take him up on it. All you have to do is ask."

"How simple you make it sound."

"It is simple. Did you listen to the tape cassette I gave you?"

"I have been rather busy, Gloria."

"Yep. Seven years all by yourself—shoulder to the wheel, nose to the grindstone. Maybe if you looked up from time to time, you would find what Paul called 'the peace of God, which transcends all understanding.' Check out Philippians 4:7 in the Bible I gave you, and pay attention to the still, small voice. God *tries* to talk to everyone."

I studied her face while she munched. Gloria radiated confidence in her faith. *What did I have confidence in these days?* Not much. I saw my future as hopelessly uncertain. For seven years I had relied completely on myself, and my achievements had been short-lived. There had to be something more. . . .

I pulled my eyes away, almost embarrassed by my own thoughts. "It's time I returned to my hidey-hole in Ellicott City," I said.

"I'll keep the bag of goodies. Something to munch on while I follow you home."

"Be careful or you'll get fat."

"Not me. I can eat anything and never gain an ounce."

"Now I really do hate you."

━━━━━━

I drove to Ellicott City watching the sun go down and feeling my courage ebb away. The shooter worked at night. I might become a target at any moment. Even though Gloria's truck stayed reassuringly close behind (I kept checking my rearview mirror!), I wondered if discretion really was the better part of valor. Perhaps I should go home to England? Once the bank foreclosed the mortgage on Hunnechurch Manor, nothing would hold me in Ryde. Why risk my life tonight and tomorrow and the day after?

Don't wimp out, Hunnechurch!

I tried the radio. Lots of news but no classical music. I was about to punch the off button when I thought about Gloria's tape cassette. No doubt it would be more religious propaganda. Nonetheless, I glanced at the radio. Indeed! A built-in cassette deck.

I dug the cassette out of my purse and slipped it into the tape player. A pipe organ played a few notes, and a choir began to sing:

What a friend we have in Jesus, all our sins and griefs to bear!
What a privilege to carry everything to God in prayer!
O what peace we often forfeit, O what needless pain we bear,
All because we do not carry everything to God in prayer.

The music stopped. Gloria's voice took over. "Pippa, I guess you didn't turn off the tape when you heard the choir singing because you hear me talking. 'What a Friend We Have in Jesus' is a familiar old hymn. I'm sure they even sing it in England, but so few of us take the words to heart. Especially you!

"I don't know what you are doing right now, and I don't know what you are thinking, but I do know that you are hurting needlessly because you try to hang on to your worries rather than give them to the Lord. 'O what peace you often forfeit, O what needless pain you bear.' Get the point? Well, that's the end of my sermon. There are two more verses to the hymn. I suggest you come with me to church one Sunday and listen to them. Hint. Hint."

I found myself smiling at Gloria's persistence and also thinking about her claims. *Could it be that simple to shed one's 'sins and griefs'? Is there really a 'peace of God, which transcends all understanding'?*

I rewound the tape and listened to the choir again.

It was a lovely concept. Carry everything to God in prayer. I certainly had a wagon full of worries to unload on him.

I arrived in Ellicott City feeling much less gloomy.

Chapter Thirty-one

I USED MY OWN CREDIT CARD to check out of the Flour Mill Inn on Thursday morning.

"Oh, my!" the innkeeper said when she saw my real name. "Another hotel person tried to reach you the other day to remind you about your medicine." She peered at me suspiciously, as if I might keel over on the spot.

"Not to worry. Miss Spitz found me."

The innkeeper puttered with my receipt, an obvious question forming behind her brow.

"Why do you use two different names?" she asked.

I had an answer ready. "Pippa Hunnechurch is my real name, while J. Huston is my stage identity. I'm an aspiring actress."

"Really?" She peered at me again. "Have I seen you in anything?"

I couldn't resist fibbing. "Possibly. I've done a few TV commercials and a bit of summer theater in Maryland."

In truth I felt like an actress that morning. My life had become a drama full of intrigue and murder, with me cast as "Little Miss Sitting Duck." The opening night at Hunnechurch Manor was less than

twelve hours away. With Gloria's help, I would give the performance
of a lifetime—in more ways than one, if the shooter caught us unawares.

I tossed my clothes into the Ford and made my way along back
roads to Maryland Route 100. I drove east toward a bright summer sun
rising in a cloudless sky. Excellent shooting weather. I accelerated to
sixty-five miles per hour, hoping that it was really more difficult to hit
a moving target.

Perhaps facing toward England caused it, but I thought of my
mother and Chloe. I hadn't considered how they would feel if the bait
didn't survive the hunt. Mum would be heartbroken, but Chloe—well,
she would also be furious to lose the opportunity to play elder, and
therefore wiser, sister. Chloe keeps up the senior-sibling charade, even
though I live an ocean beyond her clutches.

You have to stay safe, or Chloe will never let you hear the end of it.

When I reached the Baltimore Beltway, I accelerated to seventy-five.

Gloria was waiting for me outside her house. We wedged Winston's
cage into the Miata's passenger seat and squeezed my big canvas tote
into the trunk. Gloria parked the Ford out of sight, on the driveway
that circled behind the big, old Victorian.

"Perfect!" she said when I climbed behind the wheel. "Your red
Mazda is like a marquee. It shouts 'Pippa Hunnechurch is here!'"

"Perhaps we should paint a bull's-eye on the windscreen?"

"Not necessary," she said, playing through my attempt to be ironic.
"But I think you should put the top down."

"No way! I'll feel utterly starkers."

"We want you to be as visible as possible. Besides, the top isn't
bulletproof."

I surveyed the black fabric interior of the folding top that occasionally failed to block windblown raindrops. "Sorry to say, it is not."

"Speaking of bulletproof, are you wearing your vest?"

"Yes."

"Do you have my digital telephone in your purse?"

"Yes, with a fully charged battery."

"Good. Let's review your schedule one last time."

"I will make myself visible until ten-thirty in the morning, at which time I will park the Miata outside my front door, thus providing clear evidence to anyone watching that I have resumed residence at Hunnechurch Manor. While I am being seen throughout Ryde, you will reach my house surreptitiously via the back alley that connects to South Street. You will walk through the alley, enter my garden, and arrive at my back door at ten-thirty, without anyone being the wiser."

"Roger that!"

I burst out laughing.

"What's so funny?" she said.

"In Merry Old England, to 'roger' something means to, well, it's a very vulgar expression. I wish we could *roger* this whole business. I must be barking mad to turn myself into live prey."

"You can always reconsider alternatives one, two, and three."

"No," I said with a sigh. "We're doing what must be done—the only way it can be done."

━━━━━━━━

I drove the scenic route to downtown Ryde—Cove Road, then River Road, and then High Street—somewhat faster than the law approves, feeling as defenseless in the Miata's open cockpit as a metal duck at a carnival shooting range. Gloria and I had mapped out a series of errands—seemingly routine trips to a drugstore, a gas station, an office supply shop, and a computer store—that guaranteed I would be seen in all corners of Ryde. I wished we had included a tea break. A steaming mug of Darjeeling might have taken the edge off my jumpiness.

It had been great fun tweaking the superstars' noses in my office the day before, confident that Gloria (and her pistol) were listening outside the door. But I was alone this morning, not knowing if (or when) the bait might be snatched. I held my breath at each traffic light, rolled past every stop sign, and kept a wary eye on the cars that chose to tailgate me.

9:45 A.M. My play shopping was done. Winston chirped merrily when I gunned the Miata's engine. He didn't seem to mind that his swing dangled at a funny angle. Perhaps he sensed that he was going home.

"We'll be there soon, laddie, after I make another stop—this one is for you."

I wanted to replenish Hunnechurch Manor's supply of birdseed. A pet shop only a mile away sold the mixture that Winston preferred above all others. As fate would have it, David Friendly decided to visit the very same establishment at the very same time.

We parked side by side before we noticed each other.

"You call this lying low?" he growled in the chagrined tone of one who discovers that a previously solved problem has mysteriously become unsolved.

"Fear not." I rapped my bulletproof vest with my knuckles. "I've taken appropriate precautions."

He gave my midriff a hefty *thwack*.

"Wonderful! I've read a thousand stories about police officers killed while wearing body armor."

"I am antsy enough this morning without listening to your tales of horror. Please change the subject."

"Here goes! After we bury you, I'm going to get rip-roaringly drunk with James Huston and Gloria Spitz. We'll stay up all night trying to figure out why the *late* Pippa Hunnechurch was so mindlessly stubborn."

"I'll haunt you all."

"We'll have you exorcised."

"Feel free! A few sprinkles of English Breakfast tea should do the trick."

"You win!" David threw his arms up in surrender. "Pippa Hunnechurch is too clever by half to heed a foolish reporter. Well, you might as well give me advice while you're still alive. What do you know about feeding a cat?"

"One opens a can."

"Hardly very useful, and here I thought all Brits worshiped their felines."

"Not me. I have a budgie—Wait a moment! Why would petless David Friendly care about cat food?"

David began to grin. "I adopted Ginger," he said. "Gloria talked me into it, and I got Joyce to agree."

I beamed back at him. "Why, you old softy."

"She's a great cat and—" David stopped in mid-sentence and scanned the parking lot. "By the way, where is Gloria? I thought she was your bodyguard."

"I'm on my own for a few hours."

"That doesn't make any sense. Unless . . ." A shadow of concern swept across his face. "Did Reilly cook up a scheme to catch the killer using you as bait?"

I winced at the word *bait*. "I am not involved with Detective Reilly in any way," I said.

"Something's going on. I can see it in your face. I can *smell* it."

I bit my tongue. Better silence than another fib.

"Oh, I get it!" David said, his eyes brimming with anger. "You don't want to tell me what's going on. You're not playing fair, Pippa! I thought we had a deal." He mimicked my accent. "I won't hold out on you again."

"David, believe me, it's not that simple."

He waved me quiet. "What's happened to our friendship? Why won't you believe me when I say I want to help? I think you don't trust me anymore."

"Don't be preposterous, David. Of course, I trust you."

He turned and left without speaking another word.

I let him walk away. What could I say to stop him? Only the truth, but that would ruin the plan that Gloria had concocted. A friend won't let a friend be bait.

Oh David. I don't want to lose you as my friend.

━━━━━━

Gloria tapped on my back door at ten-thirty, as planned. She wore khaki fatigues and a jaunty military cap and toted a big canvas carry-all on each shoulder.

"I thought you military types traveled light?" I said.

"This isn't extra clothing, *Mizz* Hunnechurch. One bag is full of surveillance gear—a couple of night-vision cameras, a pair of wireless mikes, and a half-dozen motion detectors."

"How exciting! We can watch the telly and see the killer breaking in."

"That's the idea, if we're lucky. If not, you'll find out which of the neighborhood cats has been doing his business in your herb garden."

"What's in the other bag?"

"Material and equipment. Everything from my weapons to an army-issue coffee pot. We'll need plenty of industrial-strength java tonight."

I cringed at the enthusiasm in Gloria's voice. She might have been arriving at a pajama party rather than an ambush.

"What should we do first?" I asked.

"Reconnoiter in detail. I browsed through your house the other evening. Today I need the full tour."

I led Gloria from room to room. She studied the front and back doors, examined every window latch, tested every light and lamp, and manipulated my curtains and venetian blinds. When she finished, she put a hand on my shoulder and said solemnly, "It's amazing you haven't been burgled. An idiot could defeat your perimeter security."

"Oh dear! I'm sorry to hear that."

"Don't be. It's great news for us. We can assume that the shooter got a good look at your locks and latches the other night. She knows what a pushover this place is, so she'll probably try again. When this is all over, we'll get you some real locks and an electronic alarm system."

When this is all over. What a pleasant thought to contemplate.

We settled in the kitchen. Gloria perked a pot of coffee as fierce and foul as any I've ever smelled.

"I am amazed you can drink that witch's brew black," I said.

"Alertness counts. I'd rather lose a little stomach lining than a lot of skin."

A cogent point! I emptied my mug of English Breakfast tea and filled it full of Gloria's potent coffee. I dearly wanted to be vigilant the rest of the day.

Chapter Thirty-two

MY CHIEF JOB THAT THURSDAY AFTERNOON was to give the shooter the pip, to use one of my mum's favorite expressions.

"Why does 'giving the pip' mean getting on someone's nerves?" Gloria asked as she tugged a slender black cable under my Persian rug with one hand and grasped a sandwich in the other.

"It's quite descriptive. Think of someone goading you—being vexing enough to really get under your skin."

I had prepared *elevenses* for us both (a late-morning snack of ham, cheese, bread, and fruit) in lieu of the lunch we wouldn't have time to eat. Gloria was busy installing the surveillance equipment she had brought. I would soon be tempting crazed shooters on the streets of Ryde.

"I still don't get it," she said. "In the United States a *pip* is something special, as in 'you're a real pip.' Where in mid-ocean did the word switch meaning?"

"Oh no! You are *not* going to change the subject. This silly discussion began when I asked you if it's still necessary for me to leave the house again to give the shooter the pip. I want a thoughtful answer."

Gloria stopped wiring my room momentariliy to consider my question. "I say, yes, on the off chance that the shooter has decided not to attack you."

"Do you think that is possible?"

"You never know. Murderers can be unpredictable."

"Wonderful! The world of crime according to Gloria Spitz. Clichés spouted while you wait. A cockamamy observation for every distressing situation."

"Someone in this room seems to be getting a tad touchy."

"Of course I'm touchy. I feel rather out on a limb today. It's not every afternoon that I prance around Ryde encouraging a madwoman with a gun to take a potshot at me."

"Relax. You won't face much danger in downtown Ryde when the sun is shining. The shooter doesn't care for daylight or crowds, remember? She prefers lonely streets and dark gardens. It's part of her *modus operandi*."

"Didn't you tell me only a moment ago that murderers can be unpredictable?"

She glared at me over her shoulder. "Get out of here, Pippa. Have some fun. Order your surprise gifts. Make it Christmas in July for four lovely ladies. A *blue* Christmas."

"Ho, ho, ho," I said as I slammed my front door behind me.

━━━━━━━

I had left the safe, if snappish, environs of Hunnechurch Manor with four blue folders—each tabbed with a superstar's name and containing a note handwritten on my personal stationery:

PHILIPPA E. K. HUNNECHURCH
• 735 MAGOTHY STREET • RYDE, MARYLAND 21099 •

Dear _____,

I think it *so* unfortunate that our genial get-together yesterday ended on a *blue* note. Please accept this little gift—a *blue* item for a *"blue-chip"* woman—by way of apology. As I

see it, we must put aside our petty disagreements and learn
to work together in the coming years. We both have *so* much
to gain from a *friendly* relationship.
Cordially,
Pippa

Yes, the blue folders (and my off-the-wall notes) were blatant re-
minders of the superstars' relationship with Marsha Morgan. Three of
the women would be furious at me by the end of the day. The fourth
would want me dead. Our plan was to deliver the folders in ways that
would attract the maximum attention—*expensive* ways. Besides being
bait, I would also experience the excitement of spending a chunk of
money I could ill afford.

My first stop was the pricey fishmonger on High Street who catered
to summer tourists. He built a thriving business shipping gifts of freshly
caught Chesapeake Bay seafood throughout the country.

"I want a bushel of live blue crabs delivered to Ms. Harriet
Beardsley, at Bates-McCann Financial, in Baltimore."

"We will have 'em there in three hours," he said as he reached for a
picnic-size white Styrofoam cooler.

"No. I want the crabs packed in ice, in an old-fashioned wooden
bushel basket."

"Can do, but slatted baskets can get mighty messy."

"Indeed! My friend fancies herself a chef in the old tradition.
She mistrusts newfangled technology and especially doesn't like
plastic."

"Hey! Lots of weird people love blue crabs."

BMF had its headquarters in an elegant, marble-sided tower on
Light Street. I imagined the firm's receptionist coping with a dripping
bushel basket of exasperated crabs (who would become increasingly
frisky as the ice melted and their temperatures rose). My gift was sure
to cause a stir in the lobby and prompt an immediate telephone call to
Harriet.

"Oh, one more thing," I said. "Tape this to the basket's lid." I gave
him Harriet's blue folder.

The Ryde Flower and Garden Center, another favorite among summer tourists, occupied a renovated movie theater on High Street. I browsed the terraced aisles, looking for something blue to send to Roxanne Landesberg, master gardener. I perused hydrangea, purple penny royal, iris, blue delphinium, lavender-blue agapanthus, and morning glories, all of them much too pretty to give the pip to anyone. I finally spotted a disreputable-looking thirty-pound bag of Kentucky bluegrass seed propped against a back wall.

The sales clerk eyed me and the burlap sack with skepticism. "Well, we can certainly arrange to have your gift delivered this afternoon," she said. "Including the blue folder is no problem, but I'd prefer not to sell you that particular bag. I mean, it's *leaking*. It's bound to leave a trail of grass seed wherever it goes."

"One can only hope it will," I replied as I presented my credit card.

The manager of the Ryde Rhythms Singing Telegram Service took my request in stride. "Many of our performances are for unique occasions," she said. "We can tailor a delivery to your special requirements."

"I'm worried about your . . . ah *performer,* getting in to see my friend. She is an executive at Militet's Aviation Division and is well-protected by secretaries."

"Our forte is getting in to difficult places. We've made five deliveries at Militet over the years—the last time with a male stripper."

The idea intrigued me. "Do you have a male stripper who can also sing?"

"As a matter of fact . . ." she lifted her telephone. "What's Martin doing this afternoon?" A pause. "Good. Send him to my office." She hung up the phone. "You'll love Martin."

A gorgeous man stepped into the room. Late twenties. Tall. Athletic. Radiant smile.

"I'm sure that everyone at Militet will love Martin," I murmured.

"This gig is a toughie," the manager said to Martin. "You have to track down an executive at Militet Aviation, give her a blue folder, then sing 'St. Louis Blues' while you strip."

"She's the general manager," I added. "Her name is Susan McKenzie. She loves timeless music."

"Piece of cake!" Martin said. "Do you know what kind of car she drives?"

I remembered Harriet's comment on the gallery of the Talbot Inn. "A big, green Volvo station wagon."

"Fine! I'll call your friend Susan from Militet's lobby and tell her that I hit her Volvo in the executive parking lot. That will draw her to the lobby, and when she gets there . . ." Martin crooned "I got the St. Louis blues . . ." and began to dance.

This would be a day when legends were born at Militet Aviation.

━━━━━━━━

I traveled to the haughty precincts of Mulberry Alley, Ryde's answer to Rodeo Drive. It offers fewer trendy boutiques than its Beverly Hills cousin, but the prices are fully as outrageous. I boldly entered Scandalous Lingerie and (insisting they were for a friend) purchased a pair of amazing panty hose—iridescent blue, sheer as a spider's web, dotted with sequins, and packed in a transparent plastic pouch for all the world to see.

I took my purchase to a much-amused dispatcher at the Centurion Messenger Service, on Ryde High Street, who agreed to make a special run to Washington, D.C.

"One pair of blue stockings," he said, "the kind that Washington streetwalkers wear. Tied to a blue folder with a big, blue ribbon. Hand carried to the Department of Commerce building, on Fourteenth Street and Constitution Avenue, for guaranteed delivery before 3:00 P.M. today."

"And left with the receptionist reluctantly," I added. "I want your messenger to make a gentle fuss when the receptionist sends him away. Have him point out that the sender asked for Kathleen Isley's signature on the receipt."

"Consider the items delivered."

I knew that Kathleen, a connoisseur of classic English poetry, would understand my gift. The Blue Stocking Society, you see, was the nickname for a predominantly female literary club in eighteenth-century London.

Ta da!

Chapter Thirty-three

Waiting for the shooter to strike turned out to be nerve-wracking work, with me playacting downstairs and Gloria stationed in the "field HQ" she set up in my second bedroom *cum* furniture warehouse. A year earlier I had purchased room-darkening draperies to protect my Edwardian chests, chaise, and chairs from sunlight. At night they worked better than blackout curtains during the London Blitz. I strolled through my garden as dusk fell to make sure that not even a pinprick of light escaped the room. Anyone lurking outside Hunnechurch Manor would see a profoundly dark second-floor window, as usual. Even the little TV camera Gloria had installed was invisible from ground level.

My link to Gloria was a miniature radio transceiver smaller than a deck of cards. She had pulled a pair out of her bag of tricks early in the evening.

"This is the same kind of communications system the U.S. Secret Service uses," she said. "The earpiece hooks behind your ear and holds the microphone alongside your cheek. The radio itself clips onto your bulletproof vest at the waist."

I practiced speaking into the microphone without moving my lips.

"Pretty good," Gloria said. "As intelligible as an English accent ever gets."

I whistled loudly into the mike.

"*OK! OK!* I promise—no more Brit jokes."

At ten o'clock Gloria said, "Communications test. Report my signal."

"Loud and clear."

"Say your location."

"The living room. I'm sitting at my ladies' writing desk."

"Think back to the night of the attack," Gloria said. "When did James hear the prowler?"

"About five minutes after you left."

Gloria *hmmmed* thoughtfully. "Very clever, our shooter is. She must have recognized that I was your bodyguard and that James was merely a friend."

"James figured you out, too, while he was ogling your unjustly well-rounded hips."

"Hey! I work out a lot. I can recommend a few exercises that might help reshape your flabby posterior."

"I believe we were talking about the shooter."

"True. The shooter waited for me to drive out of sight. We're dealing with a woman who looks before she leaps."

"Is that important?"

"Definitely. She won't attack you unless she's sure that I'm not here. We'll have to convince her that you are alone in the house tonight."

"How?" I asked, although I had guessed the answer.

"Easy. You'll spend the evening working at your desk. Are you casting a visible shadow on the curtains?"

"A little one."

"Make it bigger."

I adjusted my desk lamp to emphasize my shadow, which made me feel even more at risk.

"What if she decides to shoot at me from outside the house?" I said.

"That's a chance we'll have to take."

"Ha! Ha! Ha!"

"Take a stretch. Go to the kitchen for a cup of tea, but stay close to the windows, so the shooter can see that you are alone."

"Can I watch TV?"

"No! Make like a headhunter. The sight of you working at a desk will add fuel to the fire. Use your telephone. Recruiters often call references at night."

Regrettably, I didn't have any headhunter work to do—no searches to plan, no credentials to check. When I returned with my cup of tea, I tried to write a letter to Chloe. I began:

"Dear Chum,
A quick note to tell you that all is well on my brief "holiday" with . . ."

I crumpled the letter in mid-sentence, deciding that I had told Chloe enough lies this month.

Gloria wants you to use the telephone. Find someone to call.

I thought about calling James Huston in Atlanta, but he expected me to be in Ellicott City. How would I explain I had gone back home? Unless . . .

I might not have to fib to James if I used Gloria's digital phone and steered the conversation carefully. I would have to choose each word with precision, but hearing his voice was worth a bit of fuss.

I retrieved the little phone from my purse and dialed his number.

"Huston."

"James, it's me, and before you ask, I am no longer at the Flour Mill Inn. I changed locations at my protector's request."

"I guess it's OK for you to be back in Ryde, if you are staying with Gloria."

"We've become inseparable. In fact, I'm using her telephone right now. Let me give you the number."

So far, so good. An ambiguity or two, perhaps, but no direct lies.

"I miss you," James said.

"And I you."

"It's a strange feeling for me. I haven't missed anyone in many years."

"I was about to say the same thing. When is your next trip to Washington, D.C.?"

"When would you like it to be?"

I giggled.

"You have a magnificent giggle," he said.

"I bet you say that to all the girls, which reminds me, I interviewed Angela Jennings the other day."

"Did you like her?"

"Immensely."

"Me too."

"Yes. I wondered about that. She calls you 'Jimmy.'"

"Lots of my friends do."

"Was Angela an *exceptionally* close friend?"

"My, my!" he drawled. "Now that is a question a gentleman cannot answer and a genuine lady will never ask."

"Put a sock in it, James. I have noticed that your Southern accent comes and goes."

"OK! Since you ask about Angela, I am forced to admit . . ."

"What?"

"We have been pals for years. Nothing more. Does that satisfy your curiosity?"

"Yes."

"Too bad. I like it when you are jealous."

"I am *not* jealous."

I heard a soft *beep*.

"Do you hear that?" I asked.

"Yep. The battery in your phone is almost dead. You have to hang up."

"Sorry."

"Don't be. We were about to have our first fight—about your jealous nature."

I laughed.

"Good night, James. I will call again soon." I rang off.

Gloria's voice surged through the earpiece I failed to remember I was wearing. "Holy moley! Talk about being underhanded and sneaky!"

"*Oh, my!* For one happy moment I forgot you were listening."

"I heard every dishonest word." She switched to her awful English accent. "I changed locations at my protector's request."

"I deceived James for a good cause."

"You really like the guy, don't you?"

"I suppose I do."

"Fabulous! Now get your mind back on business. There's a killer out there."

"Thank you for reminding me."

I looked at my watch. Only 10:18.

The minutes straggled by. I browsed through a fistful of junk mail (mostly brochures describing wondrous new computer programs that would surely improve my consulting capabilities) and read the current issue of *Newsweek* magazine (including the sports stories that I usually flip past).

I had run out of desktop reading materials other than my new Bible when Gloria's voice crackled in my ear. "We're approaching eleven o'clock. It's time to get ready for bed. Go for a hike around the first floor; act like you're checking the doors and windows."

I began with the living room windows. Both were wide open, but the lights inside made it difficult to see Magothy Street. Was the shooter out there looking at me? Maybe taking aim?

Get a grip, Hunnechurch.

"Oh boy!" I muttered through clenched teeth.

"What's wrong?" Gloria asked.

"Every sensible bone in my body wants me to keep away from my windows."

"Where are you?"

"At my living room window. The left one. Behind lots of glass and thin net curtains. No protection at all from bullets."

"Locking one window should be enough."

"Bless you."

"Don't act rattled. Move slowly when you back away from the window."

"No problem. My legs scarcely work."

I shuffled back to my desk, my heart thumping, feeling exposed and defenseless.

"What lights do you leave on all night?" Gloria asked.

"Only the coach light over the front door. I turn off everything else when I go up to bed."

"Good. Do the same tonight."

Once upstairs I went through the motions of getting ready for bed, hoping that my nervous jitters didn't show up on the shadows I projected on the blinds. I puttered around my bedroom, stepped into my closet, opened closed drawers, pulled back the bedclothes, and donned sweatpants and a loose-fitting sweatshirt that fit nicely over my bulletproof vest.

I could feel my adrenaline pumping as I crossed to the bathroom and brushed my teeth. Afterward I muttered to my reflection in the mirror. "When did headhunting become so perilous?"

Gloria's voice filled my ear, "The day you got involved with Marsha Morgan."

"Good work. Now I'm frightened *and* startled."

"Hey! If you really want to be scared, I'll go home."

"Don't say that, even in jest. I intend to spend the rest of the night curled up in your lap. What's next?"

"Get into bed and turn off the bedroom light."

I followed her instructions.

"I'm in my bed," I said to my microphone. "The light is off."

"OK. Join me in Field HQ. Knock first so I can douse the lights."

I left my bedroom and inched along the dark hallway, my hand against the wall, probing for the door to the other bedroom. I felt the molding and tapped.

Gloria pulled me inside and shut the door.

When the lights came back on, I saw her loading a shotgun—a side-by-side double, the kind the friendly old codger carries in a western movie.

"The perfect home self-defense weapon," she said. "Three ounces of buckshot is lethal at close range, but the pellets that miss won't travel through walls and wipe out your neighbors."

I heard a metallic click.

"Hold it for me," Gloria said, handing me the weapon.

"You want me to hold a *gun*?"

"Don't sweat it; I engaged the safety. I have to disconnect your radio transceiver. If there's any shooting, I'd rather the cops didn't find you decked out like a federal agent."

Gloria detached the radio from my vest and yanked the wire that ran up my back to the earpiece. I hefted the shotgun, surprised at its elegance—a killing machine decorated with ornate hand engravings and lovely wood inlays.

"Now we can take our positions downstairs," she said. "We should have several hours to wait before the shooter makes her move."

"Where downstairs?"

"I'll be in your kitchen doorway. She'll probably try to enter through the back door again, but there's a small chance she'll decide to use the front door. The kitchen doorway gives me an excellent view of both doors. We'll catch her with her gun in hand."

"What about me?"

"You'll be out of harm's way—on the floor in the living room."

"Bless you!"

Gloria switched off the lights.

"It seems dark," she said, "but the street lamps outside spill lots of illumination into the house. Your eyes will adjust in a couple of minutes."

We made our way downstairs and sat on the floor in the living room, our backs propped against my sofa, watching the two small TV monitors that Gloria had placed on my coffee table. One monitor connected to a night-vision camera that captured the patch of sidewalk between my Miata and my front door, the other to the camera that looked down at my garden. The images were dim, but I could make out my flowerbeds, my flowering cherry tree, my wee herb patch, and the high fence that enclosed my little estate.

"Believe it or not," I said, "I'm beginning to feel sleepy."

"Pinch yourself! I need you to help me stay alert. Start talking."

"About what?"

"Anything. Why not headhunting?"

"A grim subject," I said with a sigh. "Derek Wetherspoon seems adamant in his refusal to interview Angela Jennings. I don't know how to break the logjam."

"You don't strike me as the kind of person who takes no for an answer."

"Usually, I'm not, but Derek might be a lost cause. The rotter has the heart of a stone. He told me not to call him again. I need a way to capture his imagination and restore his faith in my capabilities."

We fell silent for a while.

"Let's keep talking," Gloria said.

"Your turn."

"I've been thinking about the shooter."

"Me too."

"No. I mean thinking *about* the shooter. She shot Missy on High Street, maybe poisoned Marsha during a party, came after you in your own home. She's nuts, but you have to admire her gall."

"The superstars are tough, committed women. They made it to the tops of demanding professions."

"True. But how many successful executives have you met who have the temperament to blow someone away at close range?"

"You raise a fascinating question." I abruptly felt wide awake. "Why don't we prepare a résumé for our shooter? We can invent an imaginary job description, then work backwards."

"Sure. We'll be all set to branch into a new business. Recruiting contract killers."

"I'm serious, Gloria. Let's flex our headhunter muscles. Perhaps we can figure out which of the superstars has set out to kill me."

"Why guess? We'll know for sure in a few hours."

"Maybe so," I said, "but you got me going. Now you have to play along with my weird ideas. Give me your impressions of the shooter."

"Well, she's cold, hard, and confident."

"Right! As you pointed out, a self-contained loner—someone who can work well independently."

"A solid strategic thinker . . ." Gloria said.

"With good planning skills."

"She reacts coolly under stress. Remember, she stopped, turned, and took a potshot at James Huston before she went over the fence."

"But she prefers to avoid risk whenever possible. She took the trouble of wearing a ski mask that night."

We were both on our haunches now, both caught up in the excitement of our game.

"I agree that she doesn't enjoy taking chances," Gloria said, "but she's unusually resourceful, willing to seize opportunities when they arise."

"Perhaps *too* willing. She often overreacts."

"In what way?"

"This whole sad business began with an overreaction that night on the *Chesapeake Belle*," I said. "She put Marsha into a diabetic stupor merely because she learned about my relationship with the Morgan Consultancy."

"Why be afraid of you?"

"Because she assumed that Marsha would tell me all about the superstars. Put yourself in her place. She imagined her most precious secret, a fact that could ruin her career, in the hands of a woman she doesn't know. She felt the risk was intolerable."

"Marsha never told anyone about the blue chips. Not even me."

"My point exactly. The killer overreacted, and then she followed suit with two more overreactions. She trashed Marsha's office to eradicate her notes, then shot Missy Morgan."

"Which has to mean that she's terrified of being exposed as a liar."

"Indeed! She must be both ambitious and fearful of a scandal—a fast-track executive with a career that would come to a screeching halt if her lies became public knowledge."

"Fearful, resourceful, opportunistic, independent, and leaps tall fences in a single bound. How many superstars fit that job description?"

"Only one."

"Who?" Gloria asked.

I told her.

"*Hmmm.* It makes sense, but like I said, you'll know for sure in a few hours."

Chapter Thirty-four

A CLINKING OF CROCKERY above my head woke me up.

"Rise and shine, Sleeping Beauty," Gloria whispered. "I nuked a cup of tea for you in the microwave."

"What happened?"

"You fell asleep at one-thirty."

"What time is it now?"

"A few minutes past three. Show time! A car drove by the house slowly. Twice."

I took several steaming sips, then peered out the window at Magothy Street. Nothing.

"She probably parked out of sight," Gloria said.

"Do you see anything on the surveillance monitors?"

"Yeah. I think a rabbit is chewing on your tarragon."

"A bunny! Can I look?"

That's when it happened. Still groggy, I set the mug of tea down too close to the edge of the cocktail table.

"Whoops!" Gloria shouted as hot tea splashed her ankles.

"Sorry!"

Without thinking, I flicked the light switch.

I squinted in the sudden brightness—my eyes capturing the tableau that anyone watching from outside my house would see through the window—the pair of us side by side in the living room, Gloria holding a shotgun.

"Well, that tears it!" Gloria said.

I doused the light, but the damage had been done. We heard the sound of running feet and the slam of a car door. Gloria raced down the hall and out the front door as an engine revved in the street. She came back a few seconds later, shaking her head.

"I didn't even manage to get a look at the car."

"What shall we do now?" I said to Gloria.

She shrugged. "Nothing, except catch a few *zees*."

═══════════

At 7:30, I cooked us a proper English breakfast: fried eggs, bacon, mushrooms, and buttered toast. Gloria served up our table talk.

"What we have here is a weird kind of Mexican stand-off," she said. "The lady is too cautious to attack you during the day, and she knows she can't jump you at night because I'm here. She also assumes that you won't tell the cops everything you know."

"Why won't I talk to the police?"

"Because you sent her a blue folder, which obviously means you plan to blackmail the superstars." Gloria chewed on a strip of bacon. "Why else would you keep your mouth shut after she took a potshot at the man standing in your back door? And why else would you invite her to an obviously staged tea party?"

"I see your point."

"She's worried about you, but not frantic. She figures she can afford to take her time."

"Your capacity for devious thought leaves me breathless."

"Yeah? Well, you make great fried eggs. What's your secret?"

"Gobs of real butter." I slid another egg on her plate. "So, what do we do now?"

"You still have alternatives one, two, and three."

"I won't run away, I refuse to destroy the innocent superstars, and Reilly would make me eat humble pie by the shovelful—assuming he doesn't flay me alive."

"Since you feel that way, we do nothing. Let's wait and see what the enemy decides to do."

My *if-all-else-fails* solution for improving a foul disposition is a top-down, pedal-to-the-metal drive along Romney Boulevard, a curvy two-lane road that the police never seem to patrol. I can wind up my Miata's engine and pretend to be Sterling Moss whipping a vintage Aston Martin through the alleys of Monte Carlo.

That Friday morning, my attempt at mood engineering didn't work. The sensation of speed gave me no pleasure, the hot sun felt unpleasant on my neck, and my bulletproof vest (which I wore at Gloria's insistence) seemed an instrument of torture. I pulled into a gas station and discovered, with a few pokes and prods, that I had twisted the straps while donning the garment. I would need to take off my blouse to sort things out.

Bother!

In the Ladies Room I recalled that my blouse was the very same garment I wore when James Huston had kissed me. The thought made me tremble. I wanted to hear his voice again, so I raced back to my car and fired up Gloria's digital phone.

"Angela Jennings called me bright and early this morning," he said after we exchanged hellos. "She's anxious to meet your English client."

"Regrettably, he hasn't agreed to see her yet."

"Oh, oh."

"Oh, oh, indeed! Derek Wetherspoon is being an annoying prat. He remains furious about Linda Preston."

An old heating oil truck rattled past the gas station.

"What's all the noise I hear?"

"An ancient diesel engine. I'm sitting in a gas station in my Miata, with the top down."

Oops! I realized my mistake too late.

"In your flashy Miata," he said. "Not my dull rental car."

"Well . . ."

"Does that mean the police nabbed the killer?"

"Not quite."

"Where is Gloria?"

I waffled. "Somewhere out of sight."

"Why did you leave Ellicott City?"

"We talked about that last night."

"Tell me again."

I hesitated an instant too long before I said, "Gloria and I decided that I should move back to Ryde."

"Move back?" His tone had become inquisitorial. "Does that mean you are living at your home, and not in Gloria's apartment?"

I tried to shift our conversation to safer ground. "Fear not, Gloria Spitz is staying at Hunnechurch Manor with me."

"The shooter got around her last time."

"We have taken better precautions this time. Let's leave it at that."

"OK, let's. You still haven't answered my first question. Why did you leave Ellicott City? What's behind the decision that you and Gloria made?"

"If you must know," I said brightly, "I missed my garden and my own bed. Being a refugee goes against my grain."

We chatted for several minutes more, but the warmth had left our conversation. We both knew that I was lying. James made a feeble excuse about a meeting he had to attend and rang off first.

I pulled the Miata's convertible top up and over and wondered how I had managed to accumulate my absurd collection of problems: the first man I cared about in seven years was angry with me, not to mention my best friend (who had walked away in a snit); my business would soon be a memory, along with my office and the little house I loved; I was about to disappoint a candidate who trusted me; and, the frosting on the cupcake of my life, I had agreed to "wait and see" if a murderer would decide to attack me again.

"Quite a list," I murmured, "and not a bloody solution in sight." I started the engine and pointed the Miata home. I drove on instinct, pondering my troubles, not thinking much about the buildings on the other end of Romney Road in downtown Ryde—until I found myself in front of the Ryde Fellowship Church.

I began to giggle. I pushed the Miata's top back down.

"OK, Lord. I appreciate your sense of humor. I agree that I'm being foolish to pretend I can go it alone any longer. I have run out of ways to deal with the various problems in my life. If you have any suggestions, I will certainly be grateful for them."

Not the most worshipful prayer, I admit, but it did the job.

━━━━━━━

There are those who will insist that what happened next was a simple coincidence, but as I drove along Ryde High Street, the traffic light in front of the Bay View Building turned red, giving me a perfect opportunity to read the gaudy sign that John Tyler's company had recently erected:

Opening in August
THE NEW HEADQUARTERS OF EUROKIT USA!
Eurokit: The Good Work Behind the Goodies

The Good Work Behind the Goodies.

A trite marketing slogan to be sure, but it set me to thinking: Why hadn't I told Derek about the good work I had done on his behalf? Why had I allowed myself to be shoved aside so easily? Why hadn't I done a proper job of fighting back when Derek fired me?

The Good Work Behind the Goodies.

Then I had an idea. I saw a way to get Derek's attention, with exactly the sort of absurd gesture that might knock a stodgy Englishman off dead center.

Could I do it? I looked at my watch. Yes—if I hurried. I tromped on the accelerator.

At the corner of Magothy Street and Arundel Lane stands the Ryde Food Mart, a neighborhood store not unlike the small "green grocers" that served Chichester when I was a girl. I parked out front and placed a call to England on the digital phone.

Chloe was bewildered by my request, so much so, that I had to repeat myself.

"It's quite simple," I explained. "I need your best trifle recipe. The one you make for the family at Christmas."

"I thought your naughty weekend begins today. With James."

"Bother James! I have had a sudden urge."

"For a trifle?"

"Indeed."

"Have you gone completely bonkers?"

"I am supremely sane, Chloe, and if you don't tell me how to make a classic Hunnechurch trifle within the next ten seconds, I will call Felicity Nelson, your culinary archrival in Chichester, and announce that I prefer her trifle to yours. I will then ask her for her recipe."

"You wouldn't dare!"

"One—two—three—four—five—six . . ."

She huffed and sniffed, then said: "One does not *make* a trifle, Pippa. One *assembles* it with respect and exaltation, in a large, elegant glass bowl—preferably an antique. Do you own a suitable glass bowl?"

"I promise I will purchase an appropriate vessel as soon as I ring off."

"In that event I suppose you do have a right to *some* of the Hunnechurch family secrets."

━━━━━━━━

I "assembled" my trifle in an oversized glass mixing bowl—the inelegant sort that comes with a blue plastic lid. For my purposes, portability was more important than beauty. Chloe's recipe turned out to be surprisingly simple:

Step 1. Line the glass bowl with three layers of one-inch-square "sandwiches" made of sponge cake and raspberry jam. (Two

one-pound cakes and an eight-ounce jar of jam make a trifle that serves eight people.) Sprinkle crushed macaroons
and slivered almonds between the layers. Add bits of candied fruit for color.

Step 2. Make a custard in a heavy saucepan. Start with four egg
yolks and two egg whites, beaten together. In another
saucepan, heat one pint of milk and one quarter cup of
sugar to boiling point. Trickle the hot milk into the beaten
eggs, stirring constantly over low heat until the mixture
thickens. Do not let the mixture overheat, or you will make
scrambled eggs. Pour the thickened custard into a clean
bowl. Add one teaspoon of pure vanilla extract.

Step 3. Moisten the sponge cake "sandwiches" with raspberry syrup
and four tablespoons of dessert sherry.

Step 4. Pour the still-warm custard over the sponge cake sandwiches, then place the bowl in the fridge to cool.

Step 5. Top the trifle with freshly whipped cream (eight ounces
of heavy whipping cream will suffice), sweetened with a
tablespoon of sugar and flavored with 1/8 teaspoon vanilla
extract.

Step 6. Decorate with almond slivers, nuts, and bits of candied fruit.

Perfection!

I was spooning the last of the whipped cream atop the trifle when
Gloria trotted into the kitchen.

"What's that?"

"A peerless English trifle. For Derek Wetherspoon." I described its
ingredients.

"Wow! You'll get his attention, all right. He'll have a massive heart
attack after his second mouthful."

"Stuff and nonsense. Generations of Brits have aged gracefully on
diets of fatty roast beef and trifle."

"So, what's your plan?"

"I will present my creation to him with a few well-chosen words designed to break through his sales resistance."

"What if he has you tossed out of his building?"

"Not a problem. Derek isn't in his office. On Friday afternoons the blighter goes to sea."

Chapter Thirty-five

Viewed from the air, Ryde Marina resembles a giant hand protruding into the Magothy River. Its five "fingers" are long docks, each accommodating a hundred sailboats. Derek Wetherspoon's *Victoria* was among them. But where, I didn't know.

I drove hither and yon through the boatyard in the marina's onshore "palm," hoping to find a directory. The serpentine pathways led me past an armada of unlaunched sailing yachts sitting in cradles close to the water—perhaps fifty beached sailboats. I wondered why so many owners left their expensive craft ashore in full summer?

On my third orbit of the marina, I crossed paths with a yardman driving a golf cart. He told me to follow the signs for C Dock and assured me that *Victoria* was still in her slip.

C Dock jutted a good quarter of a mile out into the Magothy. *Victoria*'s slip was near the tip. I tramped along the wooden planking, the trifle in my arms, Angela Jenning's paperwork in the all-purpose leather handbag that hung from my right shoulder. My clothing earned curious glances from the other boat owners on C Dock. I had changed into a dressy off-white silk business frock that looked out of place at the marina and which definitely clashed with the pair of old tennis shoes I wore (their white rubber soles would leave no marks on a fiberglass yacht). I ignored the onlookers, serene in the knowledge that I was fully prepared to do battle with Derek Wetherspoon.

Victoria, of course, was the racing sloop I'd seen in the photograph on his desk. A "StarFish 41," according to the maker's logo painted on her side, probably worth three times as much as my little house on Magothy Street. She had a white topside, a midnight blue hull, and lovely teak and bronze accents. I gazed at her with unabashed envy.

"Ahoy on board *Victoria!*" I called.

I heard shuffling inside the boat, then Derek's head popped through an open hatch in the forepeak. His smile evaporated when he saw me.

"What do *you* want?" he said.

"I've brought you a gift." I held the trifle bowl aloft.

He disappeared and then reemerged on the companionway steps, in the cockpit. "What manner of gift? And why?"

"All will be clear in a moment. May I come aboard?"

He looked at my feet. "You seem to be wearing proper shoes. All right, come aboard."

I handed the trifle to Derek and scrambled over *Victoria's* lifelines.

He hefted the bowl. "You brought me something to eat?"

"Be patient, Derek. We first have to talk about a new candidate for the post of Eurokit's chief counsel."

"There's nothing to talk about. I fired you the other day."

"Actually, you *didn't* fire me. You insulted me. You belittled my abilities. You waved Nailor & McHale in my face, but you never got around to firing me."

His lips attempted a smile. "Consider yourself actually fired. Have I made myself clear?"

"You are being foolish, old chap."

"Not at all. I'm being sensible. I won't permit you to waste any more of my time."

"You're right! Time is of the essence. Nailor & McHale may consume *weeks* of valuable time to locate a suitable candidate, but I have here in my hand the résumé of a superb attorney with all the proper credentials. You can interview her on Monday morning. It's foolish to penalize Eurokit because you're mad at Linda Preston and at me."

Derek drummed his fingers on the cabin top. "I won't deny that I find a certain perverse logic in your argument."

I dug the paperwork out of my handbag and thrust it at him. "Her name is Angela Jennings. She has had broad experience dealing with senior people in Washington whose activities will shape the destiny of Eurokit USA."

My language may have been a touch florid, but I was determined to prod Wetherspoon into action.

He opened the folder and began to read. I interjected occasional comments.

"Angela is well-educated. First in her class at Georgetown Law Center. An editor of the *Law Review,* of course."

Silence.

"She has a powerful personality and can hold her own in any debate."

Again, silence.

"Angela is a Washington insider. She knows all the movers and shakers at Commerce, the people who make the vital day-to-day decisions. And like Linda Preston, she has a good working relationship with Kathleen Isley."

Derek closed the folder. I hoped he would ask me a question about Angela, but he didn't. Instead, he picked up the glass bowl again.

"What's inside?" he said.

"A top-notch English trifle."

"A trifle? Why on earth would you bring me a trifle?"

"Because your unpleasant remarks the other day demonstrate that you have forgotten the depth and complexity of a well-made trifle. The dessert you are holding is much more than a mere concoction of sugar and foam. An English trifle is classic stick-to-your-hips food. Yes, it tastes scrummy, but there is nothing frothy or insubstantial about it." I thumped the blue plastic lid. "This blighter demonstrates a lot of 'good work behind the goodies'—*my* good work. I am committed to achieving goodness in everything I do, whether it's assembling a trifle or recruiting a superb chief counsel for Eurokit USA."

Wetherspoon started to laugh. I laughed, too, relieved at his sudden change in mood. Emboldened, I added, "What do you say, Derek? Will you interview Angela Jennings?"

He gazed at the water while I held my breath. At last he said, "I'll make a deal with you. Come sailing with me today, and I'll meet your candidate."

"Sailing? Now?"

"My usual first mate let me down. *Victoria* is too large a boat to single-hand. We'll cruise the Chesapeake Bay, eat some trifle, and work at becoming friends again."

I didn't hesitate. "Done! Although I should warn you that my sailing experience is limited to small dinghies and day sailors."

"Small boats are best for learning to sail."

"I should call my secretary before we shove off. When do you think we'll be back?"

"No later than six-thirty."

Derek prepared the boat to depart. I retrieved the digital phone from my handbag, toted it to *Victoria's* bow, extended the antenna, and called Gloria.

"A boat ride!" she squealed.

"In exchange for an interview."

The line went quiet. "I'm torn," she said after a moment. "An afternoon jaunt with Derek Wetherspoon is great for business but bad for security."

"How so? The shooter would need a pirate ship to attack a racing yacht out for a day sail on the Bay."

"Yeah, but what happens when it's over?"

"Nothing much. We'll be docked by six-thirty. I should be home before seven o'clock—long before it's dark. Please, Mommy, can I go?"

She giggled. "Yes, Pippa dear. Have fun. Your long-suffering bodyguard will meet you at the marina to escort you home. See you at six-thirty."

Wetherspoon started *Victoria's* engine. I helped him untie the dock lines, then I pushed against the pilings as he maneuvered the big boat out of the slip and into the Magothy. Scampering around the deck was energetic work; my bulletproof vest began to chafe. I would have to take it off.

"Where's the *loo*?" I asked.

"The lavatory aboard a yacht is called the *head*. You will find one beyond the main salon, on the starboard side."

I climbed down the companionway steps into a triumph of elegant woodworking. The salon had a floor planked with teak and holly, walls and built-in furniture made of light mahogany, and an overhead paneled in a blonde wood I didn't recognize.

Victoria's "head" was a cramped mini-bathroom—toilet, sink, and tiny shower stall—that provided barely enough room to wiggle out of my dress, undo my body armor, and wriggle back in. Now I had another problem. Where was I to hide the vest? The last thing I needed today was for Derek to learn that I feared being shot at, but the niches and cubbyholes in the head were too small. I scanned the salon for a place to stow the garment out of sight and decided to stuff it behind a cushion on the sofa.

"Grab the wheel," Derek ordered when I returned to the cockpit.

"Are you sure?"

"I've never met a Brit who couldn't handle a sailboat. It's in our genes." He pointed to a green buoy ahead in the river. "Keep that mark to starboard. I'll prepare the sails."

Calling *Victoria* a sailboat was like labeling a cheetah a cat—a technically correct but wholly inadequate description. My nervous hands took control of a high-performance racing machine with a steering wheel that measured four-feet in diameter and enough lines and pulleys to outfit a fleet of dinghies. To my great relief she steered as easily as my Miata. I aimed for the buoy, then turned the wheel a smidgen to the left, so that the bobbing green can would pass to our right.

I began to relax when I realized that *Victoria* would obey my slightest twitch. I pushed the throttle forward; the diesel engine chugged a few revs faster. The digital speedometer reported our speed as six knots.

It felt wonderful to be out on the water—away from land, away from business, away from the shooter.

"Helmsman!" Derek ordered. "Point her into the wind."

I held the wheel steady as Wetherspoon, standing alongside the mast, raised the mainsail.

"Halyard secure!" he called. "Fall off to starboard."

I nudged the wheel. *Victoria's* bow moved right. The mainsail caught the wind, and the deck heeled under my feet.

"Wow!" I murmured as I braced myself against the wheel.

"Hold your course!" Derek cut the engine, then yanked the jib sheets to unfurl *Victoria's* genoa jib—the large triangular sail in front of the mainsail.

Thwap! The wind filled the jib, *Victoria* heeled further to the right, and the speedometer jumped to seven-and-a-half knots. Derek continued to bark instructions. He might be a ladies' man ashore, but at sea he was a no-nonsense captain. I *ayed-ayed* crisply, corrected our course as ordered, and enjoyed the wind blowing in my face.

Out of the Magothy we flew, then south under the parallel spans of the Chesapeake Bay Bridge, and close by the U.S. Navy's old radio towers at Annapolis. The water rushing past *Victoria's* hull made a swooshing sound as she overtook other sailboats. We seemed to be the fastest yacht on the bay.

"What say I dish out some trifle?" Derek asked.

"A grand idea. But who steers while we eat?"

"The autopilot, of course." He pushed a button. I heard a motor whine, and the big steering wheel took on a life of its own.

Derek disappeared in the salon. He soon emerged carrying two blue china bowls emblazoned with *Victoria* appliqués, each containing what must have been a pound of trifle. We wolfed down huge spoonfuls while we chatted about our childhoods in England and our mutual plans to visit Chichester the following Christmas.

We devoured the last crumbs as *Victoria* steered herself past Thomas Point light, an eight-sided lighthouse atop a squat pile of rocks. Neither of us was paying attention to the time—or the weather. The wind had piped up and was now blowing out of the northwest.

"It's gone four o'clock," Derek said. "Time to turn for home."

We had soared down the bay. Now *Victoria* had to claw her way back to the Magothy River against strong winds and an opposing current. She bounced and shivered in the strong chop; her rigging groaned as powerful gusts caught the sails. The sailing was great fun, but *Victoria* was making less than five knots "over the ground." No way could we reach Ryde Marina by six-thirty.

I made several attempts to call Gloria, but my little personal phone didn't have the range to reach shore. It was seven o'clock—at the mouth of the Magothy River—when I finally saw the signal indicator appear. I punched in the number of Gloria's digital phone. A mechanical voice answered, "The telephone you have dialed is either unavailable or out of the calling area."

Blast.

The sun was vanishing behind the taller trees when Derek backed *Victoria* into her slip. I was surprised not to see Gloria waiting on the pier.

"When you find your friend," Derek said as we walked to the parking area near C Dock, "place all the blame on me for being late."

"Nonsense. I was steering the boat and having a fine old time of it."

"Well, I'm sure she will understand that all sailors are at the mercy of the wind and tides—even strong-willed headhunters."

"Indeed," I murmured. Derek plainly expected me to laugh at his amiable barb, but I couldn't. My surprise at Gloria's absence had turned to concern.

"You seem worried?"

"I am—a bit."

"Did you tell her to meet us at C Dock?"

"No."

"Ah, then I'll wager she went to A Dock. Visitors congregate there because it's the closest to the marina office."

"Yes, I'm sure that is it," I said, anxious to send Derek on his way, but I doubted that Gloria would have any more difficulty than I did navigating around the Ryde Marina.

Where is she?

Derek, trifle in arms, climbed into a lovely Jaguar sedan. Its metallic burgundy paint seemed to glow in the waning daylight.

"Goodnight, Pippa," he said. "Thank you for my gift. If I recall, a well-made trifle tastes even better after aging overnight in the refrigerator." He pulled shut his door, then opened his window. "Oh, if Miss Jennings is available on Monday morning, so am I."

Had I not been worrying about Gloria, I might have realized that three of my problems would soon be solved, but all I could think about were superstars with guns.

I started the Miata and drove to A Dock. No sign of Gloria or her pickup truck. The wall-mounted floodlights that illuminated the marina's buildings began to switch on. I turned on my headlights and circled the boatyard, checking the other docks and their parking areas. No vehicles. No people.

The evening air felt cool. I decided to raise the folding top, and then I remembered: My bulletproof vest was still aboard *Victoria*. Maybe Derek hadn't locked the companionway hatch?

Should I go back or head for home?

In for a penny, in for a pound, I thought. I wheeled my car around and drove back to C Dock. Along the way I passed a green Volvo station wagon that someone had double-parked next to a dumpster. I didn't think anything of it.

Big mistake.

Chapter Thirty-six

THE BANG OF THE GUNSHOT startled me less than the sound of the bullet bouncing off the cabin of the boat next to me. It was a coarse thunk—imagine a wounded kettledrum.

My mind processed the overlapping noises. *Susan McKenzie is at the Ryde Marina. She's shooting at me.*

"Give the dumb lady a cigar!" I muttered to myself. "You already knew that Susan drives a big, green Volvo, and the other night you figured that only Susan McKenzie completely fit the shooter's job description."

Harriet Beardsley and Roxanne Landesberg were both wealthy women. Harriet was a wildly successful back-room financial wizard, and Roxanne owned a successful consultancy. Neither would suffer much from a credentials' scandal.

Kathleen and Susan, on the other hand, both relied on their paychecks. Their careers would be dog food if their "harmless exaggerations" became public knowledge. Both women tended to overreaction, but Kathleen was a negotiator by nature, not an eliminator, and no way would her gammy leg let her jump fences.

That left Susan McKenzie, the fast-spending, risk-averse, ex-track star who made her bones as a company hatchet woman and who wouldn't let a scandal ruin her climb up the Militet corporate ladder.

I was on C Dock, about 150 feet from shore. I dropped down and pressed myself flat against the rough wooden planks.

A second shot. A second thunk.

Don't lie still. Keep moving.

I crawled forward, my heart thumping, my silk dress catching on splinters.

A third shot. This time the bullet hit something metallic, a mast or an anchor.

I risked raising my head and looked around. I didn't see Susan on the dock. She must be on land, standing in the shadows, unhurriedly aiming her pistol.

I made a superb target—a figure in white against a dark brown dock, bathed in the light from stanchion-mounted lamps that ran along its edge. Even at long range with a handgun, she was bound to hit me. Out here I'd be vulnerable even if I had my bulletproof vest. I needed to get ashore and find someplace to hide.

I slithered toward the boat on my right, a small sloop with low coamings. I counted to three, stood up, and leapt into the cockpit.

Another bang. The bullet hissed by, close enough for me to hear it. A puff of fiberglass dust erupted three feet from my head.

I crouched down. My personal phone was in my leather handbag. Maybe I could call for help?

Maybe not. I saw a circle of light dancing on the shore-end of C Dock. Susan had a flashlight. The circle began to move forward. She was coming out on the dock. If I stopped to fiddle with the phone, she'd have me cold.

"Susan!" I shouted. "Put the gun away and get out of here. Leave Ryde. Leave Maryland. You won't accomplish anything by shooting me. I don't intend to talk to the police. The fact is—I haven't told them anything so far."

My answer came as another bang.

For a bizarre instant I found myself smiling. *This was supposed to happen.* Susan had taken the bait—hook, line, and sinker. My blue-folder taunts had worked.

Too bad, old chap, but the hunted has turned the tables on the hunters. You should have paid more attention to the lessons Gloria Spitz tried to teach you.

Gloria! I thought about her again. Where was Gloria? Was she lying shot somewhere? Or dead? Was I all alone?

All alone! The terrifying notion sent an avalanche of ice roaring through my innards.

I murmured, "Oh God, don't let me be all alone. I need your help."

What had Gloria said after the tea party? "You aren't alone, because God cares for you."

"Oh Lord, I want that to be true. You took on some of my simpler problems, but nothing counts if Susan kills me. I need a miracle tonight."

Another bang—immediately followed by a sploosh of sticky wetness. *Varnish!* Susan's latest bullet had cleaved a can of varnish tied to the cabin top. Some of it had splattered on me.

The fury I felt gave me a new impetus to survive. I yanked off my shoes and quickly tied the laces around my handbag strap. I slung the strap over my head to free my arms and eased myself over the stern of the boat and into the Magothy. I sidestroked as quietly as I could through the tepid water, first away from the dock, then in a gentle turn toward shore, about fifty yards away.

By now Susan had started to walk the dock, checking every boat. I could see the beam from her flashlight light up sail covers and rain hoods and cockpits. She didn't seem interested in the river.

I came ashore between B and C Docks, clambering up the steel ladder rungs embedded in the bulkhead of railroad ties that stabilized the shoreline. Perhaps two hundred feet of open ground stood between me and my Miata. I put my shoes on, water squishing between my toes, and began to run.

The boatyard was paved with gravel. Susan heard my footfalls, turned, and began an easy long-legged lope toward me. I realized that I should have waited longer before I moved, should have let her walk farther out on C Dock. At her pace she would reach my car a few seconds after I did. I wouldn't have enough time to start the engine and take off before she started shooting.

I had to find some cover. I looked around the marina and saw the rows of cradled sailboats. I ran like the dickens.

Bang. I don't know what the bullet hit. I didn't care as long as it wasn't me. I heard Susan stop running. No need to turn and see why. She was reloading her pistol after the sixth shot.

I crouched beneath a keel. Solid iron, several inches thick, impenetrable by bullets, but also as dark as a coal mine. I lost my bearings and smacked my head against the cradle's steel framework. Susan heard me gasp and took another shot.

I held my hand firmly against my temple, willing myself not to give in to the pain. *Get out of sight! Quick!* But where? I struggled to my feet and looked around.

Ten feet away was a bulky sloop in a tall cradle with a ladder leaning against its stern rail. I climbed the ladder, dove headfirst into the cockpit, and scraped my arm against a plastic box attached to the inner coaming.

The box opened. A plastic flare gun and three flare cartridges spilled out. *A weapon.* Praise God!

I decided one flare for me, two for Susan.

The flare gun was easy to work. Swing the barrel down, insert a cartridge, swing the barrel shut, cock the hammer.

I held the gun above my head and pulled the trigger.

Woomp. A garish red glow bathed the boatyard as the flare climbed into the sky. I saw Susan about twenty feet away next to a large motor sailor. Of course, she also saw me.

I reloaded the gun, aimed at Susan, and fired. *Too high.* The flare whizzed harmlessly over her head into the Magothy River, but it spoiled the shot she took. Her bullet tore through the spray hood, well above me.

I loaded the third cartridge and aimed lower. The burning flare ricocheted off Susan's hip without slowing her down.

Now what?

I bobbed down as she shot again. I heard the bullet slam against the outside of the hull. Had it penetrated the thick fiberglass, it would have hit my head.

Don't just lie here, Pippa! Think of something!

I needed another weapon. A boat hook. A winch handle. *Anything.*

The pepper spray! I had Gloria's can of pepper spray in my handbag. I undid the clasp and felt inside for the small cylinder. My fingers touched something else alongside the little can—something small and made of metal.

The cross James lent me—the cross that had helped three generations of Hustons make it through combat in one piece. "Seek what's behind the symbol," James had said. "You'll find the stuff that miracles are made of."

Lord, I could really use a miracle about now.

I could hear Susan climbing the same ladder I had climbed moments earlier. I made sure my can of pepper spray was aimed away from me. I pointed the nozzle at the stern rail, waited until I saw hands on the ladder's top rung, and then pressed down with my thumb.

Susan screamed. I heard her feet scrabbling down the ladder. I stood up—into a fine mist of pepper-spray residue hanging in the air.

It was as if I had poked my head into a blast furnace. Molten steel stung my cheeks, my eyes, and my lips. I hiked up the front of my soggy dress to wipe my face. The fire went out.

I heard Susan cursing me. No surprise, that! I knew what a wisp of mist could do. The solid stream of pepper spray splashing on her hands and arms must have felt like liquid fire. Surely some also hit her face.

Time to go. But how? I wasn't about to use the ladder and drop into Susan's lap.

I stood on the cabin top and looked for another way off the boat. There was only one other way: move to the next boat. It was cradled about four feet away. I climbed over the white wire lifelines and leapt for my life. For an instant, I felt as if I were flying. I landed in the cockpit with a heavy thud, amazed that I hadn't broken anything. "Thank you, God," I whispered.

I moved sideways through the boatyard from yacht to yacht. The fifth boat I reached had a swim ladder on its stern. I climbed down to within four feet of the ground and jumped.

I hit the gravel hard but remained in one piece. When I looked up, I saw that Susan was already on her feet. *Blast!* I must not have hit her hands dead center with the capsaicin. She saw me and began to move forward, gun raised, her flashlight illuminating the patch of ground ahead of her feet.

The Magothy River was only a few feet beyond the cradled boats. I decided to get into the water again. Susan could never find me under the docks. I moved along the outside of the row of boats, squeezing close to the cradles, trying to stay hidden in the shadows of the hulls. I heard Susan walking in the aisle between the boats. One confident step at a time.

I bumped into a solid bar that blocked my path.

Not a bar. A mast. For the sailboat closest to the river. The mast was a hollow aluminum pole, eight-inches across. It seemed to stretch forever, although I knew it must be about forty feet long. The pole lay on its side atop three old oil drums—one in the middle and one on each end. It was aligned parallel to the shoreline, almost like a rail fence.

I ducked under the mast and dropped to the ground behind the middle drum. I listened carefully for Susan's steps on the crunchy gravel, but all I could hear was water lapping gently against the stacked rocks that protected the marina's shoreline from erosion.

Where did Susan go?

I heard a gentle thump high above my head. Susan had climbed back up on the row of boats. *Why?* Then I understood. Susan knew that height would give her a better shot at me.

Her flashlight suddenly lit up the ground beneath the mast. She was standing on the boat next to me. She moved the beam back and forth, exploring the darkness, searching for me.

If I could distract Susan for a moment, I'd have time to escape into the Magothy. I picked up a fistful of gravel and hurled it over the mast. A few stone chips splashed into the water; most clattered along the ground.

Susan wasn't fooled. She pointed the flashlight at the mast and slowly followed its shiny surface. I didn't know if she could see me behind the oil drum, but I decided not to find out. I took a deep breath and prepared to dive.

Now, Pippa. Do it now.

My feet slipped on gravel as I stood up. Instead of diving into the river, I came down hard on my knees. I ducked again behind the oil drum, but I knew that Susan had seen me.

Bang. The bullet thwacked against the oil drum, but it didn't penetrate two layers of steel. What had Reilly said? "A thirty-two doesn't have much punch."

Susan would have to come down from her perch to reach me. Maybe I would have another chance to get to the river. I had asked for a miracle; maybe this was it.

I peeked around the oil drum. Susan's silhouette was easy to see in the bits of light reflected back from her flashlight beam. I decided to make my move at the instant she hit the ground. I prayed that the jolt would upset her aim.

Susan stood at the edge of the sailboat's stern and leapt down on the mast. Her leap was gracefully athletic—the kind of leap a ballet dancer might make. However, when her feet hit the mast, the aluminum pipe rolled on the oil drums. Susan was propelled forward. She fired her gun as she tumbled head over heels into the sharp rocks that abutted the shoreline.

I ran to the bulkhead and stared at the fading circle of light as Susan's flashlight sank to the bottom of the Magothy River. It was fearfully dark and deathly quiet.

No call for help.

No thrashing in the murky water.

Not even the sounds of bubbles breaking the surface.

I knew that Susan was dead.

"God rest her soul."

Chapter Thirty-seven

WHEN THE COPPERS TELL THIS STORY, they start with the death of Marsha Morgan—how she fell off the *Chesapeake Belle* and drowned in the Miles River. Of course, Detective Stephen Reilly and his colleagues know only part of what really happened. Gloria Spitz and I know the rest, but we aren't telling.

About Gloria . . .

While I was dodging bullets at Ryde Marina, she was repelling a barrage of questions from Reilly and three more plainclothes policemen.

It seems that at 7:15, a few minutes before *Victoria* docked, a woman with a thick English accent dialed 911 and reported "a suspicious looking pickup truck parked near C Dock." The coppers investigated, found Gloria cuddling a loaded shotgun, and removed her to the Ryde Police Station for questioning, seriously suspecting that she might be the shooter.

Thus did Susan McKenzie clear the decks (literally!) in preparation for attacking me.

By the time Gloria sorted things out (*without* revealing anything about the four superstars), Susan was dead.

James Huston flew up from Atlanta on Saturday morning to help me fend off a horde of reporters, provide moral support, and (as he drawled it) "Serve you some *mahty* fine home cooking prepared by a good ole southern boy."

I told him most of the story as we barbecued two racks of ribs in my garden. He tended the grill while I applied a fiendishly delicious barbecue sauce first concocted by his *grandpappy*.

"You must be balmy," James said. "Irretrievably nuts! Had I known what you planned to do, I would have dragged you down to Atlanta, but since you managed to stay alive, I have a question. What ever happened to my rented Ford?"

"Oh my goodness! It's still parked behind Gloria's house."

As to James . . . His seminar program in Washington, D.C. is growing nicely. He expects to make frequent trips north, which will give us ample opportunities to explore our relationship. Enough said for the present.

James' gold cross . . . is safely back in his wallet. However, James (bless his heart!) had a jeweler in Atlanta make me an exact duplicate, which I keep tucked inside my purse at all times. A headhunter never knows when she may be back in combat.

As to my bulletproof vest . . . A messenger brought it to my doorstep a week later in a discreet brown-paper parcel. The handwritten note inside said:

> *I was amazed to find this exotic item of apparel in Victoria's salon. In truth, I am surprised you need a bulletproof vest. I assumed that your hide is as stubborn as your personality and that bullets will naturally bounce off.*
>
> *Regards, Derek*

Detective Reilly and Corporal Miller invited me to the Ryde Police Station for a full day "review of the facts." Reilly played the role of irate investigator while Miller watched, but I could tell that his heart wasn't in his interrogation of me.

How could it be? The obvious villain was dead. Susan's snub-nose thirty-two (which was recovered along with her waterlogged body from the muck at the bottom of the Magothy River) proved to be the revolver that killed Missy Morgan and fired the potshot at James Huston.

What seemed to bother Reilly most was the lack of an obvious motive. He kept asking me, "Why would Susan McKenzie put Marsha Morgan into a diabetic coma, loot her office, shoot Missy Morgan, and then try to kill you—twice?"

I kept answering, "I don't know. She didn't take the time to explain herself when she was shooting at me."

We went around and around like this for much of the afternoon, then Reilly surprised me by voicing the dotty theory he had invented to explain the events.

"The way I figure it," he said, "headhunters are in a wonderful position to gather dirt on successful executives. You know, the shady deals they've managed—antitrust violations they've ordered—insider trading they've done. I believe that Marsha and Missy had a nice blackmail scheme going—until one of their victims decided to fight back. They got killed and you got caught in the backwash."

What else could I do except nod at the silly clod. "I suppose your hypothesis makes sense, although I hope you don't assume that I am a blackmailer."

"Get out of here, Hunnechurch. I don't expect to see you again."

However, Reilly has seen me again. Often. He was appointed the police department's liaison to the Ryde Business Community. He never misses a monthly meeting of the Ryde Chamber of Commerce, and neither do I.

═══════════

About the Ryde Chamber of Commerce . . . At my suggestion, the Chamber endowed the Marsha Morgan Scholarship, a stipend ear-marked for worthy young women in Ryde who wish to become human resource professionals. John Tyler oversees the program—by himself. His zeal to "work closely" with me evaporated when I introduced him to James Huston.

I plan to continue as the Chamber's social chairperson. Who knows, I might even run for president in a year or two. That would provide even more lovely opportunities for "one of Maryland's leading executive recruiters" (as my new sales brochure proclaims!) to network among the Ryde business community.

═══════════

Hunnechurch & Associates has taken its first small steps to fiscal re-covery. As I predicted, Derek Wetherspoon positively swooned when he met with Angela Jennings.

"Angie is much more appropriate than that overzealous mother from Atlanta you almost foisted on me," he said. "And as you rightly claimed, we will save a pretty penny on her relocation expenses."

Equally important, Simpson Manufacturing Company hired my clever accountant after all. "It happened like the ending of a short story by O'Henry," Connie Hillman called to explain. "The hiring freeze con-vinced ten of our key employees that Simpson was on hard times. They quit and took jobs at other local companies. So you and I are back in the recruiting business."

My fee check is on the way, and not a moment too soon.

═══════════

Derek hinted at a new assignment during the lunch I bought for him the other day.

"I shouldn't speak out of school," he said, "but I am growing weary of Nailor & McHale's seeming inability to find me a Hispanic director of business development who has ten years of marketing experience, an MBA from a leading school, and undergraduate training as a chef."

Derek added, "In such a vast country as the United States, one would expect to be hip deep in suitable candidates."

Poor Nailor & McHale, I thought. But I said, "Oh yes, I agree. There must be dozens in Baltimore alone."

Derek grunted. "This might be up your alley, Pippa. I shall think on it."

═══════════

I sent follow-up faxes to Kathleen Isley, Harriet Beardsley, and Roxanne Landesberg stating that:

1. All "Morgandizing" efforts will be terminated immediately.

2. Your "special services" are no longer required.

My closing paragraph invited the superstars to forward their résumés "because it is likely that I will, from time to time, be asked to fill executive posts that fit your skills and experience."

We are still waiting to receive them.

═══════════

"We," as in Gloria and me.

I decided I needed a full-time secretary/assistant to help me build Hunnechurch & Associates. Who better than Gloria Spitz?

"You got that right," she said. "In fact, I've been thinking about an interesting business opportunity. Now that Susan McKenzie is dead, Militet is going to need a new general manager to run the aerospace division."

"Good heavens! Are you suggesting that I try to replace the woman who tried to kill me?"

"Gee. I didn't think you would be so finicky. I called the vice president of Human Resources. You have an appointment with him next Thursday, after lunch, and you might as well take the rest of the afternoon off because Thursday is moving day."

═══════════

Indeed it is! Hunnechurch & Associates plans to relocate to the suite of offices previously occupied by the Morgan Consultancy. Gloria worked out the deal.

"I talked the landlord into giving you the balance of Marsha's lease at a reduced rent," she said. "It's nicer than your old place and for less money."

"How on earth did you accomplish that miracle?"

"I pointed out that security seems to be a problem in the building. After all, the office had two different break-ins in a single weekend."

"You didn't!"

"Gotcha!" Gloria giggled. "The truth is, the landlord likes having a headhunter in the building. He thinks we add class to his tenant's list."

"Oh my!"

Gloria and I also see each other every Sunday morning—at Ryde Fellowship Church. I found Reverend Clarke's card and took him up on his offer to talk about the past. One thing led to another, and, well, I'm thinking of becoming a member.

My renewed relationship with God is still in its early days. I'm taking things slowly. "Sounds like a risky approach to me," Gloria said the other day. "God has all the time in the world. You, on the other hand, lead an absurdly dangerous life."

I threw a donut at her.

Chloe has rescheduled her trip to Ryde. She will arrive in mid-October, and we will go off to New England to look at the fall foliage. I haven't told her the whole truth yet, and I'm not sure I will. I suspect that she will be more forgiving about a nasty weekend than about her sister becoming bait for a murderer. But we will see.

Restoring David Friendly's disposition cost me a five-course dinner at Stanley's. He promised that everything I said that evening was off-the-record, so I told him the truth about the Morgan sisters and their superstars.

David listened patiently, polished off his New York cut sirloin, and then began to argue with me. He had his own conspiracy theory—as loony a notion as Reilly's.

"I don't buy your deductions," he said. "I figure that the stuff in the blue folders has to be a lot more sensitive than the details of a few harmless exaggerations. Aggressive executive types usually fly close to the edge. I'll bet those blue folders were full of juicy personal information. Sex. Lies. Rock and roll. The stuff of full-blown scandals. A reporter's dream."

His eyes gleamed as he talked.

"You might be right," I said, holding back a giggle.

"Of course I'm right." He patted my hand. "I think you did the right thing withholding your story from Reilly, even though I'm still annoyed that you didn't tell me what was going on."

"You are a highly committed professional journalist. How could you have sat on a story that good? It is your mission in life to reveal hanky-panky in high places."

"You're telling me all about those women now. Tonight you trust me to keep it off-the-record; last week you didn't. Maybe I'll break my promise and put an exposé in the next issue."

"Not without hard evidence, you won't. Everything I told you is supposition, conjecture, and a smidgen of hearsay. Susan is dead and buried. Marsha's files are history. There's no proof of any wrongdoing by the superstars." I patted his hand. "Weird Lenny wouldn't print your exposé even if you wrote one."

"You're right." He sighed. "The *Ryde Reporter* doesn't run unconfirmed stories, but I wonder . . ." David eyeballed me over the rim of his coffee cup. "By any chance, do Marsha's blue file folders still exist?"

"No! I'm sure they are gone forever."

═══════════════

Which was perfectly true.

Gloria and I entered Susan's town-house condominium at 3:00 A.M. on the Saturday morning after she died. Gloria needed less than eight minutes to pick the lock on the back door and defeat the alarm system. We found the blue file folders that Susan had stolen from Marsha's office in a cardboard box in the bedroom closet. They were all there—the four superstars, plus Linda Preston.

"Susan must have been crazy!" Gloria said. "She kept the evidence that linked her to a murder. Why take such an obvious risk?"

"Engineers are practical people. They think ahead. Who knows when you might need a little leverage over important people in town?"

"I can feel the evil radiating from these files. Let's destroy them before they can do any more damage."

We burned the blue folders in Susan's fireplace and mangled the cinders. When we left, the little white lies that had cost the lives of three people were nothing more than a heap of black ashes.